LAKEFRONT BILLIONAIRES

LOVE UNWRITTEN

LAUREN ASHER

Bloom books

Published by Bloom Books, an imprint of Sourcebooks
P.O. Box 4410, Naperville, Illinois 60567-4410
(630) 961-3900
sourcebooks.com

Cataloging-in-Publication Data is on file with the Library of Congress.

Printed and bound in the United States of America.
VP 10 9 8 7 6 5 4 3 2 1

PLAYLISTS

Love Unwritten by Lauren Asher

Scan to listen

+

Love Unwritten
Playlist

>

Forever Favorites
Playlist

>

Strawberry Season
Playlist

>

Astrid and the Treble Makers
Playlist

>

E.S. Originals
Playlist

>

CONTENT WARNING

This love story contains explicit content and topics that may be sensitive to some readers. For a more detailed content warning list, please scan the QR code or visit https://laurenasher.com/love-unwritten-content-warnings.

THE ULTIMATE
HAWAII PACKING LIST

Essentials ♫

- ☑ Guitar
- ☑ Driver's license
- ☑ Boarding passes
- ☐ Cash
- ☑ Itinerary (print out)
- ☑ Wallet and purse
- ☑ Emotional support water bottle

Comforts

- ☑ Treats
- ☑ Eye mask
- ☑ Sunglasses
- ☑ Favorite hoodie
- ☐ Comfort blanket
- ☑ The notebook (just in case)

Electronics

- ☑ Tablet
- ☑ Headphones
- ☑ Laptop
- ☐ Chargers
- ☑ Nico's gaming console

Toiletries ☆

- ☑ Sunscreen
- ☑ First-aid kit
- ☑ Shampoo, conditioner, and body wash
- ☐ Razor and shaving cream
- ☑ Electronic toothbrush and floss
- ☑ Makeup
- ☑ Makeup remover

Clothing

- ☑ PJs
- ☑ Undergarments
- ☑ Swimsuits
- ☐ Cover ups
- ☑ Sundresses
- ☑ Sports bras and leggings
- ☑ T-shirts and shorts (for Nico)

- ☑ Hiking boots
- ☐ Water shoes
- ☑ Sneakers
- ☑ Sandals
- ☑ High heels
- ☐ dress mom picked out
- ☑ new crochet outfit

Don't forget about Nico's...

- ☑ Tablet
- ☑ Metal detector
- ☐ Binoculars
- ☑ Action figures
- ☐ Bucket hat
- ☑ Back-up pair of glasses
- ☑ Second pair of emergency glasses

- ☐ Rash guard (the blue one)
- ☑ Snorkeling mask, tube, and flippers
- ☑ Matching swim trunks *Dorian bought him and Penelope*
- ☑ Snacks (pack triple!)
- ☑ Headphones
- ☑ Books
- ☐ Water Shoes

To those who see themselves as broken.
I hope you find someone who admires your scars for what they are:
A sign of your struggle and a testament to your strength.

CHAPTER ONE

Ellie

"Unbelievable." Being a glutton for punishment, I continue scrolling through the article on my computer, ignoring the way my stomach tightens with every line of betrayal.

America's sweetheart and world-renowned folk-pop star Ava Rhodes is expected to release her sophomore album this summer with MIA Records. The record label first discovered her during an open mic night at a local Los Angeles bar, where Darius Larkin found the future breakout star singing a cover of "Lies and Stolen Lullabies." Later that year, Ava released her critically acclaimed debut album, Looking Glass, *which skyrocketed her career and won a Grammy.*

The journalist goes on to boast about Ava's successful first album, which shot her to stardom and won Album of the Year. It was an album *I* helped cowrite, although the public doesn't know since my name was never listed in the production credits.

The dull pain in my chest returns, all thanks to the invisible dagger Ava embedded in my back a year ago.

"Everything okay?"

I look up and find myself pinned in place by a pair of rich brown eyes. The color and deep undertones might be warm and welcoming, but the man they belong to is anything but.

After working for Rafael Lopez as his son's live-in nanny for eight months, I thought I would've gotten used to his intimidating gaze, but it still holds the same power over me now as it did when I first met him.

Objectively speaking, my boss is handsome. With a face that belongs on a magazine cover, a deep voice that drips with quiet authority, and enough height and muscle mass to make me—the town's resident tall girl—feel small and dainty, he checks every box.

Hot single dad with more emotional baggage than London Heathrow Airport during Christmas? Check.

Brilliant tech billionaire who teamed up with his cousin to create Dwelling, the most popular real estate app on the market? Painfully cliché yet impressive nonetheless, so check, check.

A philanthropist with a life mission to find and rescue mistreated animals before fostering them in his backyard barn? Triple check *and* triple threat.

In fact, I could spend the next thirty minutes listing Rafael's redeeming qualities, but nothing, and I mean absolutely nothing, would make up for his biggest con.

He is my boss.

Whatever silly spark of attraction I felt toward him since

we were teenagers no longer mattered once I was hired as his son's nanny. While it was difficult at first to ignore the way my heart raced whenever my old high school crush looked at me, it only took a few encounters to ruin the fantasy I'd created in my head about the lonely Lake Wisteria single dad.

My change of heart has nothing to do with his post-divorce wardrobe change and the lumberjack aesthetic he has maintained for the last two years, but rather the rugged personality that comes along with it. I can deal with an ungodly amount of flannel shirts and picking up after Rafael's dusty cowboy boots, but I draw the line at his constant scowls and insistence on making me feel like an outsider despite working for him for nearly a year.

He shifts in place on the other side of the kitchen island, casting a shadow over the marble countertop. "What's wrong?"

I jerk back. "Why are you asking?"

He scratches at the thick, short beard that covers half his face and neck. "Does it matter?"

Kind of, seeing as he has never bothered asking me before. So rather than open myself up to being vulnerable, I stick to the status quo.

"I'm fine." I shut my laptop with a surprising amount of self-control.

"If you're going to lie to my face, then at least look me in the eyes while doing so."

"I am not lying." I drag my gaze away from his.

"Good try. Now do it again without breaking eye contact. That ought to convince me then."

An image of me wrapping my hands around his throat

flashes before my eyes. I'm not a violent person, but something about Rafael always brings out the worst in me.

His eyes narrow. "Are you picturing my murder again?"

"In graphic detail."

"Poison?"

"*Asphyxiation.*"

His eyes have a rare glimmer to them. "Switching it up?"

"Nico suggested it."

"My son is giving murder advice now?"

"Are you seriously surprised? His favorite comic book is about a *villain.*"

His mouth curls a fraction of a centimeter. The small, mundane gesture wipes away my bad mood about Ava and replaces my bitterness with enthusiasm.

"You smiled!"

"No." His lips press into a thin line, but it's too late.

"I know what I saw." I bite back my grin as I walk over to the magnetic dry-erase board attached to the fridge and add a tally below the pinned photocopy of his high school superlative page.

I was only a freshman when he was a senior, but everyone knew who Rafael Lopez was. The Wisteria High student body was obsessed with him, including me, although I'd deny it until my dying breath. To be fair, it was impossible not to be, with his devastating good looks, otherworldly athleticism, and charming yet nerdy personality.

During the time Nico and I have kept count of Rafael's smiles, I've yet to witness one like the bright-eyed grin from his high school years. The photo is evidence that even the brightest stars can fade away, becoming a fraction of what they once were.

It's hard to believe the person who won *Best Smile* has only done so twelve—now thirteen—times in the last three months since I jokingly invented the tracker to cut some of the tension in the house.

Between Nico keeping his father at arms' length and Rafael going out of his way to avoid uncomfortable situations with his son, they both could use a little humor in their lives.

God help them if you're considered the comedic relief.

I'm the friend people go to when they need a stiff drink or a good cry, not the one they turn to for a nice laugh, but I'm doing my best here.

"One day I'm going to tear that photo into a hundred pieces," Rafael says to my back.

"Do that, and I'll replace it with one of your baby ones." I cap the dry-erase marker and return it to its spot above the board.

His eyes narrow. "What are you talking about?"

"Turns out your aunt has a whole collection of photo albums dedicated to you."

He blinks twice. "She showed you those?"

"Yup. Right before she brought out some old home videos." My gaze flicks over him. "For someone so surly and antisocial, you sure wanted to be the center of attention when you were younger. But who could blame you with that karaoke machine of yours?"

His tan cheeks slowly turn pink. "It was Lily's machine, not mine."

"Really? I couldn't tell with how much you hogged the mic."

"She and Dahlia forced me."

Blaming both of his family friends only makes me want to embarrass him more, even though I know he is telling the truth about the machine belonging to the Muñoz sisters.

"No one asked you to go *that* hard on singing the Spice Girls. That much I can guarantee."

His blush quickly spreads to the rest of his face. "I have no idea what you're talking about."

I pull out my phone. "I have a video of it in here somewhere that could jog your memory. Just give me a second…"

"You filmed it?"

"Obviously. Whenever Nico and I are having a bad day, you dressed up as Sporty Spice always makes us laugh."

"I was an athlete."

"Who also knew every lyric to 'Wannabe.'"

He sighs like I'm the biggest inconvenience in his world. "Remind me why I put up with you?"

"Because you love your son more than you dislike me."

A long crease appears on his forehead. "I don't dislike you."

"But do you like me?"

His palm brushes over his short beard. "I'm still deciding."

"Anything I can do to speed up this lengthy decision-making process?"

"Quit?"

I chuckle to myself, and his gaze drops to my lips.

"What?" I wipe at the corner of my mouth.

He shakes his head. "Nothing."

I pull out my cell phone and double-check my teeth just in case.

"Ellie!"

My phone slips from my grasp as Nico shouts my name from the opposite side of the house. It clatters to the floor, and I curse with a hiss as I bend over to pick it up. My blond hair falls in front of my face and hangs around me, blocking my view of everything but my lit-up phone.

The base of my neck tingles, and I peek over my shoulder to find Rafael's gaze focused on my ass.

Oh my God. Why is he checking me out?

I shift my weight, and his eyes follow the length of my leggings, confirming the truth. If it were anyone else, I would take it as a compliment after spending too many years picking at my appearance and complaining about my small boobs, ass, and barely-there curves, but Rafael isn't someone else.

At least not to *me*.

Catching him checking me out isn't something I expected, but I'd be lying if I said it didn't excite me a little.

My stomach swoops as I stand upright. The sudden motion rips him out of his temporary lapse of judgment.

Before I have a chance to mutter a single word, his gaze shifts from heated to bored in the blink of an eye. If I weren't so taken aback by his interest, I would be impressed by how he schooled his features in a millisecond.

In the months I've worked for Rafael, he hasn't shown the slightest bit of interest in me or any other woman in town. Rumor has it that Rafael hasn't been with anyone since he divorced his ex-wife, Hillary, over two years ago.

After working here for eight months, I can confirm that, despite Rafael being one of the most eligible bachelors in town, he is completely disinterested in any kind of connection, including a platonic one.

Nico calls my name again, and his impatience becomes my saving grace.

"Coming!" I rush toward the kitchen exit.

"Eleanor?" Rafa's deep timbre has me turning in place.

A shiver rolls down my spine as I turn to face the grumpy giant across from me. "Why do you insist on calling me that?"

I'm surprised he can effortlessly shrug with how much his trap muscles must weigh.

I swallow back the urge to say something that could get me fired. "Everyone calls me Ellie."

"I know," he says after a long pause.

"Yet you insist on calling me by my full name for some annoying reason." Usually, I'm even-tempered, but there is something about Rafael that seems to draw out my claws.

"Do you have a problem with that?" His dry tone grates on every single one of my nerves.

I battle between speaking my mind and ignoring his obvious attempt at getting under my skin.

"Ellie!" Nico yells louder this time, deciding for me.

"Coming right now!" I take a few steps toward the hallway, only to halt midstride. "Did you need something?" I ask Rafael in a sickly sweet voice.

"Not anymore." He walks over to the fridge and yanks the door open, making the bottles on the side shelves rattle. I don't take his dismissal personally since he spoke to me more in the last few minutes than he has all week.

Rafael has always been moody, but over the past month, I can barely get him to speak more than a few words at a time. Most exchanges end as they started, with me questioning why I bothered trying to connect with him in the first place.

People like Rafael don't mix well with people like me. I feel way too much, and he barely feels at all. Opposites don't attract, no matter what propaganda teachers spew in fourth-grade science class while distracting kids with magnets.

I bolt from the kitchen before Nico comes searching for me instead. My fuzzy pink socks, which were a colorful Christmas gift from Nico because he says I wear too much black, muffle the sound of my footsteps as I walk down the long hallway toward the back of the house.

Despite Rafael having enough money to make his great-great-great-grandkids billionaires one day, he purchased land near the outskirts of Lake Wisteria, far away from the coveted lake and its million-dollar views. At first, I thought he chose this property because he needed space for a barn and the animals that live there, but I've since learned the truth.

Rafael is hiding from the world.

Despite the lack of neighbors, everything about the Lopez house feels charming, with vibrant paint colors Nico picked out himself, a movie room with the comfiest reclining chairs and our choice from the latest blockbuster releases, and a master nanny suite that is triple the size of my old Los Angeles apartment. It has everything I could need and more, with its own separate guest entrance, private sitting area, gorgeous spa bathroom, and a canopy bed that makes me feel like a princess.

I find Nico standing beside the elevator Rafael had installed to help his son navigate the three-story house easily, tapping his sneaker against the hardwood floor with an irritated expression on his cute little face. He is taller than other kids his age thanks to his father's DNA, which gives him the illusion of being older.

"What took you so long?" He snatches my hand and pulls me inside the elevator car.

"I got distracted."

"By what?"

"Your dad smiled."

"Really?" Nico stares at me with eager eyes.

That look right there is the main reason I created the smile tracker in the first place, because whether Rafael realizes it or not, his son cherishes his smiles. They're a symbol of hope and happiness—two things that have been severely lacking in this house as of late, although I haven't figured out why.

I reach over his dark head of hair and hit the button for the basement. "It was small, but I caught it."

"Wow. Two days in a row," Nico says in disbelief.

"Looks like I may win that bet after all," I tease halfheartedly. If Rafael smiles every day for thirty consecutive days, then Nico promised to let me borrow his favorite action figure for a month.

To a kid, those stakes are higher than me winning the lottery and retiring at the young age of twenty-nine.

"Oh no." He fakes distress.

"It's okay if you lose. I'll even agree to shared custody."

He hip-checks me with a giggle, and I ruffle his dark hair in retribution. The smile on his face dies as he looks up at me with narrowed eyes.

"What's wrong?" I ask.

"Nothing." His defensive tone catches me off guard. Although I'm used to that kind of tone from his father, I've never heard Nico speak like that before.

Nico pulls his glasses off with a frown and wipes the lenses with the edge of his blue T-shirt. He always loves to pick out his own outfits, and today's attire features thick red frames that match his comic book graphic tee and red basketball sneakers.

The elevator doors open, but he is too focused on cleaning his lenses to move, so I block the doors from closing and wait. He gets increasingly frustrated as he struggles with the task, but I refrain from helping him, no matter how much I want to.

Like every other eight-year-old kid, Nico wants to be autonomous, especially given the retinitis pigmentosa condition he was diagnosed with about eighteen months ago. According to my late-night Google searches, promoting independence is important, especially as his vision progressively worsens and he gets more frustrated by having to rely on others.

He places his glasses back on his face with thinly pressed lips.

"All good?" I ask.

"Yup." He squints at my face before rubbing his eyes.

"You sure?"

"Yes." His harsh tone stuns me as his body brushes against mine on his way out of the elevator, resembling his father so much in that moment.

I clear my head with a quick shake. "All right, sir. Take the attitude down a notch before I make you practice the recorder today instead."

My comment seems to pull him out of whatever funky mood he was in, and he sighs. "I'm sorry."

"It's okay. We all get grumpy sometimes." I follow him out of the elevator and into the basement.

Soon after I was promoted from Nico's after-school music tutor to his live-in nanny, Rafael converted the unfinished basement into a music studio for his son, mainly due to the drum set his godmother bought him. The large open space is decked out with soundproof insulation, state-of-the-art recording studio technology, and enough instruments to create a whole album if I wanted to.

My stomach sinks at the idea, but I'm quick to recover.

I spin the ring covering my pinkie tattoo. "What do you feel like playing today?"

Nico's gaze bounces between the display wall of string and brass instruments and the drum set before landing on the black grand piano. "Piano."

"Really?" If it weren't for Rafael insisting that Nico practice the piano and violin at least twice a week, I doubt he'd bother with anything but the drum set. Usually, I have to pry the drumsticks out of his hands.

"I want to try something new today." Nico heads for the bench with a pinched expression that tugs on my heart.

I take a seat beside him, ignoring my impulse to ask him what's wrong. "Show me what you got, little rock star."

CHAPTER TWO

Ellie

By the time I tuck Nico into bed for the night, I'm about ready to keel over from overexertion after our extra-long practice session today. Nico is supposed to be practicing for his Strawberry Festival performance coming up this July, but something about his restless energy and residual grumpiness told me he needed the additional time to work through his feelings, so I kept him company while he unleashed his emotions on the ivory keys of his piano.

If Nico's heartache had a sound, its notes would match that of a sentimental progression—achy and heartfelt and so damn wishful, it comes across as painful longing.

Even the music he listened to while taking a shower carried a melancholic tune, although I pretended not to notice while I folded laundry in his room next door.

"Can you read with me?" Nico pops out his bottom lip.

I stare at the superhero-themed alarm clock on his nightstand. "I'd love to, but it's late, and you have school tomorrow."

"*Please*." He presses his hands together. "I'll only ask for one story this time. I promise."

I've always struggled with saying no to Nico. It's one of my biggest flaws, especially when it comes to cute little kids who wield puppy eyes and good manners like a superpower. If Rafael were here, he would roll his eyes and give me a speech about it, but he is locked away in his office.

Over the last few months, Nico's bedtime routine became my sole responsibility, and I know Rafael stopped trying because of the awkward tension between him and his son. I've tried my best to encourage my boss to try again, but he claims Nico only wants to read stories with me.

Nico and I weren't always this close, especially given his trust issues with others, but little by little, our bonding over music expanded to most aspects of our lives—from having divorced parents to our love of Formula 1—we have built a strong relationship that I cherish.

"Ellie?" Nico taps on my shoulder.

I let out a deep sigh. "All right. Scoot over."

He carefully removes his action figures from the left side of his bed and lines them up on his nightstand. Compared to all his other toys that lie abandoned around the house until he is ready to play with them again, he takes extra care of the figures Rafael created with his 3D printer. My boss designed and painted them himself, a fact that I try to block from my mind solely because it makes me feel all warm and fuzzy, knowing he spent months working on each one for his son.

Nico pats the empty spot beside him with a smile.

I reach for the two newest options on his bookshelf and hold them up for him to choose. Between the newest comic book about his favorite superhero and a short chapter book in braille, I already know Nico's answer, but I give him a choice regardless.

"Which one are we feeling tonight?"

He squints at the covers for what feels like an eternity. For a kid who spent the last month talking about how excited he was for this comic, he sure is having a hard time picking today.

"I'm giving you three seconds to decide. One...two..."

My brows creep toward my hairline as he passes over the newest edition of his favorite comic book and grabs his braille book instead.

I check his temperature with the back of my hand. "Are you sick?"

"No." He pushes me away and yanks his book open hard enough to make the spine crack.

Before he has a chance to read a sentence, I pluck the book from his lap and take a seat on the edge of his bed. "Hey."

He tries to snag the book back, but I place it out of reach.

"What's going on?"

"Nothing." He stares straight ahead.

"I don't like to push..."

"Then don't."

"But I'm worried about you."

He remains silent, nearly suffocating me with the tension

building between us. If this is how Rafael feels whenever Nico shuts him out, I can now understand his bad mood a bit more, because it absolutely sucks.

I'm not ready to give up yet, so I try again. "You can always talk to me about anything. No matter how bad it is."

His gaze drops to his fists clutching the comforter in a death grip. "I can't. Not about this."

I tuck my fingers under his chin and force him to look me in the eyes. "Why not?"

"Because I'm scared." His strained voice can barely be heard over the air conditioning blasting from the vents.

"About what?" I wait patiently as he takes a deep breath, only to be disappointed when he stays quiet.

"Does it have something to do with your mom?" I ask in my softest voice.

He shakes his head hard enough to send water droplets flying off the tips of his hair.

"Dad?"

His bottom lip trembles as his eyes flood with tears.

Oh, shit. What did Rafael do? I bite down on my lip to stop myself from asking that and ten different questions at once.

His voice is barely audible as he asks, "You promise not to say anything?"

My stomach churns with uncertainty. I shouldn't make any promises of the sort, but if it means that Nico will share what is bothering him, then so be it.

I ignore my concerns and nod. "Sure."

It takes him another thirty long seconds to speak again, all while my heart beats rapidly.

A single tear slips down his cheek. "My vision is getting worse. It's harder to see in the dark lately, and the tunnel vision is getting narrower."

I feel like I just took a brass-knuckled punch to the gut. "Oh, Nico."

Another tear follows the watery path toward his wobbling chin. "I'm nervous."

"Of course." I take a deep breath. "Why haven't you told your dad?"

"Because I don't want to make him sad again."

My chest clenches as I absorb the pain on his face like it's my own.

I'm at a loss for words as I tuck him against me, wishing I could do anything other than sit around, waiting for time to steal whatever vision he has left.

One day, Nico won't be able to see much, if anything at all. It's unfair, given his young age. A kid like him deserves to experience life and the whole world without a diagnosis hanging over his head, reminding him how he is different from other children his age.

I brush his hair out of his eyes. "Your dad would want to know if you're having trouble."

"No, he wouldn't."

"Of course he would. Why would you think anything else?"

Nico takes so long to answer, I mistakenly think he's fallen asleep.

"He cried at the doctor's office," he says with a shaky voice. I freeze. "When?"

"In January." His chin trembles. "I heard him…in the bathroom."

"Are you sure?"

He nods.

My heart breaks for the two Lopez men, knowing they are suffering in silence when they could be relying on each other. Yet no matter how hard I try to push them together, they both continue to resist.

"He doesn't know that I know." His sniffle makes the crack in my chest widen.

I give him a squeeze. "It's okay for people to cry. It's normal and can be healthy."

"Yeah, but not when you're the reason." His gaze drops.

"But he wasn't crying because of you. He was crying *for* you." I'm not sure what makes my heart ache more: Rafael having a breakdown about his son's eye condition or Nico witnessing his father at a rock-bottom low that was meant to be kept private.

It's hard to pick, especially when I picture my cold, emotionally unavailable boss *crying*.

Wouldn't be the first time. I'm reminded of a memory I've kept at the back of my mind of a teenage Rafael breaking down in a parking lot one Christmas Eve long ago, completely unaware of me sitting in the car parked next to his.

At the time, I had no idea why Rafael was crying, but I've been able to piece it together after Josefina shared once that the anniversary of his mother's death lands on December twenty-third.

The memory fades as Nico speaks again. "That doesn't make it any better."

My arms tighten around him. "I'm sorry."

He snuggles into me. "It's not your fault."

"No, but I am anyway. You've been carrying this inside all this time…"

I should have pushed harder. Asked more questions. Something more than creating a ridiculous smile tracker in hopes of bringing Nico and his dad back together, thinking that would do the trick.

I take a deep breath and voice the opinion Nico will hate to hear. "You're going to have to tell him about this."

His arms tighten around me. "I will."

"When?"

He flinches. "After our trip?"

I pull back to get a better look at him. "No. You can't wait three weeks to tell him about something like this."

"Why not?"

"Because he's your dad. He deserves to know what's going on with you so he can help."

"Telling him now won't make a difference." His shoulders slump like they are single-handedly carrying the weight of the world. "My eyes aren't ever going to get better."

As much as I want to deny the truth, Nico is right. Nothing we can do will change his diagnosis, but that doesn't mean he needs to struggle by himself. He can count on us to support him through it all.

"If you're scared, I could talk to him for you."

A look of pure desperation flashes across his face as his fingers dig into my arm, right over a tiny group of butterfly tattoos. "No! Please, please, *please*, Ellie. Don't say anything yet. At least not until after our trip."

"Why do you want to wait?"

"Today, he smiled, and yesterday, he laughed!"

The chasm in my chest deepens as I remember the sound that took me by surprise. While Rafael's laugh wasn't loud or powerful, it was soft and impactful enough to make Nico smile for the remainder of the day.

"He *never* laughs anymore." Nico's misty eyes make mine tear up as well. "I don't want to ruin that before our trip."

My deep breath might not calm my heart, but it gives me a moment to clear my head. "I need you to be honest with me and tell me how bad it has gotten since your exam in January."

He asks to use my phone and pulls up an example of his current vision. It has begun to dim around the edges, as if he is seeing the world through a pair of binoculars, which was a symptom the doctor warned Rafael about given Nico's advanced medical state. His tunnel vision isn't as bad as I had originally thought, but it still worries me given how young he is.

While I don't want to risk my job for a secret, I'm not sure I have much of a choice unless I want to break Nico's trust. If his safety were truly at risk, I would betray it in a heartbeat to protect him, but I'm going to choose to believe him.

I release a heavy breath. "I'll give you until after your birthday party."

His face turns a sick shade of green. "But that's in a week!"

"It's either that or we tell him tonight."

It kills me to put my foot down, especially when Nico pouts and says, "I don't want him to be sad before our vacation."

"That's fair, but you know it's the right thing."

His reply is nothing but a deep sigh of resignation.

I lift his chin so he can look me in the eyes. "He may be temporarily unhappy, but the trip will help him feel better."

"You think so?"

"I *know* so." Okay, I may not know for certain, but I've never heard a single person say they had a bad time in Hawaii.

With all the effort Rafael put into planning this special trip for his son, including canceling the original Europe itinerary all because Nico became obsessed with Hawaii this year after watching a hundred hours of content about the place, I know he will have a good time.

Or so I hope.

"Okay. Fine. I'll tell him after next weekend."

This mini Lopez is going to be my downfall, because where Rafael is rough around the edges and keeps his heart locked behind a wall of ice, Nico wears it proudly on his sleeve for everyone to see.

I would do anything to protect it and him, even if it means making a promise about a secret that isn't mine to keep in the first place.

CHAPTER THREE

Rafael

I hate having a nanny in my private space, interfering with my day-to-day life, but for Nico, I'm willing to do just about anything. While I could easily raise my son with my family's help, Nico needs a motherly figure in his life.

He *needs* Ellie, as much as I hate to admit it.

I remind myself of just that as I lean against the wall across from my son's bedroom door and stare at my Richard Mille watch, my annoyance growing by the second. The obnoxious diamonds lining the face glint as the small hand ticks toward the number ten.

Usually, I'm not a stickler for bedtimes, but lately, Nico has been acting crankier than usual, and I only have his blond-haired, curfew-breaking nanny to blame.

Her soft laugh carries through the door and down the hall,

followed by Nico's airy giggle soon after. That heartwarming sound coming from my son is the only reason I hired someone with no nannying experience and a penchant for driving me insane to begin with.

When Hillary left over two years ago after I filed for divorce, Nico started changing. His fluctuating mood and irritability, while understandable, were unbearable, especially when I felt responsible.

I'm the one who filed for divorce, and while Nico has never blamed me for his mom leaving, I can't help assuming he does.

Our relationship only became more strained after he found out about his retinitis pigmentosa diagnosis eighteen months ago. Little by little, his condition became difficult to ignore as his eyesight worsened and he started pulling away from all the things he loved, like his friends, my family, music, and me.

Music was always Nico's outlet, so in a desperate attempt to help him, I paid for music lessons at The Broken Chord almost a year ago. At first, Nico gave me a hard time about it. He was quiet and unmotivated to pick up an instrument, but with Ellie's help, he slowly opened up again.

For a solid four months, it felt like Nico and I were finally in a good place together, but then we had another setback at the start of the year.

One that I haven't been able to overcome, no matter how hard I try. Asking him what is wrong gets me nowhere, while giving into his wishes only eases the tension between us temporarily.

Sure, changing our summer trip destination from Europe to Hawaii like Nico wanted earned me a small smile and a whispered *thank you* from him, but Nico's good mood didn't last long.

At least not with *me*.

Ellie steals me away from my thoughts as she walks out of his bedroom and shuts the door softly behind her before slumping against it.

She unleashes a harsh sigh as her hazel eyes shut. Her long blond hair rests near her waistline, the color looking more silver than gold because of the moonlight streaming through the window.

I rarely get an opportunity to look at Ellie without her noticing. Usually, she catalogs my every glance, smile, and comment, making me feel like a research subject lately with that stupid smile tracker of hers. So rather than immediately making my presence known, I conduct a drawn-out assessment of my own.

Ellie isn't one for colorful accessories or frilly, designer-labeled clothes like my cousin's girlfriend of nine months, Dahlia Muñoz. Nor is she the type to keep up with the latest makeup trend or hairstyle like Lily, the other Muñoz sister. In fact, Ellie does a good job of keeping her personality hidden, dampening it with her limited range of black, white, and gray clothing. I'm surprised that she hasn't dyed her blond hair to match the Edgy Barbie look she is going for, given how much she favors dark colors.

If it weren't for the small, dainty tattoos scattered across her body, I'd consider her as interesting as a blank canvas.

Liar.

Fine. She is as interesting as a canvas solely painted with one color.

Black.

A deep, inky shade that matches the somber music she plays late at night when she thinks everyone is asleep. She doesn't know that I listen from the shadows sometimes, but I find it hard to resist the pull I have toward her. Her music speaks to me in a way words never can, and I can't help being drawn to her in that sense.

If it's only about the music, how do you explain being drawn to her right now?

The thought has me snapping out of my daze, and a floorboard creaks beneath my boot as I step out of the dark corner.

Ellie's eyes snap open. "Good God! How long have you been standing there?"

I keep my face expressionless despite my escalating heart rate. "Long enough to notice Nico was up past his bedtime."

She stands to her full height. While she is taller than most women in town, she still only reaches my chin without shoes. "We were practicing his braille."

"Surprised you could get much done with all that laughing."

Her eyes narrow. "I'm sure humor is a foreign concept to you, but people tend to laugh when they read something funny."

"You don't say," I reply with a dry voice.

Whatever she was about to say is cut off by her yawn. "That's my cue to go to bed." She attempts to walk past me.

Without thinking, I latch on to her elbow before she has a chance to walk around me. The warmth of her skin seeps through the thin barrier of mine, sending a wave of heat up my arm.

I want to shake her off and run from the sensation, yet my hold remains strong as I ask, "How's it going?"

"What?" She stares at the goose bumps forming on her skin.

I release her and take a long step backward. "How is he doing with the braille practice?"

"Oh." She shakes her head. "Good, although he unfortunately inherited his impatience from you."

I give her a look. "Is he struggling?"

"A bit, but we're working on it. You know, if you have some time to spare, it wouldn't hurt to practice with him too."

Ever-present dread makes my stomach sink until I'm drowning in negative thoughts. I've tried so damn hard to practice with Nico, but my son has slowly closed himself off from me over the last few months, and I can't figure out why. Something shifted after the holiday season, and no amount of probing has helped me uncover the reason.

You could ask Ellie what she thinks. I shut that thought down. She wouldn't understand, seeing as she and Nico have a different kind of relationship that I love and hate at the same time.

I'm jealous of the carefree, easygoing connection Ellie has with my son. While I know it's not fair to hold their bond against her, I can't help myself.

Ellie has what I want and crave. Nico *enjoys* spending all his free time with her while he pushes me away without an afterthought, making me feel useless and dejected—two emotions I've spent decades trying to avoid.

"Why don't you join us for story time tomorrow?" she

asks in that delicate voice of hers that threatens to slip past my defenses.

"No." I sound like more of an asshole than usual.

"Why not?" The way she stares at me makes me feel uneasy, not because of how she does it but rather because of what she may see if she looks hard enough.

A coward who would rather hide his shame behind a lie.

"I'm not very good," I say.

The muscles beside Ellie's eyes soften until she is no longer glaring. "I'm by no means an expert either. Whenever I struggle with a word or sentence, I say something ridiculous instead, and it never fails to make Nico laugh."

"Must be nice." I can barely get my son to talk to me for more than a few minutes, but here Ellie is, making him laugh without trying.

Her icy gaze returns with a vengeance. "What's that supposed to mean?"

"Nothing. I'd join you, but I already made plans for tomorrow night with Julian."

Her nose scrunches like usual whenever I piss her off. "Since when?"

About ten seconds ago. "Today."

"Thanks for the last-minute notice."

"Do you have something better to do?" The question comes out all wrong.

"It's a mystery why you have no real friends."

"Some of us prefer not to waste our time on meaningless relationships."

Rather than becoming further enraged by my comment,

Ellie looks at me in the same way I've seen far too many times around town.

Pity.

"I feel bad for people like you," she says, stunning me into silence. "You work double-time to keep everyone at a distance because one person gave you a reason to."

More like three people—two of whom brought me into this world.

I don't say that, though.

I don't say *anything*.

It's easier to keep my feelings at bay when I don't acknowledge them. Call it cowardliness or repression, but I prefer the term *survival*. Because to think is to feel, and I'm not entirely sure I'll be able to control myself once I start.

My toxic trait isn't the fact that I don't have feelings; it's that I feel too much, all at once, so I suppress it instead of learning how to cope. I've always been that way, long before my mother packed her bags and left my father and me.

Ellie shakes her head. "Whatever. Now, if you'll excuse me, I should get some rest." She scurries around me, the scent of her fruity body wash lingering in the air long after she is gone.

CHAPTER FOUR

Rafael

My workday is a busy one after the real estate search engine app I own and run, Dwelling, has a glitch and an investor causes some trouble, so I don't get the chance to see Nico yet. By the time I wrap up for the night and exit my home office, he is already tucked into bed, and Ellie is nowhere near his room.

I linger outside his door while Ellie's words from yesterday come back to haunt me.

If you have some time to spare, it wouldn't hurt to practice with him too.

Before I have a chance to back down from the idea, I knock on Nico's bedroom door.

"Ellie?"

With a tight ball in my throat, I turn the knob. "No. *Soy yo.*"

Nico's smile dies. "*Hola, Papi.*"

Pain hits me square in the chest at the sign of his disappointment, but I ignore it as I take a hesitant step inside. "*Vine a decirte buenas noches.*"

He tugs his comforter up to his chin. "*Buenas noches.*"

I take a seat on the edge of his bed, feeling more like a stranger than his father at the moment. "Do you want to read a story together before I head out to see Uncle Julian?"

"No," Nico says with a rush.

The sharp sting of rejection doesn't deter me from trying again. "Ellie told me it would be nice for me to practice my braille."

A look of sheer panic flashes across his face. "Why?"

"Because I'm not very good?"

He releases a long breath. "Oh."

I chalk his unusual reaction up to him being anxious about spending time around me.

I grab the book on his nightstand. "What do you say?"

He shakes his head. "I don't want to practice with you."

His whispered statement might as well have been shouted in my face.

"Nicolas…" I muster up some courage with a deep breath that makes my lungs ache. "Did I do something wrong?"

He stares at the book in my hands with a forlorn expression. "No."

Soy yo: It's me.	**Hola, Papi:** Hi, Dad.

Vine a decirte buenas noches: I came to tell you goodnight.	**Buenas noches:** Goodnight.

"Then why do you never want to read stories together anymore?"

His lips press together.

"You don't mind reading them with Ellie."

His trembling chin makes my chest ache.

You're just making everything worse.

With stiff muscles, I place the book back on the nightstand and kiss the top of his head. "Don't worry about it. I'll practice on my own and impress you with all my skills."

He sinks deeper into the mattress. "I love you."

The dull throb ebbs a bit. "*Te quiero, mijo. Con todo mi corazón.*"

"I'm sorry," he murmurs as I near the door.

"You have nothing to be sorry for. Just know that I'm always here if you want to try reading together." Rejection of any kind hurts, but there isn't anything more painful than being on the receiving end of it from my son.

Your own kid doesn't want you around, the sick voice of self-sabotage returns at full force.

Son. Husband. Father. My list of failures is growing, and I have no one to blame but myself. I'm the one who was too busy growing my company to pay attention to my wife, so she found someone who was willing to take my place. I hadn't expected that filing for divorce would give my ex the green light to run off to Oregon with her new boyfriend and leave her responsibilities behind.

Te quiero, mijo. Con todo mi corazón: I love you, son. With all my heart.

Her superhero-loving, music-aficionado, eight-year-old responsibility.

Nico interrupts me in the middle of my downward spiral by asking, "Can you get Ellie before you leave?"

I pull on the doorknob with a death grip. "Of course."

"I was surprised when you texted me yesterday about meeting up tonight." My cousin, Julian, drops into the leather booth across from me, looking a bit haggard from a long day's work at one of his construction sites. His black shirt is covered in sawdust flakes, and his cheeks remain permanently flushed after working under the early June sun.

We may not be brothers, but we could fool anyone into thinking we are with our similar brown eyes, dark hair, and strong jawlines inherited from our fathers.

While Julian tames his wavy strands by keeping them short, mine are longer and in desperate need of a cut—something he tells me every single time I see him.

"Do you own a brush?" he asks.

"Yes."

"Need help learning how to use it?"

I run my hands through my thick hair. "Your mom is cutting it tomorrow."

"Good, because you're a week away from entering man-bun territory." He fakes a shudder.

"Like I would ever let it get that long."

He spares me another look.

"*Again*," I add. After I filed for divorce and found out about Nico's degenerative eye condition, I didn't do the best job of taking care of myself. I had too many issues on my mind to think about anything other than my failing marriage and distraught child, so my self-care fell to the wayside.

"While Ma is cutting your hair, Dahlia could come over and check out your closet. She'd love to help you pick out outfits for Hawaii too, if you let her." Julian's eyes brighten. He always gets that same goofy look on his face whenever he talks about his girlfriend and our family friend, Dahlia Muñoz.

Although I once gave him a hard time about staying away from her, my worries were unwarranted because my cousin has never been happier than he has been over the last nine months since he and Dahlia started dating.

Unlike me, Julian never jumped into bed with the wrong woman to fill an empty void. Instead, he was responsible and patient, while I was reckless and in desperate need of therapy. Heck, I still could use some, but I've put that personal journey on hold because I'm not ready to face my past. It was hard enough to discover why I clung to someone like Hillary in the first place, so I need some time to process my issues before resuming sessions.

Maybe even a few *years*.

I ignore the lump in my throat and ask, "What's wrong with my clothes?"

Sure, I used to put more effort into my appearance, but only because I cared too much about everyone else's opinion. I wanted to be liked. To be *desired*.

Now, I just want to be left alone.

He gives my outfit a once-over. "Do you want my honest opinion?"

I really don't, but that hasn't stopped Julian from voicing it anyway on more than a few occasions. I'm not sure why my family cares about my clothes and appearance, but their worries are unjustified.

Just because I don't dress to impress anymore doesn't mean I'm spiraling.

At least not *again*.

He points at my flannel shirt. "Your attire could use an overhaul before your trip."

"According to who?"

"Everybody who loves you."

I roll my eyes. "You all are just being fussy because you have nothing better to do."

"No. We fuss because we love you enough to see what you're doing."

I tense. "And what's that?"

"Disguising your insecurities with ugly clothes, a disheveled appearance, and a personality rougher than extra-coarse sandpaper."

"At least let me grab a beer first before you do a deep dive into my psychological issues."

"Screw the beer. We'd need some hard liquor to get through all of those."

"*Pendejo*," I mutter.

Pendejo: Dick

"*Cabeza dura.*" Julian lets out a soft laugh as he raises his hand to get the bartender's attention. Before I have a chance to pull out my wallet, my cousin opens a tab with his black card and orders us two beers from a brewery located a few towns over.

Julian crosses his arms over his chest, sending some sawdust flecks flying. "So, what's the real reason you called me?"

"Do I need a reason to hang out with my cousin?"

His right brow arches suspiciously. "No, but lately you're always looking for every excuse not to."

The hole in my chest widens. "Sorry. Things have been... tough."

Lately, I've found it easier to stay away from my family than answer their questions about my relationship with Nico. I know they come from a good place, and after spending the first decade of my life wishing for a family like them, I should be grateful for their love and attention, but it can be stifling at times.

Especially when it makes me feel like I'm not only failing Nico, but them too.

"What's wrong?" Julian asks.

I take a deep breath and face my fear. "Nico and I are having problems."

His eyes widen. "Really?"

I sigh. "Yes."

"Is that why you've been avoiding Sundays at the Muñoz house?"

Cabeza dura: Hard-headed person

"Yup." The Muñoz and Lopez families have spent every Sunday together ever since we were all kids, but I've done my best to avoid the family ritual lately by scheduling activities and playdates with Nico's friends.

"What's going on?" Julian asks.

"Nico's been pulling away from me and acting strange, and I can't figure out why."

He strokes his chin. "When did all this start?"

"Right around the beginning of the new year."

"So, around the same time his mother canceled her visit to town?"

I nod. "That and a few other things." Like Nico insisting Ellie join us for our summer vacation while I thoroughly voiced my feelings against it.

"Have you asked him what's wrong?"

"Of course I have."

"And?"

"He shuts down and never wants to talk about it."

"Sounds like his father."

I glare.

He stares off into the distance while sipping his beer. "Have you thought about asking Ellie about it?"

"No." The word comes out harsher than intended.

"Are you saying that no, you haven't thought about it, or no, you'd rather be a stubborn ass and avoid asking for help at all costs?"

My molars smash together.

Julian's head tilts. "So the latter, then. I thought as much."

I hate how easily Julian reads me. After knowing him for

most of my life, I'm used to it, but that doesn't make it any less annoying.

"I doubt she can help." If anything, talking to her would make me feel like an even bigger failure.

He leans forward on his elbows. "Don't tell me you're too proud to ask her."

"This has nothing to do with pride."

"Are you sure about that?"

"Positive." To care about my pride would mean having some in the first place, and I lost that along with my self-esteem a long time ago.

He chuckles to himself. "For someone who is so goddamn smart, you can sure be a real dumbass sometimes."

I raise my beer in a mock toast. "I can always count on you to lift me up."

"We've always been straight shooters with one another, so I'm not going to start lying now to save you from hurt feelings."

"True, but that doesn't mean you need to go for the jugular."

Julian's lips curl at the corners. "I'm giving you a hard time because I care."

"I know." I would do the same for him, even if it made him angry at me for a day or two.

He takes a deep breath. "Deep down, you agree with me about talking to Ellie, even if you don't want to."

I drop my head back with a resigned sigh. "Yeah. I know."

CHAPTER FIVE

Rafael

I was half hoping that Ellie would be asleep by the time I got home. Does it make me a coward? Absolutely, but at least it would have given me some more time to prepare for this kind of deep conversation.

I've always done a good job of repressing my uncomfortable emotions. At first, it was purely survival instinct because I didn't want to give my aunt and uncle a reason to get rid of me. So I learned to shield my feelings about my biological parents with toxic coping skills and a willingness to do anything for anyone.

Emphasis on the *toxic*.

I made myself so damn needed by everyone that no one could imagine getting rid of me. Soccer team captain. Senior class president and prom king. Beloved nephew, devoted father, and loyal husband.

It made me feel invincible and fulfilled…or it *had* until my life of lies came crashing down, teaching me more about myself in a few months than I had learned in the whole thirty-one years I had been alive.

The soft strumming of a guitar greets me when I walk inside the house. I head in the direction of the sound before stopping near the entrance to the living room. Ellie hasn't noticed me yet, but then again, she never does whenever she is in the zone.

I feel like I'm intruding on a private moment, but I don't want to shatter it and announce my presence before she has a chance to finish playing a popular song I immediately recognize.

My excuse for lingering in the dark sounds weak to my own ears though, especially when one song bleeds into another, and next thing I know, I've spent thirty minutes lurking.

Ellie has no idea, but I like listening to her play. Her music has a way of sneaking past my defenses and making me *feel*, and I don't want to scare her away from playing around the house if she knows I might be listening. The very idea of that happening unsettles me almost as much as my other reason for hanging around Ellie while she remains completely unaware.

There is something about her that lures me in every time, and it has nothing to do with her music. I haven't determined if my interest has something to do with her beauty or the secrets she hides behind timid smiles and songs that make my chest ache.

Partly because I don't *want* to know.

All I know is that for someone with sun-kissed skin, bright

smiles, and golden hair that looks like sunshine personified, she sure does a good job of hiding it behind heart-wrenching musical progressions and haunted melodies that stay with me long after she stops playing for the evening.

The music she plays has a chilling, melancholic quality to it that sounds completely different from Nico's upbeat song choices, and I'm always left wondering who inspires the sorrowful tunes.

I stomp my feet a few times, and the music cuts out altogether as I enter the living room.

"I'm home," I say to her back.

She turns and glances back at me from over the couch. "I thought you were staying out late."

"Changed my mind." I take a seat on the couch across from hers.

"I should get to sleep then. Nico needs me to stop by the market tomorrow before school to get his friend some cupcakes for her birthday." She rises from her spot and reaches for her incomplete music sheet.

"Wait. Do you have a second?"

"Sure."

"I need your advice."

She points at her chest. "Mine?"

"Yes," I say through gritted teeth.

She stares at me for a few seconds before nodding. "Um... all right." She reclaims her spot on the couch and places her guitar on the coffee table. "Do you want something to drink?"

"Hell yes," I say without thinking twice.

She heads toward the bar cart and tops a glass off with

my favorite bourbon without me even having to point out the bottle. When she holds the glass out for me to grab, the tips of our fingers brush against each other, sending a few sparks bursting across my skin.

She yanks her hand back.

"Thanks." I take a sip of my drink.

"Better?" She sits again.

"No."

"On a scale from one to ten, how painful was that to admit?"

"At least an eight."

That mischievous glint in her eye returns. "Better than a ten."

"Give it time. I'm sure we will get there." My lips twitch, but I catch myself before Ellie adds it to that ridiculous smile counter of hers.

"So, what sort of advice do you need from me?"

I release a heavy breath. "I'm sure you've noticed I'm struggling to connect with Nico."

Her amusement dies along with the light in her eyes. "Right."

I thought she would have a hell of a lot more to say than *right*.

You knew it was a bad idea to ask her for help.

Julian was wrong. Ellie doesn't know how to help me when her relationship with Nico is completely different.

"I'm sorry to hear that." She looks away for a few seconds before her gaze returns to me.

"Has he talked to you about it?"

"Not much."

"But he *has* mentioned something?"

She takes a few seconds to respond, adding to my unease.

Maybe things are worse than you thought.

She wraps the hoodie string around her index finger three times before speaking. "Have you asked him about what's wrong?"

"Yes, but I'm not getting anywhere with him."

"Maybe you should try again."

"What's the point? He always finds a way to reject me."

Awareness dawns on her. "Oh, Rafa. I'm sorry."

The pity in her voice makes my stomach churn, filling me with shame. "Forget I said anything."

Her skin blanches. "I wish I could tell you more. I really do."

"Has he...said anything to you?"

Her face loses some of its color. "Not really."

"That's not a *no*."

"No, but it's not a *yes* either. We don't talk much about you."

Somehow, her attempt at making me feel better backfires, only adding to my growing frustration. "So much for you being able to help."

"Hey. I understand you're angry, but—"

"Angry? You think *this* is me being angry?" My sensibility goes out the window, along with any self-preservation. "My son barely wants to spend time with me anymore. Whenever I try—whether it's reading a book together, watching a movie, or playing video games—he shuts down and pushes me away, and do you know who he asks for instead?"

She fails to meet my eyes. "Me?"

"Yes," I hiss. "And how do you think that makes me feel?" I don't bother to shield my loathing. I'm not sure who I'm more frustrated with—her or me—but the rage and helplessness become all-consuming as I direct them straight at her.

"It makes me *hate* you." Speaking the words into existence feels wrong. My aunt taught me not to hate anyone, including my parents, but I can't think of any other way to describe the burning pang in my chest whenever I look at Ellie. Jealousy, rage, and shame seem to manifest as some weird case of heartburn that no bottle of antacid can fix.

"Is that how you really feel about me?" Her monotonous tone grates on my nerves.

"Yes," I say with slightly less confidence.

She takes so long to respond, I begin to question if she ever will.

"I don't think you do, because if that were the case, you would've fired me."

I cover up the fact that I am impressed by her honesty with a clenched jaw and narrowed eyes.

Another long pause follows before she speaks again. "Regardless of your misguided anger toward me, I do care about helping you with your relationship with Nico."

"Why?"

"Because deep down, I know you're a good guy, even if you try your hardest to prove the exact opposite."

I feel like Ellie laid me out on an operating table and cut me open, revealing all the broken parts I keep hidden. Truth is, I *was* a good guy, which became a weakness and a liability rather than a badge of honor. There is a reason nice guys always finish last, and it's usually because everyone gets ahead by walking all over them.

I drop my gaze as shame snakes its way through me, squeezing every ounce of confidence from my body.

With a sigh, Ellie stands, and I brace myself for her departure like I deserve, only to be stunned when she walks around the coffee table and takes a seat beside me. Our thighs graze, sending a lick of heat up my leg.

I've never been this close to her before. I made sure to prevent any opportunity that would lead to this kind of proximity, and a quick inhale reminds me why. Ellie smells like fresh-picked strawberries and a hint of Nico's favorite bath bomb, and it screws with my head and my heart all at the same time as I take another deep breath.

I've always had this…interest in her. Every time I dropped Nico off for his music lessons at The Broken Chord, Ellie's eyes would light up to match her bright smile, temporarily stunning me. I'm pretty sure she chalked up my silence and general broodiness as part of my personality, and while she wasn't wrong, she was partially to blame too.

Whatever attraction I felt toward her quickly transformed into something far less desirable as time went on and my relationship with my son became more strained.

Jealousy.

I want to shoo her away, but then she shocks me when she places her palm against my back and rubs in a circular pattern. The motion is comforting rather than aggravating, which worries me.

Being near each other is one thing, but touching?

Completely inappropriate and unprofessional, but I can't find it in me to get up and move.

Instead, I sit there, still as a statue, while Ellie tries to soothe *me*, a man who doesn't deserve an ounce of her sympathy or compassion. At best, I've been marginally polite, and at worst, I've been a grumpy, insecure asshole who has taken out my jealousy on her.

All those past incidents fade away as she comforts me, and my body, which was rigid at first, slowly relaxes with every pass of her palm across my wide back.

You'll move in a second, I promise myself as I lean into her touch.

"I have firsthand experience dealing with bad dads, and you're not one of them, no matter how much you tell yourself otherwise." Her words sneak past my barriers and restore a fractured part of me.

I don't speak for a whole minute, although I wish I hadn't at all once I say, "I feel helpless sometimes."

"I can't begin to imagine what it must feel like to be in your position." She gives my shoulder a squeeze. It's strictly platonic on her end, but my heart jolts in my chest.

I turn to face her and instantly regret it as her eyes cast some kind of spell on me. The limited lighting brings out the darker shades of green and brown in her eyes tonight, and I can't tear myself away.

I've never seen eyes quite like hers before, and maybe it was for the best, because a single stolen glance has my skin tingling.

I want to blame the alcohol in my system, but the excuse

feels cheap. *I'm* the problem, not a few beers or a couple sips of bourbon.

Before I have a chance to dive into my reaction, a loud thud on the other side of the house steals our attention. She sucks in a breath, and my stomach lurches as a sharp cry pierces through the quiet.

"*¡Papi!*"

"Nicolas!" I bang into the coffee table and trip over my feet in my panic. "I'm coming!"

With my heart in my throat and Ellie on my heels, I take off running. Nico's room feels too far away as I rush toward the sound of his cries.

I throw open the door to his bedroom, ignoring how the knob permanently embeds itself in the drywall as I dash inside. My shaky legs threaten to give out at the sight of Nico curled into a ball on the floor. Blood is pooled around his split chin and soaking into his dinosaur-themed PJs, while tears stain his chubby cheeks.

Based on the bloody footboard and the rug being at an odd angle, I assume that Nico must have tripped and rammed his chin into the wood post before falling to the floor.

"Oh God." Ellie's voice rips me away from my stupor.

I drop to my knees in front of Nico. I'm not given a chance to warn him to stay put before he throws himself into my arms with a cry. My whole heart aches at the sound, and it tears me up inside to pull him away so I can get a better look at him. "Does it hurt anywhere else?"

"No." Nico's voice is hoarse from crying.

Ellie kneels on the floor beside him and places his glasses

back on his head. With shaky hands, I check him for any other injuries, all while he cries in pain. Each tear on his face feels like I took a bullet to my chest.

I'm stunned for a second by the blood oozing from his wound, and my stomach rolls.

Is that bone—

Ellie digs her nails into my arm, yanking me from my spiraling thoughts. "We need to take him to the hospital."

Nico cries out against it.

I choke on the lump in my throat. "I... He..."

"We need to find something to help stop the bleeding first. I'll go look while you stay with him?"

Nico crawls back onto my lap and wraps his arms around my neck, answering her question for me. Ellie searches the bathroom while I readjust Nico's position against my chest so I can carry him while being mindful of the gash on his chin.

Nico looks up at me with tear-stained eyes. "I'm sorry. So, so sorry."

"You have nothing to apologize for." Although the look on his face and his continuous insistence on apologizing have me questioning if that's true.

CHAPTER SIX

Ellie

Guilt prevents me from looking Rafael in the face. I've felt sick to my stomach ever since we entered the hospital, and it has nothing to do with Nico's bloody chin or the view I have of the doctor sewing his split skin back together.

Thankfully, Nico looks better than he did when we first found him bleeding on his bedroom floor, but his eyes lack that special glimmer to them despite the doctor doing her best to distract him with funny stories about her own children.

"All done." The doctor drops the used supplies in a medical waste bin before letting us know she will be back in a moment.

Nico entertains himself with Rafael's phone while we adults sit in uncomfortable silence and wait for the doctor.

As my anxiety grows, incriminating hives appear on my

chest. No amount of scratching alleviates the itchiness, and I release a frustrated growl.

"All good?" Rafael's gaze drops to my black hoodie.

Nico's wide eyes swing to mine, and I tuck my hands into my front pocket. "I'm fine."

"If you need to step outside…"

"I said I'm fine."

Rafael's lips purse as he refrains from asking any further questions.

A few minutes later, the same doctor reenters the room before asking a few follow-up questions about Nico's injury and pain. With every answer Nico gives, the knot in my stomach tightens until I'm about to curl over in discomfort. Rafael keeps glancing at me out of the corner of his eye, which only makes the belly pain worse.

The doctor instructs Nico to follow the path of her miniature flashlight before asking, "How's your vision?"

Nico flinches. Rafael sneaks a glance at me, but I stare straight ahead, ignoring my itchy skin.

"When was your last test?"

"January," Rafael answers for him.

"Have you noticed any changes since then?" The doctor scans the medical chart.

Rafael goes still while every muscle in my body tenses.

Nico ignores the flashlight as he stares down at his lap. "Yes."

"You didn't say anything," Rafael says.

"I'm sorry." Nico—sweet, innocent Nico—looks over at me for support while simultaneously giving me away.

I do my best to keep my face blank, although my hands tremble inside my hoodie pocket while Rafael looks at me like I'm his biggest enemy. "Did you know?"

I lose my ability to speak.

"Did. You. Know?" he asks in a rough tone.

I drop my gaze, wishing I could erase the look of mistrust and disgust from his face. "Yes."

A little over an hour later, we finally pull up to the house. Rafael kills the engine and unbuckles his seat belt softly. I do the same and exit the truck, taking in a fresh lungful of air that isn't tainted by Rafael's anger and intoxicatingly addictive scent.

Rafael pulls Nico out from the back seat and tucks him against his chest, being careful not to wake him up. My stiff movements come off robotic as I follow them into the house.

Before I walk past the foyer, Rafael speaks up.

"Stay here," he mutters in a low voice. I'm stunned into submission as I stand in the front entryway, twisting my hands in my pocket while I wait for the inevitable.

Rafael takes his sweet time getting Nico ready for bed, all while my heart feels close to launching itself out of my chest. Although I could definitely use an edible or two to take the edge off, sneaking into my room after Rafael's request to stay put would only make my situation worse.

Is that even possible?

I curse to myself as a door closes in the distance. Goose

bumps spread across my skin as Rafael's steps echo off the vaulted ceiling. He walks out of the dark hallway and motions for me to follow him into the living room.

Walking behind him feels like I'm trudging through quicksand.

"Sit."

I follow his command and drop onto the couch across from his favorite leather chair. He heads over to the bar cart in the corner and pours himself a drink before taking a seat diagonal to me. Neither one of us says anything as he brings the glass to his lips and takes a sip.

His eyes remain glued to mine while his Adam's apple bobs as he swallows. My skin flushes, and I look away as blood rushes to my ears. "I can explain."

"Don't bother."

"But—"

He balances his glass on his muscular thigh. "I have one question for you."

"Okay."

"You knew."

"That's a statement."

His jaw clenches so hard, I fear for the state of his molars.

"When I talked to you yesterday about him, you knew?" He enunciates each word with a sneer.

"Yes, but—"

"Then that's all." Ice rattles as he draws the glass back toward his mouth.

"I'm so sorry. I wish I could take it all back. I had no idea something like this could happen, or—"

He cuts me off with an icy glare. "You can't, though, can you?"

"Nico begged me not to say anything."

"If I wanted an explanation, I would have asked for one."

"I deserve a chance to—"

"You deserve *nothing*," he hisses under his breath.

If I had gone against Nico's wishes and said something like I had wanted to, this wouldn't be happening right now.

But it did.

I take a deep breath to center myself. "Regardless, I am sorry. Nico getting hurt was an accident."

"So was hiring you."

My sharp inhale only seems to annoy him more.

He doesn't bother looking at me as he says, "I should've known better than to trust someone like you."

My whole world stops as I process his words. "What?"

"You have no experience with children, and it clearly shows."

Deep breaths, Ellie. He has every right to be upset, so no need to fight his fire with yours.

My hands curl into tight fists. "In the time I've worked here, I have made one mistake—"

"A mistake that sent my kid to the hospital!"

I do my best to quell my anger like my mom taught me. "I'm so sorry."

"You're lucky I don't sue."

"What?" My voice trembles, along with my hands by my sides. I hate myself for showing any sign of weakness, but I can't stop the raw burst of emotion from overwhelming me.

He looks unbothered by my outburst as he picks at a piece of invisible lint. "If that's all…"

His cold reaction triggers a past memory of Ava doing the same. The way she dismissed me like I never mattered. Like we hadn't been friends for fifteen years before she let a man and his lies get between our friendship… God, I'll never forget the ache.

Rafael robs me of my next reply. "I'm taking Nico to my aunt's house tomorrow for a sleepover, so that should give you enough time to clear out your room."

I must have misheard him. "Excuse me?"

"I'll get Nico ready for school and drive him there myself. It's best for you to stay in your room during that time."

"Can I at least say goodbye to him?"

Rafael cuts me down with a single "No."

I rapidly blink until I regain control of my tears. "So that's it? I'm dismissed?"

"No, Eleanor. You're fired."

CHAPTER SEVEN

Ellie

Willow, who has been my best friend since I moved to Lake Wisteria in middle school, didn't ask any questions when I showed up at her lakeside bungalow in the middle of the night with tear-stained cheeks and a car stuffed with my personal belongings. I thought I could wait until morning to pack up my room, but then I considered how it would feel to stay quiet while Nico went about his morning routine, completely unaware of me no longer being his nanny.

So, similar to the time Ava fired me as her songwriter, I disappeared in the middle of the night. That option seemed better than pulling Rafael aside and begging for my job back because I'm not sure if I could survive another conversation like our last one.

I'm not a confrontational person. Sure, I can sass back

because I am my mother's daughter after all, but when push comes to shove, I'd much rather run away than stand my ground against someone who hurt me.

Even if it means never getting closure.

I wake up in the morning to find Willow already in the kitchen pouring us both cups of coffee. After a few sips of courage, I give her a short summary of everything that happened.

Willow leans against the kitchen counter with a frown. "So he just fired you without giving you any chance to explain?"

"Yup."

"What an asshole."

"Tell me about it."

"I mean, listen. He was right to be angry at you for keeping that secret from him, but he could have gone about it a little differently."

I shrug off her statement. "It is what it is. I was in the wrong, so this is my penance."

She frowns. "I know things suck right now, but you're better off without Rafael anyway. He always took you and your time for granted." The dislike is written clear as day across her freckled face. Her pale cheeks, which were already pink from her morning run, darken into a deeper shade of red as she hesitantly tucks a strand of reddish-orange hair behind her ear.

Since we became best friends in middle school, I've never known Willow to hold back from sharing her opinion, so I'm surprised to say the least. "You never said anything before."

"Because since everything went down with Ava and the record label, you seemed genuinely happy for the first time in months. You had a *purpose*. Nico was good for you and vice versa, even if his father is too stubborn to see that."

Unlike Willow, who didn't miss a beat after Ava fired her because she chose to believe my story about what happened with Darius, I struggled. *Hard.*

I still feel guilty about Willow losing her dream job as Ava's public relations manager because of me, even if she's repeatedly told me she would have left anyway because our friendship came first.

Wherever you go, I go, she had said before packing up her belongings and moving back to Lake Wisteria with me.

The dull throb in my chest transforms into a strong ache.

Willow continues when I don't speak up. "I don't care if Rafael was right to fire you. He was wrong for not letting you say goodbye at least."

"It's not like I gave him a chance to change his mind before running away."

"He doesn't deserve you." Willow gives my clenched hand a pat. "As it is, I'm surprised you put up with him for this long."

"He wasn't that bad."

"But was he good?"

Her question stumps me. In some ways, Rafael was decent to me. He gave me a job despite my inexperience with nannying and paid me well for my work, although I struggled with his grumpy attitude.

I was willing to put up with a lot from him solely because I love Nico and the financial freedom I gained thanks to Rafael's generous paychecks. With my monthly salary and a free place to stay, I was saving most of my money in hopes of suing Ava one day.

First, I needed to get over my little issue with confrontation and find a copyright lawyer who didn't run in the opposite direction as soon as I mentioned her name.

A knock on the front door startles me. "Who's that?"

"Lorenzo."

"He comes to your house now? Are you two friends or something?"

Willow recently took Lorenzo Vittori, the town's newest billionaire resident, on as a PR client. The decision was an easy one, especially since my best friend loves a good challenge, and Lorenzo was the biggest one yet, with his goal to replace Lake Wisteria's Mayor Ludlow, whose family has been here since the town was founded in the 1800s.

Unlike the Ludlows, who raise their kids on silver spoons and *Madame Virginia's Rules of Etiquette*, the Vittori name is synonymous with sinning, debauchery, and a billion-dollar international gambling empire. With luxury casino hotels located all over the world, the Vittori family specializes in all seven deadly sins.

To say he isn't mayor material is a gross understatement, but unlike me, Willow doesn't back down from adversity.

She laughs. "No, we're not really friends, but he sure could use one."

"Then what is he doing here this early?"

"I don't want anyone overhearing us talk about Operation Fake Fiancée. You know how quickly word spreads in this town."

My brows hike toward my hairline. "So getting him a fake fiancée is a whole operation now?"

"Yes, but it's still in the planning phase, so don't worry."

"Why would I be worried?"

"Because the moment Lorenzo hears you're unemployed and looking for a job, he might try to hire you, but as your best friend, I must insist that you say no. He's not marriage material. Take my word for it."

Lorenzo beats against the front door until Willow lets him inside. They share a few hushed whispers in the entryway before my best friend strolls back into the kitchen with Lorenzo trailing behind her.

The temperature in the room drops a few degrees, and a chill rushes down my spine when Lorenzo and I lock eyes. As much as I appreciate Willow's warning, there is no way in hell I would ever agree to fake-marry someone who elicits that kind of response from me, no matter how attractive or rich they are.

"Hey." He tips his chin in my direction, showing off his angular jawline as he stops in front of the outdated countertop across from me. He looks out of place with his custom suit, designer accessories, and fancy haircut, yet no one would guess he isn't perfectly at home with the confidence he exudes.

I aspire to achieve the amount of fucks Lorenzo has to give, which is none.

I lean back in my chair and cross my arms. "I hear you're looking for a wife."

He shoots Willow a withering glance. "I thought we agreed to keep that a secret."

"You can trust her."

"I don't trust anyone."

I point at myself. "Hi. I'm standing right here."

His dark eyes flick over me without an ounce of interest. "Are you single?"

"Yes."

"Would you like to become a millionaire?"

A laugh explodes out of me. "Who wouldn't?"

"I have a proposition."

"Save it. There's not enough Vittori money in the world that could convince me to be your wife."

He doesn't look affronted, because that would require feeling something other than indifference, but he does turn his nose up at my comment. "Whatever. I'm not into blonds anyway."

Willow lets out a huff. "That rules out half of the eligible women in this town."

His clinical gaze meets hers. "Or redheads for that matter."

"She's been taken since eighth grade." I ignore the twinge in my chest at the same wistful look Willow always gets whenever she thinks about her fiancé, who is completing his internal surgery residency in Washington. I'm not jealous of their long-distance relationship or anything, but I do wish for that kind of companionship. The same connection that my mom has with my stepdad.

Instead, I'm being propositioned by a sociopath to play his fake fiancée because I'm single and unemployed.

Lorenzo glances at his watch for the third time since arriving, which is my cue to go. I've been enough of an inconvenience for Willow as it is.

"As much fun as this has been…" I slide off my stool and inch toward the exit.

"Where are you going?" Willow points at my half-finished cereal bowl.

"My parents' place. I want to get there before my mom leaves for work."

"I thought you were going to stay with me."

"I'm afraid another night on your guest mattress might screw up my spine alignment." I rub at the knot forming in my neck.

"You can share my bed!"

"Thanks, but your snoring would keep me up all night."

She flips me off, and I break out into laughter.

"Add *no snoring* to my list of requests too," Lorenzo drawls.

Willow shoots daggers at him before looking back at me. "Are you sure?"

"Yeah. Positive."

"If you change your mind, you'll always have a room available here." Willow hugs me. She made the same offer when we moved back to Lake Wisteria after Ava hurt me.

I return her embrace. "I know."

"I could even get a new mattress to sweeten the deal."

I laugh despite the tears building behind my eyelids. "Save the money for your wedding. You're going to need it with your taste."

CHAPTER EIGHT

Rafael

After staying up until way too late last night working on another 3D superhero for Nico's collection, I struggle to get out of bed. I've never been a morning person, but Ellie is—

Shit.

For a second, I selfishly wish Ellie were still here to help me. It's a stupid thought, and I beat myself up over the compulsive reaction as I crawl out from underneath the comforter and head downstairs to prepare Nico's breakfast.

After last night, pancakes feel like the best choice, so I gather the ingredients and get to work on making Nico's favorite meal. Usually, I stick to making a big breakfast on Saturdays, when Ellie is gone for the day, but today calls for something special.

Bribery.

I get so caught up in thinking about how to break the news

to Nico that I end up burning two in the process. If Ellie were here, she'd shoo me out of my own kitchen and take over my task because, unlike me, she enjoys cooking. She even looks forward to learning new recipes while I stick to the tried-and-true family favorites of green spaghetti, mole, pozole, and filet mignon straight from the grill.

The earlier pang in my chest at the memory of Ellie returns with a vengeance, and I busy myself with preparing Nico's lunchbox to distract myself until it's time to wake him up.

Nico groans and yanks his comforter over his head when I open the blinds, reminding me of myself.

"I made you pancakes." I lift the comforter and tickle the bottoms of his feet.

"Stop!" he hisses while kicking his feet out.

"Not until you get out of bed."

He huffs and puffs as he rolls out of bed with a terrible case of bedhead and a scary frown.

"For someone who is about to eat blueberry pancakes, you sure are grumpy."

His eyes narrow. "With whipped cream?"

"Yes."

"And strawberries?"

"You like those?" I feign ignorance.

His head drops back with a groan.

I steer him toward the door. "Of course I added strawberries. Like I could ever forget your favorite."

He silently follows behind me, and I brace myself as we walk past Ellie's room. The same sick feeling of dread returns, my steps subconsciously slowing until Nico passes by me. I'm so distracted that I don't notice the door was left ajar until Nico throws it open.

"Ellie?" He takes a step inside and halts. "Are you here? Dad made pancakes."

Unlike Nico, I haven't been inside Ellie's room since the day she moved in, but I can quickly tell something is off. From the empty closet full of hangers to the house key left on top of the dresser, hints of Nico's previous nanny remain, although her belongings do not.

"Where's Ellie's stuff?" Nico looks up at me with pinched brows.

I don't answer him, mainly because I'm not sure *how* to. The last thing I expected was for Ellie to sneak out in the middle of the night, but then again, I didn't give her a reason to stick around.

Despite being angry about Ellie withholding the truth, I can't help feeling like a dick for kicking her out the way I did. Last night, I gave her a twenty-four-hour eviction notice without considering if she even had a place to go.

She has a best friend who lives in town—that much I know—but do they have room for her? I'm also aware that her mother lives somewhere in Lake Wisteria, but Ellie hasn't said much about her before, so I'm not sure what their relationship is like.

Why do you care? She isn't your problem anymore.

If that were true, then why does my chest feel so

uncomfortably tight all of a sudden? And how do I explain the tension building underneath my skull, pulsing with every pump of my heart?

Nico shakes my arm hard enough to pull me away from my thoughts. "Why is all her stuff gone?" His voice cracks on the final word.

My reply gets trapped in my throat as he looks up at me with eyes filled to the brim with tears. I knew this conversation would be difficult, but I was hoping it could wait until after I placated him with pancakes, a new 3D-printed superhero to add to his growing collection, and an important conversation about always telling each other the truth.

"You made her leave, didn't you?" A dark look passes over his face that I recognize too often on my own, and it instantly makes my stomach churn.

I kneel before him so we can be at eye level. "I know you care about Ellie, but I can't let her take care of you anymore after she hid the truth from me."

Rather than give in to the tears threatening to fall, Nico shoves me with all his might, and I wobble on my knees before regaining my balance. My kid has never been aggressive a single day in his life. Nico is a lover, not a fighter, so I'm floored by his reaction.

Floored *and* heartbroken, although I ignore the ache in my chest as I try to reach for him.

He steers clear of my open arms. "You told her to leave?"

"Yes."

"Why? Why? Why?" He shoves me again, but I'm better prepared this time to take the hit, both to my heart and my body.

I gently clasp his wrists. "Use your words, not your hands."

He tries to pull himself free of my hold. "No."

"Nicolas," I beg. "You know I couldn't let her stay after what happened."

"She's my best friend." Desperation bleeds into his voice.

"She was your *nanny*."

"No! You don't understand!" He tries to break out of my hold and fails. "She wanted to tell you, but I told her not to." A single tear rolls down his cheek.

I hate myself for hurting him like this, and I hate Ellie even more for putting me in this kind of position in the first place. If she hadn't left in the middle of the night, I could have had time to better prepare Nico for her departure.

"She's the adult and you're the kid. You might not have known better, but she did."

He shakes his head repeatedly. "You took my best friend away."

"I'll find you someone better—"

"No! I want Ellie!"

"That's not possible."

"You always make everyone leave!"

I let him go, too stunned by his killing blow to do anything but sit still while my son runs back to his room. He slams the door hard enough to make the frame shake.

I'm not sure how much time passes, but I don't get up until the ache in my knees matches the one in my chest.

You always make everyone leave. Nico's words haunt me.

My mom. My ex-wife. Ellie. The list continues to grow, along with my trust issues.

Since I despise letting any food go to waste after going to bed hungry far too many times, I eat Nico's serving and mine while my thoughts of self-loathing keep me company at the kitchen island.

Just a typical Tuesday.

CHAPTER NINE

Ellie

I drive to my mom's house on the south side of town, far away from the dazzling mansions lining the lakeshore and Willow's waterfront bungalow that has survived the test of time despite the town's real estate developer and Rafael's cousin, Julian Lopez, trying to buy up the property.

My mom and stepdad live at the southern tip of town, close to Nico's school and the town's fairgrounds, which host Lake Wisteria's famous festivals celebrating all four seasons. Our area is run-down and far less glamorous than the rest of town, but my mom has done her best to turn the dilapidated three-bedroom house into a home worth visiting every week.

My stepdad, Burt, opens the door with the biggest smile. "Ellie Sophia Sinclair. What a nice surprise."

"Is it?" I check out their empty living room. It's changed

a lot since I was a kid, thanks to my mom's never-ending decorating ideas and Burt's willingness to try them out despite disliking manual labor and the hour-long drive to my mom's favorite home decor store.

"To what do we owe this random drop-in? It's not even Saturday."

My smile falls. "I got fired."

His gray brows pull together. "Who do I need to speak to?"

My laugh comes out more like a sob.

"Oh no. Not the tears. I don't handle those very well." My stepdad pulls me into one of his famous bear hugs. They always make me feel like a little kid again, even after outgrowing him by a few inches once I turned twelve.

"Beatrice! Come quick. Our daughter needs your help while I go murder her boss."

"*Ex*-boss."

He squeezes me hard. "Not if I can help it."

"What?" My mom comes rushing out of the kitchen with a cloud of flour dust following her. "Ellie? What are you doing here?"

"Hi, Mom." I wiggle out of Burt's embrace and wipe the tears from my face.

Burt softly pushes me in my mom's direction. "Keep an eye on her while I go searching for my ax."

"It's in the garage. Bottom left shelf next to the paint cans."

"*Mom.*"

"What's going on?" She cradles my head between her palms before kissing my forehead.

"I'll tell you, but first you need to convince Burt not to murder Rafael."

He stands as tall as his five-foot-seven frame will allow. "I wasn't going to murder him."

"Or threaten bodily harm," I add. "What will my mom do if you end up in jail?"

Mom gives my cheeks a squeeze. "He'd wait until I found a way to end up in there with him."

"You two are hopeless," I groan before throwing myself on the sectional.

"Fortunately." Burt draws my mom into a side hug and kisses the top of her head. She melts into him with the silliest smile on her face.

When I was a kid, I used to think it was gross that my mom had a crush on my music teacher–turned–tutor who gave me free lessons because he liked her too, but now, I can't get enough of their love. It's nice to know that my mom is with someone who cares about her as much as I do, especially after the train wreck of a marriage she had with my biological father.

We don't talk about him much, mostly because we've both put in the work to move on from his psychological abuse, but that doesn't mean I never think about the man, especially when it's so easy to see how much kinder and more patient Burt is.

My mom and Burt fuss over me while they help me unload the car and carry my belongings into my childhood bedroom. I take the lead on unpacking everything. Once everything is put back in its place, I lay on my pink, ruffled comforter and stare up at the stars stuck to the ceiling.

Funny how a year ago I was sharing a small Los Angeles apartment with Ava and Willow, spending my days songwriting and my nights waitressing to cover the bills while I waited for my big break. Now, I'm back in my childhood bedroom like I never left.

Everything looks the same, with the walls covered by concert posters and fairy lights Burt hung when I was in middle school. Even my nightstand and the stacks of diaries in the bottom drawer remain untouched.

My mom checks out my newly organized closet full of hoodies, leggings, and T-shirts. "Must you wear so much black?"

"There's some white clothes in there."

"And navy." Burt winks at me.

Mom frowns. "You dress like you're in mourning."

"Perfect, since I'll be grieving my employment status for the foreseeable future."

Burt cracks a smile, along with the tension, when he asks, "What do you say we play some music together while your mom does her thing?"

"I don't know…"

"Come on. I even got a new guitar for you to test out."

My lips press together.

"Did I mention how I found it while thrift shopping at Another Man's Treasure? Turns out it was signed by Cole Griffin and Phoebe Montgomery."

"You're joking."

"Nope. The shop owner confirmed that it's real."

I jump off my bed. "Oh my God! You have to show me!"

I have no idea how a guitar signed by Cole Griffin, legendary lyricist and folk musician, and his cowriter ended up at our town's secondhand shop, but I need to see it.

Burt laughs to himself as I follow him out of my bedroom and into his makeshift music room, which doubles as my mom's home office. The space brings back many fond memories of us spending hours together while he taught me how to play the same instruments I'm teaching Nico.

Taught Nico.

My throat constricts, along with my heart.

Deep breaths, Ellie.

"What are you thinking about that's got you looking like you sucked on a lemon?" Burt asks.

"Nothing." I check out the acoustic guitar with Cole and Phoebe's signatures before remembering. "Oh no."

"What?"

"I forgot my guitar at the Lopez house."

Burt's face pales. "Do you want me to get it for you?"

"No," I say in a rush.

"I don't mind the drive. It might be nice to see how the other half lives."

"They're not the other half. They're the .0001 percenters."

"Why use math when you can just say *filthy rich*?"

I shake my head with a laugh. "I appreciate you offering to help, but no. I'm already enough of an imposition as it is."

"An imposition? To whom? Let me have a word with them." He searches the empty room for a missing person like a total goof.

Someone needs to protect this man at all costs because he is a national treasure.

"I don't want to be a bother."

He shoots me an exasperated look while holding a guitar

out for me to grab. "You're not. But if you insist on helping, then you should get a new job soon. Our water bill is going to double next month thanks to your long showers."

I strum the chords with my middle finger, earning a deep belly laugh from him.

"Are you hiring at the music store?" I ask.

"For you, always, although I've got to warn you... some of the newer kids who come in for music lessons are tough. I blame those millionaire transplants who swear their children are the next Chopin and Beethoven."

I make a face. "I hope I can handle it."

"I *know* you can. You're a Sinclair, after all."

My chest warms. My stepdad is the most genuine, kind-hearted man I've ever met, and I'd be lucky to find a partner who is half the person he is. I may have never called him Dad, but he is mine in every way that counts, which is why I took on his last name.

Burt begins strumming the opening of our favorite song, and together, we play until I forget all about my life and all the problems waiting for me later, like getting my favorite guitar back.

CHAPTER TEN

Rafael

I try three separate times to start up a conversation with Nico during the ride to my aunt's lakefront house near the northern part of town. I was hoping he would weigh in on what summer camp he wants to attend or what flavor cake he would like for his birthday party, but he completely ignores me. He even goes as far as putting on his superhero-themed headphones while I'm speaking.

Not even my aunt, who always manages to make Nico smile and laugh, is able to pull him out of his bad mood when we arrive at her house. He is so caught up in his thoughts that he almost forgets to give her a proper greeting until she reminds him.

With a reluctant groan, he kisses her cheek before turning away from both of us.

"What happened?" Josefina watches Nico retreat into the guest bedroom with his overnight bag. Her dark, professionally dyed hair and glowing tan skin make her look younger than her fifty-seven years. If it weren't for her rare scowl emphasizing the few wrinkles surrounding her brown eyes and mouth, I would guess her to be around forty.

I brush my hand through my unruly hair. "He had an accident last night and had to go to the emergency room."

"I wasn't talking about his stitches." She stares at me with a perfectly arched brow and her arms crossed tightly against her chest.

I release a deep sigh. "It's a long story."

"Perfect. You can share it while I cut your hair." She drags me into the kitchen. The sight of tamales cooking on the stove makes my mouth water and my stomach grumble.

"Haircut first. Dinner after." She pulls out a stool for me before gathering the supplies.

She lays out a few combs, a spray bottle full of water, and a pair of scissors. The silver clippers she plugs into the socket gleam from the sun shining through the window overlooking Lake Wisteria, taunting me.

Sometimes, I'm tempted to ask her to shave off my short beard, but then I'm quick to shake off the thought. Once upon a time, I shaved at least twice a week, but now, taking care of my beard feels like a massive effort. If it weren't for Nico hating when it reaches a certain length, I doubt I'd bother with trimming it.

My aunt gives my shoulder a reassuring squeeze. "*No te preocupes.* I'm only using those to clean up your edges."

That loosens some of the tension in my shoulders. Josefina has been styling my hair since a middle school haircut went terribly wrong, so I trust her not to completely botch it. She might tease me about finding a good barber since I can afford one, but I know she secretly loves helping me, so I haven't bothered replacing her.

Like Julian and me, she loves feeling useful, even with something simple like cutting my hair.

There is nothing I want more than to make my aunt happy for the rest of her days. She deserves it after all she has done for me, including taking me in and raising me like her own son when my father passed away soon after my mother had.

I take a seat at the counter and wait as she sets herself up behind the barstool.

"*¿Dime lo que está pasando?*" She picks up the spray bottle.

"I let Ellie go."

My aunt aims the nozzle at my face and shoots at my eyes.

"Hey!" I wipe the droplets away with a scowl. "What was that for?"

"How could you do that to her?"

"How could *I* do that to *her*? What about what *she* did to *me*? And to Nico?"

Her brows rise. "What do you mean?"

I explain everything that has happened in the last twenty-four hours while my aunt combs through my hair. When I finish, I peek over my shoulder.

"You're right. She shouldn't have kept Nico's condition a secret."

No te preocupes: Don't worry.

Dime lo que está pasando?: Tell me what's going on.

I didn't realize how much I needed my feelings validated until now because, with Nico treating me like public enemy number one, I was questioning if I made the right choice.

"I know," I say with a sigh.

"*Pero…*" She lets the sentence hang.

"Don't tell me you're defending her now," I mutter under my breath.

My aunt swaps the comb for the pair of scissors and shoots me a knowing look. "No. What she did was wrong, but I'm sure she had a good reason to risk her job for a secret like that."

I shake my head in disbelief. "No reason will ever be good enough."

"For you, no, but for Nico, it probably was, which is why he asked her not to say anything."

I sit with my aunt's comment for the rest of the day and question why my son hid the truth from me in the first place, and worse, why Ellie agreed with him.

The Kids' Table group chat I share with Julian and the Muñoz sisters chimes from three new text notifications. I consider ignoring them and taking my horse out on the trail like I had planned, but curiosity wins.

I pat Penelope's side and ask her to hold on a few minutes before pulling out my phone.

Pero…: But…

LILY

You fired Ellie?!

DAHLIA

What? No way.

LILY

Yes.

ME

Who told you?

My aunt promised not to say anything until this weekend, when Nico and I finally attend Sunday lunch after spending the last month filling our time with playdates, so I'm not sure how Lily found out.

I don't have a chance to consider a list of likely suspects because my phone beeps again.

LILY

Doesn't matter. Focus on the subject at hand.

DAHLIA

I liked her.

LILY

Me too. She made the best chocolate chip cookies.

DAHLIA

And homemade bread and pasta and pizza. Seriously, the woman has more recipes than Betty Crocker.

LILY

Don't forget about her pozole. If I didn't know any better, I would have assumed she was Mexican too because it's THAT good.

LILY

Dare I say it was better than Josefina's.

Lily unsent a message.

DAHLIA

Slick.

DAHLIA

Too bad I already took a screenshot.

Lily follows up with a water gun emoji pointed at a smiling face.

JULIAN

You two do realize this is a group chat, right?

They both reply with a single "yes" text message.

> **ME**
>
> I can tell you're both really concerned about why she was fired.

My cousin sends me a private text instead of replying in the group.

> **JULIAN**
>
> I take it that conversation with Ellie went well?

> **ME**
>
> Unfortunately, it was cut short by Nico being rushed to the hospital.

Julian's name and contact photo pop up on my screen. I battle between letting it go to voicemail and answering before choosing the latter.

My cousin skips past hello and asks, "Is he okay?"

"Yeah. Just needed some stitches on his chin, no thanks to Ellie."

"Thank God. What happened?" he asks in that no-bullshit tone of his.

I tell him the same story, although I go into greater detail than I had with my aunt, mentioning that I had taken his advice and opened up about how I was feeling, only to find out she betrayed my trust.

"Damn." Julian whistles to himself.

"Yup."

"What are you going to do?"

"Find someone to replace her after we come back from our trip."

"Hm."

"What?"

"Are you sure the trip is still happening?"

"Why wouldn't it be?"

"Because Nico sent me a text not too long ago asking me if I was free and interested in going to Hawaii. I thought he was joking, but now it all makes sense."

I scrub my face with a curse. "Whose phone is he borrowing?"

"Ma's."

My drawn-out sigh is one only a parent can muster. "I told her to monitor him for a reason."

"Yeah, but you know how she likes to be a cool grandma." My cousin laughs. "Anyway, Nico also let me know that his birthday party is canceled until his nanny is rehired."

"He did *what*?"

"Dahlia and Lily got a text too. Oh, and you might want to check if his mother got one as well. Not that she was ever going to come anyway since she hasn't made it to his last two."

The base of my neck throbs from an incoming headache. "Fuck me."

"Speaking of the little devil," he says, "he just asked me if we could take my private jet instead of yours. Should I say yes? I've always wanted to visit Hawaii, and now I have the perfect reason to."

I rub my pounding temple with my thumb. "Unbelievable."

"You've got to admit it's impressive how smart he is."

"Yeah. If only he applied that same effort toward his homework."

Julian lets out a soft chuckle. "What are you going to do with him?"

"I have no idea."

Much to my annoyance, it turns out Nico isn't the only one missing Ellie. I do too, although I never thought I would. Despite my best efforts to forget about her, it's impossible with all the little reminders she left around the house.

A hoodie forgotten in the dryer. The stainless-steel water bottle, which she called her emotional support bottle, left to dry on the dish rack. Her guitar abandoned on the coffee table, untouched since Nico's accident.

The last few nights, I have gone downstairs expecting to hear the sound of a guitar playing, only to be met with silence.

Perhaps if I get rid of the very reminders of her, then the guilt weighing on my shoulders will disappear as well, which is why I make a split-second decision to text her.

ME

You left your guitar and a few things here. Do you want to meet me somewhere so I can give them to you?

I spend the next five minutes waiting for a reply, only to find myself annoyed when she leaves me on read.

ME

Nico claimed your water bottle as his own now, so good luck trying to get it back.

I groan at how pathetic I sound.

To stop myself from texting her again, I busy myself with painting a new miniature figurine I designed. My latest creation took me two weeks of trial and error, and I nearly broke my thirty-thousand-dollar machine in the process of replicating Nico's latest favorite superhero, but the stress was worth it.

Once my hand aches and my eyes droop from exhaustion, I shut the desk lamp off and head to my bedroom, checking my phone for any new messages. While the Muñoz-Lopez group chat has twenty missed texts and the Kids' Table group chat has ten additional unread ones, my text thread with Ellie remains quiet.

I have no right to feel disappointed at her ignoring me, but I do, and I'm not entirely sure what to do with that.

CHAPTER ELEVEN

Rafael

My son's resolve is admirable. I'm sure I'd be impressed by the lengths he has taken to make me reconsider Ellie's position if I wasn't so frustrated by his silent treatment.

First, he canceled his birthday party and asked my aunt to contact the amusement center a few towns over to refund my original deposit. Then, he called my assistant, Ariel—a number I gave him for emergencies only—and requested our family trip to be postponed until further notice.

According to my aunt, he called Ellie too, but she didn't answer.

People say we shouldn't negotiate with terrorists, but what happens when the one causing terror is my eight-year-old son? Do I give in to his demands, or do I stand strong despite feeling uncertain about my original choice to fire Ellie? Is there a point where I swallow my pride, throw in the towel, and say screw it, Ellie made a mistake, and I should forgive her for it?

As tempting as that option sounds, I can't give in. My trust issues run deep, and Ellie's secret tore through old scar tissue like it was cheap wrapping paper.

"*¿Papi?*"

Hearing Nico's voice after his self-imposed silence startles me. I drop the paintbrush I was using and look up from the miniature villain I was working on.

"What's up?" I keep my tone casual as I lean back in my chair.

"I need to talk to you."

"Really?" Excitement bleeds into my voice, giving my emotions away.

He doesn't smile or have that special spark in his eye as he nods, but I hold out hope.

You knew he would come around.

"Let's go over here." I step away from my desk and head toward the couch on the opposite side of my recreational room. Nico drags his feet behind me before taking a seat on his favorite chair. His feet dangle above the ground as he sits all the way back, and his sneakers light up when the heels smack together.

No matter how mature he tries to act, he will always be my little kid.

I take a seat. "What's going on?"

He stares at the folded piece of paper on his lap. "I'm sorry."

I blink. "What for?"

"Keeping my eyes a secret."

"It's okay."

"No, it's not." He unfolds the paper. Bile crawls up my throat as one of Nico's tears splashes against the photocopied page Ellie made of my high school yearbook. There is a rip down the center of the page, splitting my face in two.

I was so focused on hating Ellie's stupid smile tracker that I missed how much it meant to my son.

Another way you failed him.

"I just wanted you to be happy." The paper shakes in his hand.

"I *am* happy." I ditch my seat and kneel in front of his so we can be at eye level.

"No, you're not." He shakes his head. "You're sad and angry and scared, but never happy. Not really." He points at the picture of me smiling after I won the soccer state championships during my junior year. "Not like this."

My heart has been broken before, but it never felt remotely close to this. The ache is unbearable as my gaze bounces between the photo on Nico's lap and the look on his face.

In some ways, he is right. I'm not that kind of happy anymore, but only because it wasn't real to begin with. I believed it was at the time, but life taught me better. True happiness— the carefree kind that doesn't require any overthinking or second-guessing—isn't something that comes naturally to me. It never has, and maybe it never will, but I know one thing for sure.

"I'm my happiest when I'm with you." My voice cracks. "Never doubt that."

"Are you really?" His bottom lip trembles.

I tap a finger against the photo. "Just because I don't show it like this anymore doesn't mean I'm not."

"Even if I make you cry?"

"Huh?" I question if I heard him right. "What are you talking about?"

"I heard you," he whispers to himself. "I *saw* you."

A chill shoots down my spine. "When?"

"At the doctor's. In January."

Oh fuck. I've had plenty of low points in my life, but that day made it into the top three. I thought we were going in for a routine visit for his retinitis pigmentosa, so at worst, I was expecting a new glasses prescription, only to find out Nico's condition was progressing at such a rapid rate that he is likely to go legally blind by the time he's twenty. While his vision most likely won't go totally dark, he will struggle for the rest of his life.

I always felt guilty about unknowingly passing the RP gene onto my son, but on that day, I hit rock bottom.

I swallow despite the acid in my throat. "You told Ellie about that?"

He nods.

Mierda. Is *that* why Ellie didn't want to tell me about Nico's worsening vision? Was she trying to save me from further embarrassing myself?

God. I'm ashamed and disgusted with myself for appearing so damn weak in front of both of them.

Mierda: Shit.

I grab hold of his hand and give it a comforting squeeze. "I'm sorry you saw me like that."

The apology feels insufficient, especially now that I know Nico has been carrying this heaviness with him for over five months. No wonder he kept his distance and avoided me at all costs.

I can't emotionally support myself, let alone help him, so he found someone better.

He takes a deep breath. "And I'm sorry I'm all messed up."

"You're perfect just the way you are. Retinitis pigmentosa or not."

"But if I was perfect, then you wouldn't cry. And then Ellie would still be here because she wouldn't have kept my secret."

I've never hated myself more. "None of this is your fault. Not a single thing, you hear me?"

His grip on the paper tightens. "Yes, it is. She wanted to tell you, but I made her stay quiet."

It hits me just then that I will never win this battle against my son, no matter what I say or how many times I try to reassure him. I can't expect an emotionally invested eight-year-old kid to understand my logic, so he and I can go back and forth for days—hell, maybe even weeks or months—and Nico will always blame himself for what happened with Ellie.

I'm sure if I were in his position, I'd do the same.

I need to put my trust issues aside and learn to forgive Ellie, or I can continue fighting my son on this issue, knowing I'm only hurting him more in the process.

It will be hard for me, but I'm going to try to give Ellie a second chance for Nico's sake since he is all that matters.

My only problem?

She might not want to come back.

Later that night, once Nico goes to bed, I pull up Ellie's contact information and give her a call. The ringing goes on for what feels like forever, only to be cut off abruptly by a generic voicemail system.

Instead of leaving a message with all my jumbled thoughts, I text her instead.

ME

Hey. Can we talk?

It feels like five hours before I get a response when it was really only five minutes.

ELEANOR (NANNY)

We don't have anything to talk about, so please delete my number.

I don't bother playing mind games by waiting her out.

ME

It's about Nico. He's not doing well.

Ellie's name flashes across my screen, and I answer immediately.

"Is he okay? Did the ophthalmologist have an update?" Her concern seems genuine, which only makes me feel more guilty. Regardless of my personal feelings toward Ellie, she cares about Nico even when it isn't a job requirement anymore, and that's the kind of loyalty money can't buy.

I would know, seeing as I pay his mother hundreds of thousands of dollars, and she can't be bothered to fulfill her part of the custody agreement.

"He's fine, and no."

"Did he see his doctor yet?"

"Not yet. The soonest we could get an appointment was tomorrow."

Her exhale makes the speaker crackle. "That's good. Are you keeping his chin clean?"

"Yes."

"And are you washing it twice a day?"

I don't notice the small smile on my face until it's too late. "I've been triple-washing it every day since he's a messy eater."

"Even better. And you're not using hydrogen peroxide or alcohol, right? That's bad for stitches."

"Yes."

"And did you schedule an appointment to get them taken out?"

"I did."

"Good. Hopefully it heals before his trip."

"About that..." I hesitate for a moment and don't hear anything on her end, so I ask, "Are you there?"

"Huh? Yeah?"

"Actually, on second thought, I'd rather have this conversation in person."

"No."

"Ell—"

She doesn't let me finish. "I'm glad Nico is okay and all, but I'm not interested in talking."

"What if it means getting your job back?"

She goes silent.

"Eleanor?" I ask before checking if the call dropped.

"I'm not working for you again."

"Not even if I apologize for firing you the way I did?"

"Not even then."

"Why not?"

Her sigh doesn't bode well for me. "Listen. Although I don't agree with *how* you fired me, you had every right to do so. I might not be a parent, but I can only imagine how I would react if my kid got hurt because of someone else."

I take a few moments to process her statement. While I didn't expect her to acknowledge my feelings of overprotectiveness, I'm grateful she did because I feel slightly less guilty for my reaction.

She continues, "For what it's worth, I'm sorry for keeping the secret from you. I know I should have told you, and while I don't regret not breaking Nico's trust, I do wish it hadn't affected the little trust you gave me in the process."

She hangs up, leaving me to spend the rest of my night contemplating how the hell I'm going to convince her to come back.

CHAPTER TWELVE

Ellie

"No. We had a deal." I dig my heels into the grass. The afternoon sun beats down on Willow and me, making me sweat through my leggings already after just getting out of the car.

Willow links our elbows together and steers me toward the entrance of the Park Promenade, where a crowd is forming to purchase tickets to today's softball fundraiser game. When word got around about who was playing against Lorenzo's team, people showed up early to claim bleacher seats and the best patches of grass. Some went out of their way to bring their own chairs, beer, and food, turning the park into their own tailgate party.

Everyone knows about Julian Lopez's dislike of Lorenzo Vittori, and although the two seemed to have put their differences aside for now, the rest of town hasn't gotten the memo. They're already placing bets on who will throw a punch first.

Willow pulls me toward the dugout. "Come on. I promised Lorenzo and our team that we wouldn't let them down."

"You told me I would be observing the game from the bleachers!" Her insisting on me wearing a Vittori team T-shirt makes so much more sense now.

Her face flushes. "One of our players got stuck in traffic on their way back from Detroit, so you're subbing until they get here."

"*Willow.*"

Her engagement ring glints as she throws her hands in the air. "It'll be fun!"

"According to who?"

She gestures toward the kids playing in the field behind the dugouts. "Look at all those children who are excited about raising money for their new playground."

"Do we really need to sell tickets for a game and ask for donations? Can't Lorenzo just buy them a new one?"

"He *could*, but that's not as impressive as bringing the town together for a fun game while helping raise funds to better the community, is it?"

I frown. "No, it's not."

She winks. "Glad we agree. Now, be a good sport and help me out please."

"All right." I stop dragging my feet and let her lead me toward the sign advertising today's softball championship and how the proceeds will go to building a new park closer to the south side of town, where most people live.

I huff and puff as I follow her. "I hate organized sports."

"Explains why you were the first person in Wisteria High history to flunk PE."

"The teacher hated me."

"You keep telling yourself that."

I shoot her a look, but she only laughs it off.

"Listen. All you have to do is stand in the outfield and look pretty while Burt, Lorenzo, and my brothers do all the hard work."

"Fine," I say with a sigh.

"Great! You're the best." She pulls me into a quick hug.

I return hers with one of my own. Regardless of how I feel about sports, I'm not about to let Lorenzo forfeit the game because of one missing player after Willow went through a lot of trouble planning this event.

"Ellie!" Lily Muñoz runs across the softball field, looking like a sports magazine model with her long, toned legs, pink athletic outfit, and a bright smile that reaches her honey-colored eyes. While she isn't as tall as me, she doesn't have to tilt her head back to look me in the eyes, which is nice.

"I knew it was you!" Her smile widens as she throws her arms around me.

Although Lily and I were a year apart in school, a lot of our electives overlapped since neither of us was interested in sports or learning another language. Both of us were part of the band, worked on the yearbook, and ran the school's morning show. Well, *I* ran the show while she hosted it because Lily has always been drop-dead gorgeous.

I pull away from the embrace first. "What are you doing here?"

"Julian bribed me to play since something came up with Dahlia's filming schedule."

"See? We're not the only ones doing it." Willow beams.

"What did they offer you to participate?" Lily asks me.

"A trip to Vegas."

She laughs. "Hope it's worth suffering through the next few hours in Rafa's presence."

"Rafael is here?" My head slowly swivels toward my best friend.

Her eyes bug out of her head before she pretends someone called her name and slips away before I have a chance to choke her.

"Willow!"

"Remember to stick to the outfield!" she shouts before taking off to the dugout, where Lorenzo sits and stares in our direction.

"How have you been?" Lily pulls my attention back with her question.

I shrug. "I've been okay."

She frowns. "I'm sorry I never reached out. I wanted to after I heard about Rafa firing you, but he prohibited us from asking you about it."

Grass crunches beneath my sneakers as I rock back on my heels. "Oh."

She makes a face. "I know he can be…"

"A grumpy, insufferable, paranoid asshole?"

Her eyes widen at something over my shoulder. My neck prickles before I turn my head and look back at the man staring me down like I'm the bane of his existence.

"Don't stop on my account," Rafael says. "I feel like you were just getting started."

All the blood in my body rises to my face.

"You know what? I just realized I need to use the bathroom before the game begins. See you out on the field!" Lily gives my arm a quick squeeze before she rushes toward the other team's dugout, where the players are all wearing identical Lopez Luxury shirts.

"Eleanor." Rafael's jaw ticks.

"Rafael." I take a step in the opposite direction.

He matches my stride with one of his own. "I didn't expect to see you here."

I bristle at his tone. "Why not?"

"You hate sports."

"How do you know that?"

"You and Nico bonded over it once."

My brows shoot up. "And you remembered that?"

"Hard to forget someone telling a story of how they once celebrated scoring a goal in their own team's net."

Okay, seriously though, does he remember every single thing I say, and if so, why?

I take another step backward. "Well, I'm here for charity."

His gaze drops to my shirt, where the Vittori logo is plastered across the front. "You're on Lorenzo's team?"

"Yup."

"I wasn't aware that you two knew each other." A muscle in his cheek twitches.

"Vaguely, but my best friend, Willow, is the one who planned the event."

"And you decided to participate?"

"*Coerced* is a more fitting term."

He doesn't look the least bit amused, which only adds to the tightness building beneath my sternum.

"Well, this reunion has been fun and all, but I should head to the dugout to get ready. Build up the team morale and all that fun sports stuff." I turn on my heels only to freeze as Rafael's fingers wrap around my upper arm.

He spins me around to face him again. "Can we talk for a second? Please."

I yank my arm free of his hold, hoping he didn't notice the goose bumps spreading across my skin. "I'm a bit busy."

I don't mean to be a jerk, but I can't do this with him because I don't know how. After spending so many years putting off uncomfortable conversations, I never developed the skill to handle them.

"What about after the game?"

"Sorry. I have plans."

The tiny tic in his jaw gives his emotions away. "Fine. What about tomorrow?"

"Fully booked as well. In fact, my calendar is slammed until the new year."

"It's June."

I flash a fake smile. "I have so many things to catch up on now that I have a lot of free time. Not that I expect you to understand since you're self-employed and all."

"You could at least hear me out."

"Oh, like you did the night of Nico's accident?" I might not *like* confrontation, but if Rafael pushes me hard enough, he will get one.

"I told you it was all a mistake."

I steel my spine. "Well, your mistake was my wake-up call."

"What's that supposed to mean?"

I gather up some courage with my deep breath. "Things were never going to work out. You didn't value me or my time enough, while I valued your family way too much. It would only get worse with time, so you firing me just sped up the process."

A shrill whistle and someone shouting my name in the distance save me, and I walk away before Rafael ever has a chance to reply.

After three dreadful innings, Willow shouts, "Oh, thank God you're here!" She waves at my replacement before pointing in my direction. "Ellie, you're free."

I swear I hear one of Willow's brothers cheering, but I don't take it personally. Outfield might as well be outer space with the distance I'm expected to cover.

"All good." I wipe the sweat from my brow and throw her a thumbs-up before heading to sit by my mom on the bleachers. It's unreasonably hot today, thanks to a heat wave coming in this week, and the lack of shade doesn't help matters.

At some point in the fourth inning, Lorenzo ditches his shirt altogether and earns a standing ovation from the other women watching. Burt jokingly tries to take his off too, which gets a groan from me and a whistle from my mother.

A lot of people from town have gathered on the bleachers

surrounding the softball field. I had hoped to see Nico in the crowd, but I'm filled with disappointment when I find him missing. The ache in my chest that has been present since the night of his accident worsens, always acting up whenever I think of him.

Nico has been my shadow for months, so to no longer have him around feels like I'm missing a vital organ. I long for mornings spent bargaining for him to get out of bed and afternoons hanging out in the barn with the animals almost as much as I miss our music lessons together.

I only have myself to blame for losing it all.

"You did so well out there." My mom wraps her arm around my shoulder and tugs me against her, pulling me out of my dark mental space.

"I barely did anything."

"I saw you run for the ball."

My cheeks burn at the memory. "I was running *away* from it."

"Hm. Hard to tell from this far away, so I doubt anyone noticed."

I blow a loose strand of hair out of my eyes with a frustrated huff.

Some women suck in a breath as Rafael walks past our bleachers and heads toward home plate. He wipes his face with the hem of his shirt, giving them all a good look at what lies beneath. His abs, which I had never seen before, give me eight more reasons to stay far away.

What Rafael lacks in personality as of late, he makes up for in spades physically. The man could have marble statues made in his likeness because his body is *that* sculpted to perfection.

As if he senses my eyes on him, he looks up, and our gazes connect. Something sparks in his, and I'm quick to look away, my cheeks burning at being caught in the act.

"Think he would want to be with an older woman?" Suzette, who runs the local candle shop, whispers to her friend, Gertie, who always delivered our mail up at the house on the hill.

"You wouldn't last a day with a personality like his." Gertie scoffs. "He doesn't talk. Period."

"Who said anything about talking?"

Gertie snorts while I roll my eyes.

Mom leans in and whispers, "I now understand why you had a crush on him all those years ago."

"Mom." I shush her.

"What? You had good taste, even back then."

"I didn't have a crush." I look around in a panic.

"Are we pretending that you didn't use to write *Ellie Lopez* all over your math notebook? Or that you didn't write 'Prom King' about him?"

I drag my hand across my throat in a silent request for her to shut the hell up, but it's too late. Like sharks scenting blood in the water, Gertie and Suzette turn to glance at us.

"Ellie. It's so nice to see you." Gertie pats my thigh.

I always wear leggings and pants for a reason, but they don't stop me from worrying about whether people can notice my scars through the material.

Mom has assured me they can't, but I still panic from time to time, especially when someone touches me there.

I clear my throat. "Hi, Gertie."

"I passed by the house yesterday to deliver a package, but Rafael said you weren't there anymore."

My face flushes. "Yeah."

"Is everything okay?"

Mom leans forward. "She is no longer working for him."

"What? Why not?" Katiya, a woman who owns the best Indian restaurant in Michigan, shoots me a pitiful look.

"Nico said she got fired, but I didn't want to believe it," one of the school staff members sitting on the bottom bleacher announces, making everyone gasp and mutter.

"It's okay, Ellie. Don't feel bad. You lasted longer than all the others combined." Suzette gives my hand a squeeze.

"If you need a new job, my wife and I are looking to hire a nanny," Antonio, a father of seven children, adds.

I plaster on my best apologetic smile. "Sorry. My stepdad needs help around The Broken Chord."

My mom nods enthusiastically. "That's our Ellie. Always stepping up to the plate when we need her to help at the music store."

The more I consider returning to the tutoring job I once had, the less I want to. It feels like another setback in my life, all because I made the wrong choice.

What else can you do?

I never went to college, and songwriting isn't really an option right now, so The Broken Chord is my only choice, whether I want to work there or not.

The only one stopping you from writing new songs is you.

"Did you need to announce it to everyone?" I whisper to my mom when they all focus back on the game.

She winces. "Sorry. I didn't think it would spread so fast."

"Are you kidding? I give it an hour before everyone in town knows I was fired."

"An hour? More like thirty minutes."

CHAPTER THIRTEEN

Rafael

I can't believe you convinced me to come here." Julian huffs under his breath while trying to get the bartender's attention. Last Call is packed with everyone who attended the game, so most of the employees are busy serving other patrons.

I lean against the counter. "You would've looked like a sore loser if you ignored Lorenzo's invitation."

"That's because I *am* one."

"Only because you lost to him of all people."

Julian and Lorenzo have had an antagonistic relationship ever since the casino heir tried to buy up properties around the lake. Lorenzo makes Julian wary, and while I agree that there is something off about the guy, I don't care enough to feel any sort of way about him.

If he wants to become mayor, let him. So long as I'm left

unbothered and my donations to the town are responsibly spent, I couldn't care less about Lake Wisteria politics.

The only reason I wanted to attend today's celebratory happy hour at Last Call was because I overheard someone saying Ellie was coming. After she hung up on me the other night and then refused to hear me out today, this might be my best chance to speak with her, and I'm not about to blow it because of Julian's bruised ego.

Getting Ellie to work for me is an inevitability, so the quicker she gets on board, the sooner Nico and I can move past this hiccup and begin repairing our damaged relationship. It's not going to be easy—not by a long shot, especially with how affected Nico has been by my own problems—but Nico is worth the effort.

My son is the best part of my life, and I will slay every single one of my demons to make sure he doesn't have any of his own.

Julian's frown becomes more pronounced as he points between us. "*We* lost, no thanks to you, by the way."

"I told you that I didn't want to play."

"Doesn't mean you needed to let the other team win."

My teeth grind together. "I didn't."

"Then explain why you always let Ellie steal an extra base while you stood around looking like you had never seen a woman before."

"I was…distracted."

"By what? Her ass?"

With an impressive burst of speed, I punch him in the arm hard enough to make him wince. "*Cállate.*" I look around to make sure no one heard him.

I didn't *intend* to get distracted by Ellie, but her ass stole my attention every time she ran by me with a look of sheer concentration on her face.

Julian rubs his bicep with a frown. "Fuck. How much are you lifting now?"

"Enough to make you question bringing up Ellie's ass again."

The smile on Julian's face sends warning bells ringing in my head. "No need to get defensive. Ellie is a single, good—" He cuts himself off when I pull my fist back. "I was going to say good-*hearted*, *pinche pendejo*."

I ignore the urge to punch him while he focuses on catching the bartender's attention again.

"I'll be right back," I say before heading past a group of people waiting for an open spot near the bar. I do a quick search for Ellie but come up empty, although I do notice two people I never expected to be seen together.

Lorenzo is whispering something into Lily's ear that has her nostrils flaring and her cheeks turning red. I know she can hold her own when it comes to men, but my protective instincts rear their ugly head.

Before I have a chance to interfere, she shoves at Lorenzo's chest, which only makes him laugh. He reaches for the hand that pushed him and plants a kiss across her knuckles.

I pretend not to notice the way she teeters on her sneakers. Just like I act like I don't see Lorenzo's eyes sparkle when he catches the same move a second later.

Cállate: Shut up.

Pinche pendejo: Fucking asshole.

I love Lily like a sister, but I have my own problems to deal with tonight, and none of them include Julian's nemesis.

I return to the bar to find Julian returning his black card to his wallet.

"Here." Julian passes me a bottle of Modelo before reaching for his own. "So, what's your plan?"

"I don't have one." Besides showing up here, that is.

"You could start the conversation off by sharing how much Nico misses her."

"Already tried that."

His brows rise. "Damn. I thought that would work."

"Me too." Ellie is proving more difficult than I thought, but I'm not about to give up at the first sign of adversity.

"What about giving her a raise?"

"I have a feeling her pride costs more than any offer I'm willing to make."

"Then you'll just have to play dirty. I'm sure Nico would be more than willing to shed a few tears if it meant getting Ellie back."

"I'm not about to use my son like a pawn on one of your chessboards."

"It's not *using* if he is willing."

"That's so screwed up."

"So was firing Ellie without giving her a second chance. She was the greatest thing that happened to Nico in a long time, and you can't deny it."

A spike of hot jealousy shoots through my chest.

Julian glances in my direction. "What's that look about?"

"Nothing."

"Seemed like something to me."

"Stop poking around for answers you're not getting."

His brow arches. "Sorry. Hard not to pry when you're looking a little green."

"I'm *not* envious."

"Next time, try saying that without twitching."

I release a heavy breath. "Fine. *Slightly*, but I'm working on it."

"Why would you be envious in the first place?"

"Because if someone asked Nico to pick between me and Ellie, I'm not sure I'd like the answer."

Julian's explosion of laughter makes me frown.

"Did I say something funny?"

"You truly think your kid wouldn't choose you?"

I don't answer him.

He wipes the smile off his face. "You're serious."

"They share something special."

Awareness dawns on him. "Is that why you fired Ellie?"

"No."

"You're intimidated by their relationship," he states, completely ignoring me.

"I never said that."

"Rafa." Julian clamps his hand on my shoulder and gives it a squeeze. "Come on, man. You know Nico has a heart big enough for the two of you."

I try to shake him off, but his hold remains tight.

"No one could ever replace you. He worships the ground you walk on, regardless of whatever rough patch you're going through right now."

I unleash a pent-up breath. "I wish things were better."

"Maybe the trip will help."

"If there even *is* a trip."

Julian takes a long pull from his beer bottle. "Maybe you could…"

I stop paying attention to him once I catch Ellie's blond hair out of the corner of my eye. She is surrounded by a group of people a few years younger than me, and they all cheer as two of the guys from my old soccer team show up with a tray of empty shot glasses and a bottle of tequila.

"To be young and drinking shots without consequences." Julian sighs wistfully.

"You're two years older than them."

He grimaces. "It's all downhill once you hit thirty."

My frown deepens when I catch Ellie laughing at one of the guys, and my chest constricts at the carefree look on her face as she smiles at a few people who pull her into a hug.

God. What has gotten into you?

Julian glances over his shoulder. "She looks happy." He laughs to himself. "Oh look. They're toasting to her being unemployed."

I shoot him a scathing look. "I can see that."

I see the whole damn thing, including the way some asshole I recognize from my graduating class throws his arm around her and sloppily kisses her cheek.

Is that her boyfriend? She has gone on a few dates—that much I gathered from eavesdropping and her requesting time off—but I don't remember her mentioning being in a relationship.

Don't tell me you're jealous?

No, of course I'm not jealous. Whatever discomfort I feel about her is strictly due to my anxiety about talking to her. My son is counting on me to fix things between us, and I can already tell it's not going to be an easy battle, seeing as she's toasting to me being a jerk.

Perhaps it's best if I let Ellie loosen up a bit with a few shots before demanding some of her time. So instead of heading in her direction and pulling her away from the two guys closing in on her, I spend time with Julian, who is eventually joined by his girlfriend and Nico's godmother, Dahlia.

I search the bar for her sister, Lily, hoping she can save me from third-wheeling, only to be disappointed when I can't find her.

I love Dahlia almost as much as I love my cousin, but that doesn't mean I love spending time with them *together*. Being anyone's third wheel makes my skin itch and my chest painfully clench, and I'm desperate for an escape.

Luckily, someone starts up the old karaoke machine that has been around since Julian's parents got together in this same bar decades ago, and Dahlia quickly joins the line of people who want to give it a go. Julian asks me to save him, but I only push him away with a half-assed salute.

A few people attempt to strike up a conversation with me, but their efforts die once I give only a few one-word answers. I don't actively try to be a dick, but I'm not the most pleasant conversationalist.

I scan the back of the bar where Ellie was seated, only to find the spot empty. People near the stage whistle before an "Ellie" chant begins.

"I see you all got me tipsy on purpose." A soft chuckle follows the voice I'd recognize anywhere.

A couple of confirmatory shouts follow. The first chords of a song begin to play from the speakers lining the stage.

"I love you!" a woman shouts from the side, and I follow the sound to Willow, who has her phone in the air, high above the crowd so she can record the stage.

Ellie shakes her head with a small smile. "Some of you might have heard a version of this song already—"

"Screw Ava Rhodes!" someone yells.

Ava Rhodes, as in the pop star? I knew she grew up here and all, but I haven't given her music much of a listen outside of a few popular songs Dahlia and Lily like. Most people around here aren't fans of her, although I've never bothered to ask why. I just assumed it had something to do with her turning her back on the town she grew up in.

Ellie's already flushed cheeks turn crimson. "Anyway, I don't think some of you have heard it like this before."

The song restarts, and she shuts her eyes.

Her foot taps against the worn wood floor beneath her, and her hips move to the music, drawing my gaze toward her legs again. I try to gain control of my roaming eyes, but the task proves increasingly difficult as the spotlight above her head turns on.

Like a siren calling me toward a watery grave, Ellie pulls me into a hypnotic trance as soon as her lips part and the first line of lyrics pours out of her mouth. I want nothing more than to drown in the sound of her raspy voice.

I've never heard her sing before. Anytime she plays, her lips remain sealed, although given her clear talent, I'm questioning why she doesn't more often.

> One a.m., lying in my bed, wondering which husband's coming home to greet me.
>
> Could it be the man I married, or the one who smells of cheap roses and bottom-shelf whiskey?
>
> Three a.m., bleeding red, pleading for someone to come save me and my baby.

Ominous lyrics weave a story about an abusive husband and his broken wife, and the slow buildup to the chorus has everyone swaying on their feet. Although the backing track matches the same popular song that most of the nation knows, these lyrics are different. *Darker.*

This version leans toward folk music, and I don't need to listen to the whole thing to wish it replaced the mainstream rendition.

Ellie's soft voice is thick with emotion, and her eyes have a sheen to them by the time she gets to the final verse. I don't hear her because I'm too caught up in watching a tear roll down her cheek, the evidence of her pain written clear as day across her face.

She may wipe it away with the tip of her tattooed finger, but I see it.

Just like I see *her.*

I have no right to be curious about her and the past I hardly know much about, but I can't deny the strong tug in my chest that I feel whenever I look over at her. It is the same one I felt when she first started working for me, back before I became consumed by my turbulent emotions, and one I should be wary of given my past. I'm not here because of whatever interest Ellie stirs inside me when I least expect it.

I'm here for *Nico*.

The last chord plays, and the bar breaks out in a roar of applause, prematurely ending the spell she cast on me.

Spell?

Fuck.

Ellie tucks a loose strand of hair behind her ear and holds out the microphone for the next person in line like she didn't just set the bar through the stratosphere.

"Yeah, there's no way I am going up there after that." The person standing beside the stage disappears into the crowd.

"Anyone else want to try?" She shakes the microphone.

No one volunteers, and I don't blame them. With a voice like hers, she could be doing a lot more than nannying for my family, which begs the question *why isn't she?*

CHAPTER FOURTEEN

Ellie

A hundred pairs of eyes follow me to the back of the bar, but I pretend not to notice as I disappear into one of the unoccupied bathrooms. I need to gain control over my heart rate again before I go outside and face everyone.

I'm not sure what I was thinking. That much became clear when my friends encouraged me to do something I haven't tried in years—sing in front of a crowd.

I love everything about music *except* performing, which is why I haven't tried it since I lived in Los Angeles.

Reporters always talk about how Ava was discovered at a dive bar, and that is true, but they fail to mention the other woman singing beside her.

I never wanted the fame like Ava, but I always loved the buzz I got whenever the lights were dimmed low and the music began to flow. Maybe that's why I got up and sang my heart out tonight. Maybe for three minutes of my life, I wanted to step out of the shadows and remind myself of who I was before Ava broke my heart.

Mission accomplished.

Rather than spend the rest of my night hiding in a dingy bathroom, I unlock the deadbolt and step into the dark hallway leading back to the bar. I only make it a few steps before my path is blocked by a large man taking up most of the space.

He is as wide as he is tall, and his muscular arms nearly brush against the walls when he crosses them. His expensive black leather jacket might conceal his muscles, but I can tell the man works out religiously.

I take a step forward, and the wood floor creaks beneath my sneaker. The man turns to face me with raised brows.

It takes me two seconds to place the famous musician's face.

"Oh my God! You're—"

A warm palm covers my mouth. "Please don't say anything."

His hot, minty breath hits my face as my eyes lock onto his deep blue ones. I'm so damn starstruck, I don't bother shaking him off. Instead, I stay quiet while I take in the thin, white scar cutting through his stubble and the mop of dark brown hair teasing the collar of his leather jacket.

I almost didn't recognize Cole Griffin because the last time I saw a paparazzi photo, he had a buzz cut, a thick beard, and matching black eyes after his nose was broken.

He takes a deep breath. "Sorry for overreacting like this. Shit, I really don't want people knowing I'm here, so please—"

"Get the hell away from her."

The hand covering my mouth is ripped away as Rafael shoves the wildly popular musician away from me. Cole's spine slams into a wall, and he lets out a painful *oomph* as the back of his head bangs into the bricks.

Rafael's head swings in my direction, his nostrils flaring with each heavy breath. "Are you okay?" he asks in a slightly unhinged, guttural voice.

My heart—that little, traitorous thing—squeezes as he reaches for my chin and gently lifts it so he can get a better look at me. His thumb brushes over my skin, and my breathing falters for a moment.

"She's fine, asshole." Cole rubs the base of his spine with a groan.

Whatever haze Rafael's touch put me in disappears as I push him away. I overlook the way his mouth drops open as I rush for Cole. "Oh God. I'm so sorry."

"Why are you apologizing to him?" Rafael snaps.

I ignore him. "Should I get you an ice pack or something?"

Cole gives a thumbs-up. "I've dealt with worse, darling."

"Call her darling again and I'll put that theory to the test." Rafael looms over me like a shadow.

I groan. "Can you not threaten him?"

"You're defending this guy?"

"What's your name?" Cole's smile, while charming and confident, doesn't make my heart skip or my stomach flip quite like one from the man hovering behind me.

"I'm Ellie." I hold out my hand and pray he doesn't notice the way it trembles. Anyone in my position would have a similar reaction, and whoever says differently is a liar because this is Cole freaking Griffin. Legendary vocalist. Genius lyricist. Love child of two rock gods.

Everyone with access to a radio has heard his music, and he is *here*. In Lake Wisteria!

Cole grabs ahold of my hand and kisses the back of it, all while Rafael watches with flared nostrils. The brush of Cole's lips against my skin doesn't elicit a fraction of the reaction Rafael cradling my chin did, and I'm not sure what to make of that.

"*Ellie.*" Cole tests the name in that deep, husky voice of his. "You're the woman from the stage, right?"

I nod.

"You have a wonderful voice." He releases my hand, and it hangs in the air for a second too long before I remember how to act like a normal human being.

Shame replaces my shyness. "Sorry for acting like a complete weirdo. You just caught me by surprise."

"I'm the one who should be apologizing for freaking you out."

I let out a soft laugh. "It's okay. I get it. It's not every day that someone like you shows up in town."

"Someone like him?" Rafael asks while glaring at Cole.

Seriously, what is going on with him, and why does my heart flutter at the mere idea of him being overprotective of me?

Cole chuckles. "I'm used to having that effect on people."

Rafael scoffs. "Ever heard of being humble?"

I shoot him a glare from over my shoulder before returning

my attention back to Cole. "If you don't mind me asking, what are you doing here anyway?"

"My manager suggested getting away for a while and offered to let me stay at his lake house. Thought it would help with my writer's block or some bullshit."

"How's that going?" I ask.

"Not well, but I have a feeling that will all change now that I found you."

Cole's comment earns a death-stare from Rafael. The two men size each other up while I stand on the sidelines, suffocating from the testosterone flooding the cramped hallway. They could probably go head-to-head given their evenly matched weight and body types, although I'd put my money on Rafael winning because my ex-boss looks absolutely murderous at the moment.

A few people who seem interested in using the restroom quickly turn around when they get a look at Rafael, which only fuels my embarrassment.

"Do you need something?" I ask him with a surprisingly neutral voice.

"Yes."

"Can it wait?"

"No."

Cole's amused gaze swings between us. "Boyfriend?"

"No," Rafael and I say at the same time.

"Bodyguard?"

I swallow my laugh. "Absolutely not." Although Rafael sure is acting like one with the way he stands beside me like a guard dog ready to attack.

"Then why is he here?" Cole props his booted foot against the wall, which stretches his black jeans until his knee pops out of the gaping hole.

"Your guess is as good as mine." I shoot Rafael an accusatory glance, but he doesn't notice, his eyes aimed directly at Cole's face.

The singer laughs to himself like he is privy to an inside joke I missed. "Anyway...that song. Shit, you can sing, darl—" He stops himself when Rafael's head swivels in his direction. "*Ellie.*"

Somehow, Rafael seems to hate him calling me *Ellie* more than *darling.*

I tuck a lock of hair behind my ear to give my hands something to do. "Thanks."

"Did you write that rendition of 'Late Nights' by yourself?"

His question makes me freeze. "Why?"

As much as I want to claim that it was the *original* version, I keep my lips sealed and the truth locked away, along with all the other secrets I've harbored since I moved back to Lake Wisteria a year ago.

"Because it was brilliant."

My brows jump. "Really?"

"Yeah. Honestly, I prefer it over the original."

"I agree," Rafael says, making my chest constrict. Unlike Cole's, my ex-boss's compliment worms its way through my heart and remains there.

You're supposed to be mad at him. Not swooning over him acting remotely nice after being borderline unlikable for eight months.

Maybe that's why I'm having these kinds of reactions. I

was so starved for attention from Rafael that I'm now moved by him doing the absolute bare minimum.

Right. You keep telling yourself that.

Cole continues, "I loved the rawness of the lyrics. They gave me chills."

I blink twice. "Oh wow. Thank you. That means a lot coming from someone like you."

"Do you have an agent?"

"No." The word carries a bitterness to it that makes me cringe.

"Have you ever considered finding one? You could make a lot of money if you created another song like that with the right person."

I bristle. "I'm not interested."

"Why?"

"I'm just not."

Rafael comes closer, keeping enough distance to remain respectful while staying close enough to remind me that I'm not alone. I shouldn't be grateful for his presence, but I can't help the gut reaction. There is something about his proximity that comforts me. That makes me feel like if I asked, he would whisk me away, no explanation needed.

Cole raises his hands. "I didn't mean to upset you."

I'm quick to get defensive. "You didn't." My chest rises from my deep breath. "It was nice meeting you and all, but I should get back to my friends before they think I ditched them."

His eyes flash with panic. "Wait."

Rafael tenses.

Cole scrubs a hand down his face. "I'm screwing all this up. Fuck."

My head tilts with confusion. "Screwing what up?"

"My first impression."

"*First* insinuates there will be more." Rafael's arms brush against my back as he crosses them over his chiseled chest, using the oldest intimidation technique in the book. While it doesn't seem to have any effect on Cole, it does a number on me.

That should be the first sign that something is fundamentally wrong with me.

Cole glances between the two of us before finally saying, "I'm not trying to hit on you or anything."

Rafael doesn't seem to believe him, but I do. Outside of him calling me *darling*, he hasn't appeared the least bit interested in checking me out.

Cole surprises me by saying, "I'd love to grab a coffee or something if you're free."

I blink twice. "You want to get coffee with *me*?"

He laughs. "Um, yeah?"

"Why?"

"You'll have to say yes to find out." His wink makes me laugh.

"She's busy." Rafael moves forward as he uncrosses his arms, stunning me once again as his hand curls around my shoulder. If he were anyone else, I would consider the move a quiet claiming, but this is Rafael I'm talking about. He doesn't even like me, so I don't understand why he is reacting this way.

Unless…

"Sure," I say. Screw it. I might not be interested in writing songs, but if the mere idea of hanging out with Cole bothers Rafael, then what the hell. I'll grab a cup of coffee with the singer.

It's not like Rafael cared about my feelings when he didn't let me say goodbye to Nico, so why should I extend the same courtesy to him?

Rafael struggles to mask his surprise. "What?"

"I'm pretty flexible." I shoot Cole a soft smile.

Rafael's eye twitches. "I thought you didn't have any time."

My grin widens. "Turns out my schedule cleared up."

He glares. "How convenient."

Cole's eyes light up as he pulls his phone from his back pocket. "Does Sunday work?"

I nod.

"Great. Can I get your number so we can coordinate?"

"Of course." I rattle off my number while Rafael taps his index finger against his straining bicep. My heart matches the beat, the drawn-out thumps filling my ears with a steady whooshing sound.

The angry vein above Rafael's left eye appears again as he gives Cole his back. "Can I speak to you, please? *Alone.*"

"Fine." I might as well get this conversation over with, seeing as he won't stop following me until I do.

"See you soon, Ellie." Cole tucks his phone back into his pocket and shoots me a parting wink from over his shoulder before disappearing out of the back exit, leaving me alone with the last person I want to talk to.

CHAPTER FIFTEEN

Rafael

It took me only a few seconds to put a name to the man who cornered Ellie in the back hallway near the Last Call bathrooms. I might not be up-to-date on tabloid headlines or celebrity gossip, but everyone with internet access knows about this particular musician's undesirable reputation.

Drugs. Women. Anger issues and drunken rampages.

Ellie is the last person Cole Griffin should be dragging into his destructive spiral, and I plan on reminding her of just that once he disappears through the emergency exit door.

She turns to head toward the main hallway that leads back to the bar, but stops midstride when I speak.

"You can't seriously be thinking of going on a coffee date with him?" is the first thing I say.

The very first—and very wrong—thing to say.

I can't help it, though. I'm a suspicious person by default, so even though Cole said he isn't interested in Ellie, I don't believe him, especially with the few articles I've seen making their rounds.

She spins around. "I'm not *thinking* about it. I *am* doing it."

"He's bad news."

"I'm not the kind of person who believes everything that's in the media."

"Maybe you should."

"Why?"

"He's a cheater."

She tucks her arms against her chest. "So? Not that it's any of your business, but I plan on grabbing coffee, not falling into bed with him."

An unwelcome image of the two of them doing just that makes my stomach churn. I do my best to banish the thought, but not before I picture Ellie smiling up at him, blushing the same way she did a few minutes ago when he smiled at her.

Being jealous of Ellie's relationship with my son is one thing, but feeling that same burning sensation in my gut at the idea of her with another man?

Concerning, to say the least.

I'm supposed to be thinking about Ellie as Nico's nanny, not a single woman who has every right to smile, blush, and laugh at another man.

I wipe my face with a frustrated huff.

"What do you really want to talk about, Rafael?" Ellie's tone snaps me out of my funk.

"I need you." The comment slips out before I have a chance to consider how it sounds.

Fuck.

Uncertainty flickers in her eyes. "You need me?"

"Nico and I," I amend. "If I thought things were bad between us before, nothing compares to the way he is now that you're gone."

Her shield of bravado drops. "I'm sorry."

"Me too. For a few things actually."

"You are?"

"Yeah. Your comment earlier got me thinking."

"What comment?"

"About not valuing you or your time."

"Oh." She doesn't say anything else, so I take it as a sign to continue.

"It made me realize that you've never complained about your job. Not even when I threw last-minute plans at you or acted like a dick when you didn't deserve it."

She makes a half-snort, half-scoff sound, and I shoot her a look, but keep going.

"Even though I was upset about the secret and Nico's accident, I should have treated you better after everything you've done for my family. You helped bring my son back, and for that, you deserved far more than what I did… You deserved a second chance."

She blinks rapidly, although it doesn't erase the mistiness in her eyes. "Thanks. I didn't realize how much I needed to hear that."

"I'm sorry I didn't say it sooner."

She glances away and wipes at the corner of her eye.

"Things aren't the same without you," I say earnestly.

She turns to face me again.

"*He's* not the same," I add.

Her reply is nothing but a long exhale. "That makes me feel awful." She focuses on an invisible point behind me. "But…"

I've received enough brush-offs in my life to recognize the first sign. "I'm willing to do anything to bring you back. A raise. An extra day off every week. Name it and it's yours."

"My salary or PTO was never an issue, and you know it."

"Then what do you want?"

"Something that was broken between us."

"What?" I ask.

"Trust."

My shoulders tense. "I'm going to need time."

She exhales. "I'm not only talking about you."

I stare at her in confusion.

Her eyes fall to the floor, as if looking me in the face proves too difficult of a task. "You made it clear that I'm disposable at a moment's notice, and I made a promise to myself a long time ago that I wouldn't let someone else make me feel that way again."

My teeth smash together. "I can't go back and change the way I reacted."

"I know, and as much as I hate to admit it, you were right to fire me. If Nico's accident proved anything, it's that I'm grossly underqualified to be his nanny." Her voice shakes.

"That's bullshit."

She stares at me with wide eyes.

"We went through seven nannies before you. All of them were beyond qualified for the job, yet none of them brought my kid back like you did."

Her chin wobbles. "I was doing my job."

"No. You were doing so much more than that." I take a deep breath. "I don't want to see Nico change back into the quiet boy who didn't laugh, smile, or play music. God, it would destroy me to see him like that all over again. So I'm pleading—hell, I'm even willing to beg—if it convinces you to come back."

Uncomfortable silence follows, and my anxiety spikes. Her hardened gaze seems to soften, which gives me some hope about our situation.

"You don't need to do that," she says with a soft voice.

"I'm desperate, Eleanor." My voice is strained.

She gives me a little shove, and I lose my footing, not because of her strength but because of the small laugh she lets out. "Desperate enough to stop calling me by my full name? Because although I love her, it reminds me of my grandmother."

I scoff, pretending the warmth in my chest is a result of my nerves rather than a reaction to her touch. "Anything but that."

At first, I did it solely to annoy her, but then I found myself enjoying how flustered she got each time I called her by her given name. She always did this cute little eye roll—

Cute?

Shit. Not cute.

Funny. A funny *eye roll.*

"Figures," she mutters. "Well, this little chat was great and all…"

"Okay. I'll stop calling you Eleanor."

She rocks back on her sneakers. "I should say no…"

"But you won't because we need you."

"Fine. I'll agree, but only if you repeat that again while begging on your knees."

A short but deep laugh bursts out of me, and it surprises us both.

"Oh my God."

I lift my palm in the air. "Don't—"

"You laughed!" Her smile cuts through the icy outer layer of my cold heart. I've spent months wondering what it would feel like to be on the receiving end of Ellie's unbridled happiness, and it's so much better than I expected.

But the last thing we need is me getting all soft-hearted over a single smile, no matter how much I loved it. So I look up at the ceiling and pray for help.

"I don't think I've heard you laugh since high school." She seems to speak to herself.

The comment surprises me. "Keeping tabs on me since back then, huh?"

Her cheeks turn pink. "No."

My body buzzes from the thought. "Are you sure about that?"

"You know, not everyone at Wisteria High was obsessed with you." Her cheeks morph from a rosy hue to crimson.

"It's okay if you had a crush on me." According to Dahlia and Lily, most of the school did.

"You weren't my type."

"I was everyone's type," I tease, loving the way a flush spreads to her neck.

"First, you *laughed*, and now you're making *jokes*? Who are you and what have you done with the old Rafael?"

I don't know, but I have a feeling that Ellie might push me into finding out who the new me is, whether I want to or not.

CHAPTER SIXTEEN

Ellie

I show up at the Lopez house bright and early the next morning with a packed suitcase full of my clothes and a pep in my step that was missing all last week.

My boss opens the front door in expensive denim jeans that showcase his muscular thighs, a black T-shirt that is formfitting without being off-putting, and his coveted Richard Mille watch. The diamonds sparkle from the morning sun rising behind me, although I quickly become distracted by the veins running up his arm.

Physically, Rafael is one of the most attractive people I know. Scratch that. He *is* the most handsome man I've ever seen, and that's saying a lot after spending years living in Los Angeles amongst models, actors, and aspiring musicians.

I can't help the little flutter in my stomach or the skip of my heart whenever I look at him, although I do try my best to ignore it.

I look up to find his dark eyes already laser-focused on my face.

"Don't mind me." He *smirks*. The fleeting expression reminds me so much of the senior who smiled as often as he laughed, and it takes me by surprise to see him at ease for once.

I shake my head. "I see you ditched the lumberjack aesthetic."

"Are you sad about it?"

"Marginally." Although *sad* might not be the appropriate word. *Worried for myself* is more like it, although I'd never admit such a thing to him.

He leans against the doorframe. "Is it because I won't be chopping wood for the fireplaces anymore?"

I choke on my next breath. "Why would *that* make me sad?"

"Because I caught you staring through the window sometimes."

I pray the ground opens up beneath me and swallows me whole because hell has to be better than this.

"I don't stare." My defensive tone gives me away.

"I thought it was more polite to say that rather than the truth."

"Which is?"

"You *drool*."

"You're delusional," I say with a hiss.

He shrugs without a single care in the world. "No need to be embarrassed. It's cute to see the lengths you go to sneak a peek."

Cute? I swear I've never hated a word more.

"*Pendejo.*" I curse like I've heard him say countless times before.

His brows rise. "Excuse me?"

"You heard me."

"That's a bad word."

"I know." I grin.

His lips twitch as he rolls my luggage into the foyer. "Did you forget that I'm your boss?"

"Huh. It must have slipped my mind once you started flirting with me." I saunter inside, swaying my hips with a little sass.

There is nothing more satisfying than seeing his cheeks stained pink. "I wasn't flirting." He doesn't stumble over the words, which is impressive given the flustered look on his face.

Now *I'm* the one smirking. "All right."

"I mean it."

"*Sure.*"

"Keep talking and I'll fire you again."

"No you won't because you *need* me."

He doesn't verbally acknowledge my comment, but we both know it's the truth. Rafael proved as much with my new nanny contract, which includes an overall pay increase, a reduced workload from six to five days a week, and a generous severance package should he feel the need to terminate our agreement.

His new stipulations not only provide financial but also emotional security. He is clearly trying to take what I said about his lack of appreciation into account, and for that, I'm grateful.

As I head in the direction of the kitchen, I'm overwhelmed with the smell of freshly baked biscuits and a faint hint of bacon, and my stomach makes an outrageous noise.

"Hungry?"

"Starving, actually."

"Hopefully the birthday boy is too because I made a lot of food." He rubs the back of his neck.

"Nervous?" I ask.

He drops his hand. "Is it that obvious?"

"No," I lie.

His eyes narrow. "Right."

"Everything will be fine."

"He's been…tough."

"Well, he is your son after all."

He shoots me a look. "What's that supposed to mean?"

"You're a smart guy. I'm sure you'll figure it out."

"You think I'm smart?"

"Don't go fishing for compliments. It's unattractive."

Frown lines cut across his forehead. "I was curious."

"About my opinion? Wow. You must be really desperate for company if you want that."

The little splash of pink creeping up his neck has me questioning if he was telling the truth about being curious. It's hard to believe a self-made billionaire like Rafael could be self-conscious enough to seek reassurance from others, but I guess he is human after all.

Sometimes.

With a parting glance, Rafael heads toward Nico's room. I follow him through the hallway that leads to the bedrooms at the back of the house.

Rafael stops in front of the comic book poster-covered door before stepping to the side to give me room. Not wanting to ruin Rafael's birthday surprise, I remain quiet as I knock on the door.

"Go away!" Nico shouts. "I don't want dumb birthday pancakes this year."

Rafael flinches beside me. He tries to cover it up by shifting his weight, which only makes me sympathize with him more.

I *want* to dislike him, especially after the pain he put Nico and me through after firing me, but I can't find it in me to even try. He might act cold and indifferent, but he is still a person with feelings, aspirations, and fears. One who won't be able to learn from his mistakes unless I give him a chance to.

Rafael glares at the villainous Skotos, Erebus, and Eidolon posters taped to the door, his misery clinging to him like a second skin. If we go into the bedroom with him looking like this, Nico will probably shut down again, so it's up to me to try to cheer him up.

I fake gasp before whispering, "No pancakes? This is worse than I thought."

Rafael doesn't even so much as look in my direction. I grab his arm and pull him away from Nico's door so he doesn't overhear our conversation.

"I know you said things were serious, but I wasn't aware of just how bad things have gotten between you two. What's next? No birthday cake?"

"I'm glad you're amused by all this."

Okay... Tough crowd. "What if I told you that I could make you look like a hero?"

He scoffs. "Right."

"Are you doubting me?"

"Not you."

"Then who?"

"*Me*." His cutting word slices through me, and I reach over and give his tense bicep a squeeze.

The little tingle spreading up my arm from the contact forces me to let go all too soon. "Things will get better."

"How? It's not like his condition is going to improve."

"No, but you both can face the unknown together. As a team."

Rafael's scowl melts away. "We haven't felt like one lately."

His words drill a hole through my chest. "That might be true, but it doesn't mean you can't become one again."

His long exhale fills the quiet.

"Just trust me."

His gaze connects with mine, and for the briefest second, I get a glimpse of the man who hides his fears and hurt behind hard stares and endless scowls.

I see *him*, and damn, I'm hit with the urge to pull him into a hug and promise him that everything will be okay.

But then I remember how easily he cast me aside, and whatever desire I had to comfort him is replaced by an urgency to protect myself from getting hurt again.

I look away and clear my throat. "Ready?"

He nods.

I knock a second time.

"I said to go away!" Nico shouts loud enough to be heard clearly through the door.

"I could do that, but then you'd miss out on joining your dad and me for the best birthday pancakes in the whole wide world."

Rafael's head swivels toward me. "I thought you hated pancakes."

"He doesn't know that." And frankly, I didn't realize Rafael did since he usually makes them on Saturdays when I'm not here.

"Ellie?" Nico's squeal draws a smile from me.

I open the door to find him rushing to put on his glasses. It has only been a week since I last saw him, but the days felt longer.

Something clicks into place in my chest, as if a missing piece of my heart is being returned to its rightful spot. I never thought becoming Nico's nanny would lead to a love so strong, but it did.

I never want to put myself in a position to risk our relationship again. I've learned my lesson the hard way, so from here on out, I'm going to be cautious for both our sakes.

"Ellie!" Nico jumps off his bed and throws himself into my waiting arms. "You're back!"

I brace myself for another one of Rafael's frowns, which always appear whenever Nico shows me any kind of affection, but his face bears a neutral expression instead.

A *drastic* improvement, to say the least.

Maybe there is hope for him after all.

"Your dad apologized to me."

Nico's arms slip from around my neck as he pulls away. "Really?"

"Yup. He was sick to his stomach over letting me go. Told me that he couldn't sleep at night knowing I wasn't here with you both."

Rafael sends icy daggers in my direction.

I bite back a shit-eating grin.

"He couldn't?" Nico asks. "He didn't say anything to me."

"Yup. He *begged* me to come back."

"Does that mean you're staying?" Nico's guarded gaze slides from me to his father. Whatever happiness Nico felt from my surprise appearance disappears within a blink as a frown replaces his bright, gap-toothed smile.

I'm going to have my work cut out for me with these two. There is no way we are going to spend the next couple of weeks on vacation, tiptoeing around each other while ignoring the obvious tension.

I push Nico's glasses up the bridge of his nose to get his attention. "I'll stay, but only if you want me to."

He wraps his arms around my neck and squeezes until every artery protests. "Of course I want you to!"

"Oh, great." I fake my relief. "I was worried you'd forgotten all about me already."

"Never, ever, ever!"

"Are you sure? Because you probably liked not having to eat your fruits and vegetables."

His adorable, small nose scrunches. "*Papi* still made me."

"How dare he care about your health," I say with feigned outrage.

Neither one of them laughs.

All right then.

Nico wraps his legs around my waist and squeezes as tightly as he can. "You're not allowed to leave again. You got it?"

"Never? What if you get sick of me?"

"*No.* Never. Right, *Papi*?" Nico hesitantly looks over at his dad.

I'm paralyzed when Rafael locks eyes with me. "*No te preocupes, mijo.* If she runs, I'll bring her back for you."

Goose bumps break out across my skin. Thankfully, my boss doesn't notice, although I'm painfully aware of them and what they mean.

No matter how many times I tell myself I'm not attracted to Rafael, my body will always call me out on my pathetic lie.

Doesn't mean you need to act on it.

For everyone's well-being, it's best for me to lock away whatever residual feelings I have toward him and focus on why I'm really here. Nico needs me, and I'm not about to ruin everything we have because his dad makes my stomach flip and my heart race.

No te preocupes, mijo: Don't worry, son.

CHAPTER SEVENTEEN

Ellie

Nico quickly changed his stance on having a birthday party. Although the original plan was scrapped, Josefina Lopez, the town's expert event planner, took charge and converted part of Rafael's property into the perfect Nerf gun party within a short twenty-four hours. The whole place was transformed with inflatable obstacle courses, shooting forts, and an interactive practice zone. Even the round target piñata Josefina handpicked herself while visiting family in Mexico matched the blue-and-orange theme.

Rafael was worried that not many people would show up given the last-minute notice, but the turnout was better than I expected.

After thirty minutes of Nico sticking by my side, I tell him to go play with his friends.

"You're really not leaving?" he asks.

"Not unless you want me to."

A friend yells for Nico to come play, but he doesn't budge.

I grab one of the Nerf guns off the table and kneel in front of him. "Don't spend your birthday worrying about me. I'll be here the whole time, protecting the cake from anyone who gets any funny ideas." I'd already seen a few kids eyeing the custom-made cake by Alana Castillo, and I wouldn't put it past them to sneak a swipe or two of frosting when no one is looking.

Nico hesitates to take the toy from me.

"Nico!" another kid calls out, but he ignores them.

"I promise to stay."

"You pinkie swear?" He holds it up for me.

I lock my tattoo-free pinkie finger around his. "On my life."

"Okay. But I'm going to come find you every thirty minutes just to be sure that you didn't run away with the cake."

"Deal."

It doesn't take long before I'm dragged away from the dessert table by Dahlia and Lily Muñoz. Lily passes me a magazine full of foam darts and a Nerf Hail-Fire blaster.

"Why do I need this?" I check out the toy.

"You're on our team. Adults only, and girls versus guys. And the winners get a free spa day." Lily loads her toy with foam darts.

"Seriously? Girls versus guys? Are we five years old again?"

Dahlia passes me a blue plastic breastplate. "I know, but

you weren't there. Julian looked so smug when he bet we would lose against them."

Lily raises a brow. "You know he was baiting you into playing, right?"

"Yeah, yeah. I got it." Dahlia waves her sister away. "But he didn't plan on us recruiting Ellie."

I shake my head. "Oh no. I'm the last person you want on your team."

"Why?" Lily asks.

"Because I've played with Nico enough times to know I suck?"

"Don't worry. I got you." She cocks her toy with a smile.

"Lily here used to line my Barbies up and use them for target practice," Dahlia says.

My mouth falls open.

Lily shoves her sister with a laugh. "That happened one time!"

"Only because Julian told you Lego figures make better targets."

"I hate to say it, but he was right. They always made the most satisfying sound whenever they fell and broke apart."

Dahlia and I share a look before she speaks again.

"See? Lily will have most of the guys begging for mercy in ten minutes or less."

"Um…"

"Please." Lily helps load my gun. "We need another girl for our team and you're our first draft pick."

"Great." If I'm lucky, someone will shoot me within the first minute.

A bell goes off in the distance. "It's starting! Let's go!" Lily rushes toward the field filled with a hundred different inflatable obstacles, and we quickly lose sight of her as she disappears behind one.

"The guys are wearing neon-orange breastplates. You can hit them anywhere but the eyes." Dahlia takes off running in the opposite direction to her sister.

Despite my reluctance, I run down the middle of the obstacle course maze and crawl beneath one of the small inflatable arches. I keep my toy gun drawn and focus on keeping my lunch down as I wait for someone to put me out of my misery.

"Come on out, Ellie."

I can hardly hear Rafael calling my name over the rapid beat of my heart.

"The sooner you surrender, the faster we can get this all over with and cut Nico's cake."

After spending the last thirty minutes wedged under a small archway built into one of the hot inflatables, convincing myself that I didn't really need to pee, I refuse to give up now. Dahlia and Lily are counting on me to bring home the win since everyone but Rafael and me have been ejected from the game, so I'll be damned if Rafael tricks me into surrendering.

Exploding bladder or future UTI be damned because I won't lose.

A small twig snaps underneath his sneaker as he gets

closer to my hiding spot. My finger hovers over the trigger, one millisecond away from ending the match.

"I was surprised to find out you're the last one standing," he says from a distance this time.

Maybe if I wait until he moves on, I can crawl out and sneak up behind him.

"I'll even be a nice guy and pretend to shoot you." His voice drifts as he walks away from me.

I release the smallest exhale.

Rafael stops walking.

Shit.

"Gotcha." This time, he speaks from behind me.

Fuck. Fuck. Fuck! I push forward on my elbows and army crawl toward the light at the end of the archway, only to be dragged out through the opposite end. My chest slides against grass and dirt as Rafael pulls me out from under the inflatable.

"Roll over."

"No!" I reach for my gun, only to have Rafael kick it away.

"Shooting you in the back is less fun."

"Why—" My question is cut off by Rafael flipping me over.

My self-defense training kicks in, and I use the element of surprise to bring him down with my legs. He lands on top of me at an odd angle, knocking the air from my lungs as his knees slam into the ground on either side of me.

"Well, that did not go according to plan," I wheeze.

"No shit." The hard planes of his body rub against my soft parts as he rises onto his elbows. "What the hell were you thinking?" He pokes at the scrape on his arm, completely unaware of how he is depriving me of oxygen.

My exhale sounds strained. "I'm not sure I was."

"Where did you even learn to do that?" He stares at me in utter shock, completely unaware of the way his body presses mine deeper into the ground.

"Willow signed us up for self-defense classes when we first moved out to Los Angeles." I tap his arm. "Now, if you don't mind, could you get up? I think my left lung has collapsed."

He curses at himself. "Sorry."

A wave of warmth spreads from my cheeks to my toes as his body rubs against mine one last time before he jumps to his feet and grabs the discarded Nerf gun from the ground.

"We could call a truce," I say.

He lifts his hand until I'm staring into the barrel of a toy gun.

"So that's how it's going to be?"

He doesn't smile, but his eyes soften at the edges. "It's nothing personal." His finger hovers over the trigger.

"I'll save you, Ellie!" Nico shouts from the other side of the field.

"Thank God I can count on one Lopez at least."

Nico runs directly toward his father, but unfortunately, he doesn't make it in time to save me from the foam pellet that hits me right between the eyes.

"No!" Nico cries as he raises his Nerf gun at his father and shoots. "Everyone get him!"

Hundreds of foam darts hit Rafael at the same time from all angles as twenty of Nico's friends shoot him. He mutters a curse under his breath while I explode with a giggle.

The rare sound not only takes me by surprise but Rafael as well.

His dark gaze lands on my lips. "You think this is funny?"

Another laugh erupts from my throat as a foam dart hits him in the eye.

"Screw this," he practically snarls.

One second, I'm lying flat on my back, and in the next, I'm being pulled into Rafael's arms as he uses me as a human shield.

"Cease fire!" Nico shouts at his friends, but they don't listen.

Foam darts hit me in the eyes, chest, and legs, making me hiss. "Ouch!"

Rafael's lips press against my ear. "Not so funny now, is it?"

My stomach tightens as his lips brush over the shell of my ear.

What's next? Goose bumps during a hostage negotiation? Pull yourself together, Ellie.

"You proved your point. Now let me go."

"I plan on it as soon as they stop."

"To think I once considered you a gentleman."

"That was your first mistake." Rafael lifts my feet off the ground as he hides his face behind my back. I try to break free of his hold, but the band of steel wrapped around my waist doesn't budge.

"Stop! You're hurting her!" Nico calls out in a panic.

I wiggle my way out of Rafael's hold, but only because my butt rubs against something it shouldn't have.

Something that felt *way* bigger and firmer than expected.

Oh shit!

We both try to speak at the same time.

"You were—"

"I wasn't—"

Neither one of us gets a chance to finish our sentence before Nico rushes over to me and throws his arms around my legs.

"I'm sorry, Ellie! They didn't listen to me when I told them to stop!"

I comb through his sweaty strands of hair. "It's not your fault that your dad used me as a shield."

Nico glares at his father. "Why would you do that?"

"She laughed when I got hurt." Rafael shrugs.

"What are you? Five?" Nico laughs.

I hold my fist out for Nico to bump. "Nice one."

When I look up, I expect to find Rafael glaring at us like usual, but I'm shocked to see him looking...calm. Relieved even.

While I wouldn't describe him as *happy*, he doesn't look like he might explode from jealousy either, which is a welcome change from our usual tense interactions.

I want to figure out what brought about the switch in him, but Nico doesn't give me a chance before he pulls me away from his father, claiming he will keep me safe for the rest of the day.

CHAPTER EIGHTEEN

Rafael

I didn't realize how much I needed to hear Nico's laugh until it finally happened. Just like I didn't know how important it was to see him smile at me without the weight of my unhappiness resting on his small shoulders.

By the time we are ready to cut his cake, Nico has smiled at me three whole times and laughed twice, which is more than he has in the last two months combined. I'm so taken aback by his good mood that I don't notice Ellie coming toward me until it's too late.

One moment, I'm taking a photo of Nico and his friends, and the next, a massive slice of cake is being slammed into my face. Nico's loud belly laugh stuns me almost as much as Ellie staring up at me with a sheepish expression.

Nico knows I hate wasting food, but the sound of his laughter quells my annoyance. I swipe at my face to clear my vision, only to make it worse.

Ellie makes a face. "Nico asked me to do that as his birthday present."

"Did he?" I shoot my son a fake look of outrage. He curls over, his cheeks red from laughing himself hoarse.

"You've got something right..." Ellie reaches out and smears the clump of frosting on my cheek into my short, thick beard, painting the coarse hair blue and orange. "Oops."

I'm too stunned by the graze of her fingers across my lips to do anything but stare. Our eyes meet for a brief second, and something passes between us.

An acknowledgment of attraction perhaps? It is faint but present, with my lips tingling from a single one of her touches, although I'm not entirely sure Ellie feels the same way.

Sure, I've caught her staring a few times here and there, but I've never thought much of it.

The moment is stolen when Lily comes up to my side and offers Ellie a plate with a thick slice of cake. "From the birthday boy."

Before Ellie has a chance to take it from Lily's outstretched hand, I steal it and smash the entire thing against her face. Her soft gasp of surprise fills the quiet before Nico shatters it with a loud cackle.

Ellie stares up at me in shock, with frosting clinging to her light brown lashes and soft, rosy lips. She looks so damn ridiculous that I can't help laughing.

The crowd surrounding the cake table goes quiet, and I can feel at least thirty pairs of eyes focused on me. Thankfully, my burning cheeks are hidden beneath smeared icing or else my embarrassment would be obvious to everyone around us.

Ellie's icing-covered brows shoot up toward her blue-tinged hairline.

"What?" I ask in a rough voice.

"Nothing." She shakes her head, flinging a few drops of icing in the process.

"Oh, wait. You got something right…" I repeat her words as I smear a big clump of icing over Ellie's cheeks. My thumb accidentally swipes across her bottom lip, and a spark of awareness shoots across my skin.

Ellie's sharp breath feels like it was ripped straight from my lungs.

I pull back at the sound of Nico and his friends laughing to find my family looking at us with a range of expressions. My aunt has a certain troubling smile on her face, while Dahlia and Julian are whispering to each other, their gazes darting back to us with poorly concealed interest.

My whole face heats up at the unwanted attention, and I turn back toward Ellie.

Ellie seems not to care about everyone else as she asks me, "How do you feel about getting revenge on the little instigator?"

A small smile tugs at my lips. "I like the way you think."

She smirks. "You grab him while I get the cake?"

I nod. With an impressive burst of speed, Ellie steals a slice of cake from the table while I lock my arms around Nico and pull him up high against my chest.

"No!" he shouts while squirming against me. "I'm sorry!"

To think I have spent all this time being jealous of the relationship she had with my son when I could have been trying to be a part of it instead. No one said we couldn't share experiences with Nico together, but I made it impossible with the way I behaved.

From here on out, I will work on it.

Obviously, my problems with Nico aren't going to magically go away because of a fun birthday party, but this is a fresh start. One that includes pushing my jealousy aside and appreciating Ellie's relationship for what it is.

A genuine one.

"*¡Papi!*" Nico shouts.

Ellie lets out a soft laugh I *feel* more than hear, the sound making my chest feel all warm and tingly.

We share another look, although this time I'm quick to shield my true feelings. The ones I have no right to feel in the first place because this is Nico's nanny we are talking about. She is permanently off-limits, regardless of how my heart trips up in her proximity.

Thankfully, she doesn't seem to notice my dilemma as she slams the paper plate into Nico's face while staring up at me with another heart-clenching smile that could bring a man to his knees.

I fear that, if I'm not careful, that man could most definitely be me.

Without me having to ask, my family volunteers to help clean up after the party once the last kid leaves. Lily is organizing all the food and cake leftovers while Julian, his mom, and I are on cleanup duty. Before Ellie had a chance to pick up a trash bag, Dahlia asked if they could visit the barn and go over everything the animals will need while we are away on our trip.

I didn't want to burden my family with taking care of them, but they wouldn't let me ask anyone else. I'm not the betting type, but I give Dahlia a week of mucking out stalls before she throws in the designer towel and asks Julian to take over her shift.

My phone buzzes in my pocket, so I drop the trash bag on the ground before checking who texted me.

It takes a single name to sour my stomach and ruin my good mood.

HILLARY

Tell Nico that I'm sorry I couldn't make it.

She then sends a receipt for an electronic gift card to Nico's favorite sneaker store.

I want to rage. I want to yell. I want to take my phone and toss it in the pond behind my house.

Instead, I type out a cordial reply.

ME

There's always the Strawberry Festival next month.

Hillary swore she would come since Nico is playing a special musical piece for the entire town, but I'm skeptical, given how she always confirms only to cancel right before any event.

HILLARY

Already booked my flight.

ME

Great.

I tuck my phone in my pocket and get back to cleaning. Julian spares me a few concerned glances, but I turn my back on him and internalize my aggression until the burning rage is nothing but a tiny ember of disgust.

I knew Nico's mom wouldn't show up today, but he had hoped she would.

He *always* hopes.

Nico is too young and caring to see his mother for who she is, and I'm not the kind of man who will speak ill of her to gain his favor. One day, he will learn the truth, and I'll be on standby, ready to put his broken heart back together when his mother inevitably shatters it.

Unlike my sweet, sentimental son, I've learned the hard way not to trust anything that comes out of my ex-wife's mouth. She might be the mother of my child, and for that, I will always give her more grace than she deserves, but I will never let her get close enough to hurt me again. Her or any other woman for that matter, so I keep them at a distance and prevent any opportunities for intimacy.

Loneliness might be temporary, but heartbreak?

That emotional damage can last a lifetime.

CHAPTER NINETEEN

Ellie

After the party, Dahlia asks me to go over what her family needs to do with the barn animals while we are away. Although Rafael considered hiring someone for the task so as not to inconvenience anyone, they refused to let him, claiming that the animals are part of the family.

Dahlia already knows Penelope, the racehorse who was almost put down because of an injury, so I skip over introductions and review her caretaking needs. Penelope is the only animal I didn't rename, mainly because she hated everything I came up with.

I've since come to learn that horses are rather opinionated animals.

We walk to the next set of stalls, and I motion toward the dark brown goat. "So, Jack D is afraid of loud noises. If he hears one, he might faint."

Dahlia's eyes widen with horror.

"It's not as scary as it sounds." I point out the two other goats. "Johnnie W and Jimmy B don't like to be kept apart, so make sure you let them sleep in the same stall, or else they'll keep all the other animals awake with their headbutting."

The three goats have only been here for a month, but they've made their presence known since the day Rafael saved them from an abusive owner who left them for dead inside their cages.

She stifles a laugh. "How do you tell them apart?"

"Johnnie over there has had a few too many knocks to the head, so Jimmy keeps close and takes care of him. They both have matching white spots on their left and right legs, while Jack has a white spot between his horns."

"Did Rafa name them?"

"I took creative liberties since he was still calling them goats one, two, and three."

She snorts. "Are you a big fan of whiskey?"

My nose wrinkles. "Not really, but my stepdad is."

Dahlia is then formally introduced to Jose, Patron, and Julio, the three potbellied pigs Rafael adopted right after I started working here. The day he rescued them was the first night I was trusted alone with Nico since he needed to travel a few towns over to save the pigs and Bacardi, the smallest sheep to ever exist.

"What's her story?" She kneels in front of the shy sheep.

"Wool farm incident gone wrong." My chest throbs at the various scars littering her body.

Dahlia's bottom lip wobbles. "Remind me to never buy anything with wool again."

I offer her a small, reassuring smile. "Rafael is working on shutting the place down and finding new homes for the other sheep, but he's run into a few legal issues."

She rises from the floor and picks at a few pieces of hay that stuck to her clothes. "I'm surprised he finds the time to do all this with his work schedule."

"It's important to him," I reply.

Her eyes soften around the edges. "I know. He's always been this way ever since we were kids and he wanted to save all the stray cats around town."

"He did?"

"Oh yeah. Josefina hated it."

"Why?"

"She calls them an invasive species."

My nose twitches with distaste. "Really?"

"Yeah, but that didn't stop Rafa from feeding the cats when she was sleeping."

A laugh slips out. "Sounds like his fascination with strays started at a young age."

She glances down at Bacardi. "I think he sees himself in them."

My heart acts up again, missing a beat. "How?"

"That's not my story to tell." She moves along to the next stall and changes the subject, acting like she didn't peel back one of Rafael's many layers.

I always knew Rafael had a soft spot for his animals— that much became obvious when a part of my job description included taking care of them—but I never thought to consider *why* my boss was adamant about adopting so many abused animals. I stupidly assumed it was because he saw a documentary or something equally moving, but Dahlia's statement hints at something deeper.

Something I wish to uncover, if only to get a better understanding of the mysterious man who keeps his soft heart hidden behind a thick block of ice.

I think he sees himself in them.

Everyone knows Rafael was adopted by Julian's parents, but the reason why they did it isn't public knowledge. Sure, people made their own assumptions about his upbringing, but I never paid much attention to town gossip. As it was, teenage me could barely be in the same room as him without blushing, let alone listen to stories about him without giving away my crush.

I've come a long way since those shy, awkward days, but that doesn't mean I'm immune to a man with a tragic backstory and a love for broken, discarded things.

Sundays aren't usually my free day, but Rafael gave me the day off anyway since I had already agreed to grab coffee with Cole. He offered to order for me at the Angry Rooster Café, so I walk past the counter and search the entire shop for him, only to come up empty.

I pull out my phone and text him.

ME

Hey. Are you here yet?

His reply is instant.

COLE

I slipped out the back exit.

ME

Please tell me there is a good reason you're hanging around the dumpsters.

COLE

Someone recognized me, and I panicked.

COLE

I swear.

I release a relieved breath and head toward the back. While I haven't spent much time around famous people since Ava gained popularity after she kicked me to the curb, I can only imagine how overwhelming it must feel, especially for someone like Cole, who became famous before he was ever born.

I open the back door and find the musician leaning against a wall with a ball cap drawn low over his face and a pair of sunglasses that hide his eyes.

He holds up a second cup for me. "You asked for a dirty chai, right?"

"Thanks." I happily grab the iced drink from him and take a big gulp. "You know, if you didn't want to be recognized, I would have suggested meeting somewhere else."

He makes a face. "I thought people wouldn't take notice."

I can't help laughing. "Are you joking?"

"My agent told me no one would care about who I am here."

I stare at him without blinking. "Are you even aware of how famous you are?"

Cole, despite having famous rock stars for parents, has built a name for himself in the indie-folk genre. His music is slightly different from Ava's, although they are often included in the same playlists and end up competing for awards at shows. If it hadn't been for Ava's album, Cole would have most likely won Album of the Year himself.

"Hard to forget," he grumbles.

"Must suck sometimes," I say.

"Yeah, it does, but then I remember the good things that come with a job like mine."

"Like what?"

"Connecting with people through my songs. Making them feel seen and heard with my lyrics."

"That's the best part." My lips curve of their own accord.

His smile is nothing but friendly. "I knew you'd understand."

"Yeah." I focus on a spot in the distance.

"So…" *Here we go.* "I know you said you don't write songs anymore."

"Mm-hmm."

"Is there any way I could convince you to try?"

I had a feeling that was why he wanted to meet, but a small part of me had hoped I could avoid the topic for a little while longer.

"I haven't written a song since..." Finishing my sentence proves impossible.

"Silver Scars" was the last song I wrote before Ava's music producer and new boyfriend at the time, Darius Larkin, ruined my career. It was the only one I wrote that was inspired by myself, which was one of the reasons I asked Ava and Darius to clear all evidence of it from their computers.

I didn't want people around the world to know how I viewed myself or the story behind my scars. Couldn't bear the idea of someone else singing about them either, even if that person happened to be my best friend at the time.

"Silver Scars" was and will always be *my* story, and no amount of pleading on Ava's part could convince me to let her keep it, so at least I can sleep better at night knowing the song was wiped from their hard drive.

I can't make out Cole's eyes through the dark shades, but I feel them traveling over my face.

"I'm not sure if you heard about this, but I recently lost my cowriter."

I place my hand over my heart. "Something happened to Phoebe?" Everyone who loves Cole's music knows about Phoebe, his lyrical cowriter and longtime girlfriend. They were always seen as a powerhouse in the industry.

His plastic coffee cup bends under the pressure of his grasp. "We decided to part ways."

"What? Why? She was amazing!"

His bitter laugh sends a chill down my spine. "Yeah, I thought the same thing until she fell into bed with someone else."

My mouth falls open. "She cheated on *you*?"

Everyone with internet access knew about Cole and Phoebe's romance and how much Cole loved her. The man *glowed* whenever she was brought up during interviews, so if she cheated…

"Damn," I mutter to myself. No wonder he donated their guitar to the thrift shop.

He takes a long sip from his straw. "Yup."

"I can't believe it." I chose to ignore the recent gossip headlines trying to paint Cole as a serial cheater who caused the demise of his relationship because I thought they were trying to stir up unnecessary drama.

Turns out Phoebe was the one having an affair, not him.

"The positive pregnancy test cleared things up rather quickly for me."

I nearly spit out my coffee. "You're having a kid?"

"Fuck no. I was busy finishing up the American leg of my tour."

"Shit."

"Sounds about right."

"I'm sorry."

"Sorry enough to help me write a song?"

I laugh at his boldness. "No, but good try."

"How about money?"

"I already have a job." The excuse is weak, especially since I could write songs and still remain Nico's nanny, but that doesn't mean I *should*.

Some dreams are meant to stay broken, and this is one of them.

"Is this because Ava Rhodes stole your songs?" he asks without any hesitation.

I wince. "I never said that."

"I know, but I did some digging around yesterday and found out a few things."

I shoot him a look. "That's a big claim you're making."

His right brow arches. "Yet you're not denying it."

Words escape me, so I remain quiet.

He pushes his sunglasses up so I can get a better look at his eyes. "I could get you in contact with the right person who can help you get the credit you deserve."

The world freezes as I repeat his words in my head. "That's crazy."

"Maybe, but it's also right."

I've tried to contact a few lawyers before, but everyone had the same response.

I'm not the right fit for this case.

After the third time being turned down, I've started to lose hope about ever receiving credit or royalties for my songs. Now, if Cole can help connect me to someone, it's at least worth following up on, even if it leads to another dead end.

"What kind of person?" I ask.

"The best lawyer in the industry, who would have no issue going after someone as popular as her."

"I didn't think it was possible."

"It *could* be."

"But let me guess—you'll only help me if I help you." A hint of bitterness comes out, surprising us both.

He shakes his head. "Contrary to what people might say about me, I'm not an asshole. If you want the lawyer's contact information, then I'll pass it along. No strings attached."

"Really?"

"Yeah."

"Prove it."

He pulls his phone out of his pocket, unlocks it, and taps at the screen. Ten seconds later, my phone buzzes with a new message. I double-check the text just in case.

"Still don't trust me?" He smirks.

My grip on my phone tightens. "I've been burned once before."

"I understand."

"Thanks." I fight to get the word out with how tight my throat feels.

"No problem. It's the least I could do after you agreed to meet me and hear me out. If you change your mind about writing the song, shoot me a text." He tips his chin in my direction before taking off toward Main Street, leaving me with a heavy feeling in my chest that doesn't go away.

Willow bolts from her couch. "What do you mean Cole Griffin offered you a job and you said no? Are you crazy?"

"She's just boring like the rest of this town." Lorenzo looks up from his cell phone for the first time all afternoon, finally gracing us with his attention. Having him present for this conversation wasn't my smartest decision, but I'm desperate for someone else's opinion. Willow and my parents are the only people I've told about Ava's betrayal.

I flip him off. With a shrug, he returns to tapping at his phone screen, ignoring Willow shooting daggers at him. I thought he might be able to offer insight into my issue with Ava, but clearly that isn't the case.

Willow's gaze softens when it swings toward me. "You have to call him and ask if the offer is still on the table. Like right now before he changes his mind or finds someone else."

"No."

"Why not?"

Truth is, the more I consider Cole's offer, the more I *want* to accept it...or at least I do until fear comes knocking again, reminding me all about my past.

"I haven't written a full song in a year," I say instead.

"You haven't had a good reason to," she replies.

"What if I was a one-hit wonder?"

"Technically, you had fourteen hits and three songs that went triple platinum, so that's not possible," Lorenzo says without looking up.

Willow's mouth falls open. "How do you know that?"

He shakes his phone. "The internet."

I drop onto the worn leather sofa with a huff. "Okay, but there's no guarantee I can successfully do that all again."

Willow's eyes soften. "You'll never know unless you try."

"I—"

Lorenzo's smile comes off as rehearsed and never reaches his cold, dead eyes. "Do you want my opinion?"

Willow and I both say no at the same time, which earns us a scowl.

"I'm trying to be nice," he says with a flat tone that makes the hairs on the back of my neck rise.

My nose twitches. "Well, please stop. It's not natural coming from you."

I haven't known Lorenzo for long, but I know he doesn't dish out advice because he's a nice guy. He barely tolerates Willow and me, even going out of his way to remind us that we aren't friends, although he could've fooled me with how much he hangs out around here.

At first, I was worried he might be interested in Willow, but it didn't take me long to realize their dynamic is far from romantic. He treats her like an annoying little sister, and she calls him her long-lost fourth brother.

Lorenzo is clearly lonely and looking for companionship, and it's absolutely eating him up inside to know he found it with us.

His eyes narrow. "You just want me to shut up because Willow is too nice to call you out on your bullshit."

It feels like he struck me. "Excuse me?"

"I think saying no to Cole is easy. Probably the easiest thing you've ever done besides running away from LA, if we're being honest."

Willow's eyes widen. "Whoa. Let's not jump to—"

I interrupt her by telling him, "You don't know anything about me."

"Hate to break it to you, but you're not as complex and layered as you make yourself out to be, although you artistic types sure love to portray yourselves like that." He picks a piece of invisible lint off his trousers and flicks it away. "Makes for better music, I assume."

My blood boils beneath my skin. "You're such an asshole."

"I prefer that over being a coward."

I jump to my feet and point a finger in his direction. "I am *not* a coward."

"Then why did you tell him no?"

I throw my hands up in exasperation. "Because I'm scared!"

He makes a satisfied sound and returns to tapping his phone screen, pretending he didn't just antagonize me into admitting the truth aloud.

As much as I hate Lorenzo for pushing me the way he did, he is right. I *am* a coward. A coward who is terrified of putting herself out there and getting burned again.

"It's okay to be afraid." Willow's soft voice penetrates the chill surrounding me. "After Darius took advantage of you—no, after he *assaulted* you—you have every right to be scared of returning to that scene."

Lorenzo's nostrils flare. "He did *what*?"

"We're not talking about that," I say with a strong tone, leaving no room for discussion.

Willow silently mouths *sorry* before speaking. "Cole seems like a good guy."

My head hangs. "So did Darius."

Lorenzo's eyes narrow, but thankfully, he refrains from asking any follow-up questions about him.

"But now you know better. You know what signs to watch out for, and you have the power to walk away at any moment."

I sigh. "I don't know."

Willow pulls me into a hug. "Don't let your fear of the past stop you from the future you want."

"It's not like I *want* to be afraid."

"No one does."

"But I keep thinking… What if I suck?"

Willow releases me with a scoff. "Like you could ever write a bad song."

I shoot her a look.

She huffs. "We're not counting high school here."

"Cole could hate whatever I write."

Willow's smile is small but sure. "Well, you'll never know unless you try."

CHAPTER TWENTY

Ellie

I've been on two airplanes in my whole life, and I suffered through both rides with gritted teeth, a constant cold sweat, and a churning stomach that never relented. Avoiding my fear of flying didn't take much effort since my family chose vacation destinations we could visit by car, but now I no longer have the luxury of avoiding the inevitable.

Willow suggested I take something to help with the flight, but I never gathered the courage to talk to Rafael about taking prescription medication while on the job. Admitting my fear aloud felt silly, especially to someone who has his own private jet and a passport stamped with tons of countries, so I kept my worries to myself.

When I suggested flying commercial while Nico and Rafael flew in the family's private jet, Nico vetoed the idea before volunteering them to fly with me. His father protested, but Nico didn't back down, solely because I had secretly told him that I liked bigger planes. I never explained *why*, but thankfully, he didn't ask.

Rafael, on the other hand, questioned me a few times about flying commercial versus private, but I always found a way out of the conversation before ever having to answer him.

Like today.

Thankfully, Nico does a good job of distracting me from my spiraling thoughts and his father's questions by dragging me around the airport terminal. In the short time we've been waiting for our plane to arrive at the gate, we have visited three different stores, and I've bought an overpriced pack of sour gummy worms, a neck pillow for the long flight, a coloring book, and a fifty-count pack of colored pencils.

"Ellie." The way Rafael says my name draws a sharp breath from me. By now, I should be used to him no longer calling me Eleanor, but my heart still takes a dive into my stomach every time he says it.

He holds my boarding pass out for me to grab. "You dropped this back at the store."

"My bad." My fingers tremble as I reach for the piece of paper.

"Are you okay?" He pulls back, and my fingers grasp onto air.

"Yup. Why wouldn't I be?" I plaster on a small—albeit, very tense—smile.

He scowls. "You're shaking."

"I'm cold." I wrap my arms around my torso.

"Then why are you sweating?"

My fingers twitch with irritation. How did we go from happily ignoring each other's existence to him checking in on me like he actually gives a damn, and what's the best way to politely tell him to stop?

When I don't answer, he follows up with, "Are you feeling sick or something?"

"Ellie! Look what I found!" Nico, my knight in light-up sneakers, runs over to us with the newest edition of his favorite comic book.

"Whoa. Where did you get that?" I quickly jump into a conversation with him, although Rafael's knowing gaze follows me long after we buy Nico's new comic and leave the airport bookstore behind us.

I do my best to keep calm and collected, but no amount of encouraging texts from Willow and my mom or silent prayers to a higher power save me from the overwhelming sick feeling I'm hit with when our group is called to board the plane.

Thankfully, Rafael doesn't comment on me dropping my guitar case on the way, although he does spare me another strange look when he goes to pick it up for me. I regret bringing the instrument, but I couldn't bear the thought of leaving it behind, in part because I'm still not sure if I want to take Cole up on his offer to write a song.

Who knows? Maybe I'll get inspired on our trip.

Nico remains unaware of my struggles, which is a blessing in disguise since the last thing I want to do is worry him about a plane. He leads the three of us, looking far older than his nine years of age with the way he manages to roll his suitcase while talking to his grandma at the same time.

"*Si, Abuela. Yo te llamo cuando lleguemos.*"

My heart hammers in my chest as Nico goes before us and hands his first-class boarding pass over to the smiling airline employee.

Despite usually traveling on Rafael's private jet, Nico acts like a pro as he tucks his boarding pass into the front pocket of his miniature carry-on suitcase before taking off to the jet bridge.

Acid climbs up my throat as the employee beckons me forward. My feet remain frozen to the carpet, my body paralyzed by fear until my fight-or-flight response kicks in.

Nope. Can't do it.

The thought of getting on that plane—of spending hours trapped in a small metal tube with hundreds of people at the mercy of turbulence and a pilot I don't know—seems impossible.

"Ma'am?" The employee frowns. "Your boarding pass, please?"

"I got it." Rafael slips his hand into my hoodie pocket, replacing the cold dread in my stomach with a wave of heat. A cotton barrier prevents his fingers from grazing my skin, but my body reacts anyway.

"Just breathe," he whispers in my ear as he holds the boarding pass out toward the woman. "You're going to be fine."

Si, Abuela. Yo te llamo cuando lleguemos.: Yes, Grandma. I'll call you when we get there.

Am I? Because I don't exactly feel anything remotely close to *fine* at the moment.

"Nico is waiting for us. See?" Rafael reminds me.

I was so busy panicking, I forgot all about Nico. We haven't even made it to Hawaii yet and I'm already messing up.

It'll be a miracle if I still have a job by the end of our two-week vacation.

"Miss, are you all right?" the employee asks.

"Define *all right*?"

She makes a face.

"She's joking." Rafael swaps my boarding pass with his. With a quick scan, both of us are cleared to board.

Too bad my shaky legs won't cooperate.

Rafael places his hand on the small of my back and gives me a small push. "I know this part is hard, but you're going to be okay." His palm remains a warm, soothing presence against my spine, grounding me to the world.

Rafael offering me comfort was not something I ever thought possible, but I'll never say no to an emotional support buddy during a plane ride.

He lightly pushes me with one hand while rolling both of our carry-ons with the other. "Come on. The sooner we get on the plane, the quicker you can get settled in."

He leads me down the never-ending jet bridge that feels hotter than hell thanks to the June sun beating down on the metal tube. "You didn't tell me you were afraid of flying."

"You didn't ask."

"Fair enough." His low chuckle tickles my ear and sends

a shiver down my spine. "Now I finally understand why you didn't want to take the private jet."

"Have you seen the size of that thing? It's tiny." The massive plane we are about to board makes Rafael's jet look like one of Nico's toys.

"It's not nice to insult a man's size." There's a hint of a smile in his voice.

"Rafael Angelo Lopez. Did you just make a dick joke?" I sneak a glance at my boss, whose cheeks turn pink.

"How did you find out my middle name?"

"The same way I find out most things."

"My aunt needs to learn how to keep her mouth shut." His blush intensifies.

I used to be a glutton for Rafael's smiles, but I prefer the way his cheeks flush with embarrassment even more, especially when I'm the cause of it.

"Hey, slow pokes! Let's go! It's hot in here!" Nico shouts.

Rafael sobers, and his serious mask returns as he gives me another little push.

"Are you okay?" Nico looks at me when we finally make it to the door of the plane.

"Yeah. Just feeling a little sick."

"Oh no!"

I plaster on my best reassuring smile. "Yeah, but I'll be fine."

"Good, because it's gonna be a long flight." He really enunciates the word *long*, which further fuels my panic.

Rafael seems to notice my cracking composure and gives the back of my neck a reassuring squeeze. The gesture is far more intimate than he probably intended, and it makes my heart jolt.

A flight attendant waves to get our attention, and Nico grabs my hand and pulls me toward the open cabin door. "Let's go!"

I follow behind him without protesting because, regardless of my personal fears, I'm willing to do just about anything for Nico Lopez, including suffer through ten hours of misery and motion sickness if it makes him happy.

Nico talks my ear off throughout the entire plane boarding process. I try to keep up with the conversation, and he seems to have forgotten about me feeling sick until I rip my sweaty hoodie off and pop a Dramamine into my mouth.

"Are you still feeling bad?" he asks in the loudest whisper known to man.

"Kind of?"

"What's wrong?"

Thankfully, I'm saved from having to answer by none other than Rafael.

"Nicolas?" his dad calls from the seat behind me.

"¿Si, Papi?"

"Do you mind switching seats with me?"

He makes a slight frown. "Ugh. Why?"

"Because my window screen won't open."

"Mm." Nico leans in and whispers in my ear, "*Papi* likes keeping it open because he's a scaredy cat."

Well, Rafael is going to be mighty disappointed when he learns I'd much rather leave mine closed.

"*Nico*," Rafael says in that serious tone of his.

"Fine."

They swap seats. Since Rafael bought four tickets so he didn't have to sit next to anyone, Nico stretches across the two large seats.

"Put your seat belt on, please." Rafael stands and waits for the confirmatory click of the two metal pieces locking together.

My heart, which was already racing, threatens to burst as Rafael slides through the gap between me and the seat in front of mine.

I've never been so acutely aware of someone else before, and my body goes haywire as he brushes past me to get to his seat.

"Hey," he says once he settles into the chair beside me.

"Hi." I stare into his dark brown eyes.

We rarely have a chance to be this close to one another, and I'm not entirely sure how I feel about it. On the one hand, I find it difficult to look away, while on the other, I'm desperate to evade his gaze.

Fortunately for both of us, he ruins the moment by lifting the window covering.

"No!" I rush to cover his hand with my own.

"You don't like to look out the window?"

"Absolutely not."

He frowns. "Why?"

Since my self-preservation was lost somewhere between the loading bridge and the first-class cabin, I have nothing to lose by being honest.

"It makes my anxiety worse."

"Hm."

"What?"

He takes a moment to think. "What is it that you're most afraid of? Claustrophobia? Crashing? Turbulence? Takeoff or landing?"

"Is there an *all of the above* option?"

His lips curl ever so slightly at the corners. "You hate flying that much?"

"Absolutely despise it. This entire process is a nightmare from beginning to end, so maybe it's best if I switch seats with Nico and let you two enjoy the whole first-class experience."

He ignores my offer and asks, "How many times have you been on an airplane?"

"Twice."

"In your life?"

"No, in the last month."

He makes a face.

"Of course twice in my whole life. One trip was enough to last a lifetime."

His head tilts. "But you agreed to go on this trip."

"Because it's important to him," I whisper while pointing my thumb at the row behind us.

I had never anticipated Nico wanting me to join him and his father on a trip to create lasting visual memories, but once I was invited, I couldn't exactly say no. Not even after Nico encouraged his father to switch the original Europe trip for a tropical vacation ill-suited to someone who wants to hide their scars for as long as humanly possible.

Rafael stares at me for the longest five seconds of my life. "Thank you." His throat visibly tightens from his thick swallow. "It means a lot to him."

A tidal wave of warmth spreads through my chest, only to be cut short when the takeoff message cuts out and the plane jerks backward.

My breathing becomes shallower as the plane starts moving toward the runway, and my bone-crushing grip on the armrests tightens until my knuckles turn white from lack of blood flow.

Rafael's gaze lifts from my hands. "You should have told me about this."

I laugh to myself. "What could you have done?"

"Suggested some Xanax?"

"Do you happen to have some?"

"No, but I would have pointed you toward someone who could have helped. Or at the very least, I would have taught you some strategies before the big flight."

"Oh, because you're an expert on aviophobia now?"

"Seeing as I once felt the same way, yeah."

"Really?" I thought Nico was joking because I find it hard to believe Rafael is—or was—afraid of something mundane like planes. He seems so…strong and stoic.

"Yup. Why do you think I like to keep the window open?"

"If you want…" I swallow the lump in my throat. "You could…"

"I'm fine."

The takeoff announcement begins to play on the large screen in front of me, reminding me of everything that can go wrong on the flight. I can't look away from the short film that discusses safety rafts, emergency exits, and the importance of putting my oxygen mask on first before helping anyone else.

The engines roaring to life only make my anxiety worse as the plane and my heart rate pick up speed.

"Let's play a game."

"Cute idea, but I'm going to have to politely decline because, I'm not sure if you've noticed, but I'm about two seconds away from losing my goddamn mind."

He ignores me as he asks, "Would you rather never play an instrument again or lose the ability to sing?"

My gasp can barely be heard over the noisy engines. "Excuse me?"

"You have to pick one."

"I don't want to." My heart jolts as the wheels lose touch with the ground.

You're stuck in here for hours, and there is nothing you can do—

"I bet you'd choose to give up your voice."

Wait. What?

"Which would be a damn shame if you asked me."

I'm struggling to breathe, and it has nothing to do with the plane taking off.

"You have the most beautiful voice I've ever heard."

My whole face probably resembles a tomato. "You're just saying that to distract me."

"Since when have I been the type to give false compliments?"

I'm too stunned to reply.

"So what would you pick?"

I decide to throw him a bone and answer since he is clearly doing this for my benefit. "It's not like I'd want to stop singing, but never playing an instrument again isn't an option. They make my soul sing in a way."

His head tilts in silent curiosity. "What's that like?"

"What's *what* like?"

"Having something that makes you feel alive."

I struggle to come up with a suitable reply, so I stick to silence as I process his question. Does Rafael not have anything that sets his heart on fire, or has he closed himself off from the opportunity of ever feeling that way?

I'm not sure, but I'm afraid of what might happen if I search hard enough for an answer.

CHAPTER TWENTY-ONE

Rafael

Ellie eventually fell asleep, which I didn't think was possible, especially given how anxious she was about the whole flight. Her body gave out once the adrenaline wore off, and she chose my shoulder as her pillow while the one she bought remained on her lap. I could push her away, but I'm still feeling guilty after her earlier admission, so I remain still as a statue while she leans on me.

When Nico strong-armed me into inviting Ellie on our summer trip, I assumed she had agreed because of the all-expenses-paid vacation, but that couldn't be further from the truth.

Like me, she is here for Nico. Travel anxiety be damned.

Her dedication to making the most of this trip for my son fills me with gratitude so strong, it overwhelms me—as does the idea of Ellie doing more for Nico than his mother ever has.

If my ex-wife had a similar fear, I wouldn't find her anywhere near a plane, let alone powering through a ten-hour flight for our son.

"How long is she going to sleep for?" Nico whispers through the hole between our seats.

"I don't know," I reply in a soft voice.

"Shouldn't we wake her up soon?"

"We still have a few more hours left." I sneak a glance at the woman I once found annoying as she cuddles up to my side, pressing her warm body up against mine.

It doesn't take long until her soft snores slowly lull me to sleep too.

Someone's hand clamps around mine, and I jolt awake.

"What the…" I look down to find Ellie's fingers locked between mine. The plane shakes as we hit a bit of turbulence.

"Rafael." Her panic-laced voice sparks me into action.

"It's fine."

"It's not freaking fine!" Ellie's already-ashen face pales even more as the plane shakes.

"Is she okay?" Nico whisper-shouts.

"She will be in a little bit. How about you?" I ask him.

"Yup! It's like that space ride in Dreamland." Nico speaks in that upbeat voice of his, which helps me relax a bit. Ellie doesn't seem to share the same sentiment, as her grip on my hand tightens until it tingles from the lack of blood circulation.

Blood circulation. Right.

Her heavy breathing drags me away from my thoughts. It's been a long time since anyone but Nico sought to be comforted by me, and I quickly become aware of how rusty I am as I say, "The statistics are in our favor. Only one in every eleven million planes crashes."

She stares at me in horror. "One in eleven million?"

"According to Google, yeah."

"But aren't there at least a hundred thousand flights in a given day?"

Fuck. So much for comforting her.

The plane dips a little, and my stomach lurches. Her bone-crushing hold on my hand doesn't relent, and I offer a reassuring squeeze despite my joints protesting.

"We could—"

She doesn't let me finish my sentence. "If you suggest we play a game, I will kill you."

"I was going to recommend taking a few deep breaths, but if plotting my murder distracts you, then be my guest. I'll even offer ideas."

"Do you have a will?"

"Why are you asking?"

"Just want to make sure Nico is set for life and all."

There must be something wrong with me because that's the only plausible explanation for how my chest warms at the idea of her caring enough about my son to make sure he is taken care of if I'm not around.

The plane rocks again.

"Oh my God." She groans. "We're going to die."

A few other people in the first-class cabin stare at Ellie

with a mix of judgmental expressions, and I glare at them from over the top of her head until they drop their eyes.

Who knew my scowl could be turned into a superpower?

When I look back down, I find Ellie staring straight ahead with a single tear rolling down her face. It affects me more than I'd like, and I instinctively find myself brushing the droplet away with the pad of my thumb.

"Ellie."

Nothing.

"Hey."

Her silence eats away at me as she takes a big gulp of air.

"Elle?" I speak the nickname into existence without thinking much of it. "*Háblame.*" My use of Spanish pulls her out of whatever anxious spiral she was in.

She turns to look at me. "What does that mean?"

"Talk to me," I translate.

"I can't," she rasps.

"You're crying."

She rushes to wipe at her cheeks. "This is so embarrassing."

"I agree. If you keep this up, I'll have no choice but to use it as blackmail one day."

She laughs. It's nothing special, but it relieves some of the growing tension in my body until the plane shakes again. While I got over my fear of flying years ago, I still hate turbulence, so distracting Ellie will benefit me too.

"What's this tattoo about?" I trace over the thin band of stars that circles the entirety of her middle finger.

"Huh?"

"Your tattoo." I tap the permanent black ring.

"Oh. That." Her brows furrow. "I made a promise to myself when I was younger."

"What was it?"

She stares at our hands. "That, no matter what happens or how hard life gets, I won't give up on myself."

Thunder rumbles outside as rain beats down on the plane.

I try to distract her with another question. "Why did you choose this finger?"

She swallows thickly before glancing up at me. "Middle fingers are associated with our life and identity, so it seemed right."

"Huh. I just thought they were good for flipping people off."

Another laugh pours out of her, only for the sweet sound to be cut off by another clap of thunder.

"What about this one?" I point at the triplet note located on the inside of her right wrist.

"It represents my family. Burt, my mom, and me." She points to each part of the note. "They got matching ones."

"I didn't know you were an only child."

"You never asked."

"I've been an asshole." Guilt replaces my curiosity. After knowing Ellie for nearly a year, I should be able to answer a simple question like that myself.

"Just a teensy, tiny bit."

I shoot her a look.

"But to answer your question, I was raised like an only child, but I have half-siblings on my father's side. I've never met them, though."

I know better than to broach a conversation like that, especially with how anxious she is.

"And what about this one?" I turn her arm and follow the path of blank skin to the crescent moon near her elbow.

Her already-pale face completely loses all its color, and she yanks her hand away without warning. "I just liked the way it looked."

"If you want us to start trusting one another, you should stop lying."

Her eyes narrow. "You want the truth?"

I nod.

"It's the one and only tattoo I regret." She reaches for her headphones and covers her ears, effectively shutting me out.

Ten minutes later, the summer storm has officially passed, and the captain promises that the rest of the flight will be a smooth one. Ellie acknowledges me with a whispered *thank you* for helping her through her anxiety before tuning me out again.

I'm used to Nico's nanny being quiet. It was one of the main reasons I hired her in the first place, because unlike the other ones, she wasn't actively trying to impress me or force me to open up. We both did our own thing, with us only interacting when it related to Nico.

It was a match made in heaven...until now.

I should be grateful that Ellie established a clear boundary again, but instead, I'm left with the bitter taste of loneliness as we go back to ignoring each other's presence.

You could always suggest being friends.

Except nothing says *pathetic* quite like asking my son's

nanny, who is on my payroll, to be my friend. God knows I could use one, but that doesn't mean I'm going to force Ellie into being mine.

No matter how much I want to.

CHAPTER TWENTY-TWO

Ellie

nearly burst into tears as we step off the plane in Honolulu. Not to be dramatic or anything, but I saw my life flash before my very eyes during that random storm. A highlight reel of my favorite moments and biggest regrets played in my head, which was a bittersweet reminder of all the things I've left unfinished.

"You did it." Rafael's praise makes my heart want to burst.

Seriously? We're swooning over a simple "you did it"?

"You were such a big kid," Nico taunts.

I give him a little shove. "Not all of us can be as brave as you."

"Obviously, because I'm awesome." His big, goofy grin draws out one of my own.

We follow his father to the baggage claim area. Nico and I play a racing game together on his portable gaming console while Rafael waits with all the other people near the ramp. Both of us want to pick our favorite Formula 1 driver as our playable character, so three quick rounds of rock-paper-scissors determine that Nico gets Elías Cruz. Nico ends up winning both races we play, in part because I'm distracted by everything happening around us.

Rafael and Nico's checked bags are some of the first to come out, so we have to stand around for my overweight suitcase to make its appearance. I knew it was a bad idea to let my mom and Willow pick my outfits for the trip, but they strong-armed me into choosing clothes that wouldn't give me a heatstroke in Hawaii.

Five excruciatingly long minutes later, Rafael lifts my suitcase off the conveyor belt without straining a single muscle, although he does rip the *heavy* tag off the handle. "What did you pack in there?"

"A body."

Nico giggles while Rafael makes a face.

"Kidding! Just a few things."

"Like?"

"Five pairs of shoes, a couple of books, Nico's metal detector, seven of his action figures, and half of my closet." So, I'm an over-packer. Sue me.

"Are you moving?" Rafael asks in that dry voice of his.

"I'm seriously considering it because there is no way I'm getting on another plane."

Nico gasps. "But what about getting to Kauai?"

"They don't have ferries?"

Nico looks up at his dad for an answer.

Rafael shakes his head. "No."

My hope dies, along with Nico's excitement.

"Don't worry, Ellie. We don't have to do a helicopter or plane ride. We can stay here in Oahu instead." Nico covers my hand with his.

If this little guy didn't already own a big part of my heart, I would have gladly given it up for him in this moment because this trip is supposed to be about him and everything he wants. I'm not going to let my fear of planes get in the way of that and him creating special visual memories while he can still enjoy it.

I give him a reassuring pat on the shoulder. "That's sweet of you, but there's no need to change our plans. If I survived the flight here, I can make it through those shorter ones."

He wraps his arms around me with a smile. "You're the best and bravest person I know!"

Compliments from not one but two Lopez men have me feeling emotional. I must be getting my period soon or something, because there is no other reasonable explanation for the overwhelming swell of emotion taking up real estate in my chest.

The back of my neck heats, and I look up to find Rafael staring at me with a strange look on his face.

Thank you, he silently mouths, making my chest get all tight and tingly yet again.

It is the same feeling I had on the plane while he was doing everything in his power to make me feel better. My anxiety was too big to handle on my own, and I clung to the first person who could help me feel safe. But now, without my fears fueling my actions, I'm left with a grim reminder of our circumstances.

I can like Rafael as a *person*, but it can never go further than that because of the little guy who clings to my legs like another appendage. For him, I'm willing to do just about anything, including pushing his father away for the sake of keeping my job as his nanny.

Because I have a feeling that if I let someone like Rafael get close, I wouldn't be able to stop myself from wanting the same in return. From wanting *more*.

And that will never happen, so I need to get my confusing feelings under control and remember who is important here.

Nicolas Lopez.

Rafael places the hotel key over a sensor, and the elevator whirs to life as we begin our ascent.

"What floor am I on?" I ask as the numbers keep climbing.

"You're staying in our suite," he says in that annoyingly bland, nonchalant voice of his that I'm quickly realizing is used whenever he is defensive and uncomfortable.

Good, because he isn't the only one.

We may share a house, but a hotel suite is different. Back in Lake Wisteria, Rafael's place is the size of a palace and provides us with enough space to steer clear of one another. If I don't want to see him, I can simply stick to a different floor.

A hotel suite is going to be tiny in comparison. I won't have anywhere to hide from him.

Unlike me, Nico seems quite taken with the idea based

on his bright smile. "Yay! We can stay up all night watching movies, telling stories, and playing games!"

Rafael shoots him a *good luck trying that* look.

"Um…" I bite down on my bottom lip.

Rafael stares at me for so long, I'm sweating by the time he speaks again. "If you'd feel more comfortable having your own room, I can ask my assistant to book one."

"No! Stay with us! *Please.*" Nico puts his palms together. "It'll be fun. I swear."

I *should* take Rafael up on his offer and stay in a separate room, but my resolve crumbles when I remember how much he paid for five nights here. For two hundred grand—yup, that's right—I thought we would at least have separate suites to call home for the next few days.

It goes against my entire character to ask Rafael to pay even more, regardless of his billionaire status.

"All right," I concede.

Nico pumps his fist in the air. "Yes!"

I face forward and focus on the numbers flashing above the elevator door.

It's just a suite, I tell myself.

The doors slide open, revealing a massive penthouse.

To think you were worried about sharing a small space.

I take a shaky step out of the elevator and into the massive living room overlooking the Pacific Ocean. The light wood tones, expensive white furnishings, and tasteful splash of blue accents immediately put me at ease, blending coastal chic decor with luxury living.

Growing up with a store manager for a mother and a

music tutor for a stepdad meant my family booked RV spaces and chain hotels, not five-star "suites" that have a chef's kitchen, sauna, and a private balcony with a hot tub that could comfortably fit ten people.

All those details are amazing, but nothing gets me more excited than the white grand piano facing the lagoon below. I can't begin to describe the serene view of the shoreline, but it is different from our lake back home. Whitecaps as far as the eye can see. Colorful umbrellas and towels lining the sandy beach. Palm tree fronds swaying with the breeze, casting shadows over pedestrians stopping to take in the view.

A sense of tranquility washes over me like one of the waves crashing against the shore, and I want to write about it.

I want to *write*.

I'm not sure what the song would be about, but the feeling is familiar, and one that makes me happy I packed my guitar after all.

My fingers itch for a pen. "This is…"

"Amazing." Nico presses his face against the bifold glass door that takes up the entirety of the wall.

"I spy something blue," I say, using our game as a way to check in on his vision. Asking him bluntly only leads to his discomfort, so I learned long ago to use games like "I spy" to gather information instead.

Nico's smile widens. "Waves I can't wait to ride!" He does the shaka sign, making me laugh.

"You got it."

He strokes his chin. "I spy…something green."

"Palm tree fronds?"

He shakes his head.

I scan the beach looking for something green before spotting it. "Trash cans!"

He presses his forehead against the glass and squints. "No."

"The bushes?"

A dark look passes over his face. "Isn't it obvious?"

"Um..." Fuck.

I don't have the heart to tell Nico he is struggling with color discrimination again because of his diagnosis. In a panic, I glance over my shoulder, hoping Rafael answers my distress signal.

Our eyes connect for a brief second before he walks over and stares down at the shoreline. "Hm. Maybe Ellie is the one who needs to get her eyes checked because I think I figured out the answer."

"Maybe!" Nico laughs, making Rafael's eyes widen, along with mine.

Some of the pressure in my chest lessens when Rafael answers, "Beach towels."

"Yes!" Nico holds his hand up for his father to smack.

Rafael looks stunned for a second before he returns the high five.

"Oh. The beach towels." I fake a huff.

"It's okay, Ellie. You'll win next time." Nico pats my arm with a smile before abandoning us.

"Thank you for helping," I whisper to Rafael as Nico veers off to the left and runs into the only room on that side of the suite.

"He's had trouble discriminating between pink and orange before, but green and blue is new."

"I know."

His frown says more than words ever could.

"I call this one!" Nico shouts from the room before letting out a small giggle.

Rafael's sullen mood seems to fade away at the sound, his son's happiness acting like a healing balm for his aching heart. Gaining control over his emotions is no small feat, and I'm overwhelmed with pride at him obviously pushing aside his own worries to make his son happy.

"That's supposed to be mine," Rafael grumbles.

"Too late!" I hear rather than see Nico climbing onto the bed and jumping on it. "All mine now."

Both Rafael and I look to the right side of the suite, where there are two doors a foot apart.

"I guess those are ours," I say in a cheery voice.

Rafael surprises me by silently disappearing behind the door on the right, leaving me with the ocean-view room.

I can't help the squeal that pours out of me when I walk inside. The panoramic window facing the lagoon is great, but not as amazing as the four-poster bed with a gauzy, white canopy fit for a fairy tale.

I battle between wanting to drop onto the bed with a sigh—airport germs be damned—and exploring the opulent en suite bathroom.

"If you're still unsure about sharing a suite, I can look into another room."

"Are you crazy?" I turn on my heels to find Rafael leaning against the dresser near the door.

"Depends on whether Mercury is in retrograde or not."

My lips curl as a small, amused huff of air escapes me. "You're funnier than I thought."

"Is that a good thing?"

"I've yet to decide."

He doesn't laugh, but his eyes brighten with amusement.

If I'm not careful, I could become addicted to the way he looks at me, especially during times like these when his guard lowers enough for me to peek at the man hidden behind the grumpy exterior.

Rafael breaks the stare first as he tucks his hands behind his back. "Anyway, if you change your mind, I can have Ariel book a room for you."

I shake my head. "And have you spend another hundred thousand dollars here? Absolutely not." I'm not about to take advantage of him like his ex-wife does. I've overheard enough conversations to know how much she affects Rafael.

Instead of looking relieved like I had hoped, his gaze hardens. "Money isn't an issue."

"Clearly, if you're dropping two hundred thousand dollars on a hotel room we'll barely spend time in."

"Nico only deserves the best." His voice has an edge to it.

"I don't think it gets better than this." I counteract his grumpiness with a soft tone.

"You think so?" His hesitancy shouldn't be endearing to me, but after spending eight months thinking he had the emotional range of a brick wall, I can't help enjoying the bits of humanity peeking through.

"Yup. You're going to have a hard time convincing him to leave in five days." With all the fun activities Rafael planned, like beach days, deep-sea fishing, and a hike to a famous waterfall, Nico is going to adore this place.

"It's *you* I'm worried about, not him."

"Me? Why?" I ask.

"There is only one way off the island, and you happen to be terrified of it."

"But with you holding my hand, I can accomplish anything!" I clasp my hands against my chest and bat my lashes.

He scratches at his beard with his middle finger. "Dinner reservations are at seven."

He turns to leave my room, but not before I catch the hint of a smile on his face. If things go my way, it will be the first of many during our trip, so long as I keep doing little things to draw them out.

CHAPTER TWENTY-THREE

Rafael

Nico is still getting ready for our first dinner in Honolulu after spending twenty minutes giving Dahlia, Lily, and my aunt a tour of our suite during their video call, so I take a seat on the sectional and wait for him and Ellie. The stunning view of the ocean should keep my attention, but my thoughts quickly drift back to my responsibilities.

Spending the next two weeks away from work is supposed to be good for me, but I still feel guilty about leaving Julian alone to handle Dwelling while I'm gone. He has enough on his plate with his own business to run, but when I suggested taking a vacation last year, he took it upon himself to call my assistant and ask her to block the time off my calendar.

Two weeks doesn't sound like a lot of time, but for me, it is the longest vacation I've taken in years. Time off was long overdue, although I'm not sure how relaxed I can be knowing Ellie is joining us the entire time.

Like I conjured her up simply by thinking about her, Ellie's bedroom door opens, and she steps out. Thankfully, she is distracted by something on her phone, which gives me a moment to recover from my shock.

Ellie Sinclair has always been pretty, but right now, she looks absolutely gorgeous in a floor-length gauzy white dress that highlights her soft curves and sun-kissed skin. I can only think of one word to describe her, and it is *ethereal*.

I become a man fighting against the clock, trying to take in as many details as possible before she notices me staring at her like she is mine.

Fuck.

There it is. That deep feeling of want that I've spent the last eight months denying. Ignoring my attraction toward her wasn't difficult, especially when jealousy was the dominant emotion I felt, but now, with that stripped away, I'm left with something far worse.

Desire.

I felt it at Nico's birthday party and little sparks of attraction here and there, like when I held her hand, secretly listened to her playing music, or found myself staring for extended periods of time, but now that we are removed from our lives in Lake Wisteria, I allow myself to really acknowledge it.

To *feel* it.

I will never act on it, but for a few seconds, I pretend Ellie and I are two different people. I'm not some jaded single dad with abandonment issues, and she isn't my son's nanny.

In this fantasy, she is a woman who would steal my attention the second I saw her. She would pretend to be disinterested at first, claiming I wasn't her type, but I'd know better. I've seen the way she looks at me when she thinks I'm not paying attention. The way she sucks in a breath whenever I touch her.

She desires me just as much, whether she wants to acknowledge it or not.

"Ellie! Look at my new shoes!" Nico comes barreling out of his room, shattering the illusion.

Ellie looks over at my son with a blinding smile, and I swear my whole world stops for a second.

I shake my head hard, erasing the thought from existence. For a minute, I forgot myself, but as I watch Ellie with my son, I'm reminded of our biggest issue.

She will always be his nanny, just like I will always be her boss. So while I can desire her from afar, acting on my attraction goes against the rules.

Despite how much I want to break them.

The drive to the restaurant is a quiet one, with Nico playing a game on my cell phone while Ellie spends the majority of the trip taking in the view of the beach. I watch her out of the corner of my eye while I drive the Jeep I rented for our time in Oahu, although I force myself a few times to look away.

She and Nico keep the conversation flowing throughout dinner, only stopping to take bites of their fish dishes.

I've never seen Ellie so relaxed in my presence. Sure, the

two mango martinis she had after I insisted it was fine helped loosen her up a bit, but I'd also like to selfishly believe she feels comfortable because of me.

Ever since she came back last week, I've been making an effort to be less…well, less like me, and I think it's working. Truth is, I'm not sure who I am. After spending so many years trying to become the person I thought people wanted me to be, I am struggling with an identity crisis.

Despite my internal dilemma, even Nico seems happier around me, although I still catch a few flickers of concern from him.

Like right now.

"*¿Papi?*" Nico asks.

"*¿Si, mijo?*"

"*¿Qué piensas?*"

"*¿De qué?*"

He shoots Ellie an exasperated look. "I told you he wasn't paying attention."

I sit up in my chair with a wince. "Sorry. I got lost in my head a bit."

"Sounds scary," Ellie jokes, effectively cutting the tension.

I glance over at her, but she is quick to avert her gaze, giving me a side view of her profile and the flower tucked behind her ear.

On our way to dinner, Nico handpicked the flower for her, and the pink petals stand out against her blond hair. I'm pretty sure Nico learned the slick move from one of my

¿Si, mijo?: Yes, son?	**¿De qué?:** About what?
¿Qué piensas?: What are you thinking?	

aunt's favorite telenovelas, and it earned him a radiant smile from Ellie.

For a fleeting second, he made me wish I had thought of the idea first.

I turn to my son. "What were you trying to ask me?"

Nico shrugs while looking down at his plate. "It was dumb."

"I told you no question is a stupid one so long as you're brave enough to ask it."

"I said the same thing." Ellie takes a sip of her drink.

Nico shoves his food around with the tip of his fork. "I was wondering why you like saving animals."

His question is innocent and one that he hasn't asked me before, so I'm taken aback by it.

A ball of tightness grows in my throat. "What brought on that question?"

"Have you not noticed the chickens walking around throughout dinner?" Ellie asks.

Seeing as I was a bit distracted by her, no.

"Oh, right," I say instead. "The chickens. Who could've missed them?"

She spares me a knowing look that I ignore.

"I told you it was a dumb question," Nico grumbles to himself.

I reach over and uncurl his fist. "It's a good one, but I won't answer it if you keep talking like that."

He looks up. "Really?"

"Yup."

"Okay. Sorry."

A swell of panic builds in my chest, but I do my best

to shield it…and I think I do until Nico's eyes flash with concern.

"It's okay if you don't want to answer."

I take a deep breath and begin. "You know I love animals."

He nods with enthusiasm.

"I may not have chickens—"

"*Yet*," he interrupts with a smile.

"We'll see about that." I continue with my story, "But when I moved to Lake Wisteria, I found something better."

"What?"

"*Cats*."

Nico makes a face. "The stray ones?"

I nod.

"Gross." His nose twitches.

"Hey. That's not nice. They're still animals."

"Sorry. *Abuela* told me they have germs and bugs and it's best to stay away."

A small grin tugs at my lips. "She's just scared of them."

"But you're not?"

"No."

"Oh."

"When I was a little older than you, I started saving up my allowance money to buy food for them."

Ellie's eyes spark with interest. "Your aunt didn't mention that."

"I'm a man of many mysteries."

"I can see that." Her mouth pulls up at the corners, sending another wave of warmth through my chest.

"So, it all started because you like cats?" Nico asks with an incredulous tone. His simplistic view of life makes it easier for me to open up, although I hesitate for a whole different reason. Sharing my past with my son is one thing, but doing so in front of his nanny?

It *should* make me pause, yet I only feel an urge to continue with my story. Ellie's presence is strangely comforting, although that is a concern for another day.

I push the thought aside. "It was because I felt bad for them."

"Why?"

Relax, Rafa. "You remember that *Tía y Tío* adopted me?" We had a conversation about it last year, but I had never specified *why* I was adopted. Just that I moved from Mexico to Lake Wisteria when I was about his age, after both my parents died.

Nico confirms with a nod.

"My life before I moved to Lake Wisteria wasn't the best."

"What do you mean?"

"You know how all the animals have sad stories?"

Nico's eyes fill with tears, and I hold his small hand within my larger one.

"I had one kind of like that too."

"You did?" His voice cracks.

"Yeah. My parents had...problems." Gambling. Drugs. Infidelity. *Me.* "They didn't take care of me the way they should have."

Ellie leans forward and gives my shoulder a squeeze I didn't

Tía y Tío: Aunt and Uncle

realize I needed. I turn to look at her, noting the sympathy pouring out of her in thick waves.

She briefly mentioned her *bad dad* in passing while trying to make me feel better, but I don't think I truly processed what she meant until now. We share a matching look full of festering pain that never seems to fully go away, no matter how much time passes.

With every whispered confession, Ellie collects another one of my heartstrings in the palm of her hand, keeping me permanently tied to her.

I'm already struggling with attraction, so if she were to break through my emotional defenses, I'd be a lost cause.

I break eye contact first and meet my son's watery gaze. "I don't like to talk about it, mostly because I'm okay now, but that's the reason I like saving hurt animals. Because I was hurt too, so I know what it's like."

My son surprises me as he hops off his chair, crawls onto my lap, and wraps his small arms around my neck. His embrace warms the cold part of my heart that has always dreaded the idea of having a conversation like this with him, in part because I didn't want him to see me as weak or broken.

I want him to view me as a strong, capable parent who will always be there for him, even in the worst of times.

"I'm sorry you got hurt, *Papi*." Nico hugs me.

I return his hug with one of my own. "It's not your fault."

"I know, but I'm still sorry. And sad."

I look over at Ellie to find her staring at us with misty eyes.

"You're a real-life superhero," she says.

I've never considered myself to be a hero in anyone's story, least of all Nico's, but Ellie's statement makes me wish I were.

CHAPTER TWENTY-FOUR

Ellie

I volunteer to put Nico to bed. When I step outside of his bedroom after two bedtime stories, I find Rafael sitting in front of the piano. He hesitantly hits one of the keys before pulling his hand back, acting like he was caught doing something he shouldn't.

Damn. It's kind of cute to see him so out of his element.

"If you're worried about waking Nico up, don't be. He sleeps like the dead," I say, startling him.

He smiles to himself. "I know."

"Are you interested in learning how to play?" I ask without thinking much of it.

He stares at the keys. "I'm not sure yet."

I walk toward the piano bench and motion for him to scoot over. Our sides brush as I take a seat beside him, and his thigh remains permanently pressed against mine as I run my hands across the keys. "The piano was the first instrument I learned to play."

He turns slightly to get a better look at me. "It was?"

"Yup. My mom taught me herself."

"I thought your stepdad taught you."

"Not at first. He did later, once my mom and I moved to Lake Wisteria."

Rafael's head tilts with interest. "You weren't born there?"

"No. I'm from Lake Windermere. Once my mom filed for divorce, she wanted a change of scenery, but she couldn't go far because of custody reasons, so Lake Wisteria was the obvious choice."

"Hm. Close, but not too close."

"Exactly." I begin playing a simple melody to fill the quiet, and my body softly sways to the music. Rafael bristles whenever I brush against him, but eventually he loosens up as one song blends into the next.

"I wanted to join the band. Back in high school."

I'm so surprised by his statement that I accidentally hit the wrong key. "You did?"

He nods.

"What stopped you?"

He clams up again, but I refuse to let this bit of information go until he shares more. "Don't tell me you were worried about ruining your reputation or something silly like that," I tease. Being part of the Wisteria High band wasn't the most coveted elective, but people liked our performances enough to stick around for the halftime show and attend our seasonal showcases, so I never felt embarrassed to be part of the drumline. If anything, I was proud, especially after we won the state championship.

He glares at me out of the corner of his eye. "And if I was?"

"I'd say that's incredibly cliché." *And disappointing.*

Rafael and I were never part of the same circles, not only because of our age difference but also because he was the popular jock who lived in the spotlight while I was the nameless girl playing the drums on the sidelines. He had no clue who I was, and honestly, I'm starting to think it was better that way because he kind of sucked.

"I was a shallow teenager who was obsessed with everyone's opinion of me, so yeah, cliché doesn't begin to cover it."

I continue playing, using the song to process his confession. "Maybe it was best you never joined the band after all."

His forehead creases with confusion. "Why?"

"Because I would've ended up hating you if you had."

"No one hated me." A sly smirk tugs at his lips.

My eyes roll. "That attitude right there would have earned you a drumstick to the eye."

"Having confidence isn't a bad thing."

"No, but too much of it makes you annoying. Especially at that age."

"No one seemed to mind."

"Only because no one recognized your confidence for what it was."

Overcompensation.

I don't realize how my statement comes off until he stares at me with a pinched expression.

Shit.

Him learning about my crush would be embarrassing to say the least, so I need to do a better job at hiding how much I knew about him back then.

It is easy to forget sometimes, at least until my heart starts acting up in his presence like I'm a teenager again. I'm pretty sure fifteen-year-old me would have had a heart attack at the mere idea of sitting this close to him. Of playing *music* for him.

But now, I just feel comfort in his presence. Sure, there is this undercurrent of energy whenever our sides brush, but I'm no longer overwhelmed by being next to him.

I play off my statement with a shrug.

"Did we ever meet? Back then?" he asks before I have a chance to start a new song.

"No," I answer. Our paths never really had a chance to cross until now, after our lives were fundamentally changed by our choices and circumstances.

I might have seen him countless times—might have had a ridiculous crush on him when he didn't know I existed—but we never met. Not formally at least.

I might have known how he looked when he cried and how he liked to hide out in the computer lab during lunch to get away from everyone, but that was as deep as our one-sided connection went.

I channel the ache in my chest into my music. Rafael starts slightly swaying to the melody, looking at peace with his eyes closed and his shoulders relaxed.

"Now you got me thinking too," Rafael says without opening his eyes.

"About what?" I'm hardly breathing as he continues.

"If we had met back then, I would have done everything possible to make you like me instead of hate me."

He wouldn't have had to try too hard.

Just like he doesn't have to try too hard now.

CHAPTER TWENTY-FIVE

Rafael

Our second official day of vacation goes to hell when I get an emergency call from my assistant, Ariel, notifying me that my ex-wife is attending today's Dwelling board meeting. Canceling on Nico was the last thing I wanted to do, especially with how excited he sounded about us visiting the North Shore to watch big wave surfing, but I don't have a choice. Being absent from today's meeting will only cause me more problems since my ex rarely attends unless she wants something from me.

Unfortunately, my broke twenty-year-old self didn't fathom ever needing a prenup, seeing as Hillary was the one with money, not me, so a judge had no choice but to award her fifty percent of my Dwelling shares.

Hence her ability to attend virtual meetings like the one taking place right now.

My assistant unmutes her microphone. "Mr. Lopez?"

I snap out of my daze and stare at the webcam. "Yes?"

"Ms. Wilson asked you a question about the recent financial report."

Pull yourself together.

"Would you like me to repeat it?"

My teeth grind at the sound of my ex's shrill voice, but I take a deep breath and remind myself that, one day, she will get bored or desperate enough to let me buy her remaining company shares.

I glance out the window overlooking the lagoon and families down below. Nico is probably getting a kick out of watching surfers tackle the ocean while I'm trapped up here, disappointing him.

This whole trip is meant to be about helping create visual memories that he can keep forever, and I'm already letting him down on day two.

He may not understand it, but you're appeasing his mother for him.

I push any thoughts of Nico out of my mind and face my ex, ignoring the ache in my chest as I take her in.

Hillary's beauty was never an issue. Her narcissism was, but I was too blinded by her glittering brown eyes and picture-perfect smile to notice until it was too late.

"What was your question?"

"What about the increased profits stated in the latest report?" She fakes a smile for the other staff and board members. Some return it, but Julian remains scowling through his webcam.

For a woman like my ex, appearances are everything, which is the only reason why she started dating me back in high school. I was the popular guy who bent over backwards trying to please everyone, regardless of whether it was healthy or not, and she was the posh new girl from Oregon who was more than willing to put up with my suffocating adoration and chronic insecurities in exchange for attention and increased social status.

Things weren't always so toxic between us. It all turned ugly once I learned why she stayed married to me despite her growing affections for another man. Sure, infidelity played a huge part in our divorce, but it really was her *pretending* to be happy with our marriage that screwed with my head.

The only genuine emotion she had during our last year together was her happiness about my company finally going public, and I didn't need a divorce lawyer to explain why that was.

Money was the reason we got married in the first place, so it was only fitting that it led to our divorce as well.

With a long exhale, I refocus on my laptop screen. Sitting through the meeting and reviewing the latest quarterly report is painful, mostly because I can see the dollar signs in my ex-wife's eyes. No doubt she will be contacting her lawyer by noon to request a meeting with mine.

My mood quickly devolves into something dark and ominous after we end the call. Julian's name flashes across my cell phone screen, but I ignore it while I wait for the email I know is coming.

Our divorce settlement dictated that on the first of January each year, my ex-wife would receive a lump sum of five hundred thousand dollars to cover her yearly expenses and child support.

I could fight her on the child support payment since she hardly spends any time with Nico, but I consider it well-spent hush money. Neither one of us wants her to follow through with the court's split-custody agreement, so funding her expensive lifestyle is a small price to pay for Nico's well-being and my sanity.

Even if it puts me in the foulest mood for a day or two.

My inbox chimes from a new email three minutes later.

URGENT: Request for Increased Spousal and Child Support.

"So much for today being a good day."

The dark cloud over my head churns when Nico and Ellie show up three hours later, laughing themselves hoarse as they walk into the suite with a trail of sand in their wake.

I try my best to fake a smile, but it falls flat.

"Are you okay?" my son asks with a big frown.

"Yup." I shut my laptop and turn in my chair. "How was the beach?" My question was supposed to sound light and carefree, but it comes out stilted instead.

Nico's shoulders slump. "You never showed up."

"A few things came up that I needed to fix." *Like your mother manipulating me into funding her shopping addiction and wannabe hedge-fund manager boyfriend.*

"Okay. Whatever," he says with a bit more bite in his tone.

Ellie gives his shoulder a squeeze. "Maybe we can all spend time together now? What do you think?"

"I'm tired." Nico walks into his room and shuts the door softly.

Ellie's mouth twists. "I texted you asking when you were showing up, but you didn't answer."

"I was busy," I snap.

She doesn't even flinch. "He was really looking forward to today. He didn't stop asking about you—"

"If I wanted to know, then I would have asked."

She stumbles back a step, as if my words physically injured her.

What I *want* is to punch myself in the mouth. Actually, screw the mouth. A good kick to the balls is what I deserve for a comment like that.

"So that's how it's going to be, huh?" Her brows rise along with her voice.

"Shit. I'm just angry, but that isn't an excuse for talking like—"

She silences me with a single slice of her hand through the air. I've seen Ellie upset and frustrated, but I've never seen her look at me like she wants to flay me alive.

"I'm not interested in hearing another one of your apologies because, clearly, you don't mean any of them." Her brows pinch together. "For someone who can be such a nice guy sometimes, you sure don't have any trouble reverting to being an asshole, which is making me question who the real Rafael is."

"Elle, I—"

She softens for a second before her gaze hardens again. "You know what my biggest issue with your apologies is?"

"What?"

"I don't trust them." Like Nico, Ellie disappears into her room, leaving me alone to handle the nuclear-level fallout of my poor choices.

After upsetting Ellie and Nico, I spend the rest of the day in my bedroom, discussing alimony and child support with my lawyer while stewing in self-loathing. In painful summary, unless Hillary gets married again to someone else, I'm stuck paying for her lifestyle, whether I like it or not.

While Nico and Ellie have dinner at one of the resort restaurants without me, misery keeps me company as I evaluate the decisions that led me to this point. Hillary will continue finding new ways to piss me off and ask for more money, so it is up to me to learn how to stop caring.

If I don't, I'll keep disappointing those closest to me.

My son. Myself. *Ellie.*

I've worked so hard to create the life I have. I spent my twenties trying and failing to acquire the wealth and security I have now, and what do I have to show for it? Sure, I can afford a fancy hotel and anything my son desires, but what good is any of it if he doesn't want to enjoy it with me?

When I wake up the next morning, I'm not surprised to receive the silent treatment from my son. It hurts to be rejected after we had a good first day here, but surprisingly, it doesn't bother me as much as Ellie's silence during our hike to Mānoa Falls.

Nico is easy to spot from a distance with his colorful swimsuit and hiking shoes while Ellie blends into the tree line with her dark leggings and athletic T-shirt. She keeps close to my son and helps him a few times when he stumbles due to his vision difficulties, all while I walk behind them in case they need me.

Nico is independent to a fault, but he can't hide how he struggles at times to keep up with us given the low visibility during parts of the hike and the general newness of the trail.

When I catch him stumbling for the third time, an uncomfortable tightness in my chest returns, and I take a few deep breaths and focus on what is within my control.

He is okay.

Ellie has him.

He will only get upset if you try to single him out for being different, I remind myself like a mantra.

We finally make it to the waterfall, and Nico squeals as he rushes toward the water.

"No swimming!" Ellie shouts.

Nico glares over his shoulder. "I heard you the first ten times."

Ellie laughs, only to swallow the sound when I stop beside her. Outside of asking me a few basic questions about the trail, she's been pretending I don't exist. It triggers the old me who hated making other people unhappy, although I'm self-aware enough to know it doesn't come from an unhealthy place this time.

It stems from my shame at lashing out the way I did and letting her down.

Nico begins chatting with another kid whose family started the hike fifteen minutes before us, sharing all the facts he knows about the waterfall and its famous filming history.

"I don't know how he does it," I say to break the silence.

She stiffens at the sound of my voice. "What?"

"He can talk to anyone so easily."

"Must have picked it up from his aunt or someone likable." Her eyes flicker over me before shifting back to Nico.

"Listen—"

She gestures toward my son, who is standing thirty feet away. "Is now the best time?"

"Seeing as he is occupied making a new friend and I don't want to spend the rest of my day in awkward silence, yeah."

"What's the point?"

"I have a few things I want to get off my chest."

She cuts into me with a disinterested look. "I think you said plenty yesterday. Don't you?"

"I should have never said what I did."

Her jaw tightens.

I take a deep breath. "I'm ashamed of letting my emotions get to me like that." My gaze lands on the water crashing against the surface of the small pond. "I don't know what to do." My next breath comes out shaky. "Every time I think I'm taking a step in the right direction—that maybe I can finally be happy for a change—something happens that ends up dragging me back into that same dark place."

I brace myself for her disgust and pity as she turns to look at me, but I'm surprised to see something else entirely.

Admiration?

No. That can't be right, because who would admire a mess like me?

I look over at Nico, who is reenacting some movie scene for the other child. "I took my anger toward Hil—toward someone else—out on you, and that was uncalled for."

"Yeah, it was."

"I know you were trying to make me feel better, and I acted like a dick."

"That seems to be a recurring theme for us."

"What if I don't want it to be?" I ask softly.

"We can *want* a lot of things, but that doesn't mean anything if we don't put in the effort to make any of it happen."

I stay quiet.

Her sigh of discontent makes my chest twinge. "Listen. We've been down this road before, and it always leads to a dead end, so let's agree to stay in our own lanes and keep to ourselves."

"What do you mean?"

"You never wanted to be friends with me, and honestly, I used to be offended by that, but now I'm starting to think I prefer it that way."

I won't deny how much her words sting, although I do my best to ignore it. I'm not even fully sure why they bother me, but perhaps it is because I thought she was talking about something…more.

I guess whatever I feel about her is one-sided.

She seems to take my silence as an invitation to continue. "You're angry—and rightly so, based on what I've heard about your ex. No one is denying that, but the way you let her affect you matters because it has an impact on everyone around you. So until you learn how to control your emotions and channel them into something else, you'll always be repeating the same harmful patterns." Ellie wields her tongue like a blade, cutting me open and exposing my weaknesses.

"How would you know that?"

Her condescending laugh grates on my nerves. "You're not the only one who has struggled with a toxic relationship."

My curiosity is piqued. "You've been through a bad one?"

She releases an unsteady breath. "No, but I was the result of one, which comes with its own list of problems."

"Like?"

She chews on the inside of her cheek in quiet contemplation. I can tell she doesn't want to open up to me, and I don't blame her, given my struggles with the same issue.

But then she surprises me by speaking up again.

"My biological father, whom I refuse to call anything else, was a terrible person. Like Hillary, he used money to control my mom and forced her to stay in an emotionally abusive relationship because he threatened to leave her with nothing."

I'm not sure I'm even breathing right now.

"He said he would fight her for full custody, which was the main reason she stayed for as long as she did."

I recognize the pain in her voice. The *guilt*.

"It's not your fault she made that choice."

Her soft laugh can hardly be heard over the rushing water

in front of us and Nico giggling at something the other kid said. "I know. It took a couple years of therapy, but I finally accepted that I shouldn't feel guilty about my mom's decision to stay, just like she shouldn't feel the same way about the choices I made."

"What choices?"

Her gaze falls to her feet. "Just dumb teenage stuff."

Her lie is obvious, but I don't call her out on it.

She looks up. "The point is that I understand your anger more than you think, which is why I know you need to start channeling your feelings into something healthy before your negative emotions consume you."

"What if it's too late for that?"

"Do you feel sorry for how you reacted yesterday?" Her question comes out of nowhere.

"Yes. Of course I do."

"Then it's not too late for you." She pauses. "Yet."

"What do you suggest I do?"

She shrugs. "That's up to you to figure out."

"Okay. What did you do?"

A smile, small but so damn beautiful, appears on her face. "Isn't it obvious?"

"Would I be asking if it was?"

"*Music.*"

CHAPTER TWENTY-SIX

Ellie

I wake up the next day with a better understanding of my boss. In some ways, I was like Rafael. Closed off. Unbearably irritable. Silently suffering while my mom helplessly watched her only daughter take her anger and sadness out on her body.

It took therapy, a music tutor who wouldn't give up on me, and a judge ruling in favor of my mother receiving full custody for me to finally start healing, both physically and mentally. So while I may not understand everything Rafael is going through, I know enough about anger issues to understand how everyone needs an outlet.

We just need to find his.

Spoiler alert: It's not building sandcastles.

Rafael looks so damn sad building a pathetic excuse for a castle all by himself while sparing longing glances at his son, and I can't help feeling sorry for him.

Nico is still keeping an uncomfortable distance from him. I tried to validate Nico's feelings while also making it clear that Rafael wouldn't skip out unless it was extremely important, but Nico wasn't receptive. He is still disappointed in his dad for not joining us to see big wave surfing, and he is afraid he will ditch him for work again.

When I told Rafael that, he seemed more motivated to prove Nico wrong. So while Nico befriended a couple of other kids and volunteered to help them with their sandcastle, Rafael stayed where Nico left him.

I've been stuck on the same page of my book for the last ten minutes, no thanks to the lonely father sitting ten feet in front of my beach chair, looking completely lost in his head. He didn't bother removing his shirt and going into the water like I expected once Nico left, instead choosing to linger nearby in hopes of his son returning.

"Screw this." I toss my book on the chair and head over to him. My crochet top and pants swish in the wind, providing me with ample coverage while still keeping my skin cool.

He shields his eyes from the sun as he looks up at me. "What?"

"You look like you could use some help." I kneel in the sand beside him and push a bucket out of the way.

"I'm fine." He brushes grains of sand off his shirt.

"I'm not sure you'll be saying that in a few minutes when this whole thing falls apart." Somehow, he used both too little water on one side and too much water on the other, which will cause both sides to crumble for opposite reasons.

On cue, one tower collapses in on itself while another completely breaks in half.

Rafael unleashes a deep sigh that rattles something in my chest. "You don't need to try to make me feel better."

Nico giggles in the distance, and Rafael frowns as he catches the group of kids helping the other parent dig a moat out to the ocean.

"You know, we could totally make a castle better than that," I bait him, hoping to spark his competitive nature.

A lot of people in town talk about Julian and Dahlia's competitive streaks, but many overlook Rafael. The man always wanted to be the best at everything. From sports to clubs, he always strived for greatness, which was one of the many reasons people flocked to him like they did.

Me. I'm people.

He just had no idea.

I speak again when he remains silent. "Our reputation is at stake here."

His lips twitch. "Who knew you were so passionate about sandcastles?"

"Are you kidding? I placed first for three years in a row during our family trips to northern Michigan."

He passes me a shovel. "My mistake then. I didn't know I was in the presence of a champion."

I laugh as I grab the plastic tool from him. Our fingers brush, sending sparks scattering across my skin.

I'm quick to add some space and take a stab at the sand. "By the time we're done, those kids are going to be wishing they helped us instead."

"You sure about that?"

I scan our tools before passing him one. "Yup. Now get to digging."

After three hours laboring under the unrelenting sun, Rafael and I finally finish the sandcastle. Compared to the kids' crumbling disaster fifty feet away, ours is a masterpiece. A few people even stop to take photos of our creation, which feeds my ego until my head threatens to explode.

My sunburnt cheeks stretch from my smile. "What do you think?"

Rafael doesn't answer, so I turn to find him focused on me rather than the castle.

My stomach swoops as he looks away and clears his throat. "I thought you were bluffing about first place."

I laugh. "Really?"

"Yeah."

"Why would I do that?"

"To trick me into accepting your help?"

I stare at him. "There's absolutely no good reason for me to lie about something like that."

He scratches at his short beard. "I know."

"But you assumed the worst anyway."

"Unfortunately." His flinch is nearly invisible, but I notice it.

"Well, then I take great pleasure in proving you wrong."

"I'd expect nothing less." He doesn't smile, but his eyes glimmer like the ocean in front of us.

"Whoa!" Nico kicks up sand behind him as he runs toward us. "This is awesome."

"Too bad you were too busy to help us," I tease while shooting Rafael a look.

Just follow my lead, I try to convey.

He keeps his lips sealed, so I take it as a silent confirmation.

"I wasn't too busy." Nico's gaze drops.

"Hm. It sure looked like it from here. Your dad tried to get your attention, but you must not have heard him."

His cheeks turn pink underneath the layer of sunscreen I went over to slather on his skin thirty minutes ago. "Yeah." He looks over at his dad. "I thought you were going to work."

"I told you I wasn't."

Nico shrugs.

"He didn't touch his phone once," I add.

Nico bites down on his bottom lip while circling our castle. "You built all this?"

Rafael nods. "With Ellie."

"Wow." Nico assesses it from every angle.

Rafael hesitates, and I nearly jump in to fill the silence but stop myself right before he speaks.

"I'd love it if you joined us tomorrow. We could use your skills building a moat."

Nico stops midstep and stares down at his sandy feet. "What about work?"

Something in my chest twists as Rafael gets down on his knees in front of his son. "I know you're disappointed about the second day, and I'm sorry things didn't pan out how we both wanted, but if you give me a chance, I'd like to make it up to you."

"What if work calls again?"

"I won't know because I threw my phone in the ocean."

Nico laughs. "No, you didn't."

"No, you're right, but I sure thought about it," he teases in a way I haven't seen before.

"Good. It's cracked and old like you."

"Take that back."

"Never!" Nico lunges away, but not before Rafael locks his arms around him and reaches for the ticklish spot beneath his arms.

"Stop!"

"Nope. You're all mine now," Rafael says in his best villainous voice.

"Ellie! Save me!" Nico reaches out for my hand.

I take a big step back. "Sorry. No can do."

"*¡Para!*" Nico squirms in the sand, but Rafael ignores him. "*¡Papi!* Ellie's ticklish too! Even more than me!" he shouts between big gulps of air and giggles.

That little brat.

Rafael's head snaps in my direction, turning that small, devilish smirk on me.

I take a big step back and nearly trip over a bucket. "No, I'm not."

"Yes, she is. Especially her feet." Nico bats his father's hands away.

I check my empty wrist. "Well, would you look at the time…"

Before I can finish my sentence, Rafael releases his son, who comes running at me with his hands fully extended, his smirk reminding me so much of his father's in that moment.

"Get her!" Nico rams into me, successfully knocking me

¡Para! : Stop!

over. My ass hits the warm sand first, followed by my back as he tackles me.

"I got you!" He reaches for my rib cage.

I could easily slip out from underneath him, but the way Nico looks over at his dad stops me.

"*¡Papi! ¡Ayúdame!*"

Rafael drops to his knees beside my legs and reaches for my right foot. His fingers brush the back of my calf, making me freeze before instincts kick in.

"No!" I attempt to yank my foot away from him, but his grip tightens. Invisible flames shoot up my leg, straight toward a place that should not be throbbing.

I consider kicking Rafael away, but my body freezes when his hand locks around my ankle like a shackle. He brushes the bottom of my foot with the tips of his fingers, and all hell breaks loose inside me.

Rafael is touching me, and instead of running away, I'm practically inviting him to continue.

I squeal when he teases my foot, ignoring the tightness in my belly that has nothing to do with being tickled.

"I told you she was ticklish!" Nico's unhinged laugh spurs Rafael on.

I stare at the man holding my legs hostage. "I hate you."

"Good." He *grins*, and all hope is lost. I'm a goner for every single one of Rafael's rare smiles, their scarcity causing an emotional supply-and-demand issue.

¡Ayúdame!: Help me

Being ticklish is the least of my worries because that strange tingling in my chest? The one that doesn't stop, even after Nico loses interest in me and Rafael releases me from his hold?

It tells me I'm absolutely screwed.

CHAPTER TWENTY-SEVEN

Rafael

On our way to grab some Hawaiian shave ice after our beach day, I receive a new text from Dahlia.

DAHLIA

As requested, here are your weekly proof of life photos.

She attaches a photo of Jimmy B and Johnnie W passed out in their pen with miniature whiskey bottles thrown around them, one of Penelope with a set of purple and pink bows in her mane, and a blurry image of Bacardi hanging out in the corner of her stall like always.

ME

What's happened to Bacardi's coat?

DAHLIA

Lily and Josefina tried to even out her cut yesterday, but she wasn't having it.

ME

She's afraid of the sound clippers make.

DAHLIA

So we learned after Lily got kicked in the face.

I knew it was a bad idea to have my family take care of my animals, but they assured me it would be okay.

Guilt makes my heart heavy as I type out my next message.

ME

Fred can check on them instead.

DAHLIA

I knew you'd overreact.

ME

It's called caring.

Lily and Dahlia are the younger sisters I never had, so I can't help my reactions sometimes, especially if I'm the one to blame.

DAHLIA

I know, and we love you for it, but relax. Seriously.

DAHLIA

Bacardi is fine. Lily is fine. Everyone is fine.

ME

How is Lily's face?

DAHLIA

Besides a small bruise on her cheek, she's all good.

I release a heavy breath and start to type out a message to Fred, a farmer and my closest neighbor, but Dahlia's next text makes me pause.

DAHLIA

BUT maybe you should hold off on adopting any more animals for a bit.

I laugh to myself.

ME

Too late.

One of the farmers in a neighboring town is struggling to keep up with his animals since his wife died, and I already agreed to foster them while I find them a more permanent home. Julian has begun working on the expansion plans for the barn because he thinks I'll outgrow the space by next year.

DAHLIA

...

DAHLIA

I pity Ellie. I can't believe she willingly puts up with nine animals.

ME

I only have eight.

DAHLIA

You forgot to count yourself.

I send a middle finger emoji while biting back a smile.

Now that I think about it, Ellie hasn't complained once about taking care of the animals. If anything, she has taken it upon herself to care for them, even going as far as naming them.

I never thought much of it, but now, after listening to Dahlia and Lily's struggles with managing the barn, I'm ashamed to admit I unknowingly took advantage of her. I even said she was underqualified for her job when that couldn't be further from the truth.

Ellie could be doing so much more with her life. That much became obvious after Cole Griffin expressed an interest in her song, but she chose to take care of Nico instead.

She chose *us*.

Not us. Nico, I correct myself.

Disappointment tugs at my chest, impossible to ignore, because for a fleeting second, I wanted it to be true. I *wanted* her to choose me too.

With only a few more nights left in Honolulu before we head to Kauai, I thought it would be a good idea to finally use the hot tub after Nico fell asleep, only to find out it was already occupied by his nanny.

Having a physical reaction to seeing Ellie in a bikini is normal, but getting a hard-on because of it?

Embarrassing and inconvenient to say the least.

Unfortunately, the foam and bubbles caused by the jets block me from getting a full view of her body, but the sight of her chest is enough to send a rush of heat toward my groin.

I thought she would be hiding in her room playing the guitar tonight, so I'm surprised to find her out on the balcony, staring up at the stars with deep longing.

Thankfully, she is so enraptured by the view that she doesn't notice me at first, which is a blessing, seeing as I'm too distracted by her chest. Her breasts are small and perky, and I picture them fitting perfectly in the palms of my hands.

Based on Ellie's modest clothing choices so far, I didn't

think she owned a swimsuit like *that*, but the lime-colored bikini might as well be a green light with the way my dick is acting.

I shield my growing issue with a towel as she turns to find me staring at her.

"When you're done checking me out, do you mind turning the dial?" She points at one that controls the jets.

I ignore her first comment and do as she requested, extending the timer by fifteen minutes.

Well played, Ellie. Well freaking played.

She returns to looking up at the moon, disinterested in watching me fumble through getting inside the hot tub without her noticing my stiffening cock. The hot water hits my sore leg muscles first, and I sigh.

"Feels great, right?"

"I need one of these at home."

"I'd like that."

My dick seems to agree.

For a few minutes, we sit in comfortable silence until Ellie breaks it with a question. "Do you ever wonder what's out there?" She stares up at the sky with a sigh.

"Have we officially reached the point in our relationship where we discuss conspiracy theories?"

The sound she lets out makes me smile.

"We don't really have a relationship. At least not a normal one."

"On that, we can both agree." The feelings she is slowly dragging out of me don't feel normal. In fact, they feel pretty damn scary.

Her heavy exhale draws my gaze toward her chest again.

She clears her throat, and I look up without a hint of shame. Pretending I don't find her attractive is useless, so why bother hiding it?

"Are we going to have a problem here?" she asks with a hint of a rasp.

"Do you want there to be one?"

She is the one to look away first. "This was a bad idea."

Good thing she doesn't have access to my thoughts because I have a hundred bad ideas playing on repeat.

"You could leave," I suggest without actually meaning it.

"So could you."

"Yeah, not happening."

"I was here first." She kicks her leg out and splashes my face with water.

Before she pulls back, I latch on to her foot and yank hard enough to send her sprawling. She curses as she is pulled underwater, only to break through the bubbling surface with a scowl a couple of seconds later. "I was trying to keep my hair dry."

"My bad."

Next thing I know, water splashes against my face and hair. I fake a gasp. "Ugh. There goes my blowout."

The look of pure outrage on her face makes me laugh.

Her upper lip curls. "You're such an asshole."

"We've got to work on your insults, Elle. They're growing a bit stale."

"Don't call me that," she seethes.

"Why? Are you afraid you'll start liking it?" Based on the way she softens every time I use it, I already know the truth. She can pretend to despise the shortened name, but her eyes give her away.

"It's dumb."

"The nickname? Or the way you react every time I say it?"

Her eyes narrow. "You're in a mood tonight."

After Nico asked me to tuck him into bed tonight *and* read him a story, I feel like I'm living on cloud nine, so hell yeah, I'm in a mood. A *great* one, in fact.

"It's called being happy. Try it with me."

"Are you high?"

"No, but that could be fun."

She gapes at me.

"What?"

"I'm just…shocked."

"Why?"

"I didn't peg you as the type to smoke."

"Did you expect me to like edibles like you?"

She looks stunned. "How do you know about that?"

"I saw that you Googled if it was legal to bring them on a plane."

"There's a valid explanation for that."

"I'm sure."

"I have anxiety!"

"I think the three hundred passengers on the plane were aware, yes."

"It was a legit question!" Her defensiveness is charming, especially with her cheeks turning red.

"I didn't say it wasn't, but next time, delete the search history from the main computer."

She slaps a hand over her mouth. "I'm so sorry. I thought I did."

"Just for your information, if Nico ever asks you what an edible is, you need to answer 'cookies.' Got it?"

The best laugh pours out of her, and a sense of satisfaction rolls through me, knowing I'm the reason behind the sound. "I mean, you're not wrong."

"No, I guess I'm not." I catch myself smiling at a memory of Julian and me trying to make pot brownies, only to get busted by his mom, who then proceeded to keep the weed for herself.

I catch Ellie staring at me a few minutes later. "What?"

"I was trying to imagine how you would act while high."

"Chill?"

"Really? I was going to guess paranoid."

"I take personal offense to that."

She bats her lashes. "No need to feel bad. There's always one of those types in the group."

"Yeah, and their name is Julian Lopez."

Her whole face lights up. "Julian? Really? I didn't expect that!"

"Neither did I. The first couple of times we tried it in high school, he was chiller than usual, but then Dahlia hung out with us once..."

"Oh no."

I nod. "Yup. You know how he gets with her."

"It's sweet," Ellie says with a hint of wistfulness that tugs on something in my chest.

"It's annoying, is what it is."

"What happened next?"

"She was so relaxed, Julian was worried that she overdosed."

Ellie smiles. "That's ridiculous."

"Hence the paranoia. I had to physically stop him from driving her to the hospital after she fell asleep."

Ellie's shoulders shake with silent laughter.

"What kind are you?" I ask.

She looks up at the sky. "The dreamer?"

"AKA the person who won't shut up while stoned? Noted."

She splashes me again, although this time I don't let her get away with it as I stand and yank on her hand. She loses her balance on the built-in seat, and I pull her against me to keep her from tumbling face-first into the water.

Ellie falls against me and accidentally brushes up against my erection. A soft groan slips past my lips, and her eyes flutter shut with a sigh before they snap open again.

Neither of us is breathing as we stare into each other's eyes. I'm not sure who leans in first, but I can't bring myself to pull away, instead choosing to close the gap between us.

Ellie feels good in my arms. She feels *right*. Like she was made to perfectly fit there, which makes it impossible to let her go.

With our faces only a few inches apart, I take advantage of the opportunity to memorize every single detail. A trio of beauty marks near her jawline. The way her lashes flutter as her gaze drops toward my lips. How her sharp cheekbones balance out her sultry lips and heart-shaped face.

I dip my head, but before our lips touch, Ellie pushes at my chest, ruining the moment before there really was one.

I forgot myself for a second. Ever since I entered the hot

tub, the world around us faded away until it was just Ellie and me.

No Nico. No employment contract. And no emotional obstacles getting in our way.

I was *happy*. Genuinely happy, and it was because of her.

In a rush, I let her go, and she teeters for a moment before catching her balance on my shoulders. Carefully—and somewhat reluctantly—I remove her hands and take a step toward the stairs.

"I'll let you enjoy the rest of your night."

"Rafael," she calls out while reaching for me.

I turn away and exit the hot tub while Ellie remains, a look of confusion on her face as her eyes shift between me and the churning water splashing around her.

"Where are you going?"

Back to the place I'm still trying to escape.

My personal hell.

ME

> I almost kissed Ellie.

I pace the confines of my room. It's late, so I don't expect him to reply, but I'm hoping he is up doing who knows what.

I don't have to wait too long for a reply, thankfully.

JULIAN

> It's late.

ME

Yet you're up.

JULIAN

Because you woke me up...

ME

Sorry.

ME

Make it worth the sacrifice and help me?

JULIAN

Who pulled away first?

ME

She did.

JULIAN

Did she say anything?

ME

No. I walked away before
she had a chance.

JULIAN

Hm.

ME

What?

JULIAN

Nothing. That was probably
the best choice.

I'm flooded with disappointment, but that is exactly why I texted Julian. Out of the two of us, he is the more responsible cousin. He is level-headed and always seems to have an answer for everything, while I made a few reckless decisions that changed the entire course of my life.

Hence my hesitancy now.

ME

I made the right call, right?

JULIAN

Do you feel like you did?

Yes. No. Fuck if I know, which is why I'm asking.

I'm both relieved I didn't kiss her and pissed I didn't take advantage of the chance, because who knows if it will ever happen again.

With a shaky breath, I reply.

ME

I'm not sure.

JULIAN

Then you made the right decision.

JULIAN

For now.

ME

What do you mean "for now"?

JULIAN

You shouldn't kiss her until you know that you won't regret it. Because once you take that step, there is no going back.

I hate to admit it, but Julian is right, even if I wish he wasn't.

CHAPTER TWENTY-EIGHT

Ellie

I nearly let Rafael kiss me tonight, and worse, I wouldn't have stopped him if he had. Knowing I would have kissed him right back makes me feel guilty.

I swore that after Darius Larkin kissed me without my consent and destroyed my friendship with his girlfriend in the process, I would never put myself in a situation where a person in a position of power could take advantage of me again. Yet here I am a year later, risking my job for a quick thrill.

I flirted with Rafael. I let him *hold* me. Hell, I was considering kissing him, but thankfully, I remembered myself before that happened.

Deep down, I know Rafael wouldn't fire me over a kiss, although I don't know if it would stop at just that. I would want more than he would ever be willing to give, and that in itself is a reason to stay far, far away.

But telling myself that doesn't stop butterflies from exploding in my stomach whenever I think about the way Rafael looked at me. At the way his body felt when pressed against mine, his co—

No.

In a panic, I text Willow, half hoping she is still awake at this hour since she hardly sleeps. Thankfully, I don't have to wait long since my phone vibrates a few minutes later with a new message.

WILLOW

What do you mean Rafael almost kissed you?

ME

Well, we were in the hot tub.

Before I'm able to follow up, Willow's next message comes through.

WILLOW

HOT TUB? With your BOSS?

My cheeks heat.

ME

I was there first.

WILLOW

But you didn't leave when he got there.

ME

No.

WILLOW

Interesting.

WILLOW

What bathing suit were you wearing?

ME

...

WILLOW

I'm a visual person, so help a girl out.

With an eye roll, I reply.

ME

The green one.

WILLOW

No wonder he joined you. Your boobs look phenomenal in that one!

I answer with a blushing emoji.

WILLOW

So what happened next?

ME

We talked. Joked around a bit.

WILLOW

Flirted?

ME

Kind of.

WILLOW

It's a yes or no question.

ME

Fine.

ME

Yes.

WILLOW

I knew it!

WILLOW

Go on.

ME

Anyway, he ended up holding me and looked like he was about to kiss me.

WILLOW

Whoa whoa whoa. You skipped all the good stuff.

ME

Like?

WILLOW

Did you cop a feel?

ME

No!

WILLOW

I'm disappointed in you.

ME

I did feel his...

She sends three eggplant emojis before another text.

WILLOW

Was he hard? Please say yes.

My body temperature spikes, and my heart jolts in my chest at the memory of just how turned on he was.

ME

I am not answering that.

WILLOW

So he was! Good to know.

ME

I'm suddenly too exhausted to text... Talk to you never.

WILLOW

Wait! Don't leave me on a cliffhanger!

When I don't answer right away, Willow resorts to threatening me.

WILLOW

Tell me what happened next or else.

ME

Nothing happened. I snapped out of the moment first, and then he let go of me and left in a rush.

WILLOW

No speech about how he wants
you but can't have you?

ME

No.

WILLOW

Well, that was anticlimactic.

Tell me about it. With a groan, I type out another message.

ME

How am I supposed to look
him in the eyes tomorrow?

WILLOW

He was the one who almost kissed
you, so that's his problem, not yours.

It feels like it's both of our problems, because while we could deny our chemistry before, I'm not sure that is possible anymore.

At least not for me.

After last night's hot tub incident, I think it's best for me to spend Sunday by myself while Rafael and Nico go deep-sea fishing. I need time to recuperate and think of my next step, but unfortunately, Nico won't let me get away with avoiding his father.

"But I want you to come." He grabs my hand and tries to pull me out of bed. Despite his height, he barely manages to drag me a few inches.

"I want to sleep in." I groan before throwing a pillow over my head.

"But you're already awake!"

I'm having a hard time fighting that logic, so I roll over and play dead.

"What's going on?" Rafael's deep voice cuts through Nico's pleas.

"Ellie refuses to get out of bed."

"Why?"

"She says she wants to sleep in."

"That makes two of us."

"*Papi*," he says with a groan.

"If she doesn't want to go…"

It's obvious *he* doesn't want me to, which only adds to my embarrassment about last night.

"You've got to come!" Nico yanks the pillow off my head, forcing me to stare into his father's deep brown eyes. The same eyes I was gazing into last night when he was holding me tightly against his chest, looking at me like I mattered.

Like I was *his*.

Rafael's gaze drops to my lips. The glance is fleeting, but

it feels as if he yanked on an invisible string wrapped around my heart.

Something shifted between us last night. The energy is different. Electric. *Dangerous.*

The blood rushing to my lower half is just another reason I need to stay away and collect myself today. I need to regroup and reassess our situation until I remember why I'm here and what I stand to lose if I allow myself to get swept away with lust.

I would be risking not only my job but also my relationship with Nico, because there is no way in hell Rafael would let me continue working for him if we ever crossed that line. I wouldn't if I were him, which means I need to control myself and focus on why I'm even on this vacation.

To help Nico have the trip of a lifetime.

Nico points at me. "Tell her she has to come."

I silently beg Rafael to ignore his son, but the bastard doesn't listen.

"Elle."

There we go again, dropping the nickname that makes my heart stutter. It's stupid, really, the hold a single syllable has over my heart, but it isn't the nickname itself that gets to me.

It's the fact that Rafael gave me one in the first place that is exclusively *his.*

"Oh. Elle! I like it." Nico claps his hands.

Rafael spares his son a look. "I call her that."

Nico's eyes roll. "So I can't?"

"Glad you understand."

I swallow my laugh while Nico stares at him, looking more confused than ever.

"I like it when you call me Ellie." I pat Nico's shoulder and pretend my cheeks aren't betraying just how much I like his father's nickname.

"Then Ellie it is." Nico grins before hitting me with his best serious look. "But if you don't come hang out with us, I'm going to start calling you Eleanor."

"Are you—"

Nico stands proudly. "Blackballing you? Yes."

Don't you dare laugh...

"*Blackmailing*," Rafael corrects while ruffling his son's hair. "I've taught you well."

"For the record, I prefer it when you two aren't getting along." I point at both of them.

Nico holds his fist out, and Rafael bumps it.

These two boys will send me to a premature grave. That much I can guarantee.

"Are you feeling okay?" Nico asks.

I slump over the side of the small fishing boat with a groan. Rafael's hold on my hair doesn't loosen, which matches the one he has on my heart today. His other hand, which found the small of my back and never left, rubs in a soothing circle.

I was supposed to be steering clear of him and sticking to one side of the boat, but then my stomach decided to revolt after suffering through twenty minutes of unrelenting nausea. Thankfully, I made it to the side of the boat in time, with Rafael on my heels. He pulled my hair away from my face in a second and kept the strands in his tight grip while I vomited. He even ran a wet towel over my face and whispered reassuring phrases under his breath, only for me to hear.

Rafael is being so gentle—so damn soft and caring and patient—that tears spring to my eyes at the unfairness of it all. Of craving the comfort of the one person I can't have.

Thankfully, I'm turned away from him, so he doesn't notice me getting emotional, but it doesn't make the tears any less real.

Rafael isn't just rekindling the crush I had on him all those years ago. He is fanning the flames and making them burn stronger than ever before, and he has absolutely no idea.

I've never been cared for like this by someone who wasn't my family or Willow, and it makes me feel so much all at once.

Burning desire. Crippling fear. Unbridled sadness, knowing this is all our relationship will ever be.

After channeling a bit of strength and wiping at my mouth with the back of my hand, I stand and lean against the boat. "I told you I should have stayed at the hotel."

"It's my fault we didn't charter a bigger boat."

"Your modes of transportation are severely questionable." I'm desperate to ease some of the discomfort I feel at ruining their fishing expedition because if there is something I hate more than confrontation, it's inconveniencing people.

I explored that issue in therapy, but that doesn't mean I don't slip back into that kind of guilty mindset from time to time. It's impossible not to after feeling like a burden for so long. My mom has always vehemently disagreed, but that hasn't stopped me from blaming myself for her staying with my father because she wanted to protect me.

Another wave crashes against the side of the boat, and I stare at the horizon while praying that the sudden bout of nausea disappears as quickly as it came.

Nico passes me the mint tin from Rafael's backpack, and I pop three in my mouth.

"*Mijo*, can you get Elle some water too? And ask the captain for crackers, please."

"Sure. Anything for *Elle*." He sticks his tongue out at his father and takes off toward the front of the boat. It's not a big one, which Rafael explained only makes the rocking worse.

My stomach churns. "This is miserable."

"I already asked him to turn back."

"No!" I face him with wobbly legs. The next wave that comes barreling against the side of the boat throws me off-balance, but thankfully Rafael stops me from falling over. It takes me back to last night and the way his hold tightened around me, especially when he lets me go in a rush again.

He crosses his arms against his chest. "You've thrown up twice already."

"Perhaps the third time's a charm."

He doesn't even crack a smirk.

"Stop fussing over me. At worst, I'll be dry-heaving because I have nothing left in my stomach."

His scowl deepens. "You're probably dehydrated."

"And you're overreacting." I point at Nico, who struggles to keep the water inside the plastic bottle as he walks toward the back of the boat. "I just need a little water, and I'll be good to go."

Rafael seems unimpressed. "You look pale."

"That's my sunscreen."

He doesn't seem to buy my answer. "Why are you pushing so hard to stay?"

Because I hate being a burden.

The frown lines beside his eyes soften. "It's okay to say you don't feel well. You're not ruining our day if you ask us to go back."

I smile through the nausea. "I'll be good as new in a few minutes. Just wait and see."

I'm not good as new. Not even close, although I breathe through the discomfort and pretend I'm having the best time because Nico is enjoying all the one-on-one attention from his dad. Watching the two of them finally getting along warms my heart, and I refuse to be the reason they cut today's special activity short, regardless of feeling shitty.

At the captain's suggestion, I sit near the back of the boat while they hang out in the front, casting lines while learning all about Hawaii and its local wildlife.

Rafael keeps glancing over at me with knitted brows, but I wave him off and continue flipping through my notebook as I try to distract myself from the deep sea and my anxiety by working on a new song.

I haven't bothered writing music since I left Los Angeles, but I feel like putting my pen to paper today, especially since it usually quells my nerves.

My hand trembles, not because I'm anxious about

writing but because of what scribbling the very first line represents.

My fresh start.

Even if I never agree to Cole's songwriting opportunity, I'm going to reclaim the person I was, one song verse at a time.

While Nico and Rafael spend their time fishing, I alternate between staring at the horizon to fight my nausea and scribbling random lyrics I think up in my head. Most of my lines don't make sense, but one sticks out amongst all the others.

> It was snowing hard on Christmas Eve,
> When our paths crossed that first time.

I'm so caught off guard by it that I scribble over the lyrics until they are no longer recognizable. I expect to feel relief at erasing the evidence of my first meeting with Rafael, but something tugs at my chest instead.

Something that feels a little like regret.

I haven't written a song about my personal life since "Silver Scars," yet here I am, starting a new song off by referencing *him*.

I close my notebook and pull out my phone to distract myself with a random game, but nothing can make me forget how Rafael inspired a lyric.

And I'm not quite sure what to make of it.

Nico wants us to take a stroll on the beach after dinner. While

I'm happy to walk off our meal, Rafael doesn't appear to share the same sentiment. He seems grumpier than usual, and I can only assume it has something to do with me and the cursed boat day.

When I asked him to take a picture of me earlier so I could prove to my mom that I wore the dress she picked out, he could hardly look at me.

I blame the unique retro pattern and bright colors. My mom found it while sifting through the racks at the consignment store in town, and I didn't have the heart to tell her no, so I packed the floral frock despite it clashing with my entire closet.

When I put it on, I felt pretty, but one look at Rafael's pained expression made me question my fashion choice.

Thankfully, Nico seems to have a completely different reaction from his father's as he stops by one of the hibiscus bushes and yanks on an orange flower.

He turns and holds it up for me. "A pretty flower for a pretty girl."

"Thank you." I tuck the flower behind my ear with a smile. "These are quickly becoming my favorite."

Nico tries to be slick by going behind my back, but I catch him motioning for Rafael to do the same. My cheeks, already warm from today's sun, flush as I pretend not to notice Rafael struggling with the idea.

With a soft huff, Rafael scans the bush twice before he appears satisfied with an option. He gently grabs a flower that reminds me of the sunset, with the ombre petals resembling the sky around us.

It's a perfect match for my dress.

Unlike Nico and his sweet words, Rafael doesn't say anything, but he doesn't need to.

Not when he looks at me with so much want it makes my body tremble.

I'm not sure he even notices, but for a brief second, his guard drops, and I finally see what he has been trying to hide all night long.

Lust.

My core pulses with need, and I press my thighs together and pray for it to go away.

Instead of waiting for me to reach for the stem, Rafael curls a loose strand of my hair behind my other ear before placing the flower there. His fingers graze the sensitive shell as he pulls away, and I suppress a shiver.

The whole exchange doesn't last more than a few seconds, but time feels like it stops to give us a moment. His eyes roam over my face, soaking up every detail while I make out bits and pieces of the man who hides behind a beard and constant scowl.

I find myself disappointed when he pulls away all too soon, taking his spicy scent with him as the world roars back to life around us.

Our eyes meet again, and my heart jerks in my chest as I'm hit with a strong, forbidden sense of yearning for someone I can't have but will always want.

I wanted Rafael Lopez when I was in high school, and I want him now. But just like back then, I know he will never be mine.

Not then. Not now. Not ever.

Nico and I convince Rafael to grab Hawaiian shave ice with us after dinner. The drive to a local spot is a short one, although the line is longer than the other day.

We wait behind a family with the cutest baby. When I tell the mom that, she comments on how she hopes her son is half as cute as mine. I laugh off her statement before correcting her, although Rafael doesn't seem to share my amusement.

He is unusually quiet, being borderline rude with the way he stares straight ahead, glaring at the line like it personally offended him.

Nico seems unaware, although Rafael's strange behavior doesn't relent, even after we get to the front of the line and order, and his scowl remains permanently in place as we find a free table.

"Ellie?" Nico steals a scoop of mine before ever touching his.

"Yeah?"

"I have a question."

"When don't you?" I tease.

He giggles. "Do you want kids?"

I choke on a spoonful of shave ice. "What?"

Rafael shakes his head. "That's a personal question."

"So?" Nico asks innocently. "Ellie and I are friends."

"Doesn't mean you should ask people questions about wanting kids."

"Why?"

I interject, "Your dad is right. I may not mind you asking, but someone else could."

"Oh." Nico's smile transforms into a frown. "Sorry."

"It's okay. But to answer your question, yes. I'd like to have a family."

"So you want to get married too?"

Rafael pinches the bridge of his nose with a sigh.

"Sure. If the one I've been looking for comes along, I would."

"The one? Like a prince?"

I laugh. "No. *The one* isn't going to be a prince, but I'm sure he will make me just as happy."

Rafael's plastic spoon snaps in half. "I'll be back."

Nico doesn't think anything of his father's abrupt departure, but my stomach churns, ruining my appetite.

I don't know why our conversation triggered him. Rafael is well aware that I go on dates, so I'm not sure why he would be surprised by the idea of me wanting to get married and start a family.

I can't shake the feeling that my answers disappointed him somehow, which only adds to the complicated emotions building inside me whenever I think about my boss.

CHAPTER TWENTY-NINE

Rafael

I have absolutely no right to feel disappointed by Ellie's answers to Nico's questions about marriage and starting a family, but I can't help it, which both confuses and angers me at the same time.

Despite walking away for a few minutes to gain control over my emotions, I can't seem to.

I had a good idea about Ellie's stance on marriage and wanting a family. While she has mostly kept quiet about her personal life, I know she has been actively dating people. I've even overheard a few hushed phone conversations that confirmed as much.

I'm the complete opposite of what she wants, and if it wasn't apparent before, the conversation she had with Nico tonight made it crystal clear.

Ellie wants a husband, a baby, and a future that doesn't align with mine, so it's best I come to terms with it now.

My conflicting feelings remain as I return to the table and finish my shave ice without sharing more than ten words. If Ellie notices my mood shift, she doesn't say anything during the drive back, although she spares me a few glances out of the corner of her eye when she thinks I'm not paying attention.

Despite being focused on the road, my skin always tingles with awareness whenever she does that. Just another unfortunate side effect of being in her proximity, along with my heart rate rising whenever we touch.

It could be for the briefest second, but the power she has over my body and mind is concerning.

Fuck. I need to get this control over myself, not only for her benefit but for *mine*.

Surprisingly, I wake up before Nico and Ellie the next morning, which may be a first. Instead of checking my work inbox, I spend some time sending my family photos of our trip.

My aunt forgoes texting and calls me instead.

"Hola, *Tía*." I sift through my luggage for a swimsuit.

"*¿Cómo andas?*"

"*Bien, ahí vamos. ¿Y tú?*"

"Good. Nico seems to be enjoying the trip so far."

I smile to myself. "Yeah. I'm going to have a hard time

¿Cómo andas?: How are you doing?

Bien, ahí vamos. ¿Y tú?: Good. And you?

getting him to leave."

"Leave that to Ellie. Wherever she goes, that boy will follow."

My grin dies. "Yeah. Sure."

"Hm," she says.

"What?"

"How is everything going with her?"

"Fine."

"We all know what that means."

I frown.

"Are you still upset with her about what happened with Nico?" she asks without any judgment.

"No. I've let that go."

"Then what's wrong?"

My lips press together. "Nothing."

She chuckles to herself. "*Right*. Well, if you ever want to talk about it, I'm here."

My aunt said the same thing all my life, but I've never taken her up on the offer. When I was younger, I did it to protect her from knowing the truth about me, but now I am too proud to admit my struggles.

In some ways, I'm just like my uncle and Julian, with a hubris that has caused me nothing but trouble.

Only because you're too stubborn to ask for help.

I run my hand through my hair. "I appreciate it."

Her small sigh of disappointment makes my chest uncomfortably tight. "Of course. I know you're all grown up now and don't need me—"

"I never said that."

"You didn't have to."

I consider changing the topic but decide against it at the last moment. "To be honest, I don't know *how* to talk about everything."

"Well, you'll never learn unless you try."

I take a few seconds to think up my reply. "Things between Ellie and me are…"

She sucks in a breath. "Yes?"

"*Tense.*"

"Oh." Her earlier enthusiasm is wiped away.

"It's not that I don't like her as a person…"

She jumps in to talk when I don't finish my sentence. "But you're not interested in her as more."

That isn't true, but just because I'm attracted to her doesn't mean I can do anything about it. Yesterday's conversation made that perfectly clear.

"I can't be," I answer honestly.

Her confirmatory noise eases some of the tension in my shoulders. "After everything you've been through, I understand why."

I'm surprised by her statement. "You do?"

"Yup. If I had my heart broken by someone I loved and trusted, I wouldn't be willing to part with it again."

My aunt may not know all the sordid details of my divorce, but she can connect the dots on her own with whatever information she has.

"*But…*" She lets the word linger in the air, earning a scowl from me. "If I met the right person, I might end up changing my mind."

The problem is that Ellie may be the right person, but that won't change the fact that I'm all wrong for her.

Even though I'm wishing that wasn't the case.

CHAPTER THIRTY

Ellie

Despite being worried about tomorrow's flight to Kauai, today *was* supposed to be spent enjoying our last full day in Oahu while avoiding my anxious thoughts, but life had different plans for me.

From the moment I wake up, I'm a walking, talking disaster. First, I misplaced my favorite guitar pick, and then I ruined my outfit after my macchiato was introduced to my shirt.

Neither of those calamities compares to the third and final stroke of bad luck. Not even close.

Ava has clearly run out of good song ideas, which explains why she betrayed me one more time with her newest release.

Like a masochist, I replay Ava's latest song for the fifth time before lying back on my bed. I tuck my tear-soaked pillow underneath my head, fold my legs into a fetal position, and shut my eyes.

"Silver Scars" was never meant to see the light of day, let alone shoot to the top of the music charts overnight, but I should have anticipated that Ava would pull one last killer blow.

Like a gunshot wound to the chest, I'm bleeding out, but no one is around to witness a part of my heart dying.

WILLOW

> I had to talk myself out of committing murder since you haven't been answering your phone.

WILLOW

> According to the dark web, there are people you can contact for those kinds of jobs.

WILLOW

> Their fees are a bit out of my budget, but who needs $200,000 anyway?

I lock my phone and stare up at the ceiling in an effort to keep the tears at bay. The air feels thinner, and I fight to fill my lungs with oxygen.

"Screw her and Darius," I wheeze.

Having Ava release an album full of my stolen songs destroyed my whole world a year ago, but I thought I was healing from the betrayal and moving on.

Don't let Ava get you down again.

I brush a finger across my thighs, tracing the outline of my scars. The midthigh tattoo that I begged my mom to let me get when I was only sixteen keeps me grounded and serves as an important reminder whenever I feel the urge to unleash my emotions on my body to make the ones in my head settle down.

This too shall pass.

The cursive writing always comforts me, helping me center myself.

I hate that whenever I feel like I'm moving on—that I'm finally making positive steps toward a better future—something drags me back into a dark pit of self-doubt and loathing.

Is this how Rafael feels? Because it's *terrible*.

With a shaky finger, I outline my newest scar, which is only a year old. It's one that always fills me with shame, because after years of therapy and positive coping strategies, I crashed from the heavy weight of my emotions and returned to unhealthy patterns I fought so damn hard to overcome.

Unlike the last time though, I don't give into temptation. I even test myself by grabbing my razor from the bathroom, but I put it on the nightstand and there it remains, untouched and intact.

It's just a song. You can always write another one, and she can never steal any of yours again.

Except it wasn't *just* a song. It was *the* song. "Silver Scars" was my story to tell, not hers, which was why we both agreed to wipe the recordings and lyrics from the hard drive.

God. How could I have been so stupid and trusting? I should have double-checked the server to make sure Ava had deleted any record of it, but at the time, I believed her because she hadn't betrayed me yet.

My phone buzzes again, but I can't find the energy to check my messages, so I silence my notifications and cover my head with a pillow. It doesn't take long for the tears to come again, and once they start, I can't seem to stop them.

A faint knock five minutes later interrupts my sobs. My body turns to stone despite my brain screaming for me to run.

"Is everything okay?" Rafael's question draws more tears.

Nope. "Yup!" My high pitch is painful to my own ears.

"You've been in there for a while."

I will the tears to stop, but my eyes refuse to cooperate.

"I'm not feeling well today." My voice cracks. "Maybe it's best for me to stay away from you both, just in case it's contagious."

Great idea, Ellie. Isolate yourself from the people who could make you feel better. That'll really make you happy.

He doesn't pause before asking, "Is that why you got sick on the boat yesterday?"

"Maybe!"

"Do you need anything?"

"Nope."

"I could get you medicine or—"

"I'm fine! Thanks for offering, though." My voice sounds harsh to my own ears.

Stilted silence follows, and I pray Rafael leaves me alone and takes Nico down to the beach like we had originally planned. They should build sandcastles together and spend our last day in Honolulu having fun, not dealing with me, the human downer.

"Okay. Text me if you need anything."

A relieved sigh follows. "Thank you."

The door to the hotel suite shuts not too long after as Rafael and Nico leave me alone to wallow in my sadness.

Turns out Rafael isn't the only one who hates themselves for trusting the wrong person.

I do too.

My pity party lasts all of one hour. Once my alarm goes off at the sixty-minute mark, I crawl out of bed, splash some water on my face, and call the one person who assured me they could help.

After speaking to both my mom and Willow about the subject, they both agreed that the best way to deal with a bully like Ava is to make them regret ever choosing me as their target in the first place.

Ava may be America's sweetheart, but I found someone better.

Nashville's bad boy, Cole Griffin.

While I don't want to begin my working relationship with Cole on a bad note—pun not intended—I don't have a choice. I'm done being an invisible footnote in someone else's story. I deserve recognition for my work, even if it means facing one of my biggest fears and finally confronting Ava for all the hurt she has caused me.

It's time for me to accept that I'll never have a bright future if I'm always feeling like a victim of my past.

My phone lights up not ten minutes after I texted Cole to ask if we could talk.

"Hey," Cole greets me with that drawl of his. "How are you doing?"

"Fine. You?"

"Hm."

"What?"

"My sister taught me better than to take that particular word at face value."

"You have a sister?"

He clears his throat. "Yes."

"I had no idea."

"My parents preferred to keep it that way."

"Oh." *Oh? That's all you can manage to say? Really?*

Unfortunately, I'm emotionally tapped out and lacking any kind of people skills at the moment, so that's the best Cole is going to get.

He chuckles to himself. "Anyway, talk to me. What's going on?"

"Remember how you sent me the lawyer's information?"

"Yeah."

"I never called them," I admit with a whisper.

"Why not?"

I struggle to get the words out. "I'm scared."

"Fair enough, but you're only asking for a meeting. It's not like you have to move forward with anything if you don't want to."

"I know." I fall back onto my bed.

"Do you want my advice?"

"Have you been through this kind of thing before?"

"Uh, no. I prefer to give people credit for their work and pay them well, so they *want* to partner with me again, but I've heard from others who weren't as lucky."

I frown. "At least I'm not alone."

"No, but it goes against industry standards, so whoever made you believe differently deserves to be sued for every penny they're worth."

My shoulders slump. "Even if it ruins my career and reputation in the process?"

"Did you steal someone's songs?"

"No!"

"Then you're not the one who needs to worry. Ava does."

I bite down on the inside of my cheek. "But she's so popular." And I'm a nobody.

"Great. That means she should have had the funds to pay you for your work."

"Yeah, but I don't have a lot of evidence to prove—"

"You won't need it."

That surprises me. "No?"

"The chances of a case like that ever going to trial are slim."

"Why?"

"Because Ava is most likely going to want to settle before word gets out and ruins her pristine good-girl image."

I can't help the deranged laugh that escapes me. "I spent the last year worried about going to court for nothing?"

"I said they *most likely* will want to settle. Not that they actually will."

My confidence dies. "Oh."

"But don't worry about any of that yet. First things first, you need to get in contact with the lawyer."

"I know."

"Would it help if I set up a meeting for you?"

"You'd do that? For me?"

"Sure."

My mouth drops open. "Why?"

"I like seeing good people win."

"That's altruistic of you."

"I wouldn't go that far…"

Laughing feels impossible given the heavy weight pressing against my chest, but I do smile. "Thanks for listening and offering to help. That's really kind of you."

"Thank me by writing a song for my next album?"

I don't hesitate before answering. "Sure."

"Really?"

"Yeah. I like helping good people too."

Cole has proven twice already that he isn't the wild man the media makes him out to be, so it's time I give him a chance.

"Great!" He sounds extremely excited by the idea.

"I'm going to play around with my guitar and a few ideas while I'm on vacation."

"You're not in town?"

"Nope. Hawaii."

"Beautiful place. Maybe it will inspire you."

I sigh. "We'll see."

"If it does, awesome, but if not, there's no rush. Good music takes time."

Let's hope it doesn't take too long because I don't only want to write one song.

I want to write a whole comeback *album*.

CHAPTER THIRTY-ONE

Rafael

When Ellie told me she couldn't join us because she was feeling sick, I was nervous about spending the day with Nico. I know it sounds ridiculous to be intimidated by my own kid, but it's the truth. Ellie has been a buffer during our time in Oahu so far, and without her, I'm worried everything with Nico will revert to the way it was the last six months before our trip.

The bright sun turns my vision spotty for a few seconds before my eyes adjust.

"Pool or beach?" I ask my son.

He waves his metal detector in the air in a silent answer.

I lead him toward an unoccupied area near the shore, far from other children who could try to strike up a conversation with my son and steal him away.

Is it petty? Probably, but efficient nonetheless.

For the first twenty minutes or so, we both do our own thing. Nico plays with the metal detector Ellie packed for him while I pass the time reviewing the plans Julian sent me for the barn expansion.

Eventually, the temptation to check my work inbox becomes too great to ignore, so I open our work app and spare it a quick glance. I've never been away from work for longer than a week, and while I know Julian and my assistant are more than qualified to take care of everything, I still struggle to let go.

Julian calls me out on just that by pinging me through the app.

JULIAN

> I see you're online. If you answer a single message, I will take Nico up on his offer and replace you.

With that, I tuck my phone into the beach bag I brought and get up.

He's your son. Stop being a nervous wreck and spend time with him.

With a long, extended breath, I walk over to Nico.

"Hey."

He squints in my direction. "Hi."

"What do you say we work on a sandcastle together?"

"But you're busy."

Great. In my effort to give Nico space and not come on too strong, I messed things up even more.

"Your *tío* told me if he caught me working again, he'd come here and kick my butt."

Nico giggles. "No, he didn't!"

"Yeah. Even threatened to send me back to Lake Wisteria."

"Really?"

"Yup. So there's no way I'm working anymore on this trip."

His whole face lights up. "Good! Work is boring." He practically sings the last word.

"True, but work also paid for all this."

"So? Aren't you a gazillionaire?"

"Nicolas," I say in that no-bullshit parenting voice I picked up from my uncle.

He rolls his eyes. "What? All the kids at school say you have a million dollars!"

Just a few thousand of them, give or take.

But still, it is never too early to teach my son the importance of money and how growing up without it not only influenced me but his entire life. "You know that wasn't always the case."

His eyes widen. "Yeah?"

"Yeah. My parents struggled a lot, so I didn't have a lot of things while growing up. We never went on vacation or had a nice house."

"What about music lessons?"

I shake my head. "Definitely not."

"Did you have a TV?"

"Yes, but it only had a few channels."

My life was a far cry from Nico's, which means I did my job as a father, even if it meant sacrificing love and time to make it possible.

"I may have money now, but it wasn't always like that, which is why I work hard to make sure you have all the things I always wanted but couldn't have."

"Oh." His frown deepens. "I'm sorry for making fun of work."

"It's okay. I'm not telling you so you feel bad. I just want you to understand why working is important to me."

He throws his arms around my waist and gives me a hug. "Thank you for working hard so we could come on vacation."

My chest tightens as I ruffle his hair. "You're welcome."

I steer him away from the ocean and bring him back to our area. The tension between us becomes a distant memory as we each grab a bucket and our tools.

"Are you sure you know what you're doing?" he questions me thirty minutes later.

"Kind of?"

On cue, part of the castle's east wing crumbles.

Nico curls over and laughs. "I knew Ellie made that castle!"

"Hey! I helped."

His brow arches into a perfect, condescending curve. "*Si tu lo dices.*"

"Are you calling me a liar?"

His eyes narrow. "Mm. Was your nose always that big, or does it grow every time you lie?"

I throw the bucket aside and grab him. After making sure his glasses are secured with the strap wrapped around the back of his head, I throw him over my shoulder.

Si tu lo dices: If you say so.

"No!" He bangs his fists against my back as I rush toward the ocean.

Water hits my toes, followed by my calves, as I quickly submerge half my body. "This is what you get for saying I have a big nose."

"I was kidding!"

I fake confusion. "Huh. You were?"

"Yes! I swear!"

I squint. "Hm. Your nose looks bigger now too."

Nico's response is cut off by his squeal as I toss him in the ocean with an evil laugh.

He surfaces a few seconds later with a death glare. "Not fair."

"Neither is life, but you'll get used to it."

My son shows an impressive amount of strength and speed as he tackles me. I take him down with me as we both fall back, our bodies sinking beneath the surface. The salt water makes my eyes sting, and I screw them shut as I stand.

I'm greeted by a fresh ocean breeze and Nico's deep belly laughs. I haven't heard him like this in months, and it fills me with a burst of fatherly pride.

You did that.

And if things go my way, I hope to do it again.

Nico and I spend thirty minutes in the water together before he asks if we can head back to the beach.

"Let's go." I turn and give him my back.

He climbs on and wraps his arms around my neck. "Do you think Ellie is okay?"

Before Hawaii, a hot spike of jealousy always stabbed me

in the chest whenever Nico brought up Ellie's name. But now, I'm nothing but neutral as I pull out my phone and send her a text asking if she needs anything, along with a short video of Nico saying he misses her.

If you're nothing but neutral, then why is your heart skipping a beat?

The betraying organ calls me out on the lie, reminding me exactly how I feel toward Nico's nanny. A feeling I shouldn't be having in the first place, for a few different reasons, but most of all for the kid who is the center of my universe.

While I'm not winning any Father of the Year awards, Nico makes me feel like I'm in the running again. He doesn't seem as tense or withdrawn while we talk during lunch about this afternoon's plan to head to the North Shore for our ATV tour.

Everything is going great until Nico shocks me with a whispered confession halfway through our meal.

"I had a nightmare last night."

My world tilts as I try to process this new piece of information. "You did?"

He nods. "I get them sometimes."

My throat feels tight. "I didn't know that."

His eyes drop to the remaining shrimp he has yet to eat. "That's because I didn't want to upset you."

Rather than allow my sadness and self-loathing to take over, I reach for his hand and give it a squeeze. "I'd never get upset about something like that."

Knowing Nico was struggling with nightmares in silence reminds me so much of myself, and it makes me physically *ache*.

"I appreciate you telling me."

He squints at me. "You do?"

"Of course. I'm not sure if I told you before, but I used to have nightmares too."

"About what?"

Despite feeling like I'm being choked by my T-shirt collar, I plaster on a small, reassuring smile. "Things that scared me from my past."

His brows knit together behind his glasses. "Really?"

I nod. "What are yours about?"

"I have dreams about not being able to see *anything*. I can hear everyone. Can smell and touch things too, but my vision is gone."

I want to pull him into my arms and never let go, but I remain in my seat. "That does sound scary."

His chin trembles. "One time, I was lost at the mall. All of a sudden, everything went dark. No one could help me find you."

I reach for his hand. "I'm sorry you've been having nightmares like these."

He stares down at his lap. "I don't want everything to go black."

I shake my head. "The doctor told us that won't happen."

"I know, but what if they're wrong?"

"No doctor can tell the future, but they have the science that shows you'll be able to still see. And there are things we can do to help you."

"But it won't be the same. It'll just keep getting worse."

"You're right." Another sharp pain ricochets through my chest, but instead of allowing my grief to consume me, I channel it into helping my son process his fear. "But we will make the most of the vision you have."

His frown morphs into a smile. "Does that mean we can go on vacation all the time?"

I laugh, which only makes his grin widen. "I'll think about it." While I can't go on vacation as often as Nico would like, I can make them a top priority for us, ensuring he makes as many visual memories as possible.

We move on to lighter topics, like our future trip to the Mexico City Grand Prix with Ellie in October, before heading to the pickup location for our ATV tour.

Nico and I have a blast exploring the scenic valleys, dirt roads, and iconic movie locations in our two-passenger buggy. Nico's smile never drops, his laughter is constant as I drive us around, and I enjoy making him squeal with sharp turns and small jumps.

We haven't had this kind of long-lasting fun together in months, and I'm reluctant to drive us back to the drop-off location solely because I don't want today to end.

You don't need ATVs or a beach to make Nico happy. You just need to be you.

"You've got some dirt in your beard." He laughs as he brushes my chin.

"Maybe I should shave it all off." While I keep my beard nicely trimmed, sand or dirt like today's still get caught in it, making for an itchy experience.

"Really?" His eyes go wide.

"Yeah." I scratch at my cheek.

His smile expands. "Yay!"

"You don't like it?"

His face turns red. "I didn't say that."

He didn't have to.

"Okay then. Do you like it?"

He bites down on his bottom lip.

"I thought so." I pull him in for a hug and rub my face against his, earning a loud laugh and a hard shove against my shoulder.

"Stop!" he squeals as I spread dirt across his cheeks.

"What did you say?"

"I said stop!" He speaks louder this time.

I release him. "You should have told me you didn't like it sooner."

A dark look passes over his face before he stares down at his feet.

My stomach muscles clench. "What's wrong?"

He stays quiet.

"I was just kidding," I say to put him at ease.

"I know," he whispers.

"Did I say something to make you upset?"

He shakes his head.

"You can talk to me. I'm not going to get mad or anything."

He takes a deep breath. "I overheard Dahlia and Lily talking about you."

My lungs feel as though they're being crushed by some invisible weight. "What did they say?"

"That you're handsome, but you hide it because you're sad."

Mierda.

Hearing the truth from my son's mouth hits hard. I internalized my despair and became someone else until I no longer recognized my own reflection.

It was easy to ignore the failure of a person I was by making him disappear altogether.

Nico's comment sparks a new flame of hope in my chest.

I kneel in front of him. "Lily and Dahlia were right."

His head snaps up. "They were?"

"Yeah. I stopped caring because I was sad."

His bottom lip trembles.

"But I do disagree with one thing," I add.

"What?"

"Being called handsome."

He laughs. "Now you're just being silly."

"No. This is me being happy."

His wariness remains. "Really?"

"Yeah, and I'm going to prove it to you."

I park the Jeep back at the hotel an hour later. Nico struggles to carry the bags of supplies we—okay, mostly *I*—picked out for Ellie, but he refuses my help as he lugs them all the way back to our suite.

He leaves my room to go take a peek inside hers, only to return with a frown. "She fell asleep."

"Maybe she's still feeling sick?"

"Is it because we're going on a plane again tomorrow?"

Shit. I didn't even think of that, but it could explain some things. "Give me a minute."

I call the concierge desk and request to speak with the hotel's travel agent. Nico rifles through the bags of supplies we bought, waiting patiently for me to finish up.

While I'm busy on the phone, he accidentally sprays blue shaving cream all over my comforter.

"Oops! Sorry!" He rushes into the bathroom before coming back with a towel. "I got it!" He means well, but the mess only gets worse as he proceeds to spread it everywhere. I'm not sure how he even managed to get it in his hair, but a few strands are stuck together from the residue.

Thankfully, I hang up the phone a few minutes later and can finally give him my full attention.

"Let's get you cleaned up." I lead him into the large en suite and place the bag of supplies on the counter. Nico pulls out his kid's shaving kit and passes it to me.

"Can you open it?"

I spare him a look.

"Please."

I help open the package enough for him to get the plastic shaver and shaving cream out for himself.

"This is fun." He giggles as he covers the bottom half of his face. "Ho. Ho. Ho."

I swallow my laugh as I run my new shaver under some hot water after splashing my face with it.

"Is it going to hurt?" He checks out the blades.

"No, as long as I don't cut myself."

"Does that happen?"

"Sometimes. I'm a bit out of practice."

"Maybe you shouldn't then."

My chest clenches at the hint of fear in his voice.

"I'll be fine." I kiss the top of his head before I follow his lead and cover my beard with shaving cream. Nico quickly moves on from worrying about me, instead choosing to make squiggly lines across his face with the plastic razor.

"This is awesome!" He laughs.

I press my lips together to stop myself from smiling. With a steady hand, I run the razor from the middle of my neck upward. The swift stroke reveals skin that has been hidden for two years.

Two long, agonizing years.

I didn't think a simple task like shaving could have such a visceral effect on me, but my next breaths prove otherwise.

It's time for a change. I repeat the same motion, revealing another clear patch of skin.

You're doing this for you. Me. Not Nico, although I'm happy he will no longer associate my lack of upkeep with my sadness, and I'm most definitely not doing this for my family, who will be happy to see my whole face again regardless.

Every swipe of the blade leads me closer to letting go of the old me. The broken me. The me that spent the last two years in a haze, hardly living at all.

I couldn't be happier about the change. I want to look better because *I* care. Because I want to look past the person I *was* and accept the man that I can be.

Correction: the man I *want* to be.

CHAPTER THIRTY-TWO

Ellie

had intended on joining Rafael and Nico outside at some point, but the heavy weight pressing against my shoulders and chest has me sticking to the confines of my bedroom, where I can fully embrace my emotions through music.

I toss the guitar pick on the bed and reach for my notebook. The page is covered with a mix of unfinished lyrics and song ideas that failed to pass my first round of edits.

I've always written songs from a woman's perspective, weaving my personal stories into purposeful lines and relatable lyrics. While it shouldn't be a challenge to write from Cole's point of view, I'm struggling. *Hard.*

I drop back on my mattress with a sigh and end up falling asleep for a couple of hours until I'm woken up by heavy knocking against my door.

"Ellie?" Rafael asks.

"Yeah?" I rub at my tired eyes.

"Can I come in?"

My heart picks up speed. "Sure?"

The doorknob turns before the door opens to—

I gasp. "Oh my God." My hand instantly reaches out toward Rafael's clean-shaven face, only for me to snatch it back.

His slightly pale cheeks, which I haven't fully seen in the whole time I've been working for him, turn pink as his gaze meets mine. "You don't like it?"

I most definitely *shouldn't*, but I'm single with an active sex drive, so of course I like Rafael's clean-shaven face. In fact, I like it a whole lot more than I should.

"It's…nice," I manage to say with an even voice.

He rubs at his cheek. "Just nice?"

"Are you fishing for compliments again?"

"Only because you're starting to give me a complex."

"Would you rather I say you're hot?"

"See? Was that so hard to admit?"

I roll my eyes with a smile. "Anyone in town could tell you that."

His eyes lock onto mine. "I don't care about anyone else's opinion."

My stomach takes a dive into dangerous, butterfly-inducing territory. "Now you're giving *me* a complex."

I have to glance away because I can't bear the weight of his stare. See, Rafael has always been hot, even with his rugged aesthetic, but this is different.

He is different.

I'm afraid to hope, just in case he takes another major step back, but at the same time, I am so proud of him. The idea of him reclaiming parts of the old him while becoming someone new makes me incredibly emotional. How can it not when I'm getting a front-row view of him pulling himself up off the ground after spending the last two years buried underneath his sorrow?

"Ellie?"

"Huh?"

"Jokes aside, are you feeling okay?" A worried line appears down the middle of his forehead.

"Oh. Yeah." I clasp my hands together to hide the way they tremble.

"Nico wanted to get you some medicine." He places a paper bag on the edge of my bed. "He was worried about you. I…uh…was too. I texted you to check in, but you didn't answer."

A part of me dies inside at the hint of self-consciousness in his tone.

I've done my best to keep my feelings toward Rafael in a locked box with a massive *do not touch* warning label. It was easy when he was so unlikable, but now that he is doing and saying things that make my heart skip more beats than a damaged vinyl record, I don't stand a chance.

Most definitely not when he is looking at me like my well-being matters to him and checking in to see if I'm okay.

"I know you weren't feeling well, so I wasn't going to bother you…" His voice trails off.

"*But?*"

He doesn't smile. He *beams*. "Nico and I had an amazing day today, and I need to talk about it with someone."

His happiness is contagious, and I find myself smiling for the first time today as well. "Tell me everything."

"I don't remember the last time we had so much fun together." He starts pacing beside my bed, stopping right next to me before turning in a hurry. "He wanted to build a sandcastle with me, so we tried. It wasn't half as good as the one you and I made two days ago, though."

I flick my hair over my shoulder. "Obviously. I am a champion after all."

He chuckles to himself, adding to the growing list of things he does that tug on my heartstrings.

"We missed you," he says next, taking an invisible battering ram to the wall protecting my heart.

I glance away. "You're just saying that."

He abandons his pacing and walks up to me. "No, I— Wait. Why are your eyes all red and puffy?"

"Huh?"

I'm hit with an overwhelming sense of loss as his smile is replaced with a frown. "Were you...crying?"

I shift my gaze toward the window that overlooks the vast ocean. "No."

He clasps my chin and twists my head until I look up at him. "I thought you said you were sick."

Heartsick is more like it. "I am."

"Is everything okay?"

"It will be."

His fingers tense against my skin. "What's going on?"

"Nothing you need to worry about. I'll see you at dinner?" The change of topic is far from smooth, but I hope he takes it as a hint that this conversation is over.

He stares at me for a few hard seconds, his mouth opening and closing once before he releases my chin with a nod, turns around, and leaves my room like he just saw a ghost.

I wait until Rafael storms out of my room to open the bag he dropped off. Although he said Nico chose the items, the truth becomes clear within the first ten seconds.

Rafael handpicked most of these items himself but gave Nico all the credit.

I've been grocery shopping with Nico before, so he knows I love cookies with rainbow sprinkles and that I prefer snacking on clementines and kettle corn, but his attention to detail usually stops there. Anytime I've sent him into another aisle to get me something, he always comes back with the wrong brand, which is an impressive feat in itself, seeing as we usually only have three options back home.

Nico can't pick out my favorite sparkling water, let alone my favorite *flavor*, but Rafael apparently can. I'm surprised he even remembered since the strawberry-lemon ones are impossible to get because they are always sold out.

I always thought Rafael was too stuck in his own head to notice little details, but he keeps proving me wrong.

So very, very wrong.

With each item I pull out of the bag, I quickly come to the conclusion that Rafael doesn't only pay attention.

He *cares*.

From afar, at least. That way, no one can ever hold it against him.

The truth becomes painfully obvious as I pull out a box of my favorite chamomile tea, my preferred brand of saltine crackers that have the little elf on the packaging, and some fuzzy socks.

While it was probably Nico's idea to buy me a new pair since it's become a running joke between us, the pattern has Rafael's name all over it because there is no way a nine-year-old kid would think to choose socks with alcohol bottles on them.

I press them against my chest and smile at the reminder of home and the eight crazy animals waiting for us to come back.

Rafael even got me more Dramamine pills, plus a few off-brand options for motion sickness with a hotel-branded sticky note that says, *Sorry it's not Xanax, but you can still hold my hand.*

I fall back on the bed with a huge grin on my face and my heart swelling to twice its usual size. A care package shouldn't make me feel so happy I could cry, but the more I think about it, the harder it is to control my emotions.

And I have no one but Rafael Lopez to blame.

CHAPTER THIRTY-THREE

Rafael

Nico taps on my shoulder and asks, "*¿Papi?*" Nico asks.

"*¿Qué?*"

"Do you like Ellie?"

The question comes out of nowhere, or at least I think it does until I realize who Nico caught me staring at. Ellie hangs out at the bar, looking beautiful in a floor-length tropical dress while the bartender prepares our second round of drinks.

"You keep looking at her," he adds, unknowingly saving me from having to lie about his question.

I turn my attention to my son. "She's pretty."

He grins. "You think so?"

"Yes," I admit, naively thinking it would get him to stop asking questions.

"Do you want to marry her?"

Thankfully, he didn't ask that particular question in the

middle of me sipping the last bit of my drink, or else he would have been coated in bourbon.

I rub my smooth cheek. "I don't plan on marrying *anyone*."

He frowns. "No?"

"No. Sorry."

His happiness fades like the sun setting behind me. "Is it because of Mommy?"

Yes, but also because of me. The idea of loving someone enough to commit to them for the rest of my life terrifies me after my first marriage disaster.

I sigh. "Marriage is hard."

"I know, but if you like someone, you get married. Right?"

"Yes, but not always. And I never said I liked Ellie."

His eyes roll. "But you said she was pretty."

"Because she is, but that doesn't mean I like her like that."

"Then why do you keep looking at her all the time like *Tío* does with Dahlia? He likes her. A lot."

I lose the ability to form a coherent sentence. I knew was Nico smart, but I didn't think he could make these kinds of observations at his age.

It's not like you did a good job of hiding it.

I've had a hard time keeping my eyes off Ellie tonight ever since she walked out of her room wearing another dress, this time in a shade of teal that brings out the shades of green in her hazel eyes. Finding a flower to match it was nearly impossible, although I tried my best to match the pink one Nico chose for her hair.

My self-control was put to the test during our night attending a traditional Hawaiian luau and tearing my gaze away from her has been a difficult task. When Ellie volunteered to dance amongst the hula dancers a little while ago, I couldn't stop staring, not even after she caught me *twice*.

Nico lowers his voice as he says, "It's okay if you like her. I can share."

"How generous of you," I deadpan.

"Do you want me to ask her if she likes you too?"

"Nicolas—"

"I got drinks!" Ellie announces.

"Finally," I grunt.

My nine-year-old son *winks*, although it looks more like a twitch. To think that all this time, I was concerned about my aunt being the matchmaker when I should have been taking note of my son.

Nico tips his head back. "Ellie?"

I hand him a glass full of his favorite fruit drink as of five days ago—Hawaiian Sun Pass-O-Guava. "Here. You should drink this."

"In a minute." He pushes the tall cup aside. "I've got a question."

"Look, Nico. Why don't you go check out that chicken over there?"

Ellie shoots me a strange look. "You want him to go hang out with wild chickens?"

I bite back a groan.

"Do you like my dad?" Nico asks in a singsong voice. "Because he likes you."

Ellie's eyes collide with mine. "He said that?"

Nico lets out a puff. "Well, no, but he said you're pretty."

Her cheeks flush. "He's never said anything to me."

"He's shy." Nico fails to keep his voice at a whisper.

"Not true," I say.

"Just a coward then?" Ellie's eyes spark with quiet challenge.

If she wants me to call her pretty, then I'll do just that, but later, when my son isn't present to hear what else I have to say.

After dinner, I drive us out to a lookout spot the resort manager recommended for watching the sunset, since it is our last night in Oahu. Nico loved the idea, only to fall asleep after a few rounds of "I spy." Ellie and I spend the remainder of the ride listening to the soft crooning of Frankie Estelle, one of Nico's and her favorite artists.

I park the Jeep in the small dirt lot and hang out near the trunk while Ellie grabs a notebook from her purse and heads to an empty bench facing the sky, streaked with ribbons of orange and pink. Waves crash against the rocks below, creating a soothing soundtrack to listen to while I sift through my thoughts.

My mind and body are at war with one another, with my head warning me away from getting close to Ellie, while my hands itch to hold her and never let go. It's a battle, wanting someone to the point of pain yet knowing it can't happen for a multitude of reasons.

She wants to find *the one*, and I'm not him.

"While I'm flattered you want to stare at me, you're missing the whole point of us driving out here." She turns to look at me with an arched brow.

Busted.

With more confidence than I feel, I walk over to the bench and sit. "What are you working on?" When I try to peek at the page, she shuts her notebook.

"A song."

"Really? I thought you didn't write music anymore."

"I've decided to give it another try."

"Why the sudden change of heart?"

She readjusts the flower I tucked behind her ear earlier tonight before dropping her hands. "I don't want to stop doing things I love because I'm scared."

"What are you scared about?"

Her lips remain firmly pressed in a thin line.

Fine. I deserve her shutting down, especially when I've been a closed book, but it *bothers* me. Just like it did earlier when I noticed she had been crying.

That's twice in one day that I'm finding myself getting annoyed over Ellie keeping me at arm's length, and I'm not sure what to make of it yet.

Not sure I *want* to, either.

I snap a photo of the sunset for my family before tucking my phone back into my pocket.

"What was up with Nico tonight?" she asks a minute later.

"I don't know." I tried to press him about it when Ellie went to the bathroom, but he didn't take the bait and moved on to another subject altogether.

"Is it true?" Her eyes flicker with amusement.

"What?"

"Did you say I was pretty?"

My mouth curls at the corners. "Who's the one fishing for compliments now?"

"I'm curious."

"Why?"

She glances away, her cheeks turning as pink as the sky. "Forget it."

I stare at her until she meets my gaze again. "I wasn't about to tell my son what I was really thinking, if that's what you were wondering."

She releases a shaky breath. "What was that?"

"That you looked so damn gorgeous, it physically hurt me to look at you because I knew you could never be mine."

Her sharp inhale fills the quiet. "Is it because I'm Nico's nanny?"

"No, it's because of *me*."

CHAPTER THIRTY-FOUR

Ellie

What's that supposed to mean?" My notebook falls to the ground as I jump off the bench. I'm not a confrontational person, but Rafael always draws this fire out of me that I find hard to extinguish, even with deep breaths and Willow's yoga mantras.

His eyes flick up at me. "You're a hopeless romantic."

"I prefer the term *hopeful*."

He squints. "That there is exactly my point."

My frown becomes more pronounced. "Is that such a bad thing?"

"In theory, no."

"But you seem to think so."

"Only because I'll never be *the one*," he says it with a sneer, making my cheeks flush with embarrassment.

Sure, I've said I'm looking for *the one* in passing, like when we were getting some shave ice the other night, but it didn't sound as childish as he makes it seem. It's not like I'm out there searching for some kind of soulmate, rejecting people left and right because they don't meet an unrealistic set of expectations.

I cross my arms tightly over my chest to shield the way they shake with anger. "There is nothing wrong with being picky and knowing what I want."

His head tilts in silent understanding. "No, there isn't."

"Then what's your problem?"

"What you want and who I am are two completely different things."

"Sounds like an excuse."

"Or is it just a reality check?"

I frown so hard, my forehead muscles strain.

"I can think you're pretty—can think you're the most gorgeous woman I've ever seen, inside and out—but that doesn't change our reality."

"And what's that?"

"We want very different things out of life."

"How do you know what I want when you haven't even asked me?"

His eyes drop to my mouth. "You said enough the other night."

Is that why he looked so angry after snapping a spoon in half? I had a feeling it had to do with what I said, but I didn't realize just how much it impacted him until now.

He stands and closes the space between us until our chests brush and our ragged breaths synchronize. His hand reaches out to cup my cheek, sending a zing down my spine that then ricochets toward my chest.

For someone who claims he isn't *the one*, he sure has a way of making me feel like he is with every single touch.

He brushes his thumb across my cheekbone. "Tell me you don't want to get married then."

I try to avoid his gaze, but he lifts my chin and forces me to look him in the eyes.

"You can't, can you?"

"No." I meant what I said the other night. I *do* want to get married, but that doesn't mean I wouldn't wait for someone like him to come around to the idea. If I knew the person was special, a ring is only a symbol—a symbol I would want because of the commitment it comes with—but there wouldn't be a due date for it.

I'd wait, if it made someone like him happy. A partnership is what matters most to me in the end, not some legally binding contract.

His next words make my stomach sink. "Tell me you don't want kids after all."

"I can't." After growing up as an only child who ached for the siblings I would never have, I want at least two, maybe even three, depending on life's circumstances.

"I got a vasectomy when I found out about Nico's condition." My heart squeezes.

He doesn't look away as he speaks. "I love him, but I didn't want to risk having another kid who could struggle with RP one day. Didn't want to pass that burden on out of selfishness, so I took care of the problem."

"That's okay."

"Is it?"

"Of course. You of all people know adoption is always an option."

His eyes narrow, and I can immediately tell he doesn't believe me.

Can tell he doesn't *want* to either.

"So you don't want kids of your own?" he asks.

"I mean, I've thought about it, but who hasn't?"

The muscles around his eyes soften. "I thought so."

His resigned tone fuels my frustration. "Why are you asking me all these questions in the first place? What point are you trying to prove here?"

"That touching you…" He cradles my cheeks between his palms. "*Wanting* you… It may *feel* right, but we couldn't be more wrong for each other."

I don't realize how much his words hurt until they affect my breathing.

His sad smile is meant to soften what comes next, but it has the opposite effect, making the dread building inside my stomach worse. "I don't want to get married again and have more kids. I've been there, done that, and barely made it out alive the first time. Hell, I'm still paying the price every single day and probably will be for the next nine plus years, all because I had a kid with someone who doesn't deserve him." His voice cracks toward the end.

"Rafael," I say in a broken whisper.

He brushes my cheek soothingly, which makes the ache in my chest feel unbearable. "One day, when you find the one you've been looking for, he better do everything in his power to keep you because you deserve the kind of love that they write songs about." A single tear slips out of the corner of my eye, and he brushes it away with the pad of his thumb.

He pulls back, but not before he steals the flower he gave me straight from my hair.

My heart splinters right down the middle, a thousand cracks forming as he walks back to the Jeep, taking whatever misguided hope I had about the two of us with him.

The next morning, I wake up to Nico bouncing on my bed, shouting for me to get up before the yacht takes off without me. I have no idea what he is talking about until I check my phone and read a cryptic message from Rafael.

RAFAEL

> Slight change to our travel plans.
> We will be taking a boat from Oahu
> to Kauai instead of a plane.

With that confirmation, I pack both Nico's and my suitcases, all while he keeps talking about this massive yacht and all the activities we get to do over the next day.

Only Rafael would pay a seven-day retainer fee for a yacht he plans on using for twenty-four hours. I should find it obnoxious, but then again, if he wants to spend millions to help his kid have the trip of a lifetime, I can't fault him for trying.

I'm not sure what brought on the drastic change to our plans, but I'm not about to complain about spending the day on a yacht, although it does make me a little queasy when I think about Rafael's bank statement and the fishing boat from the other day.

An hour later, the hired car drops us off at a private marina. Nico is already a hundred feet in front of us because he wants to analyze every single boat before we find ours.

"Did you take your Dramamine?" Rafael asks while rolling our luggage.

"No?" With this morning's craziness, I completely forgot about it.

Rafael reaches inside his carry-on duffel bag and pulls out a tube. "Here."

"You have some too?"

"Since you forgot it on the last boat, I thought it would be good to have some on me just in case."

"How thoughtful." Usually, I would find something like that romantic, but after last night's conversation, it angers me.

He looks at me with a frown. "You're still upset about last night."

"No. I'm *upset* that you keep sending me mixed signals," I say with a bit of bite.

His face crumples. "I'm just trying to be nice."

"Well, maybe you should stop, because from my point of view, it's coming off like you're interested, even though we both know you won't do anything about it." My voice shakes at the end, and I wish I could take back what I said immediately. I don't want him to know how much his words from last night affected me. How much they *hurt*. It feels like I'm betraying myself and opening up my heart even more to someone who doesn't want it.

He rejected me. Simple as that. The sooner I accept my new reality, the better for both of us.

I'm not even sure why I'm so upset, especially when this is the best option for my job, but I am. Maybe it's because I was willing to put my position as Nico's nanny on the line for Rafael, only for him to put me right back in my place while single-handedly making me feel like a fool.

Rafael mutters something to himself in Spanish that I don't understand before passing me an unopened can of strawberry-lemon fizzy water from the same carry-on bag. "Here."

My heart does a little jolt at the sight, but I squash the feeling of hope with a mental fist.

If our conversation taught me anything, it's that Rafael can be nice and thoughtful, but it is up to me to keep my head on straight and remember it can never be more than that.

I don't protest as I throw a Dramamine pill into my mouth, take a sip of my drink, and resume our walk. We easily catch up to Nico, who remained standing in front of a gray superyacht.

"Is this it?" Nico asks.

Rafael shakes his head. "Keep going."

Nico pauses a few boats down, this one even bigger than the last few. "What about this one?"

"No. We're all the way down there." Rafael points toward the end of the dock, where a yacht the size of a cruise ship is currently docked.

I stop midstride. "You're joking."

"Hopefully you find the size satisfactory this time." His lips quirk.

The bastard didn't rent a yacht to take us from Oahu to Kauai. He chartered a *ship*.

Nico takes off running toward it, and I follow behind him and his father, my steps mechanical and my spine stiff.

The fiberglass and metal handrails gleam under the sun, temporarily blinding me until I put on my sunglasses. A small crew waves at us from the different levels while a few of the members are already hopping off the boat and grabbing our luggage from us.

I look over at Rafael, whose eyes are hidden behind a pair of black Ray-Bans. "You chartered *that* to take us from here to Kauai?"

"Yes."

"Isn't that a bit…excessive?"

He shrugs. "It's much more fun than a plane for you."

My chest feels uncomfortably tight all of a sudden. "Please tell me you didn't do this all for me."

"Okay. I won't."

Nico grins. "But he did!"

"*Nicolas*," Rafael says his name with an exasperated sigh.

"It's true! He didn't want you to be scared about the plane."

I'm not sure what to make of all this. I would have survived a forty-minute flight from Oahu to Kauai, but Rafael planning this instead makes me…

Angry? Happy? So damn sad, knowing he may be thoughtful but it will never extend beyond that?

All of the above seems like a fitting answer.

Rafael sends him a scathing look that sends his son rushing up the gangway with a giggle. "See you inside!"

"You can't say what you did last night and then do things like this anymore," I say in a hushed whisper, not to draw attention from the crew smiling down at us.

"Why not?"

"It's giving me emotional whiplash."

He seems to sit with my statement for a moment. "I'm sorry. I'll try to be more...cognizant of that."

Now, *I* feel like a major jerk, so I offer an olive branch. "I appreciate the thought, though. Thanks to you, I can officially scratch *someone rented a two-hundred-foot yacht for me* off my bucket list."

I can't see his eyes, but I can tell he is rolling them. "Elle?"

"I hate when you call me that."

"Yet you haven't asked me to stop."

I frown.

"I'm sorry for the mixed signals, but just try to enjoy it. For me, please?" He walks onto the gangway like it's his own personal billionaire runway.

I stare at it without responding.

He sighs. "If it makes you feel any better, Nico was the one who picked this boat out."

I look up at him. "This isn't a boat, Rafael. It's a *vessel*."

"Well, you *did* ask me to charter a yacht."

"I was joking!"

He scratches his head obnoxiously. "Huh. You seemed serious."

I shoot him a look from behind my sunglasses as I follow him onto the back platform.

"We're ready when you are, sir." The captain tips his hat in Rafael's direction.

Twenty-four hours on a yacht with Rafael and Nico sounds like a fun expedition, so what could possibly go wrong?

If I had to guess, based on the way Rafael keeps looking at me when he thinks I am not paying attention, the answer is simple.

Everything.

CHAPTER THIRTY-FIVE

Ellie

It takes exactly thirty minutes after we left Oahu and the glittering shoreline of Honolulu for my heart to start acting up again. The little skip in my chest began as soon as Rafael sauntered out of his cabin in nothing but a bathing suit and that same pair of Ray-Bans.

I was supposed to remain strong, but one look at him applying sunscreen like a social media thirst trap sent my thoughts straight into the gutter, and I haven't been able to find my way out since.

I fight to keep my tongue in my mouth as I check him out. His body is something most people *wish* to achieve when they hire a personal trainer and are blessed with the right genetics, so I can't help marveling at it.

The first thing I notice are his abs, followed by his bright lobster-print swim trunks that match the ones Nico selected to wear this morning. It's a silly pattern that Dahlia purchased for the two of them, and one I imagine Rafael only wears because it makes his son happy.

The swim trunks stop halfway down Rafael's thick thighs, showing off a set of Herculean-sized calves he has earned from his daily workouts.

At some point between him finishing his sunscreen application and walking over to me with a smile, I've lost my ability to speak.

"Eleanor?"

"Hm?" Those damn butterflies in my stomach start acting up again, their invisible wings fluttering uncontrollably as I rip my gaze away from Rafael's toned, glistening chest.

"You good?" He wields his smile like a weapon aimed straight for my heart.

"Why wouldn't I be?" My stomach flips, and it has nothing to do with the boat rocking to the side as we break through another wave.

"Because you didn't even make a fuss when I called you Eleanor."

"Mm-hmm." I'm too distracted by the defined muscles of his hips to pay attention to the words coming out of his mouth.

"Nico should be out in a couple of minutes. He's on the phone with my aunt, who says hi, by the way."

"Great." I try to keep my gaze above his shoulders, but it dips toward his abs.

He leans against the rail beside me and looks out at the rippling waves. "It's a nice day."

"Yup."

"Your speechlessness is doing wonders for my ego, by the way."

I turn with heated cheeks and stare out at the horizon. "I was…assessing."

His knowing smirk could make me drop dead right here, right now.

At least my last view would be nice.

"Is that what we call *checking someone out* nowadays?" he asks.

Part of me wants to flirt back, but after last night, I need to keep my distance for my heart's sake.

"I should see if Nico needs any help," I say instead.

He turns to look out at the sea with a frown. "Yeah. Good idea."

I take advantage of my moment of clarity and head back inside the yacht before I say or do something else I'll regret, although I struggle to forget the look on Rafael's face before I left.

He was the one who made his stance about us clear, so why should I feel bad about him appearing rejected?

Because you like him, whether he feels the same way about you or not.

According to Rafael, whatever Nico wants on the yacht, Nico gets, so long as it doesn't require me doing anything that could make me sick. Rafael thinking of my well-being was sweet and a gesture I greatly appreciated after Nico wanted to go wake-boarding and tubing.

Just the idea of being on the smaller boat made my stomach turn, so I hung out on the back deck, watching the two of them from the yacht instead. Nico is decent at wakeboarding since Rafael and Julian have been taking him out on the lake for years, but his father is something else entirely.

I should expect nothing less from someone so athletic, but watching him was an experience I didn't know I needed to witness firsthand. Strained muscles. Bright smiles. Washboard abs clenching and muscles straining with every jump, turn, and spin.

At one point, I'm wondering if Rafael was trying to show off with all his flips and tricks, but I keep my suspicions to myself when he comes back aboard with a smile. Nico becomes excited by whatever he sees on the horizon and disappears into his cabin for the binoculars he packed.

Rafael finds me on the deck—accidentally, it seems, based on the way he freezes midstride before walking over to my spot.

"What have you been up to?" Rafael asks.

I pretend to be consumed by whatever doodles I drew beside a few half-finished song lyrics. "Not much."

He folds his arms against his chest. "Working on the song?"

"Trying to." I shut my notebook and look up at him. Water drips down his face and hair before trickling across his tanned torso, but I don't let my eyes linger there for long.

No matter how much they want to.

"How's it going?" He looks at the cover of my notebook, completely unaware of the lyrics hidden between the pages inspired by *him*.

I tuck it under my leg just in case. "Why does it matter?"

His eyes narrow. "I'm being polite."

"No need to try so hard on my behalf."

His lips press together. "Are you still upset with me about last night?"

Yes, but I'd rather die than listen to him bring up that subject again. "Nope. Just struggling with Cole's song."

Shit. I did *not* mean to admit that.

A frown line appears between his brows. "So you two are working together now?"

My heart beats harder in my chest. "Yes, but it won't get in the way of my current job, so don't worry."

"That's not what I'm worried about." A dark look passes over him.

I know provoking him is a terrible idea, but after the way he pushed me away last night, I want to get under his skin like he does mine. To leave a permanent mark like the one he left on me.

Using his jealousy against Cole is petty, immature, and a strategy I've never employed before, but screw it.

I throw my hair over my shoulder and flash a smile. "Yeah. Cole's been so great and supportive with the whole lawyer thing. He even went out of his way to set up a meeting for me."

Rafael's left eye twitches. "I wasn't aware you needed to speak to a lawyer."

"I know."

"I could have helped."

"Yeah, but Cole offered. Can you imagine someone being that nice without wanting something in return?"

"Oh, I'm sure he wants something," he mutters under his breath.

"What was that?" I bat my lashes.

"He wants *you*."

"Huh. That could be fun, plus, who knows? Maybe he's *the one*."

"You deserve better than a guy like him." His sour expression makes me want to smile.

Rafael Lopez is jealous of another man because of *me*. My heart does a little squeeze at the idea because being the cause of his jealousy for once makes me downright giddy.

Based on the tension in his face and shoulders, Rafael most likely hates himself for it, which only makes the realization that much sweeter. He may not *want* to feel this way, but he can't help it.

Rafael is good at hiding his true feelings behind a mask, and I desperately want to tear it off, even if it gets me in trouble.

"Keep talking like that, and I may start to think you're jealous."

"I'm not jealous."

"No?" *Liar*, I tell myself as I stand and rake my nails over his chest.

His hands curl into two tight balls. "*No.*"

A small laugh breaks free, and before I have a chance to stop myself, I ask, "Is it that hard to admit you care about someone besides Nico and your family?"

"Yes," he says with a hiss.

"Why?"

He doesn't pause to think. To breathe. To even second-guess his killer blow before he delivers it. "*They* haven't given me a reason not to trust them."

I stumble back a step. "I thought…" I'm so hurt by his statement, I can't even finish the sentence without giving myself away.

"What? That you would magically have my trust again only two weeks after you broke it?" His harsh words make me feel foolish because I *did* think that.

I was living in a fantasy, thinking we could rebuild whatever trust we both broke. If I'm being honest, I should have taken him thinking I would lie about winning a stupid sandcastle championship as a warning sign, but I ignored it, just like the others I turned a blind eye to.

Rafael was absolutely right when he said we were wrong for each other, but I didn't listen. Instead, I wanted to make him jealous about Cole to prove some stupid point that didn't need proving in the first place—and look where it got me.

A whole bunch of heartache. *Again.*

Tears of frustration spring to my eyes, and I blink them away. Crying in front of someone is bad enough, but doing so in front of the person that brought the tears out in the first place?

Embarrassing.

Rafael reaches out, a silent apology written across his face, but I take another step back.

"You're right. I did think you could trust me, but it clearly was a big mistake." I grab my notebook, turn toward the stairs, and walk away with my head held high, pretending Rafael didn't rip my heart out for the second time in twenty-four hours.

Hopefully, I learned my lesson for the final time.

Rafael Lopez keeps his inner circle tight, and it's time I realized I will always be on the outside looking in.

CHAPTER THIRTY-SIX

Rafael

I screwed up big time. That much becomes painfully clear when Ellie walks away, pretending my words didn't affect her when I know for a fact that they did. Her pain was as obvious as the tears threatening to fall, and instead of feeling satisfied at driving her away, I feel a huge sense of loss.

I haven't been able to shake the same feeling since last night, when I told her we were all wrong for each other, and her attempt today at making me jealous only amplified the sensation.

I like Ellie, but I'm terrified of giving in to my feelings and getting hurt after the way my last relationship turned out, so I keep pushing her away. Keep making up excuses and finding a million different reasons why we wouldn't work. Some may be valid, but that doesn't make the truth hurt any less.

If I were a different person, I would date her in a heartbeat, but I'm not.

I'm a screwed-up orphan with enough trust issues to keep a therapist on speed dial, while she is beautiful, compassionate, and far too perfect for someone like me. I would break her before she ever had a chance to do the same to me, and the thought of that happening makes me sick to my stomach.

Despite my reasons for keeping her at a distance, I'm still hit with guilt that is so overwhelming, I feel like I'm being choked by it. It grabs me by the throat, making it impossible to breathe.

With a heart full of dread, I head downstairs to find my son on the front deck, looking out at the ocean with a pair of binoculars pressed against his glasses.

"*Hola, Papi.*" Nico offers me a chance to use them, but I shake my head and take a seat on the chair beside him instead.

"Are you okay?" he asks.

"Mm." I don't want to burden my child with my problems, so I fake a smile and try Ellie's favorite trick to distract him.

"I spy…"

Nico beams. "What?"

I look around the yacht. "Something red."

Nico drops the binoculars and scans the deck. "Um…the towel?" He points at the pink-and-white striped one beneath me.

My chest, which was already uncomfortably tight after my conversation with Ellie, aches.

"Nope."

He frowns. "Hm."

I readjust my position on purpose, drawing Nico's attention to the lobsters on my swim trunks.

"Your bathing suit!"

"You got it." My small smile doesn't reach my eyes.

His roll. "Only because you gave me a hint." He taps his chin. "I spy...something white!"

"The clouds?"

"Nope."

"The fiberglass on the boat?"

He shakes his head, and I spend the next few minutes looking around for something white before choosing something that is pale yellow.

"The deck chairs?"

"Yes! Finally!"

My chest twinges again. I'm not sure how to continue our game, especially given Nico struggling to differentiate between similar-looking colors. If Ellie were here, she would say something to lighten the mood and make me feel better.

Too bad you pushed her away yet again.

Nico frowns. "What's wrong?"

I break eye contact and stare out at the ocean. "I made a mistake."

"Oh." He frowns. "What happened?"

"I hurt someone's feelings."

"Did you say sorry?"

"No."

He laughs to himself. "But you've got to say sorry first! You taught me that."

"I don't know if sorry is going to work this time." I seriously doubt Ellie would accept any apology from me that doesn't come with a personality shift.

He cuddles up to my side. I prop my chin on the top of his head and wrap my arms around him, and together, we stare out at the ocean for a few minutes before he loses patience.

"Why did you hurt the other person's feelings?"

I'm so caught off guard by his question, I ask him to repeat it.

"The person you hurt. Why did you do it?" he asks.

It takes me a few seconds to consider a good enough response for a nine-year-old kid. "I was scared."

"Of what?"

"Getting too close to them."

"Hm." He snuggles deeper into my chest.

"What?"

"I get scared of getting close to people too."

"You do?"

He starts tracing invisible patterns on my chest. "I don't want them to leave one day." He pauses to take a shaky breath. "Like Mommy did."

I crush his body against mine. "I don't want that either."

Seeing as my own mom left my dad and me, I understand Nico's fear. It was one that I never truly got over, in part because my father never helped me process it in the first place. I wasn't allowed to grieve my mother, let alone show any sadness about her leaving.

Boys don't cry, he told me whenever I thought about my mom.

I'll give you a real reason to shed some tears if you keep it up, he said while high as a kite on whatever he scored that week.

Unlike my father, I want to give Nico a safe space to talk out his feelings, regardless of how I personally feel about his mother. In the end, we were both to blame for our marriage failing.

Instead of understanding myself better before getting into a serious relationship at only seventeen, I picked the first woman I formed a bond with, whether it was a good one or not, and clung to her. And just like my parents, I've allowed my negative relationship with my ex-wife to impact the way I connect with others.

With Ellie.

I tighten my hold around my son. "Sometimes people leave, no matter how much we want them to stay."

His shoulders slump with defeat. "That's not fair."

"I know."

"What's the point of letting people get close, then?"

I consider his question. I've done a thorough job at keeping people at a distance, but what has it gotten me besides chronic loneliness? I've spent so much time avoiding people in general because I thought I would be better off not forming connections, but I'm far from happy.

I kiss the top of his head. "Because life is about finding the right people who *want* to stay and making sure neither of you ever let go."

I stare out at the ocean with Nico tucked against my side, wishing I could save him from any more hurt while also acknowledging that there isn't anything I can do to stop it from happening.

All I can do is be a positive role model for him so he doesn't fall into the same harmful patterns I did. I don't want him to be wary of everyone because that is no way to live. I've spent the last two years doing that, and I have been nothing but miserable.

I want to be better. For Nico. For Ellie. For *me*.

And I want to start now.

The rest of the day is spent feeling uncomfortable, with Ellie only speaking to me when absolutely necessary. Nico carries the conversation throughout dinner while Ellie answers his questions without trying to include me. It is painful to know I stole her happiness, especially when I compare the way she is acting to our previous dinners.

Before, she was bright-eyed and expressive, pulling me into conversations whether I wanted to engage or not, but now she can hardly look at me.

It makes me feel like absolute shit, and I need to fix things before they spiral out of my control.

Later that night, once Nico falls asleep, I knock on Ellie's cabin door. She doesn't answer right away, but I can make out the faint sound of a strumming guitar through the crack.

I tap my knuckles against the door harder. "Ellie."

The strumming stops, but the door remains shut.

"Can we talk about earlier, please?"

No response.

"I want to apologize," I say a minute later when she still hasn't opened the door. "I know I don't deserve it, but if you give me a chance, I'd like to explain the real reason why I said what I did today."

My heart beats faster in my chest as I silently wait. The vein in my neck pulses with each rapid thump of my heart, and I consider giving up and walking away, but my feet won't move.

Thankfully, I don't have to. The sound of a lock turning, followed by hinges softly creaking as the door opens, makes my stomach lurch.

Ellie blocks the entrance to her cabin with a frown. Her black and white striped pajama top and pants are a perfect match, and while I like the outfit, I miss seeing her tattoos.

She crosses her arms. "I'm tired, Rafael."

"We can talk tomo—"

She doesn't let me finish my sentence. "No. I'm *tired*." She emphasizes the word. "It's exhausting trying to get to know you, and honestly, I don't know if it's worth it anymore."

She doesn't need a weapon to tear into me and do some damage. Her words are enough, cutting me off at the knees.

I deserve it, but that doesn't make it hurt any less.

She continues, "I was wrong for how I behaved earlier. I let our...um"—she gestures between us without saying the damn word I know she means—"cloud my judgment, and for that, I'm sorry. It was inappropriate for me to push you like that."

"Regardless, I shouldn't have said what I did."

"Why? You were just being honest. I know you don't trust me and never will, so you might as well put me in my place so I don't embarrass myself anymore."

"I hate that I made you feel that way," I say with a frown.

"Why?"

"Because I care."

Her bitter laugh sounds all wrong. "You have a funny way of showing it."

"What do you want me to do?"

"Leave me be."

"I can't."

"Why? You've done it for eight months already, so it can't be that difficult."

"That was before."

"Before *what*?"

"I realized just how *much* I care."

CHAPTER THIRTY-SEVEN

Ellie

I told myself that I wouldn't fall for another one of Rafael's apologies. I've done it before, and look what it got me.

Disappointment. Frustration. *Heartache.*

I'm done letting him pull me in, only to shove me away the moment things get a little too real between us. It isn't fair to keep putting myself in that position in the hopes of us moving forward.

He was right all along.

I *do* deserve the kind of love they write songs about. Not sad ones like the ones I enjoy writing, but the happy kind that people dance to at weddings because they flawlessly describe what it feels like to love and be loved.

"You know what I want?" I ask with a hint of anger.

He seems confused by my question. "What?"

My anger emboldens me. "Someone who cares about me so

damn much, they would do everything possible to *protect* me rather than *hurt* me, and I'm quickly coming to realize you're not that man. At least not with me."

I've seen the way Rafael acts toward people he cares about. The way he treats Nico, Julian, his aunt, and the Muñoz family. His support, patience, and loyalty are unwavering, and he trusts them enough to let them in.

Because they never gave him a reason not to, I remind myself, echoing his earlier words.

A deep-rooted sadness takes hold of his expression. "What if I wanted to be that man? For you?"

"What?" Shock replaces whatever frustration I felt before. He was supposed to agree with what I said, not challenge me.

"I did a lot of thinking today." He lets the statement hang.

I stick to silence.

"Do you mind if we take a seat for this conversation?" He tips his chin toward the sitting area inside my cabin.

"Is that such a good idea?"

"I'd rather not open up to you in the middle of a hallway, if that's all right."

I consider telling him no and sending him away, but my curiosity won't let me. With a sigh, I open the door wider, giving him enough room to enter. "Don't make me regret this."

He keeps close, intentionally brushing against me as he walks inside. "You won't."

I shut the door harder than necessary, closing us off completely from the rest of the ship. His gaze flicks between the couch and the chair before he chooses the former.

I take a seat on the chair, cross my legs, and wait.

Rafael uncurls his clenched hands and looks up at me. "About what I said earlier…"

I don't speak. Don't breathe. Don't even blink while he gathers the courage to continue.

He stares at his hands like they hold all the answers to the universe. "I have trouble trusting people."

I nod.

"I've always been that way, ever since I was a little kid." He releases another shaky breath. "I thought if I kept people at a distance, they wouldn't be able to hurt me."

I dig my fingers into my knees to stop myself from reaching out and grabbing his hand. "Sounds lonely."

"It was for a while…"

"But?"

His mouth opens, only to slam shut before he wipes a hand down his face. "I haven't told anyone this before."

I blink twice. "No one?"

"Not a single soul besides my previous therapist."

"What about your family?"

He shakes his head. "I didn't want them to look at me differently."

My fickle little heart clenches at the revelation.

At the *trust*.

But the tiny voice in my head reminds me that I've been burned too many times by Rafael to get my hopes up. "Why are you telling me, then? You don't even trust me."

He takes a few moments to meet my gaze, but when he does, I can see his guard dropping. It starts with the softening of his frown, followed by the lessening of the tension lines by his eyes, all before he reveals the broken man hiding behind a grumpy exterior.

I see him, not as a weak person, but as someone strong enough to be vulnerable with me, knowing I could possibly hurt him. That I could take his secret and use it against him if I wanted to.

I've always thought he was handsome, but in this moment...

He is *beautiful*.

His short inhale breaks the silence. "I can't expect you to earn my trust if I don't give you a chance to keep it."

I look away first, unable to bear the weight of *that* particular stare for longer than a few seconds. "Okay."

Saying anything else would betray how much his statement means to me, and after how he behaved earlier, he hasn't earned my vulnerability.

Yet.

His deep breath fills the quiet. "I developed this screwed-up mindset at a young age about relationships. That if I became the version of myself that I thought people wanted me to be, then they wouldn't ever want to leave me."

My bottom lip wobbles, so I bite down on it to hide just how much his words affect me. Was any of it real, or was the man who caught my attention in high school and earned the Best Smile superlative always faking it solely because he didn't want to be abandoned again?

The thought of it being the latter makes my heart feel like someone stabbed it with a thousand needles.

He continues, "I was a people pleaser to a fault, but it didn't feel like a sacrifice because I had what I thought I wanted.

Family. Friends. *Security.*" His upper lip curls. "Moving to Lake Wisteria gave me an opportunity to reinvent myself, and in the process, I convinced myself that I was happy."

"But you weren't."

"No, but I tricked myself into believing I was."

"Why?"

"Because I didn't want to give my aunt and uncle a reason to get rid of me."

My chin trembles.

He looks away. "I'm not telling you this for you to feel bad for me."

I don't feel bad. I'm *heartbroken*, knowing he struggled with so much at such a young age. Knowing how much it still affects him all these years later.

A wrinkle appears between his brows from how hard he frowns. "That kind of mindset applied to a lot of my relationships, including the one with my ex-wife."

The knot of dread in my stomach tightens.

"I already had trust issues before her, but she only made them worse."

I can't speak.

"And then she accidentally got pregnant despite promising me she was on birth control."

Breathing becomes an impossible task, and my lungs burn as if I just inhaled a bucket of water. The knee-jerk reaction to speak hits me, but I press my lips together and sit quietly while he takes a few more breaths.

His laugh is rough and bitter. "I was already screwed up before, but that made a bad situation ten times worse." He pauses before speaking again. "But despite the *surprise*, I felt… happy."

He looks through me rather than at me, clearly lost in a memory from the past. "I was twenty-two and scared as hell, obviously. It wasn't like I had a fancy future at an Ivy League university like Julian and Dahlia, and I was fine with that because I never bothered applying to college in the first place, but I still had dreams. The small paychecks I earned while working for my uncle's construction company were enough when I was only worried about myself, but everything changed after that positive test."

"Did you want to be a dad?"

"I hadn't given much thought to it before, but once Hillary told me the news, I realized how much I wanted it. The pregnancy wasn't planned, *obviously*, but it didn't matter to me because I knew from the moment I heard that heartbeat that Nico would change my life forever, and I was right."

"That you were." I can't help my smile.

He tries and fails to match it. "Hillary seemed excited about becoming a mother too, but I eventually realized her reasons were different from mine."

An eerie chill slithers down my spine. "What do you mean?"

"Before she got pregnant, things were…tense between us."

Shock steals my ability to speak, so I stare at his face and wait for him to continue.

"We had already broken up twice before—both times because she wanted to—so our relationship wasn't exactly solid and ready for the next step. If anything, I was the one who was questioning if we could make it long-term."

"Do you think…"

"That she got pregnant on purpose?"

I nod.

"I had my suspicions, but I never voiced them because it didn't seem worth the trouble. What was done was done, and I had Nico because of it, so getting angry at her seemed hypocritical when I was so damn excited."

"You didn't think it was *worth the trouble* to find out if the mother of your child tricked you into having one?"

He shrugs, but I can tell the idea bothers him, whether he wants to admit it or not. "She said she forgot to take her pill for a few days, and I took her word for it." He shakes his head. "Mistake number one, but whatever. We were going to be parents, whether she really thought out her choices or not."

"But why did you marry her?"

He makes a face.

"What?" I ask.

A flush crawls up his neck and bleeds into his cheeks. "Her parents insisted."

"What century were they born in again?"

"The one where they would disown her and liquidate her trust if I didn't do what they wanted. It wasn't a huge sum of money, but she had enough that getting cut off financially would hurt."

"What about your uncle's construction company?" I forgot the name before Julian rebranded it as Lopez Luxury.

"My aunt was struggling with depression after my uncle died so suddenly, and Julian was trying to help her and run a whole company at twenty years old with hardly any experience. I helped as much as I could, but the business was going under."

"Sounds like a nightmare."

"Marrying her was a temporary solution anyway. I never wanted a handout, especially from her parents, but with Julian struggling to make the construction company profitable and my first few app ideas being massive failures, it was either accept her parents' help or become exactly like my parents."

"That's…"

"My worst nightmare." His gaze falls to his empty hands. "Even though I knew I'd never turn to drugs or other vices like them, the idea of struggling with money and bills like they had pushed me to make a desperate decision that I'm not proud of."

"That's not fair." My voice cracks.

His smile doesn't reach his eyes. "If I learned one thing, it's that life never is."

My mom taught me long ago that people make big sacrifices for security and peace of mind, and we can't judge them for their choices unless we have walked in their shoes, but I can still hurt for him and the fact that he married someone he wasn't sure about because of his past trauma.

And I hurt a lot.

I stop pulling at a loose thread on my sleep pants. "Why did you stay married to her after you became a billionaire, then? It's not like you needed her parents' money anymore."

He stares at me.

"What?"

"Do you really want to hear that answer?"

"Yes?" Or at least I *thought* so until he asked me that.

"It took some time, but things got better between us. Nico brought us together, and we were this happy little family for a few years. I thought we were both committed to making the marriage work." His disapproving laugh cuts through me like a knife. "But once Nico went to Pre-K, cracks started forming again, this time worse than before. She went back to work, and I was focused on managing a construction job while trying to get the Dwelling app off the ground. We were growing apart, but it was easier to ignore the signs and hope things would get better like last time. I even suggested having another child at one point, which seemed to freak her out."

"But things didn't get better."

He shakes his head. "No. They weren't bad, but only because she was biding her time until my app finally became the success her father claimed it would be." His voice *shakes*. "He was my first investor, so he had been there since the beginning. He knew exactly what was happening behind-the-scenes and how much Hillary stood to earn if the company went public, although I had no clue until I filed for divorce." His bitter laugh sends a chill down my spine.

Bile churns in my stomach. "She stuck around because of money?"

His throat tightens as he nods. "Her parents said she owed them for helping us from the beginning. That's why she stayed despite falling in love with one of her coworkers."

Before I speak, he continues, "I think part of me loved her, which is why it hurt so much. I thought she *cared* about me, only to realize she was a better pretender than I was."

"Rafael..." I want to pull him into a hug, but I remain

seated, my heart physically aching at not being able to provide him with some type of comfort.

I've never felt this way before. Never wanted to soothe someone so badly that it pained me to stay away. I don't know what to make of it, but the burn in my chest doesn't relent until I walk over and take a seat beside him.

I wind my arms around him and pull until we are pressed against each other. At first, he stiffens, but after a few passes of my hand down the center of his back, his muscles loosen, and he lets out a sigh. His hand rests on the inside of my thigh, sending tingles up my leg that I do my best to ignore.

He tries so damn hard to disguise his shaky breath. "Her affair had been going on for over a year, but I was so focused on my damn company going public that I hadn't noticed. I should have known it was strange that she kept working since we finally had the money to support her being a stay-at-home mom like she wanted, but I just assumed she liked her job." His laugh is bitter and full of self-loathing.

I press my palm against his cheek. "It's not your fault someone took advantage of your trust."

"I try to tell myself that, but the signs were all there. If I had just stopped to pay attention, I could have saved myself a lot of pain, time, and money."

"It was an honest mistake."

"I seem to make a lot of those."

"Do you know what that makes you?"

"Stupid?"

"*Human*."

He stares into the distance while I look at him, taking in every single detail of his face.

Rafael may be handsome, but what makes him truly breathtaking is his heart. It's no mystery why he wants to protect it, especially after everything he divulged about Hillary and her family.

Do I blame him for his issues trusting others? No. Not at all, especially after what he went through. If I were in his position, I'm sure I'd struggle to do the same, which only makes me empathize with him more.

I'm not sure how long we sit there in silence, but he is the first one to speak.

"What I said about not trusting you earlier…"

"I understand why you can't." I didn't know all the details about his divorce before, but now that I do… No wonder he never wants to get married again. I'm not sure if I could either.

He shakes his head. "That's not what I mean."

"Oh."

His inhale is a long, drawn-out one that makes my heart stutter. "I spoke to Nico today and realized that he and I have a certain thing in common."

"What?"

"We both struggle to let people get close."

A small laugh escapes me. "Oh, tell me about it. Do you remember how much hell Nico gave me during his first month of music lessons?" I considered pawning him off to another tutor, but then Burt reminded me of the little terror I was when I first started at The Broken Chord, so I persevered.

Eventually, Nico opened up just like I had hoped, and his love has been a gift ever since.

Rafael's gaze locks onto mine. "Yeah, which reminded me that if my son learned to let you in, then so can I."

"You don't have to."

"I don't, but I *want* to." He gives my thigh a squeeze that goes straight to my heart, and it has nothing to do with my fear of him noticing the scars hidden underneath my sleep pants. "Just like I want to forgive you for keeping Nico's worsening vision a secret."

The pressure valve in my chest opens. "Thank you."

His head drops back with a sigh as he leans against the couch. "Talking about this…it feels better than I thought."

"People say *the truth will set you free* for a reason."

His laugh is soft yet so damn strong at the same time. My eyes dart toward his lips. The slipup lasts only a second, but Rafael seems to catch it before his mouth pulls into the cockiest smirk to ever exist.

I want to kiss it right off his stupid face.

"You've got a terrible poker face," he says.

I tap my temple. "Maybe that's what I *want* you to think."

"So you don't want to kiss me right now?"

Well, shit.

CHAPTER THIRTY-EIGHT

Ellie

blink a few times. "Would it matter if I did?"

"Maybe."

"Why? It's not like you'd do anything about it."

The imaginary crowd in my head goes wild.

Rafael's fingers flex before forming a fist, and I, the *hopeful-slash-hopeless romantic*, believe it's because of me.

"We shouldn't," he states carefully.

I nod. "Nope."

His eyes drop to my mouth. "It's a bad idea."

"I agree. A terrible idea that could have serious repercussions for both of us."

His thigh brushes against mine as he sits up. "Plus, it could be the worst kiss I've ever had."

"Yeah, you're right. You look like the type who uses way too much tongue anyway."

He half scoffs, half laughs. "If you find me using too much tongue, it better be while my head is between your legs."

My soul leaves my body.

He twists so we're fully facing each other. "No comeback for that one?"

"Give me a minute. I'm sure one will come."

"No pun intended?" He cups my flaming cheek.

"What are you doing?" I pull back, but his other hand snakes around my back and secures me in place.

"I have a reputation to uphold."

"*A reputation to uphold?*" I gawk. "What in the *Jane Austen* hell is that kind of statement?"

His lips quirk. "You're the one who accused me of using too much tongue."

"Fine. I take it back."

His thumb delicately brushes over my cheekbone. "Too late." His hand moves to the back of my neck and presses until our mouths are hovering a few centimeters apart. "My honor is at stake."

"Are you talking like a character from a regency novel on purpose or…"

"Elle."

"Yeah?"

"Shut up and kiss me already."

Him giving me the power to decide if I *want* to kiss him means more to me than he will ever know.

I nearly give in, but then I remember why I should be saying no in the first place. After today's spout of jealousy on the boat,

I learned my lesson, and it's time I redraw the professional line in the metaphorical sand.

With a deep sigh, I say, "I don't think it's a good idea."

The girl who had a crush on him seems to disagree.

What's the harm in a single kiss? I've kissed plenty of guys before, and some of them I had hardly known at the time, so it doesn't have to be a big deal until I make it one.

Right?

His hand around my neck tightens, sending a zing of pleasure down my spine before he releases me and starts to pull away.

Shit.

No.

My heart sinks faster than a stone in the ocean, forcing me to act now, face the consequences later.

I hold up my index finger. "Fine. One kiss. For research purposes."

His palm slides up my spine, making me suck in a breath before it returns to the spot he favors at the base of my neck. "You're something else."

"You can call me crazy. It's okay."

"You're more than that." He kisses the corner of my mouth, making my heart jolt like I just took some electric paddles to the chest.

I don't get to ask him to elaborate because my mind goes completely blank once his lips press against mine.

My thoughts quiet and my body turns numb as the whole world ceases to exist before it comes roaring back to life.

My toes curl. My spine tingles. And my heart could simply

burst as Rafael Lopez kisses me like he was born to. Like his lips were created to perfectly match the shape of mine.

He is slow at first, and I follow his pace. It is torture of the best kind, especially when he groans against my lips and sinks his fingers deeper into my hair.

When he doesn't show an initiative to explore more, I'm the one who teases him. First, with my hands running over his chest and arms, and then with the flick of my tongue across the seam of his mouth.

His soft groan, barely audible over the sound of our breathing, spurs me on. With a scrape of my teeth against his bottom lip, he opens, and things shift.

One moment, we are sitting face-to-face. The next, I'm underneath him with my back pressed against the couch cushions and his mouth devouring mine. It isn't a soft claiming but rather a full-blown takeover of my mind and body.

I absolutely love every single second of it, and the thought of it only happening once makes my heart heavy.

I'm not sure how long we kiss, but a knot forms in my throat as I feel Rafael slowing down. I cling to him without meaning to, and he rewards my burst of need with another deep, toe-curling kiss that leaves me breathless and aching for more.

Kissing him feels so damn *right* that I fear everyone else will always feel *wrong*.

It hits me then that our deal was a stupid one from the moment we made it. A thousand kisses wouldn't be enough, let alone *one*.

I can't find it in me to regret it, though. I *refuse* to because I'd rather know what it feels like to kiss Rafael once than to never have experienced it at all.

He pulls back to look me in the eyes.

"Did I disprove your hypothesis?" he asks with that sexy smirk of his.

"I'm afraid not," I lie.

His eyes narrow jokingly. "You liar."

"There, there. Not everyone can be good at everything." I pat his chest, noting how fast his heart is beating. It fills me with satisfaction to know I'm not the only one affected by a single kiss.

"I'm not everyone."

"Nope, you're just the someone who uses too much tongue."

He leans in, and I sharply inhale as his lips nearly touch mine. "Let's try again."

"We agreed to only one," I say, a little too breathless.

His burning gaze meets mine. "I'm open to renegotiation."

"No." Especially not after he made me feel like *that* with a single kiss. My head is still spinning, and it doesn't look like it'll be stopping anytime soon.

"If that's what you want…" He rotates his hips, and I suck in a breath as his hard length presses into me.

Stopping him from doing more isn't what I want, but it's what we *need*. That and some new boundaries because this man has been tearing them down left and right.

We don't have a future, or at least not one that includes kisses like *that*. It becomes painfully clear that Rafael can be my *friend* but nothing more, for not only my sake but for his son, who needs me.

With a reluctant sigh, Rafael rolls off me and stands before offering me his hand to help me sit up. He doesn't let go even after I'm upright, so I'm the one who has to pull away this time.

"Where do we go from here?" He tucks his hands behind his back.

"Perhaps we could be friends." I hate the idea as soon as it leaves my mouth, but it's too late.

"Friends?" He sounds as surprised as he looks.

"You do remember what it's like to have one that isn't related to you, right?"

His gaze sharpens. "Do you kiss all your *friends* like that, or am I an exception to the rule?"

My whole face becomes engulfed in invisible flames.

"Just teasing you, Elle." He pauses to think. "If you want to be friends, then I can do that." He *smiles,* and my heart rate climbs until I can feel my pulse racing in my neck.

I've made a huge mistake tonight. Well, *two* mistakes, to be exact. The first was thinking I could kiss Rafael once and end it at that, while the second was even worse.

We could be friends.

I want to smack my head and mouth at the same time for suggesting such a thing. Men like Rafael aren't the type you befriend. They're the kind you could *fall in love with*, whether you want to or not, because they have this magnetism that draws you into their orbit.

I fell into this black hole in high school when I first

developed a crush on him, and I'm falling into a similar pattern, although this time, I'm not crushing on a person who never truly existed.

I'm developing feelings for the real Rafael, and it absolutely terrifies me.

CHAPTER THIRTY-NINE

Rafael

Friends. The idea sounds as stupid now as it did two minutes ago when I left Ellie, seeing as my cock has yet to settle down because of my new *friend*. My frustration follows me all the way back to my cabin, where I remove my pants before climbing into bed.

There is no way in hell this platonic Hail Mary is going to work, but the alternative of us hooking up to get each other out of our systems is likely to fail. Just the thought of her lips pressed against mine and her hands in my hair sends another rolling wave of pleasure through me, as if she is right here next to me doing the very damn thing I'm daydreaming about.

My lower half aches with a need so strong, I can't ignore it.

With a sigh, I push my boxers down and reach for my cock. The tip is already moist, and with a few pumps, I gather enough to slicken my shaft.

Pleasuring myself over the last two years has felt more like scratching an itch than something I did for enjoyment, but tonight is different.

I shut my eyes and allow my mind to drift. My pumps are lazy—

No.

It's not *my* hand wrapped around my cock but *Ellie's*. She is the one in my bed, looking up at me with those sparkling hazel eyes that haunt my dreams while she teases my shaft with the tip of her tongue.

I'm downright depraved to imagine my cock sinking into her mouth, inch by inch, until she can't take any more. She wants to—I can tell based on the way she tries and fails—but she can't.

Some guys get excited by gagging someone, but I don't need that to get off. I'd much rather watch Ellie swallow as much of my cock as she can while I sit back and enjoy her show.

And what a performance it is.

She alternates between kissing, sucking, and pumping, all while I do everything possible to stay sane. My girl is a tease, taking me to the edge only to push me away.

My girl.

Yeah, I could get used to the sound of it.

Ellie tormenting me is both the best and worst kind of payback. I would do the same thing as I take her to the edge before pulling back over and over again until I finally decide that she can come.

My cock jerks at that particular visual, and more of my arousal oozes from the tip.

I shut my eyes again and concentrate. Ellie's pumps, which were slow at first, switch to a faster tempo that sends a blindingly hot rush down my chest and straight toward my balls.

My ears ring as I come all over my hand. Some of my release shoots out and lands on my T-shirt, making a mess of the black fabric.

I can't find it in me to care, let alone move, as I blink up at the ceiling. "Fuck."

I've pleasured myself plenty of times before, but I'm not sure I've ever been able to come that hard and fast before, and most definitely not just by imagining someone.

There is no way in hell I can be *friends* with Ellie, who can make me come without ever having to touch me. And it's clear that she wants me just as much but refuses to act on it, so where do we go from here?

"I feel bad for you," Julian says the next morning after I bring him up-to-speed on everything with Ellie.

I switch the call to speaker so I can start shaving my face. "I'm looking for advice. Not pity."

"Why would you ever think being friends was the best solution to your problem?"

I grind down on my molars. "It wasn't *my* idea."

"So you kissed her, and then she suggested you should be friends?"

"Yes."

Julian laughs.

I consider tossing my phone against a wall for a brief moment. "I hate you."

He is still wheezing by the time he says, "Have you considered that maybe you've lost your touch with women?"

"Based on the way she was kissing me back, I seriously doubt that." I don't want to expand any more on the moment we shared, and thankfully Julian doesn't ask for more information.

"I don't know where you go from here." I hear some rustling as he covers the mic, although I can make out a female voice.

"What does Dahlia suggest?" I ask with a sigh.

There is a brief pause before a little shuffling.

"How was the kiss?" she asks a little too eagerly.

"You sure you—"

"Just describe it to me. But skip the nauseating bits that could ruin my lunch, please."

If she were here, I'd glare at her. "All I know is it physically hurt me to stop."

Ellie brought a small part of my soul back to life and lit a fire in me that I haven't felt in a long time.

"Well, that says it all, then."

"Meaning?" I ask.

"You like her."

I take a seat on my bed. "I never said I didn't."

"Then what's your issue?"

I clear my throat. "I might have told her a few things that would make her not like me back."

Dahlia groans.

"It sounds worse than it is."

"I seriously doubt that."

I rub the back of my neck. "I just said that we want very different things in life. That we're all wrong for each other, even if it feels right."

"Do you seriously blame her for friend-zoning you? You were practically begging for it!" Dahlia shouts at the phone.

I can't help sneering. "Either way, being friends is a stupid idea."

"Yeah, maybe it is, but it's safer than giving someone like you a chance."

"What's that supposed to mean?"

"You're a handsome, closed-off, grumpy single dad with a tragic backstory, which makes you hazardous for her heart."

"You think I'm handsome?"

"No," Julian answers in the background, and I crack a smile.

"I know you may not want to be her friend, but unless you're ready to be more, that may be the best you're ever going to get."

The idea of Ellie and me remaining friends doesn't sit right. "I don't like it."

"I didn't expect you to, but it's the truth. You pushed her away, so now you have to find a way to draw her back."

"How?"

"Be her friend. Let some of your walls down. Give her a fighting chance to earn your trust, and I'm sure she'll let you do the same."

"I'm trying to be more…open." The last two nights were a good start—hell, a *great* start—for someone like me.

"I know how hard it is for you to trust people, let alone someone who broke that trust once before."

"She made a mistake."

"The fact that you're calling it that says a lot about your progress."

I take a deep breath. "I *know* she is one of the good ones…"

"But you're still worried about letting her in."

My head hangs. "Yeah."

"I understand. I felt the same way about Julian after my broken engagement."

"But you eventually let your guard down."

I can hear the smile in her voice. "Yeah, and it was the second-best decision I ever made."

"What was the first?"

"Letting go of the past and building a future *together*."

The idea sounds great in theory, but I can't simply snap my fingers and forget everything that made me the person I am today.

Maybe you don't have to.

Letting go doesn't mean erasing the past. It means acknowledging the person I was while working to become the man I want to be.

This is my second chance to get things right. My previous relationship was never meant to last, and I take partial responsibility for it falling apart because our foundation was never solid to begin with.

I wasn't solid, but I won't make that mistake again.

I'm going to figure out who I am and what I want in life, so the next time Ellie gives me a chance—and she will—I won't throw it away.

I'll make sure of it.

CHAPTER FORTY

Ellie

Rafael and I officially enter a new—and slightly strained—phase of our relationship once the yacht docks in Kauai the following morning. We may have agreed to be friends, but there is no denying the undercurrent of sexual tension that passes between us whenever we lock eyes or accidentally touch each other.

Thankfully, Nico provides the best distraction, and we spent our first day on the island zip-lining and hiking. The hike we went on made Nico tear up, which then made my own eyes water because watching him come to terms with his worsening eyesight breaks my heart.

Do you think I'll remember what it looks like? he asked me with a sniffle.

If you don't, you can always come back and see it, I replied.

What if it doesn't look the same? he followed up.

The best part about sunsets is that you'll never see the same one twice. Rafael wrapped his arm around Nico's shoulder, and the three of us stuck around the cliff until the sun disappeared, leaving behind a pinkish hue that guided us back to our rental car.

Today, Nico wanted to jet-ski, so he and Rafael went while I hung out by the beach, frustrated at myself for not joining them.

As if he sensed my interest, Rafael asked me point-blank if I would like to go with them, but I came up with an excuse about wanting to work on my song.

Truth is, I can't prance around in a swimsuit. The night Rafael joined me in the hot tub was a close call, and without bubbles and foam to hide my body, I'd risk revealing my darkest secret and stirring up a hundred different questions I'm not ready to answer.

Sticking to the beach is my best bet, even if it feels like a losing one.

After they return from jet-skiing, Rafael and Nico spend the rest of the day in the water, playing games while I stay out on a shaded lounge chair and work on the song I'm writing for Cole. My fingers hurt from how long I've been playing the guitar, but I'm so close to finishing.

Or at least I *was* until I got distracted by Rafael. My inattention isn't because he is shirtless, although that sure doesn't help matters.

No. I'm completely, unabashedly interested in Rafael, *the father.* The caring, enthusiastic, patient, and doting parent who hasn't taken a single break since Nico asked him to go swimming over an hour ago.

I can't hear them from my spot on the beach, but I wish I could, based on the way Nico throws his head back from time to time at something his father says.

Rafael may not want more kids, but he was born to be a dad. That much I know.

Nico shrieks as Rafael tosses him into the air for what has to be the fiftieth time, only to be cut off when he lands in the water with a splash. Rafael's arms must be burning from the workout, but he hasn't stopped yet.

Until now.

Nico follows him, chanting, "*Again*!"

"Give me a few minutes."

Once I apply another layer of sunscreen to Nico's skin, he grabs his binoculars and heads back to the beach while Rafael falls onto the empty lounge chair behind me. After spending all that time in the water with Nico, throwing him around and acting like a dolphin for him to ride, I would need more than a few minutes, but then again, Rafael is a machine.

Rafael looks over at me and squints. "What's got you smiling like that?"

"You," I answer honestly.

"What did I do?"

My smile only brightens. "You're a really amazing dad."

His already sunburnt cheeks darken. "You think so?"

"Are you kidding? You just spent thirty minutes pretending to be a dolphin."

"First off, I was a *shark*."

I giggle. "My bad."

He smiles, and my heart misses a beat.

"I haven't seen Nico this happy in a very long time." The light in his eyes fades a bit.

"What?" I ask.

"I'm just worried it could all disappear."

"No one can be happy forever. It's not sustainable."

He looks out at the ocean again. "Trust me, *I know*."

My chest tightens uncomfortably at the reminder of his past choice to make others happy at the expense of his own happiness.

I twist in my chair until I'm facing him. "Nico is going to have great days like today, but he's also going to have shitty ones like the night of his accident. All you can do is support him through the good and the bad."

He sighs. "I hate the bad days."

"Me too, but they happen, especially with the rapid progression of his condition."

"Being out of control makes me edgy."

I frown. "You're not going to be able to control everything, but you are able to control how you react to situations."

He scowls. "I didn't mean to have a breakdown at the doctor's."

I wasn't planning on bringing *that* up, but if he wants to, then okay.

"I know that," I say in a soft voice.

"I'm still embarrassed he heard me."

"Why?"

"Because I'm supposed to be strong, and he saw me at my weakest."

I blink a few times. "Is that the lesson you want to teach

your kid? That crying or feeling emotional about something that clearly matters to you makes you *weak*?"

He stares at me.

I look down at my lap. "When Nico made me promise not to say anything about his worsening vision, I thought it was because he didn't want to make you sad again. But maybe it was because he didn't want to look *weak* to you either."

"Fuck." His head drops back a few seconds later. "I never even thought of that."

I hadn't either until he started describing himself as weak because he had a moment of vulnerability.

Rafael blinks up at the striped umbrella a few times and *sniffs*.

Oh shit.

Did I make him cry? I never did that to anyone except my mother, and it makes me feel awful. "Are you okay?"

He rubs his eyes. "I've got some sand in my eye."

Damn this man for making me fall a little bit more for him. We are supposed to be friends, goddammit. Friends who think about kissing each other but friends nonetheless. Except now he is upset, and I want to console him.

Shit.

His muscles tense as I take a seat beside him and brush his hair out of his eyes. I'm not sure if he notices how he leans into my touch, but it makes my whole chest warm.

"It's okay." I cup his cheek.

He glances away with glassy eyes. "Elle?"

"Yeah?"

"I lied."

My heart sinks. "About?"

"I don't really have sand in my eyes."

A small laugh escapes me. "I had a feeling, but I didn't want to assume." My own vision turns cloudy as I bear witness to his walls crumbling.

"I'm sorry." He adds another piece of my heart to his growing collection.

I cradle his cheek in the palm of my hand. "I forgive you."

"My dad…" His breathing is shaky at best. "He used to tell me to stop crying. To *act like a man*." He seems to subconsciously lean into my touch. "When I found out that Nico's condition had worsened, my gut reaction was to hide before he could watch me fall apart."

"You don't have to do that anymore, though. You can break the cycle and teach him that it's okay to feel. That it's good to depend on others when we can't support ourselves."

"I didn't even realize I was sending the same message to my son until now." His voice cracks, and I wrap my arms around him.

His hand brushes down my back. "Thank you."

"For what?"

"Being you." His hand presses into the small of my back, and I suck in a breath as I look into his eyes.

Warmth explodes in my chest and my lower half at the same time as his gaze drops to my mouth.

"Elle—" Whatever he was about to say is cut off by Nico yelling, "Group hug!" He throws himself on top of me, and I squeal at his swimsuit soaking my clothes.

"No!" I push, but Rafael wraps his arms around the two

of us, effectively trapping me between Nico and him. Nico returns the hug with his own, crushing me farther into his father's chest with a laugh.

For the first time since I started working for this family, I wonder what it would be like to be a part of it. Not as a nanny, but as something *more*.

CHAPTER FORTY-ONE

Rafael

O n our third day in Kauai, Ellie—sweet, too kind for her own good, and *should really learn how to say no* Ellie— agrees to join Nico and me on a helicopter ride despite her crippling fear of planes. I told her a few times she didn't need to come with us, but by my third attempt to talk her out of it, she politely asked me to stop talking.

Nico holds her hand the entire time while I wish I could do the same. Instead, I keep mine tucked against my lap while my son distracts Ellie with random facts that he learned about the island from watching hours of videos.

"Where are the dinosaurs?" Ellie hesitantly leans forward.

Nico smacks her shoulder with a giggle. "There are no dinosaurs!"

She scrunches her brows. "Really? You promised me there would be some."

"No! I told you they *filmed* them here."

"So they still exist?"

He shakes his head in disbelief. "Did you go to school?"

"Of course."

"Then didn't your teacher tell you about the big comet that killed all the dinosaurs?"

"I thought they brought them back with mosquito blood and frog DNA," she teases.

Nico drops his head back with a dramatic sigh, and Ellie cracks a smile. Despite my protests about her coming on this trip, I'm glad Nico insisted because I can't imagine being here without her.

It takes a special person to raise other people's children like their own. Nico's mother doesn't show the same amount of care and affection toward her son, and she gave birth to him, so I understand how special Ellie's unconditional love truly is.

I've spent the last ten days witnessing it firsthand, but today is the first time I wish she shared a bit of the affection she has toward my son with *me*.

Is it pathetic to be jealous of my own kid? Probably, but I'm hitting all new lows lately, seeing as I spent part of our day trying to compete for Ellie's attention like a child.

I'm not even sure when I went from being jealous of Ellie with Nico to being jealous of my son instead, but it is pitiful.

My attempts at stealing her attention continue long after our helicopter ride and into dinner.

"*Papi*, I'm full." Nico pushes his plate away from him and pats his belly with a groan.

I blink away my thoughts. "What about your veggies?"

"I ate most of them, but I can't take another bite." He puffs his cheeks with air.

Most of his plate is cleared, but a few pieces of fish and his least favorite vegetable in the medley mix, broccoli, remain untouched. My eyes flick over to Ellie, who is finishing the last bite of her own food.

A normal man would let the staff take Nico's plate away without thinking twice about it, but the idea of leaving food behind makes my own dinner crawl toward my throat.

Old habits die hard, and trauma seems to last forever.

"You did well." I reach for his plate and place it on top of my empty one.

"Ew. That has my germs."

My cheeks heat at the feeling of Ellie's eyes on me, and I wonder what she is thinking. Is she disgusted by me eating my son's leftovers? Or would she find me weak for being unable to overcome a fear that will never be a problem again, as long as I live?

My ex-wife *despised* my compulsive behavior once she discovered I wasn't eating her leftover food because I was still hungry. It took her an impressively long amount of time to realize my *habit*, and only because it was harder to hide once Nico was born and I was eating whatever they both left behind.

Eventually, as Nico grew older, I became better at predicting how much food he would eat in a given meal, but vacations put the control back in the hands of the chefs who cook for us.

Funny how I have enough money to have Wagyu beef flown in from Japan and have it prepared by a private Michelin star chef for every meal for the rest of my life, but here I am, staring at Nico's dinner plate like it could be my last.

I've never felt weaker than I do in this moment, knowing not only Nico but Ellie too will witness my embarrassment.

Ellie surprises me when she stabs her fork through one of the pieces of fish.

"Ellie! Not you too!" My son looks over at me with an exasperated look. "Tell her not to do that, *Papi*. Please."

I'm too shocked to speak, let alone command Ellie to stop.

With a small smile, she pops the piece of fish into her mouth. "Delicious. Dare I say it tastes better with your germs on it."

Nico looks absolutely horrified. "Yuck!"

My mouth falls open for a completely different reason, but words continue to escape me as Ellie reaches over again to take another piece of fish from Nico's plate.

Before she has a chance to steal another forkful, I clasp my hand around her wrist. "You don't have to do that."

"Weren't you going to eat it?"

"Yes."

"Then so can I."

"Why?"

"Because it's important to you," she says with a casual shrug, all while I feel like she stabbed her fork through my heart instead of Nico's leftovers.

I've never had someone take on the burden of my irrational fear with me. My family is aware of my *quirk*, and Hillary was vocal about her dislike of my *psychological issues*, as she so unkindly phrased it, but people usually keep their heads down and their mouths shut about it.

They don't comment. They don't look. And they sure as hell don't participate because it's *important to me*.

My lungs feel as if they could explode at any second, unable to bear the weight of Ellie's actions and my heart expanding.

Ellie seems completely unaware of my struggle—or she at least *pretends* to be—as she pops her fork into her mouth before slowly dragging it out.

"But you said you were too full for dessert." Nico groans at Ellie.

"I wasn't in the mood for ice cream."

Nico throws his hands in the air. "Who even says that?"

A very special woman with a heart two sizes too big.

My fork trembles in my hand as I spear through the second-to-last piece of fish on Nico's plate. Ellie—fucking Ellie, with golden hair to match her golden heart—reaches underneath the table and gives my thigh a reassuring pat.

Before she has a chance to pull back, I latch on to her hand and keep it secured to my thigh as I finish Nico's vegetables.

The usual shame that accompanies my weakness fades away, and the condescending voice in my head is silent as I clutch Ellie's hand like a lifeline.

Whether I like it or not, she is quickly becoming mine, and rather than fear the consequences of letting someone get close to me again, I want to embrace the possibility of finally sharing my burden.

Of finally dropping my walls and allowing myself to just be *me*.

Nico asks both Ellie and me to tuck him in tonight, so together, we help him get into bed and read him a story. At his request, Ellie and I read his latest book like a play, with her reading the parts of the mom and me the dad. He sits between us on the big bed, along with the five action figures Ellie packed in her oversized luggage.

Ellie fits so easily into our lives, it is hard to remember what everything was like before she entered it. Nico adores her, and I'm quickly understanding why.

Still, I don't want to ruin the special thing we have going for us by pushing harder against her friendship idea, but that doesn't mean I'm not still tempted, especially when she looks at me like I'm someone special.

Like someone *worthy*.

Nico snuggles under the comforter with a sigh. "*Papi*."

I shake my head and turn to face him. "Yeah."

"Why do you eat my food?"

"Huh?"

Ellie's eyes drop to the mattress.

Nico can hardly keep his own open. "I was just thinking about Mommy and how she doesn't eat all my food."

The rosy color of Ellie's cheeks fades.

I lift Nico's comforter to his chin. "No, she doesn't."

He looks over at Ellie. "But you did."

"Yeah."

"Why?"

I clear my throat. "Remember how Penelope came to us and you could see her ribs?"

Nico's bottom lip wobbles as he nods. "Yeah."

"And she was so hungry she kept trying to eat your hair?"

That seems to break the tension. "Yeah!"

"I was like that once."

"So hungry you could eat someone's hair?"

My cheeks burn. "Not quite, but hungry enough that you could count my ribs too."

Ellie gives my hand a squeeze. When she moves to pull away, Nico places his hand on top of both of ours.

My heart is full to the point of bursting. Never has it yearned for someone to the point of pain before, but something about Ellie makes me want more.

More of what, I haven't decided yet, mostly because I'm still working through my issues, but I do know what we currently have isn't enough.

Nico looks up at me. "I'm sorry I laughed at you."

I kiss his forehead. "No need to say sorry. I know it can be...gross."

Ellie's eyes soften, and I have to look away because I can't take the pity in her gaze.

Nico smiles. "I like that you like my germs."

I laugh. "No, you don't."

"Yes, I do! Maybe I'll steal some of your food too."

"Not if I steal it first," Ellie says with a smile I feel straight to my heart.

CHAPTER FORTY-TWO

Ellie

When Rafael invited me to have a nightcap on the balcony, I couldn't refuse him, especially after the moment the three of us shared while putting Nico to bed.

Little by little, Rafael has been opening up to those closest to him, and I'm honored to witness so many big moments for him. Watching him become more comfortable with himself and his past truly is incredible.

We settle on a set of lounge chairs underneath the night sky, with the moon casting a glow over the shoreline down below.

Similar to his company, the silence is comforting, so I don't push to start talking right away, and neither does he.

A few minutes later, Rafael is the one to break first.

"About tonight…"

I twist in my chair to see him better. "What about it?"

"I'm sure you have some questions."

"You don't owe me any explanation." The one he gave Nico was sufficient for me.

"It's not that." He scrubs a hand down his face. "I want to talk about it with you."

My heart does a little skip. "Okay."

He stares out at the ocean, his jaw clenching and unclenching with each deep breath. "You know how long it took Nico's mom to notice my *habit*?" He says the last word with a sneer, and my mouth stops working temporarily.

"Nico was two years old already," he says when I don't speak.

"That is…" A very long time.

"Pathetic." His gaze swings from me to the stars.

The fact that it took *years* for Hillary to notice that gives me so much insight into their marriage. I hadn't shared many meals with Rafael back at the house, so I didn't pay much attention before, but once we got to Hawaii, I started picking up on the clues.

First, I noticed how he would ask waiters for specific serving sizes and be very purposeful about which meal he chose, which would have made him look like a hard-ass if it weren't for his extremely generous tip and the simple *thank you* he wrote at the bottom of every receipt.

Then, he kept saying he was full after every meal, only to eat the small leftovers on Nico's plate. He didn't look happy about it. In fact, he appeared pretty damn miserable, which was the biggest glaring sign.

"She thought I was just hungry because of my workouts

and all the physical labor I did at work." He doesn't look at me. "She didn't even ask me why. Didn't *care* to." A shaky breath follows. "If anything, she was annoyed."

My bottom lip quivers, but I ease the tightness in my chest with a joke. "Well, it doesn't bother me."

"No?"

"Nope."

He releases a heavy breath before speaking up again. "My parents didn't have a lot of money. Whatever they earned was quickly spent on booze, gambling, and whatever made my mom happy that week. Sometimes, because of their irresponsibility, we didn't have enough money for food, so I learned to not let anything go to waste."

Our dinner sits in my stomach like a lead block.

His eyes dart away. "It became a habit, or a *compulsion*, as my therapist said. Some kind of trauma response, and one I can't control despite having more money than I could ever spend in a lifetime. I didn't know my limits when I was younger, so when I first moved to Lake Wisteria, I would eat to the point of making myself sick, which then triggered that same fear of my aunt and uncle getting tired of my issues. I was convinced they would wake up one day and decide they were done with me."

"How old were you?" I ask in a neutral tone despite my heart aching.

"I was only a little older than Nico, and I had seen so much shit in a short amount of time. I was a mess."

"You were a *child*."

He glares at the sky like he wants to yell at it.

"Did they know how bad things got with your parents?" I ask.

"No. My uncle and his brother weren't on speaking terms before his death, so they weren't aware of the situation until they got the call about me needing a new home."

"Oh, Rafael."

He can't look me in the eyes anymore. "They drew their own conclusions based on a medical chart and a couple of questionnaires, but they never pushed me to open up."

He clenches and unclenches his hands a few times before speaking again. "I got away with avoiding the topic for a year, but it wasn't like I could hide my nightmares or compulsive behavior. Then one day, I overheard my aunt and uncle talking about how they were thinking of sending me somewhere to get help."

His breath, like my own, comes out shaky. "Lake Wisteria is a small town, and I had heard of a couple of kids in school who went away because they had issues, so I panicked, thinking my aunt and uncle were getting sick of me."

An invisible vine covered in thorns wraps around my heart and gives it a squeeze. "They just wanted to help you."

"I realize that now, as a grown adult with a kid of my own, but back then, it felt like my whole world was ending." Rafael's despondent smile makes my chest ache.

I yearn to hold his trembling hand in mine, but I remain seated, not wanting him to lose his nerve and shut me out.

"So, I changed little by little, that way no one became suspicious."

"What do you mean *you changed*?"

"I didn't want my aunt and uncle to worry about me, so I pretended I was getting better. That I wasn't having nightmares about my parents or that I was no longer struggling to keep my dinner down because I was overeating."

"How?" The question comes out a whisper.

"Some things were easy, like making an actual effort to have friends or focusing on the positives while ignoring every negative thing that happened to me, while other things were more difficult, like controlling my nightmares. I couldn't do much about those, but I found that if I stuffed a blanket through the crack between the bottom of my bedroom door and the floor, and slept inside the closet, then no one could hear my cries." His voice breaks, along with my self-control, as a tear slips down my cheek.

I brush it away quickly so he doesn't notice. "I'm so sorry."

"What are you apologizing for? It's not like you did anything."

"No, but that doesn't make me any less sorry for what you've been through." The temptation to curl up next to him and pull him into my arms becomes too great to ignore, so I follow that unraveling heartstring in my chest toward the one who keeps pulling on it.

"Scoot over." I motion with my hands.

"Why?"

"I want to hug you."

"This is becoming a habit for you." He shoots me a look I serve right back. With an arched brow, he shuffles over a bit, hardly giving me much room at all.

Well played.

I snuggle up to his side and place my cheek against the spot right over his heart. The beats are strong, although a little faster than normal.

That makes me smile.

Rafael tucks my head underneath his chin and wraps his arms around me. "I didn't tell you this so you would pity me."

"It's called *empathy*, but if you don't want it…" I start to pull away, but his arms tighten around me instead.

"On second thought, let me share more tragic stories from my past. I've got plenty to pick from."

I know he means it as a joke to lighten the mood, but my chest tightens.

I tap on the spot over his heart. "You don't have to pretend to be okay with me."

A crease appears between his brows. "I'm not—"

I press my finger against his mouth. "I'd rather you say nothing at all than lie to my face."

His gaze drops to my hand, and I pull it away, noticing the tingle left behind from touching his lips.

"Thank you…for trusting me," I say while ignoring the knot in my throat.

His bravery makes me want to open up to him too, although I'm not sure where to start. Telling the story behind my scars is never easy, but Rafael sharing parts of his past wasn't either, so it's only a matter of where to start with mine.

Fate seems to step in when Rafael brushes a hand over my hip, and I flinch.

"Sorry." He removes his arms from around me and places them back on the cushion.

I make a decision then. It isn't a hard one—not after he opened up to me the way he did—but it still makes me nervous. I'm never quite sure how people will react or what they will say, but I have a feeling Rafael will take the time to understand me.

I place his palm back before moving it over the raised skin. "My reaction wasn't because of you."

"What's that?"

"A scar."

He stays quiet while he softly rubs his thumb over the same spot. If he presses a little to the left, he will find another scar... and then a different one next to that. It isn't difficult since my body is riddled with them, although my long dress does a good job of hiding them from plain sight.

"What happened?" he asks while stroking my skin through the fabric of my dress.

I remember that first cut like it was yesterday. The anger. The hate. The pressure building inside my head without any kind of outlet.

My mom couldn't help me, at least not yet. She was struggling with her own demons, and the biggest one of all was Anthony Davis.

Father. Deputy. *Abuser.*

"You don't have to tell me," he says a moment later.

"I was thinking about where to start, not whether I wanted to talk about it."

We both stare up at the stars and a night sky that reminds me so much of my own thighs and the stars I had tattooed around my scars.

A shooting star races across the sky, and I take it as a

sign. "When I was younger, I had difficulty controlling my emotions."

His thumb keeps rubbing against my scar, back and forth, giving me the reassurance to continue.

"My father was a mean man who took pleasure in belittling his wife and daughter. No one knew that about him though, because to the public, he was an upstanding citizen. A deputy with a bright future ahead of him. The doting husband and father that they show in movies or magazines." The words are tainted with my obvious disgust.

Rafael's heart stutters against my ear.

"He had absolutely no control, at least not with *us*. It was only a matter of time before I picked up on his propensity to explode." I flip my palm over on his chest so he can see the scar. "I was only eleven when I had my first…incident."

His heart picks up speed again. "Incident?"

"Self-harm." I run my thumb over my first scar on the palm of my hand. "It started as an accident. Someone had bought me one of those vintage hand mirrors, and one day after my father exploded on me for drawing on my skin with a permanent marker, I broke it. Just threw it at a wall and watched it shatter into a hundred different pieces."

"What did he say?"

"That only ugly girls draw on their skin like that."

"What a bastard."

"When he came in and saw it, he told me to pick it up myself. Forbade my mother from helping too. Said that if I wanted to be an angry brat, then I needed to learn my lesson by cleaning up my own mess." I tense up at the memory.

Rafael brushes a hand down my spine. "You were only eleven."

"Regardless, I shouldn't have thrown something out of anger. That was something *he* would do."

"You were a *child*." His words mimic mine from earlier. "You're allowed to make mistakes and get upset."

"Yeah, well, not in my house. Everything had to be *perfect*, including me."

There is a fire behind Rafael's eyes, his anger simmering just below the surface. "Did he ever hit you?"

"No, but he didn't have to because his words always packed a punch."

Rafael traces the fine bones in my hands. "I think your tattoos only enhance your beauty."

I can hardly manage a *thank you*, given how tight my throat feels. I've never had someone look at me or talk to me the way he does.

"What happened?" he asks.

"When I was picking up the pieces, I accidentally cut myself." My breathing is shaky. "My hand hurt like hell, but the pain in my head was finally quiet, at least for a little while." I trace over one of my hand tattoos. "I felt *relieved*." A sad laugh escapes me. "It didn't last long, but it didn't matter. A new coping mechanism was born." My scarred hand forms a tight fist.

"The cutting only got worse when my mom moved out before my twelfth birthday and filed for divorce. Spending weekdays with her and weekends with a living nightmare of a father nearly wrecked me, but thankfully, my mom was finally awarded full custody right before I turned fourteen."

Rafael lifts my palm with the scar to his mouth and kisses it. The gesture is small, but it has an incredible amount of sway over my heart.

A heart that Rafael is slowly earning, piece by broken piece.

He doesn't release my hand, and I don't try to pull away either.

I don't think I could, even if I wanted to, based on the way his grip tightens when I speak again. "I saved the piece of the mirror until I found better...alternatives."

"Do you still have them?"

"What?"

"Your *alternatives*."

My body turns rigid against his. "Why?"

"I'm not going to judge you for your answer. I'm just curious."

"A couple of years after I stopped for good, I got rid of almost everything."

"What did you keep?"

"A piece of the mirror. I tried to get rid of it, but I just couldn't yet."

He sits in silence for a minute, and I don't push to fill it, instead allowing him to process everything I threw at him.

"How long did this go on?"

"Long enough to do some damage to my body."

"Did you ever..." His voice drifts off.

"Try to kill myself?" Might as well ask it point-blank.

He nods, and a muscle in his neck tics.

"No, probably because my mom got me the help I needed and a full-custody agreement we both desperately wanted.

It was a long battle because my father had connections and his hometown rallying for him, but eventually, after a physical and psychological evaluation, the judge ruled in my mom's favor. I'm not sure how much longer I would have lasted spending time with my father. Without my mother, he was..."

A monster. My mom was a buffer, so once she left, I faced his wrath on my own, and it was truly a miserable place to be.

The arm wrapped around me tightens. "He was *what?*"

I fiddle with one of the buttons on his shirt and accidentally graze some of his chest hair.

"Actually, you don't have to tell me." He stumbles over the words. "I know it's not easy to talk about the past."

"That's the thing. Opening up to you isn't difficult at all." When he isn't fighting tooth and nail to keep me away, Rafael makes me feel *safe*. Like the demons from the past can't get me, no matter how much I talk about them.

He makes my head quiet.

Rafael seems to sit with that for a few minutes before we continue talking. This time, we stick to safer subjects, talking about the plan for the rest of our trip, how the animals are doing without us, and how excited Nico is about performing at the Strawberry Festival soon.

I nearly forgot about that one, in part because I didn't want to think about Hillary coming to visit. For Nico's sake, I hope she does make it, but that doesn't mean I have to like it.

Rafael's deep, soothing voice eventually lulls me to sleep, and I don't even wake up when he carries me to my bed.

In my dream, he fussed over my strappy heels before

tucking me in. He might have even kissed my forehead and whispered something against the top of my head, but I was asleep again before I ever heard the words.

CHAPTER FORTY-THREE

Ellie

So, you were friends with Ava Rhodes ever since she moved to Lake Wisteria when you were fourteen?" Ms. Copper, the lawyer Cole referred me to, asks without looking up from her notebook.

My head swims with memories I've tried so hard to forget. Breathing is becoming progressively more difficult, and if I'm not careful, I could pass out from lack of oxygen.

We are only five minutes into our allotted meeting time, but it feels like an hour already.

"If you don't mind, I just need a few minutes." I mute my microphone and turn off my camera.

Deep breaths, Ellie.

I try so damn hard to calm myself down, but I'm only working myself up more with every ragged breath.

I should have known today was going to be a bad day based

on the gloomy weather. But still, I held on to my hope and talked myself into a consultation with Cole and the lawyer despite the warning sign.

When Cole reached out yesterday, asking if I could meet with the lawyer while I was on vacation, I said yes. I thought I could handle it without my family or Willow being there to support me, but I was wrong.

I'm not sure why I thought this was a good idea. There is no way I can—

No.

I *can* do this, and I will, but I just need…someone. Anyone really. I don't care who, but my options are limited to only two, and since Nico hearing my story is out of the question, I'm left with only one person.

Rafael.

Goose bumps spread across my arms. After he tucked me into bed last night, I haven't talked to him other than to ask him if he could entertain Nico while I attended an hour-long meeting, so the idea of calling him makes me jittery.

With a shaky hand, I pull out my phone and do it anyway.

"Ellie?" Rafael answers.

"Are you in the living room?"

"Yeah. Is everything okay with the meeting?"

"Um…about that. Do you mind coming to my room?"

He doesn't hesitate. "Sure. I'll be there in a minute. Let me just get Nico his tablet."

"Thanks."

He hangs up, and I spend the longest sixty seconds of my

life pacing the layout of my room until there is a heavy knock against my door.

"Elle."

I flip the lock and open the door.

"What's wrong?" He steps inside and assesses the room.

"Remember when I mentioned Cole and that copyright lawyer?"

His eyes land on the computer. "Yeah."

"Well, we're in the middle of a meeting right now, but I'm kind of having a bit of a freak-out and don't know if I can do it." Panic bleeds into my voice.

His scowl deepens. "Do you need me to do something or talk to someone?"

I shake my head. "Can you just…be here while I talk? You don't have to say anything. I just—"

"Whatever you need."

He follows me to the couch and sits. After I take a few deep breaths, I turn my microphone and video back on before introducing Rafael, who waves with a grunt. I'm sure his lack of enthusiasm has everything to do with Cole smiling back at him.

"Rafael. Nice to see you again."

He tips his chin. "Cole."

"So, Ellie." The lawyer doesn't smile, but her eyes soften a bit as our gazes connect. "I was asking you about your relationship with Ava."

"Right. Ava." I subconsciously rub at the crescent moon tattoo on the inside of my arm, right above my elbow. "We became best friends in high school, after she moved to Lake

Wisteria during middle school. We were both new to town, so it was easy to bond over that."

My hand trembles, and I tighten it into a fist. Rafael uncurls my fingers one by one before intertwining them with his.

A simple squeeze of Rafael's hand gives me the confidence I need. I don't look at him while I share my story about moving to Los Angeles and all the songs Ava stole from me, but I can feel his anger rolling off him with every new piece of information I share.

It takes a while to get through all the little details and pieces of evidence, but once I get to speaking about Darius Larkin, Rafael's mood goes completely dark.

"Darius was well aware of my involvement in creating the album but didn't credit me for my work." I take a deep, painful breath. "I don't know if this matters for the case, but he…" I can't find the strength to continue.

Rafael stiffens beside me.

Cole leans forward, looking absolutely enraged. "I know about Mr. Larkin's reputation with women."

"Well, I don't." Rafael's lethal tone sends a shiver down my spine.

The lawyer speaks up. "He tends to scout out younger talent. Typically, women who don't have much experience in the business or know much about him." Her sad smile makes my chest clench to the point of pain. "They don't have the resources to fight back, even if they wanted to."

"I wasn't aware." My voice sounds so small and distant.

I never knew Darius had a *reputation*. Never even thought to ask anyone about it because him signing Ava onto the record label was supposed to be our big break after spending a few years struggling in Los Angeles.

When I came back to Lake Wisteria, I drove myself crazy, thinking that maybe I did something to lead Darius on and make him think I was interested in him romantically. That if I had kept my head down, my mouth shut, or worn less eye-catching clothes, he wouldn't have been interested in me.

God. I spent so many months blaming myself when I should have blamed *him*. Willow told me as much, but it is different hearing the truth from a complete stranger.

Tears rise to my eyes, and no amount of blinking saves me. Rafael's grip on my hand tightens, keeping me grounded as the truth tumbles out of me.

"I didn't want to kiss him, but he..." I stumble over how to phrase what happened. "I wasn't given a choice, but I didn't make one either. I just stood there, completely frozen, while he... Ava walked into the recording studio and saw us—saw *him* touching me. *Him* kissing me."

Once the tears start, I can't stop them. "All hell broke loose when Ava showed up. She had to physically be restrained after slapping me, but that didn't stop her mouth. She called me a dirty slut. A *whore*."

The veins in Rafael's neck look ready to explode.

"She told me she was going to steal my songs like I stole her boyfriend," I say between sobs, totally unfazed at the idea of Cole and the lawyer watching me break down. "She was my best friend for over a decade, and it was like I didn't even recognize her anymore."

Rafael wraps his arm around my waist and crushes my body against his. I press my cheek against his chest and cry, all while he whispers reassuring words against the top of my head and rubs my back.

I feel instant relief in his arms, and it's everything I needed and more. He doesn't stop rubbing my back—doesn't stop making his presence felt—while I cry.

Once my tears stop flowing and my breathing evens out, he presses his mouth against my ear and whispers, "When I'm done with him, that piece of shit is going to wish he never laid eyes on you."

My body vibrates as I look into his dark eyes. "Please don't murder someone on my behalf."

"There are plenty of ways to destroy someone without ever committing a crime."

"Like?"

"Why ruin the surprise?"

"Keep talking like that, and I may consider something like that romantic."

His lips curl at the corners. "Maybe I want it to be."

My heart pauses before picking back up again.

Cole clears his throat. "As entertaining as it is to watch you flirt, some of us have things to do and songs to write."

I turn with bulging eyes to find him grinning.

He winks.

The lawyer clasps her hands together. "Well, Ellie. You provided me with a lot of information about Ms. Rhodes, and while it is a very interesting situation legally…"

I've been through three rejections already, so I recognize

the beginning of another letdown. I *told* myself not to get my hopes up this time, and I should have known better.

After spending so many years in the dark, I like to hope. It may make me naïve, but I'd rather be a dreamer than a pessimist any day of the week.

"I'm very sorry that you've been taken advantage of like that. By both Ms. Rhodes and Mr. Larkin." Ms. Copper's red lips press into a thin line.

I tense against Rafael's side and prepare for the next blow.

"Given the information you shared, along with the logs and detailed notes you kept of your writing sessions, I think we can start looking into establishing a case," she continues, but I'm not listening.

Oh my God.

After a year of trying and failing to find someone to represent me, I'm finally going after Ava for what she did to me. I don't even care if I win the settlement or prove that I helped write her songs.

I just want a chance to *fight*.

I don't even realize the meeting is over until Rafael shuts the computer after promising I'll return the lawyer's email as soon as possible.

"Elle?" He waves his hand in front of my face.

I blink a few times. "Yeah?"

"Thank you for asking me to join you."

I look up at him. "I don't know if I could have done it without you."

"You would have. I have no doubt about it, but I'm glad you wanted me to be here anyway."

My heart threatens to tumble straight out of my chest. "I was about to have a meltdown before you came in here."

"But you held yourself together. All I did was hold your hand."

He did more than that, and we both know it.

He tucks a loose strand of hair behind my ear. "Ava mistook your kindness and silence for weakness, and I can't wait for you to prove her wrong."

"What about Darius?"

"Don't you worry about him." I've seen smiles like Rafael's before, and they always spell trouble.

Rafael tells me to take some time to unwind after the meeting, and I had planned on it, but then I was inspired to finish the song I was working on for Cole. After all he has done for me, I want to give him something in return.

I channel my sadness from earlier into a new song. It isn't the one I was originally working on, nor is it the one inspired by Rafael, but the lyrics seem to pour out of me with no sign of stopping.

> I'm a decorated soldier winning a war against life.
>
> Collected endless scars like medals of valor
>
> Until my body became a symbol of my fight.

A melody comes soon after, and within a few hours, I have a song. It's the first one I have finished since Ava betrayed me, and because of that, it holds a special place in my heart.

Fitting really, seeing as it's similar to the one she stole from me but *better*.

If Cole doesn't want to use it, I won't be offended in the slightest, but at least it proves that I still have what it takes to write songs.

I set my phone on the coffee table and record myself singing and playing the guitar. It takes a few tries, mainly because I reword some lyrics and change a few chords here and there, but once I'm done, I send Cole the recording and hope for the best.

ME

> Thank you for everything you've done to help me until this point. I'm not sure I would have worked up the courage to talk to a lawyer without you.

I busy myself with taking a shower, shaving, and blow-drying my hair. Keeping my mind occupied takes the edge off my anxiety, so by the time my phone buzzes thirty minutes later, I'm more excited than nervous.

COLE

> I told you. I like watching good people win.

He doesn't mention anything about the song, so my mind starts to spiral.

Did he hate it so much he doesn't want to comment on it?

Does he like it but not love it?

So much for thinking about writing a whole album.

My heart sinks with every negative thought, only to bounce back at his next message.

COLE

> I know we only agreed on you writing one song, but I've changed my mind.

Oh no. That doesn't sound good.

COLE

> How do you feel about trying out an album?

I screech so loud that Nico and Rafael both come barreling into my room.

"What's wrong?" Rafael asks while Nico shows off a fighting stance he learned from his one and only tae kwon do class.

"Sorry. I just got excited."

Nico exits the room with a cartwheel while Rafael looks me over once more.

"You're good?"

I nod.

"What happened?"

"Cole liked my new song."

His smile is small but genuine. "You finished it?"

"Yeah. And he wants to work on more!"

A look passes over his face, but I can't make out what it means. "I knew he would love anything you wrote."

"How?"

"Because he may be annoying, but he's no fool."

"I—" My phone chimes from an incoming call. "I should take this."

Rafael shuts my door behind him. The slight pressure in the air remains after his departure, but I decide to focus on it later.

I answer Cole's call.

"I hope I wasn't too forward."

"No. Not at all. I'm just relieved you liked the song."

"Liked it? It's fucking amazing. My drummer teared up, and he's not even a crier."

I laugh before Cole starts explaining his writing process, impending deadline, and the expected amount of money I could make.

I nearly pass out at the rough figure he gives me.

The rest of the call is an information overload, and my head is spinning by the time he hits me with the catch.

"I could fly you out to Europe so we can spend whatever free time I have during the European leg of the tour writing. The turnaround time will be tight, especially with the number of shows I'll be playing, but I have a feeling we can pull it off. I'm always better on a tight deadline anyway."

"The European leg?"

"It kicks off in the mid-July."

"How long is it?"

"Five weeks."

Shit. "I have a job."

"Will they let you take a leave of absence?"

"I don't know." The knot in my stomach becomes unbearably tight.

"You don't have to give me an answer right now. Take the weekend to think about it and get back to me by Monday."

Monday? That's in three days.

"Can I have a week instead?"

"Sure."

Seven days may not seem like a lot of time, but I would rather not ruin the rest of our vacation by bringing up my new job offer. While I hope Nico and Rafael will be happy for me, I'm not a hundred percent sure my boss wouldn't make me choose between two jobs I want.

And the idea of that happening makes my heart want to break.

CHAPTER FORTY-FOUR

Rafael

Ellie seems lost in her own head tonight. I imagine after the day she had, she doesn't want to talk much, so we order room service, and Nico and I carry most of the conversation during dinner, with her offering a little input here and there.

When she excuses herself from the table after all three plates are cleared, Nico looks over at me with pursed lips.

"Is Ellie okay?"

"I think so."

"She looks sad."

I give his shoulder a squeeze. "She just had a long day."

He seems satisfied enough with my answer to let it go, although I'm still thinking about her long after I put Nico to bed.

With a reluctant sigh, I text the one person who can help me with the Darius Larkin situation. I've heard enough about him to know he has connections I don't.

I can already hear Julian yelling in my ear, telling me this is a bad idea, but I don't care. Ellie is worth making a deal with the Lake Wisteria demon, so long as that piece of shit producer is irrevocably destroyed.

LORENZO

Isn't this a lovely surprise.

ME

Just answer my question.

LORENZO

I *could* do what you want.

ME

What would you want in exchange?

LORENZO

What are you willing to give me?

Answering a question with another question? The man really was born for politics.

ME

Depends on how much you help me.

LORENZO

Give me a week and your endorsement.

ME

Done.

LORENZO

From you AND your cousin.

Fuck.

I text Julian about the request.

JULIAN

No.

ME

Please?

JULIAN

Everyone knows I can't stand him.

ME

Exactly why he wants your endorsement.

ME

I wouldn't be asking you for
this if I didn't need him.

The dots appear and disappear twice before his next message pops up.

JULIAN

I could help you.

ME

Help me by saying yes?

His text pops up a couple minutes later.

JULIAN

For the record, this is a terrible idea.

ME

But you'll do it?

JULIAN

Yeah. I will.

My throat feels thick with emotion as I pull up the other text thread and reply.

ME

We're in.

LORENZO

I'll be in touch.

❀

Today's meeting with the lawyer not only filled me with anger about Ellie's situation but it also made me curious about the songs that were stolen from her.

Rather than support Ava by streaming the music, I pull up the lyrics for each one and read them instead. One in particular called "Half Truths" catches my attention because of the lyrics that craft a story about a person who struggles to be honest with themselves and those they love.

Although I know it isn't the case, it *feels* like this was written for someone like me, and I see avid fans praising Ava for her lyricism and vulnerability. For her *courage*.

It makes me sick to my stomach to know *Ellie* was the one who poured her heart out without ever getting recognition for her work. My revulsion intensifies as I pull up Ava's latest song, "Silver Scars." It's clear to me that the newest hit was written by Ellie, and just like the others, she isn't listed in the credits.

> Tried to numb the pain with the bite of steel,
>
> But only created new scars that never truly healed.
>
> Turned my body into a broken masterpiece,
>
> All because I needed temporary release.

I can't make it past the first verse. It isn't that I don't *want* to continue reading, because I do, but doing so without Ellie's consent feels wrong, especially when she had no part in releasing the song in the first place. While I have no idea why Ava chose to release it now, I can only assume it was meant to hurt Ellie one last time.

I lock my phone and stare up at the ceiling.

Fuck.

Is that how Ellie views herself? Like a *broken masterpiece*? Knowing she has spent God knows how long seeing herself like that makes me so angry that I lose all sense of control and head directly to Ellie's room.

She isn't a broken masterpiece, and if I need to prove it to her, I will.

Fuck boundaries and lines in the sand. My unrestrained emotions are like a wave, erasing them from existence.

I lightly knock on the wood door so as not to wake Nico. It swings open a few seconds later, and Ellie stands in front of me in another matching set of pajamas that hides her tattoos and scars from my view.

I hate it, especially now that I have a better idea of why she wears them.

"Are you okay?" Ellie asks.

"No." I spit out the word before reminding myself to calm down. "Sorry. I'm just upset and needed to see you."

She motions for me to enter before shutting the door behind me. "What's wrong?"

"Will you do something for me?"

"Now? It's ten p.m."

I search the room for her guitar and hold it out for her to grab. "Here."

She looks down at the instrument in confusion. "You want me to play a song?"

"Yes."

"Why?"

"Because I don't want to *read* about your silver scars. I want to hear you sing about them."

Her grip on the guitar slips before she readjusts it. "No one was supposed to know about that song."

I swallow back my anger. "But Ava betrayed you. *Again*."

She nods.

"Will you sing it for me?" I ask in a soft voice.

"No." She takes a step back and shakes her head. "I write songs—I don't perform them."

"What about the time you sang at Last Call?"

"That was an exception."

"Then make one again. For me."

She shakes her head.

I slip my hand beneath her shaky chin and lift it. "One time. That's all I'm asking." When she doesn't answer me, I follow up with a strained, "Please?"

She stares up at me with glassy eyes. "Why?"

"Because it's the one and only time I ever want to hear you call yourself a broken masterpiece."

I need to hear her sing the lyrics once so I can confirm whether she really believes them herself.

I grab her hand and lead her toward the sitting area, where she gets settled while I take the couch cushion beside her. She drops her pick twice before she takes a deep breath and rolls her shoulders back. "I haven't sung it in a long time."

"I don't care."

"But I'm out of practice—" Her darty gaze lands on everything but me, so I cradle her face between my hands and force her to look at me.

"I. Don't. Care." Reluctantly, I release her and sit back on the couch, silently willing myself to take a few deep breaths.

I have no idea how the song is supposed to sound, but I should've known the melody would be somber.

"One time," she says after pausing her fingerpicking.

"That's all I need." I shut my eyes and concentrate.

Her singing starts out so soft, I can hardly hear her over the guitar, but slowly, her voice, raspy from unuse at first, grows stronger, along with her confidence. It's a stark contrast to the words she sings about herself.

I listen to the way she views her body and the men who disappointed her by making her feel *undesirable*. I even pick up on the reference to the mirror fragment she has kept for over a decade because she can't seem to let it go.

I hear every single word of every painful verse, memorizing the lyrics.

Her voice wavers a few times while singing, but I don't open my eyes. If I do, then I'll tell her to stop, and I can't. No matter how much my heart hurts.

The pressure in my chest becomes unbearable, but thankfully, she plays the final chord, and blissful silence follows. When I open my eyes, I find hers screwed closed, her emotional pain etched into every fine line on her face.

I pluck the guitar from her shaky hands and put it on the coffee table before holding her face between my hands.

"I never want to hear you call yourself *broken* again."

She tries to look away, but her face is caught between the palms of my hands. "You don't understand."

"I understand more than you could ever know."

"Oh, because you have fifty plus scars all over your body?"

"I may not have ones you can *see*, but that doesn't make them any less real." I tap on my heart.

Whatever defiance she had dies, and she crumples in my arms. "I'm jealous that you can hide them while mine are always there. Every single day I see them, and I'm reminded of all the mistakes I've made. Of how weak I was and always will be."

I want to shake some sense into her, but I kiss the top of her head instead. "You're one of the strongest people I know."

"You wouldn't be saying that if you saw them. They're... hideous." Her voice breaks, along with whatever restraint I promised to have before I entered her bedroom.

Screw holding back.

"I want to see them." My heart beats harder against my chest.

Her head snaps up. "What?"

"Let me get a look at them before you assume the worst."

"Rafael."

"Show me just how hideous they really are," I say with a bit more grit. That word—and whatever memory is clearly attached to it—pushes her over the edge.

"Fine. You want to get a look at them?" She stands, her body rippling with anger. "Let's see how quickly you change your mind." She grabs the band of her pajama pants and pushes them down.

I prop my arm against the back of the couch to stop myself from reaching out and grabbing her. My fingers painfully dig into the material, and my nails threaten to rip a seam.

I don't drop my eyes as I stare into hers and say, "You're beautiful."

She shudders. "You're not even looking."

"It won't change the way I feel about you."

"You're just saying that."

I stand and walk over to her. "Would you rather me prove it instead?"

She sucks in a breath as I slide down to my knees in front of her. I can see the scars, yes, but they are surrounded by a countless number of beautiful tattoos. A *This too shall pass* tattoo is written in thin cursive across one of her thighs, hardly noticeable amongst the galaxy of stars.

When I glance up, she is looking straight ahead.

I grip her legs. "Look at me." When she finally slides those pretty hazel eyes toward me, I speak. "You may see a broken masterpiece, but I only see *you*."

I lean forward and press a kiss against one of her scars. My lips brush over another one and another after that until, soon enough, I lose count of how many times I've kissed her thighs.

The tears she tried so hard to keep from falling betray her as I whisper sweet praises against her skin. Her body trembles when I get closer to the hem of her pajama top, which hangs past her panty line, but I don't lift the material.

I only have so much self-control, and I have a feeling it would snap the moment I saw her most intimate place.

Based on my cock straining in my pants, I made the right choice, even if it feels like absolute torture to stay away.

Her clenched hands shake. "This isn't a good idea."

My lips hover over a patch of skin. "I know."

"We should stop."

I don't miss the way she clenches her thighs while saying it. If I lift her top, will I find her wet for me?

I bet if I lean forward, I could probably—

"Rafa." Ellie sounds both pained and aroused, which strokes my ego while simultaneously doing the exact opposite.

That's my girl, always turning me into a walking, talking contradiction of mixed emotions.

Against every fiber of my being, I rise to my feet and step away. My heart protests against taking a step toward the door, but I power through and rely on my critical thinking.

Where was that critical thinking a few minutes ago when you were getting down on your knees in front of her?

"Where are you going?" Her question is laced with panic.

"If I stay any longer, I'm going to end up doing something you'll clearly regret." I turn back to the door.

"Who says I'll regret it?" she asks.

My next step is unsteady. "I'm your boss."

"What if you weren't anymore?"

I look over my shoulder. "That's not an option."

"What if it was?" She drags her eyes down my body, lingering on the area throbbing with need.

A flush of warmth spreads through my body before I shake my head. "It isn't." *And neither is she.*

"I can't be his nanny forever." Something flickers in her eyes, but I can't make sense of it.

The idea of her walking away—of her *leaving*—is unbearable, and not only because it would affect Nico. *I* want her to stay, even if it means putting my own needs aside to keep her.

I'm not sure how long we can keep this platonic sham of a relationship going, but I just need her to give me time.

Time to sort through my issues.

Time to figure out what I want in life and who I really am.

But most of all, time to come to grips with the idea of not only letting my walls down but also the possibility of opening up my heart.

I never thought I could fall in love with someone after everything that happened with my marriage. Never even entertained the idea.

I was ready to spend the rest of my life raising my son alone, but throughout this vacation, I've been put in situations that have me questioning my stance. Ones that make me wonder if a life of solitude is really what I want after all. Sure, it is the safe choice, but it is also the loneliest one.

Nico keeps me company, and my family is a huge presence in my life, but I'm starting to wonder if that will be enough.

"Rafa?" Ellie asks.

"Just...give me time."

She looks at me with an expression I can't quite place.

"Please, Elle?"

She glances away and nods.

I should be relieved, but something about the look on her face makes me question just how much time I have left.

The next morning, I wake up to find Nico already dressed in his swimsuit for today's snorkeling trip. Neither he nor Ellie have noticed me yet, so I watch her rubbing sunscreen onto his skin with a grin.

"Are you sure you don't want to come?" he asks.

Her smile falters. "Yup."

The strain in her voice makes me pause.

"But you love sea turtles," he whines.

"I know." Her long exhale adds to my growing suspicion.

"Then why won't you come?"

She stays quiet as I walk into the living room.

"Do you want to join us?" I ask.

Her eyes fall to her lap. "I can't."

After listening to her "Silver Scars" song last night, I know exactly why she sticks to the sidelines, and the idea of her continuing to avoid activities because of her scars, despite clearly wanting to join us, upsets me.

I should have known there was a good reason why Ellie refused to go in the water. Originally, I thought it was because she couldn't swim, but clearly that isn't the case.

I should have connected the dots myself after she told me about her scars and self-harm, but I didn't realize just how much it all affected her mentally until I heard her sing that song.

I don't want her to hide from me.

Once Nico disappears into his room to answer a video call from my aunt, Ellie moves toward hers to get dressed, but I stop her before she disappears inside.

She blinks up at me with a face. "What?"

"Do you know how to swim?"

"Of course I know how to—" She looks at me with a pinched expression. "Wait. Why are you asking?"

I fail to hide my smile. "Do you trust me?"

Her eyes narrow. "What's with the interrogation?"

"Just answer me." The urge to tuck a strand of her golden hair behind her ear becomes too great to ignore. I wish I had a flower too, solely so I could have another reason to touch her while tucking it behind her ear.

Now that's an idea.

"Yes." She sighs. "I trust you."

"Will you do something for me, then?"

"What?"

"Will you join us today? *In* the water."

Her panic-stricken face makes my heart squeeze uncomfortably in my chest. "I thought we had an agreement."

Back when I reluctantly invited her on the trip months ago, she made her stance on swimming and water activities clear, and I was more than willing to go along with her request.

Until now.

I don't want Ellie to spend the rest of our trip hiding her scars. To me, they're beautiful because they represent what she has overcome in life, and I'll continue to make that point known until she finally believes me.

"It could be fun," I say.

"Nico will ask questions."

"I'm okay with that, but only if you are too."

She bites down on her bottom lip. "What if he looks at me differently?"

"He won't. He may be curious because he's only a kid, but he would never judge you or treat you differently because I taught him better than that."

Her head dips toward her chest, so I tuck my hand under her chin and lift it until our eyes meet.

"Trust me on this?"

With a single nod of her head, she offers me a gift I plan on protecting from here on out.

Her trust.

CHAPTER FORTY-FIVE

Ellie

I search my luggage for the one-piece swimsuit I bought strictly for this trip. The lime-green one I wore that night in the hot tub was supposed to be for special—isolated—occasions, while the black one I bought is more family-friendly.

While rifling through my suitcase, I come across a swimsuit I most definitely *did not* pack, so I pull out my phone and text Willow a photo.

ME

Seriously?

WILLOW

Are you going to wear it?!

ME

No!

WILLOW

I have a feeling you'll be changing your mind pretty soon.

It takes me a few minutes to finally understand Willow's text.

ME

Please tell me you didn't get rid of my other swimsuit on purpose.

WILLOW

Of course not!

WILLOW

But I'm not about to tell you where I hid it either.

I spend the next couple of minutes searching for the swimsuit, only to get progressively more frustrated when I can't find it.

WILLOW

> Just put the pink one on first. If
> you still hate the idea, then I'll tell
> you where I put the other one.

With a sigh, I reach for the modest but bright one-piece I bought on a whim. The back dips low, showing off the *Bend but never break* quote I had tattooed along the curve of my spine. The straps are dainty, with short ruffles fanning out in a way that flatters my shoulders and neck.

The color brings out my new tan and pairs nicely with my blond hair, but I feel ridiculous wearing something so frilly and soft with the number of tattoos and scars I have.

I snap a photo of myself in the pink swimsuit and send it to Willow.

ME

> This was a terrible idea. I'm never
> going shopping with you again.

WILLOW

> DAMN.

WILLOW

> You've been hiding those hips underneath
> mom jeans and hoodies this whole time?

WILLOW

Also, did you get a new tattoo on your hip bone? I don't think I've seen that one before.

ME

Yes, and stop changing the subject.

WILLOW

Sorry, your boobs distracted me for a second.

I knew I shouldn't have bought a few swimsuits from this one boutique in town that we love, but at the time, Willow's endless compliments gave me enough confidence to buy three bathing suits from this year's summer collection inspired by different sorbets.

That should have been my first clue that this was a terrible idea, but I couldn't resist the pink one-piece with feminine sleeves. It was too cute to pass up on. I had intended to save it for a boat day on the lake with our friends, but Willow clearly had other plans.

ME

I look like a doll.

WILLOW

> Hell yeah. Do you think Rafael
> will want to play with you?

She adds a winking emoji.

With a groan, I toss my phone on the bed. I wrap a sarong around my hips to give myself some coverage. The mesh see-through material doesn't hide much, but it makes me feel more comfortable in my own skin, so it's staying for now.

Do you trust me? Rafael's question from earlier bounces around in my head.

Seeing as I'm about to step outside dressed like this, the answer is painfully obvious.

With one last glance in the mirror, I head to the living room with my head held high. Nico is distracted by whatever game he is playing on Rafael's phone, but his father is completely, irrevocably focused on me.

His eyes darken as they slowly trail down my body. Not knowing his thoughts drives me mad, and I'm tempted to break the spell and ask him for his opinion.

When he gets to my legs, his hooded eyes flick back up to mine before he traces his bottom lip with the tip of his tongue.

For a brief moment, I wish we didn't have to fight our attraction. That we could just exist without any kind of issue holding us back.

As much as I love Nico, I'm slowly developing serious feelings for his father that can't be ignored, no matter how hard I try, which can only lead to one thing.

Trouble.

Rafael pauses our walk toward the beach to pluck a hibiscus flower from a bush. I've quickly grown to love Nico and him competing for the prettiest flower, although the one Rafael picked today may be the best yet. Not because it's my favorite color—bright pink—but because of the way he looks at me while he tucks the flower behind my ear.

"Thank you for trusting me." His finger grazes the shell of my ear before he pulls away.

Goose bumps spread across my skin. "I'm going to miss receiving all these flowers when we go back home."

His head tilts. "You are?"

"Yeah. I've been saving them all."

"Why?"

"Wanted to have something special to remember this vacation."

He makes a face as if he wants to say something, but then Nico tugs on my hand.

"My turn!"

I squat so he can place his flower on the opposite side of my head. He takes his time, making sure to double-check that it won't fall out of my hair.

When he is done, I drop a sloppy kiss on his cheek. "Thank you, little rock star."

He grins.

The back of my neck prickles, and I glance up to find Rafael looking at us. "What?"

"Nothing."

He says that out loud, but the look of pure yearning on his face?

It says *everything*.

Last night, when he learned about my song and the scars associated with it, I thought Rafael was being kind for the sake of it. He *said* my scars are beautiful because they're a part of my story, but I've heard a variation of those words before. I've had a few boyfriends who all seemed to feel the same way, but then I caught them staring when they thought I wasn't looking or wincing when they brushed their hands over them. Felt them hesitate whenever they kissed my thighs. Saw them handling sharp objects differently whenever I was in the room, acting like I might grab a blade at any second and pick up where I left off years ago.

But today, I *feel* the truth behind his words, and I've never felt more beautiful in my whole entire life.

It doesn't take long for Nico to notice my scars. We haven't even made it onto the boat for our snorkeling expedition yet, and I already caught him staring once, although he was quick to look away with flushed cheeks. Thankfully, he refrains from asking me about them while we are getting settled on the boat, but he sneaks glances every now and then during the ride out to the snorkeling area.

At one point, while I'm popping a Dramamine pill in my mouth, he pulls Rafael aside and whispers something into his ear while I pretend not to notice. I knew it would happen, but

Nico knowing about my past fills me with more trepidation than it ever has before.

I don't want him to look at me differently or be afraid of me. The anticipation of what could happen next ruins my excitement about seeing sea turtles in the wild, and I spend most of the boat ride stressed about what Nico will ask.

It's not until we reach our destination and Rafael excuses himself to use the bathroom that Nico finally gathers up enough courage to ask me the question I've been dreading.

"Ellie?"

"Mm." I school my features as I look up at him.

"Are you happy?"

I blink a few times as I register his question. "Happy how?"

"Like in general. Do you feel good?"

"Mostly, yes. Not everyone can be happy all the time because that's impossible, but I feel good most of the time."

"That's nice." He readjusts his snorkeling mask until his glasses sit comfortably against his face.

"Why are you asking me that?"

"*Papi* told me sometimes, when people are really, really sad, they hurt themselves instead of others."

So that's what Rafael and Nico were whispering about while I pretended to be fascinated by the ocean. Rafael and I agreed on that response back at the hotel, but I still feel anxious at the idea of Nico knowing.

I take a deep, cleansing breath. "He's right."

"So you did hurt yourself?"

My eyes fall toward my lap. "Yes."

"Because you were really, really sad?" He frowns.

"I *was*, but I don't do that anymore. I talked to someone who helped me get better and taught me what to do instead."

That seems to soften the tension in his shoulders. "I'm sad you were hurting that bad."

My heart feels like it's shrunk to half its size. "I'm better now. I promise."

He holds out his pinkie. "Do you swear?"

I lock my pinkie finger with his and promise before saying, "You don't need to worry about me."

"*Papi* told me it's okay to worry about people we love because that means we care."

My eyes mist over. "I love you too."

"More than sour gummy worms?"

I nod. "And strawberry-lemon fizzy drinks."

The plastic flippers on his lap fall to the floor as he jumps up and pulls me into a hug. "I love you more than pianos, superheroes, and Duke Brass."

"Wow. That's a lot of love from such a little guy."

"*Papi* says I have the biggest heart he knows."

Second-biggest heart to exist, right after his father's.

CHAPTER FORTY-SIX

Rafael

After a long day out on the water, snorkeling until our muscles were sore, we call for room service and eat dinner together in the suite's dining area.

Ellie is so tired by the end of it that she can hardly keep her eyes open when she takes a seat on the couch.

Nico holds Ellie's guitar out for her to grab. "Will you still play a song? *Please.*"

"How about I promise to play two songs tomorrow instead?"

"No." Nico switches strategies by climbing onto the couch and tickling the bottom of her foot.

"Stop! I'll seriously throw up if you do that again."

"*Mijo.*" I look up from the photo I was sending to the family group chat.

"What?"

"Leave Ellie alone."

"But she promised me." He sticks out his bottom lip, but that strategy stopped working on me years ago.

With a sigh, Ellie sits up. "All right. One song."

"Yay!" Nico bounces on the cushion a couple of times before settling down.

"He needs to learn no means no."

"Good thing he has a dad who loves the word. He'll be a pro in no time." She grins.

I scratch my nose with my middle finger, and Ellie laughs while tuning her guitar.

My phone vibrates against my thigh, and I check the Muñoz-Lopez group chat. I sent a group of photos and a couple of videos of Nico snorkeling, hiking, and riding around on the back of an ATV with me.

TÍA

Nico reminds me so much of you and Julian when you were younger.

Rosa, Dahlia and Lily's mother, follows up with a text thread full of different emojis.

DAHLIA

Is anyone going to address the obvious?

Most of the pictures I sent are of Nico and me, except for one that Ellie loved from our snorkeling trip. Nico is sitting between us with his arms wrapped around our middles, wearing the goofiest grin. Ellie is looking at the camera with a small smile and her body positioned in a way that hides her scars behind the plastic flippers.

I stare at the photo, looking for any possible clues. If I zoom in, there is a faint mark Ellie missed, but then the person would have to risk my wrath by admitting they were looking that closely at her legs.

ME

What?

DAHLIA

You're smiling!

I completely overlooked that small but crucial detail in the photo.

LILY

I forgot what his smile looked like.

LILY

And half his face.

JULIAN

Still the least handsome Lopez cousin by far.

DAHLIA

Is it too soon to get rid of the flannel?

LILY

I vote no. I'll volunteer as tribute to go through your closet myself.

ME

Elle never complains about my clothes.

DAHLIA

Are we officially caring about ELLE's opinion now?

Fuck.

ME

Typo.

TÍA

Elle! ¡Me encanta!

ME

Please don't call her that.

¡Me encanta!: I love it.

TÍA

¿Por qué?

LILY

It's adorable.

DAHLIA

I mean I think you can do better than a nickname like that, but it's still cute.

ME

Settle down, Strawberry Sweetheart.

Julian sends a middle finger emoji.

I'm quickly distracted from my phone by Ellie softly strumming.

"What about the new song you've been working on?" Nico asks.

While I'm happy she is getting back into songwriting again, my chest tightens at the idea of what could happen if Cole wants more songs from her.

It's one song. Relax.

Ellie's eyes pop. "No."

"It sounds so good." My son smiles.

"How do you know?"

¿Por qué?: Why?

Nico's cheeks turn pink. "I might have listened a little bit."

I make a face. "I told you it's rude to go sneaking around like that."

"I didn't mean to…at first."

That's my son.

Ellie pauses her strumming. "It's not finished."

I clear my throat. "I didn't know you were working on another one."

Way to not sound like a self-conscious asshole.

She glances down at her guitar. "Yeah. I'm just messing around with a few ideas."

"Can you play what you have so far?" Nico asks.

Ellie looks over at me before her eyes flick back to her guitar. "How about another one instead? Maybe one of your favorites?"

Nico makes a face, and Ellie, being the sweet, kind soul she is, complies.

"You don't need to give in to him."

"You try saying no to that face."

On cue, Nico pops his bottom lip out and wobbles it.

"See?"

I shrug.

Seriously, Ellie spoils Nico way too much, but seeing as I can't tell her no either, who am I to judge?

Ellie starts playing her new song, and both Nico and I become enraptured by her storytelling.

My momma says to look toward the future,

But I can't see in the dark.

So I move around in a stupor,

Without ever hitting my mark.

My friends say tomorrow's a brand-new day,

but I'm trapped in a never-ending night.

With no stars in the sky to point my way,

back to the missing light.

The doctor says to keep moving forward,

but I can't seem to get out of reverse.

So I'm stuck in an endless torture,

With no way to break the curse.

Her voice is hypnotic and weaves a picture so vivid, I can't help but wonder if what she's saying is real. She continues singing, although the next verse has me questioning her lyrics even more.

I'm tired of hearing them tell me

how I'm supposed to live.

That if I want to be happy,

I need to learn what it means to forgive.

Ellie's voice tapers off as the music stops altogether.

"That's it?" Nico whines in disappointment.

Ellie's cheeks turn pink. "So far, yeah."

"I like it." He nods. "But…"

She gives him a look, and he lifts his hands up. "I know, but I was thinking you could change it to sound like this instead."

He holds his hand out, and Ellie places her guitar in his open palm with a frown.

Nico sets her guitar on his thigh and plays Ellie's original chords. "This is how it sounds right now." My son replays the same chords from the opening verse without messing up.

"Right." She nods.

"But what if you did this?" He changes the sound slightly, altering the speed at which the chords are plucked, which seems to add a bit more buildup before the first bridge.

I don't know much about music, but whatever Nico did makes Ellie's face brighten.

"Do that again."

Nico repeats the same sound, and Ellie beams. "You're a genius."

"I am?"

"Yes! I need my notebook and my phone." Ellie scrambles off the couch, kisses the top of Nico's head, and takes off running toward her bedroom.

"So much for not being able to move!" Nico shouts at her back with a big grin on his face.

"If you keep up the sass, then I'll never tell Cole Griffin you helped write his song!" she shouts from the hallway.

Nico's mouth falls open as he looks over at me. "Wait. The Cole Ellie was talking about before is *Cole Griffin*?"

"Yup."

Nico nearly drops the guitar. "*Dios mío*. And you didn't say anything?"

"I had no idea you knew who that was."

"Everyone does! He's Cole Griffin!"

Knowing my nine-year-old kid listens to songs with lyrics centered around depression, anxiety, and broken hearts doesn't exactly make me a happy parent, but Nico has always been interested in music, so I can't expect him not to be curious about our generation's greats.

"His songs aren't for kids your age."

"Neither are Ellie's, but you let me listen to hers."

"She's different."

"Because you like her?"

"Nicolas." My cheeks flush.

He has the mischievous glint in his eyes that always gets me into trouble. "Oh. You're getting embarrassed."

I drop my head into my hands and groan. "Stop talking. Right now. Please."

"Only if you admit that you like Ellie as more than a friend."

"Fine. I like her."

"Okay, but do you *like* her, or do you *like like* her?"

For fuck's sake. "*¡Por el amor de Dios, si!* I *like like* her. Are you happy now?"

I don't need to look up to know that Ellie returned with her notebook. The way my neck prickles with awareness is enough of a tell, but I still check anyway to confirm that she heard my comment.

Based on her wide eyes, I have my answer.

Dios mío: My God.

Por el amor de Dios, si.: For the love of God, yes.

418

CHAPTER FORTY-SEVEN

Ellie

I feel just as confused this morning as I was last night about my situation with Rafael after overhearing him confess to Nico that he *likes* me. While I'm happy to know how he feels, it complicates matters because I like him too.

I may even more than *like* him.

I haven't wanted to admit it to myself, but denying the truth isn't doing me any favors. He and I are going to have to come to terms with what this development means for our relationship.

If there even *is* a relationship.

While Nico seems less of an obstacle now that he at least knows his dad likes me, it doesn't address our biggest issue.

Rafael is still my *boss*.

That truth is hard to avoid, which is why I ignored him knocking on my door last night until I could talk to a voice of reason.

My mom.

"Ellie! I got your photos!" my mom gushes. "They're absolutely gorgeous."

"You'd be proud. I went on a boat yesterday and didn't throw up once."

She laughs. "Look at you conquering motion sickness and your fear of planes all in two weeks! What's next? Snakes?"

"Over my dead body."

She chuckles. "I miss you so much! I can't wait to see you and hear all about your trip when you come back."

"Yeah, me too."

"But you're not calling me to talk about it, are you?" My mom always had that special sixth sense when it came to me.

I fall back onto my bed. "Not exactly."

"What's going on?"

"So, you remember how Cole Griffin hired me to write him a song?"

"Who could forget? I've been listening to a few of his albums since you mentioned his name during our last call, and he's really good."

"I know."

"His songs are sad, but he's a perfect match for you lyrically."

"Well, I'm glad you think so because he asked me if I wanted to help him write his next album."

"He did?" My mom squeals, and I can hear Burt rushing into the room to check on her.

"Cole Griffin asked Ellie to help him write an album!" she tells him, and I smile. Mom has been trying to push me to get back out there and try songwriting again, but I've obviously been resistant.

"I had no doubt it would happen," Burt says.

"I'm excited."

"Of course! This is huge!" Mom shouts so loud, my speaker crackles.

I pull my phone away from my ear. "There's only one problem."

"What?"

"He wants me to join him in Europe while he's on tour."

"If going to Europe is a problem, I'll happily take your place," Burt jokes.

Mom shushes him. "What's the matter?"

"I don't know if I can go."

"Why not?"

"Because I already have a job, and there is no way I can take five weeks off like that."

"Ellie, dear." Mom's soft voice makes me pause.

"What?"

"I know you like the Lopez family and are loyal to a fault—"

"I think I may more than *like* them."

"Them or *him*?" she asks in that knowing tone.

"Him."

She makes a confirmatory noise. "Well, that sure complicates matters a bit."

"I don't know what to do." I curl the string of my hoodie around my index finger. "I didn't expect him to bring out old feelings, let alone new ones."

"Hm."

"And he likes me too." I think back to yesterday and how he admitted to Nico that he liked me. I felt so damn excited before our reality came crashing back down around us.

"Well, then, that's an even bigger reason for you to consider another job."

I knew she would suggest it, but hearing it still makes my chest clench. "I know it's wrong to feel that way about my boss…"

"I didn't say that, but is it in your best interest to keep working for him if you're developing real feelings?"

No, which only adds another layer to our issue.

"I'm scared of change."

"If you weren't, I'd be concerned because you love to second-guess."

"And triple-think," Burt adds.

"What did she always say when she was younger?" my mom asks him.

"Four times to be *for sure*?" he suggests.

Mom laughs. "Yes! I knew it was something like that."

I can't help chuckling with her. "Okay. I get it. I like to really consider my options."

Mom sobers. "We're just teasing you. Anyone in your position would hesitate about accepting a job like that, especially after what you went through last time."

"I mean, I *want* to agree to Cole's offer, but I don't want to lose Rafael or Nico in the process."

"Because you care," Mom replies.

"Exactly."

"Well, my sweet girl, if they truly care for you too, then they will be happy and supportive of you chasing after your dreams because you of all people deserve it."

I release a shaky breath. My mom does have a point, whether I want to agree with it or not.

Mom continues, "You gave that family more than eight incredible months of your time as their nanny. Taking a different job doesn't negate that, but it could open the door for a new kind of relationship instead."

Our last day in Hawaii is bittersweet. For the last two weeks, we've lived in our own three-person bubble, and while I can't wait to get home and back to my routine, I'm going to miss this feeling as well.

Despite taking Nico kayaking around the island, having both Hula Pie *and* shave ice for dessert tonight, and watching the sunset from a special lookout point while listening to his favorite Duke Brass album, morale is still low by the time we get back to the hotel suite.

"Can we watch a movie?"

Rafael and I shoot each other a look.

"It's late," Rafael says.

Nico runs up to his dad and pops his bottom lip out. "Please."

Rafael glances down at him and says, "No."

Damn. He doesn't even flinch when he says it.

Nico is a man on a new mission as he abandons his father and rushes over to me. "What do you think, Ellie? I'll even let you pick the movie."

I bite down on my lip. "I don't know."

Rafael rolls his eyes, and I flip him off behind my back.

"Please?" Nico presses his hands together in a silent plea. "You'll be the bestest nanny ever."

After the conversation I had with my mom earlier, I know my time as his nanny is coming to an end, so I'm feeling extra sentimental tonight.

When we return to Lake Wisteria, Rafael and I will have to have a talk about my job, but tonight I can pretend nothing will change.

I look back at his father. "Maybe we can decide on the movie together?"

"You could say no."

My right eye twitches.

With a sigh, he nods. "Fine."

Nico throws his fist in the air. "Yes!"

Rafael and I choose a movie neither of us have seen before while Nico grabs some snacks from the chef's kitchen. I pick the side of the couch with the chaise while Rafael settles on the opposite side and kicks his feet up on the cushions, only to have Nico drag his dad over to my side so we can "share a blanket."

Neither of us calls him out on his clinginess as he settles between us with a sigh, although we share a look from over his head.

Rafael eventually props his long legs on the coffee table and lays his arms on the back of the couch. It may be the oldest flirting trick in the book, but it makes my heart beat faster when his fingers tease my neck and shoulders.

I suck in a breath, earning me a smirk. When I shoot daggers at him, Rafael pretends to be watching the movie.

Fine. Two can play this game.

I reach over and start running my nails across the back of

his head. He leans into my touch and groans, but Nico misses it thanks to an action scene playing.

Whenever I pull away, Rafael drags my hand back, and I spend the next five minutes scratching his head.

Nico eventually catches me and then proceeds to beg me to do the same. Like a cat, he leans into my touch with a silly smile. "That feels so good."

He and Rafael spend the next thirty minutes vying for their turn. Nico asks me to brush my nails across his arm, back and forth, before determining that I give the best *cosquillas* ever, after which Rafael asks me to do the same so he could decide if that's true.

Eventually, I tell them my hand is tired and to try again next time when we get back to Lake Wisteria.

I'm wondering if there will be a next time.

Any doubts I had about quitting were erased tonight because I can't take this push and pull anymore.

I want Rafael Lopez, and I'm done pretending otherwise.

So later that night, before I go to bed, I text Cole two words that seal my fate.

I'm in.

Cosquillas: a light tickle done using the the tips of fingers.

CHAPTER FORTY-EIGHT

Rafael

Aside from Ellie being anxious during our red-eye flight home and me staying up with her for a couple of hours, talking about everything and anything, until she finally dozed off, we make it back to Lake Wisteria without any issues.

Ever since we returned to my home and the eight animals who are thankfully still alive, Ellie has been abnormally quiet, to the point that I forgot that she was even in the house. It wasn't until she popped into my office around dinnertime to let me know that the food was ready that I realized she hadn't taken Nico out to the pond or to the park in town.

As much as I want to spend time with them, I needed to start catching up on two weeks' worth of work. I am so busy answering emails, checking Dwelling app analytics, and reviewing tasks with my assistant that I don't get around to eating what Ellie prepared until long after they are done and their dishes are put away.

After spending fourteen days in Hawaii, sharing almost every meal together, the kitchen is unnervingly quiet today.

I despise it.

Distracting myself with work doesn't lessen the loneliness like it used to, and tonight I can't seem to focus on anything but the empty void in my chest that Nico and Ellie's company seems to fill.

I miss Nico's giggles and Ellie's small smiles. Miss the way she loosened up a bit after a cocktail and shared interesting stories from her childhood and the time she spent living in Los Angeles. She always made the cutest half-snort, half-scoff sound whenever I made a snide remark, and her deep laughs—which don't happen often—always filled me with unbridled pride.

I miss her like she isn't currently in the basement with Nico, helping him practice his Strawberry Festival musical piece. Like I didn't spend the last two weeks constantly around her and soaking up her attention.

In the past, it would have concerned me to care about someone outside my family like that, but I'm not afraid.

I'm *motivated*.

Starting tomorrow, I'm going to prioritize eating dinner with Ellie and Nico, even if it means staying up a little later to finish my tasks for work. I'll even stock the wet bar with mango margarita supplies, since she loved them, and every single flavor of Hawaiian Sun since they're Nico's favorite.

After I finish my food, pack away the leftovers for tomorrow, and help put Nico to bed, I seek Ellie out. I remember her telling me that she wanted to go check on the animals once Nico fell asleep, so I head outside.

I walk over to the barn, only to stop near the entrance once I hear her talking.

"I'm going to miss seeing you every day."

One of the goats bleats.

Miss them? Why?

"I just got back here and now I'll be leaving again." She sighs.

Leaving? Where?

"I love spending time with you too." She chuckles to herself as a second goat makes a noise. "I'll try to come back as often as possible…if he doesn't hate me, that is."

Is she talking about *me*? Why the hell would I *hate* her?

I'm thinking about all the ways I can spend more time with her, and this is what she is thinking about?

Nothing she's saying makes sense, so I mentally flip through today's sequence of events, searching for clues as to why Ellie would be talking to the animals like she plans on not coming back.

Just the other night I told her she can't—

I can't be his nanny forever.

Something about that statement seemed off in the moment, but I ignored it because I assumed she was talking about way down the line. Not *now*.

Feet shuffling in the goat's pen, followed by their door closing and the lock sliding into place, has me stiffening. Ellie hasn't seen me yet, so I marvel at her like she's a work of art.

She may not be wearing a dress like on all those nights in Hawaii, but she isn't wearing her usual leggings and hoodies either.

My heart swells with pride. Her outfit is casual, but her T-shirt and shorts carry so much meaning. It might have taken her time to become comfortable enough to do so in Nico's and my presence, but I would have waited as long as it took for her.

"Rafa?" Her voice snaps me out of my thoughts.

"Elle." My voice is rough and guttural.

"How long have you been standing there?"

I push away from one of the barn's support columns. "Long enough."

I don't have all the facts, but I've gathered enough to know she owes me a few answers.

Her face pales. "Oh."

I drag my eyes away, hoping it eases the ache in my chest. "Are you quitting?"

She bites on the inside of her cheek. "Maybe we should go inside the house—"

"Just tell me."

She looks around the entire barn before her eyes land back on me. "I'm afraid of how you'll react."

"I may not have…had the best control over my reactions in the past, but I won't get mad at you for being honest with me."

She looks at me like she doesn't believe me, and I stare back until she does.

After a long sigh, she finally says, "Cole wants to fly me out to Europe so I can help him write an album while he is on tour."

A sharp pain shoots through my chest, strong enough to make my next breath hurt. Ellie crosses her arms as if she is bracing herself for me to lash out.

So I take a few deep breaths and school my features. I had a feeling it could happen, especially after reading the lyrics to all the songs she wrote for Ava, but reality hits me harder than I thought.

"How long?" I ask with a neutral tone.

She shoots me a quivering smile. "Five weeks."

Fuck. That is a lot longer than I would like, although she would still be able to make it in time for our trip to see the Mexican Grand Prix.

"And when would you leave?"

"After the Strawberry Festival."

"So you'll still be around until then?"

"Yup. I wouldn't miss Nico's performance for anything." Her smile is small but sure.

I don't *want* her to go, but I also want what is best for her. She is brilliant and talented, and it's time someone recognizes that, even if that person happens to be Cole.

I want Ellie to shine like she was meant to, but that isn't possible if she stays with me in the dark.

It hurts like hell to know I will have to let her go, but at the same time, I understand it is the best decision for her, which makes it the right choice for me.

Even if it feels *wrong* now.

My head may be spinning, but my heart is *calm*. No skipped beats. No racing pulse. No blood whooshing in my ears or temples throbbing. Honestly, if it weren't for the fact that I'm still breathing, I would question if it was working properly.

My smile is honest. "I'm happy for you."

Her brows hike up toward her hairline. "You are?"

I nod despite the tension in my neck. "I'm incredibly proud as well. I knew you were talented, but to score a job working for Cole? That's a career-making opportunity."

"Um…"

I walk over and pull her into my arms. "It's okay to be happy about this."

Her face crumples. "But I feel so conflicted."

"I can help make the decision easier."

"How?"

My hand finds the small of her back. "For starters, I'm not going to make you a competitive offer."

"You're not?" She tilts her head.

"No."

A frown appears between her brows. "You could at least *look* torn up about me leaving."

I am, but in a way, I feel free to do what I want now that we no longer have her job or Nico standing between us, and that in itself is a reason to celebrate.

I wrap my hand around the back of her neck. "Elle?"

"Yeah?"

"You know I like you, right?" I brush my thumb across her cheek.

"Well, I did hear you tell Nico that a few days ago, yes." She looks confused as she tries to follow my train of thought.

"Remember that in a second, okay?"

"Wha—"

"You're fired."

Her protest dies when I crush my lips against her and kiss her like I've been wanting to.

Like I've been *dying* to.

Without anything holding us back, I pour everything into our kiss, showing her exactly how I feel without ever uttering a single word.

With her in my arms, I'm happy and hopeful. Like I'm no longer stuck in reverse because I found the brightest star to guide me out of the dark.

Elle Sinclair.

CHAPTER FORTY-NINE

Ellie

Rafael and I shared a kiss before, and while it was incredible, it wasn't like *this*, and I know nothing will ever compare again.

Power and passion clash as our kiss becomes a battle of possession, and I quickly end up on the losing side of the war as Rafael dominates my mouth like he does my heart. He is an army of one, claiming every fragmented piece of my mind, body, and soul as his while I wave the white flag of surrender.

Whatever he wants, he can have it, so long as he never stops kissing me like this.

My heart threatens to give out altogether, along with my legs, but Rafael holds me upright.

In his arms, I forget about the world around me and allow myself to *feel*. His adoration. My desperation. And the hope blossoming in my chest like a weed with roots that never seem to end.

I'm not sure how long we stand there, lost in each other, but eventually Rafael grabs my thighs and lifts me up. My legs instinctively wrap around his waist before he pushes me into one of the barn's support columns.

He returns to kissing me, all while his cock presses into me. I grind against him, earning a moan from him while my tongue teases his in a dance of languid strokes and fleeting touches.

He pushes into me, and my head drops back with a moan. "God."

His deep chuckle makes my insides clench as he moves on to kiss my jawline. Neck. Collarbone and chest. He marks my skin with invisible tattoos in the shape of his lips.

Hm. I'll have to save that line for our song.

With a groan, he tears his mouth away and carries me toward the ladder below the hayloft while I leave a trail of kisses down his neck.

He puts me back on my feet. "Get up there."

When I remain standing in place, he smacks my ass before pointing up at the loft above. "Now."

I shoot him a look that earns me smack on my other butt cheek.

"I should have let you quit." He narrows his eyes.

Mine roll. "No one asked you to fire me."

He places his arms on both sides of the ladder, effectively crowding me. "I wanted to."

I glare.

He kisses the tip of my scrunched nose. "How else would you get your severance pay?"

I blink.

And blink some more.

I never even *considered* the severance clause in our newest employee contract or the hundred thousand dollars I stood to gain if he ever fired me again.

My eyes bulge. "Oh my God."

"I prefer to go by the less formal *Rafa*, but in your special case, *God* does seem to have a nice ring to it."

I swat his shoulder. "You should have just let me quit!"

"I want to make sure you're taken care of." He kisses the corner of my mouth, and I lose it.

This man may say he likes me, but I'm not a fool. I know his feelings are more complex, so it is up to me to nurture his affection and help it bloom until he has no choice but to acknowledge it.

I wrap my arms around his neck and kiss him so hard he forgets his original mission to get me up the ladder. I'm not sure how long we stand there, making up for lost time and growing sexual tension, but I pour everything into that kiss.

My appreciation, devotion, and *love*.

No conditions. No agenda. No expectations but the chance to show him how things could be with us, so long as he is willing to take a risk.

With a reluctant groan, I pull away first and reach for the ladder. My limbs tremble as I climb up to the second story. The barn's loft is small but charming, with a full-size daybed facing the window overlooking part of Rafael's property. There is a distressed writing desk in one corner with his latest barn expansion plans and a couple of books I forgot to take back to the house.

We have both hung out here on plenty of occasions, but never at the same time—until now.

Rafael wraps his arms around me from behind and rocks his hips into my ass. "We should go slow."

"Your body seems to say the opposite."

He spins me around, and my skin pebbles with anticipation. "I'm trying to go about this the right way."

"Can you start tomorrow? Because I really, *really* want to choose the wrong way." I reach for the hem of his shirt and start lifting it.

His nostrils flare. "Elle."

I brush my fingers across his abs. "Say it again."

"*Elle*." He groans this time when I slip my hand inside his joggers.

"Still want to go slow?" I grip his cock and pump once.

Next thing I know, I'm airborne before landing on the daybed with an *oomph*. My hair falls in front of my eyes, and I shove the strands away with a laugh.

The bed dips from Rafael's weight as he places one knee on the mattress. "I'll touch you on one condition."

I rise to my elbows. "What?"

"Let me take you on a date tomorrow."

My answer is easy. "Sure."

He smirks. "You're not going to play hard to get?"

I bite back a laugh. "Do you want me to?"

"You *could* make me work for it."

"What do you think I plan on doing now?" I wink while spreading my legs.

His eyes drop toward my parted thighs, and his nostrils flare. My confidence remains strong as I drag my top over my head, revealing my simple bralette, scattered scars, and array of tattoos.

I never imagined I would be seducing Rafael Lopez, let alone talking about going on a date, but here I am, with my legs spread and my heart in my throat.

"Fuck." He wipes a hand down his face.

"Already having regrets?"

"Only one."

"What?"

"That I've waited this long to taste you." He undoes the button of my jean shorts, and my heart jolts in my chest as he tugs them off.

My typical apprehension about my scars is still there. I had my tattoo artist add stars around the scars, not to cover them but to turn my thighs into a canvas inspired by one of my favorite songs.

Still, I can't help being self-conscious about the older ones. Eventually, I learned to be more discreet, choosing places that could easily go undetected by almost everyone. My stomach. The insides of my upper thighs. Behind my panty line.

God, what will he think if he sees those? I think as I look away with a flinch.

He slides to his knees and brushes his hands across my thighs. "*Mírame.*"

Mírame: Look at me.

My wide-eyed gaze swings back to his. Rafael brushes his hand across my flesh, but this time, I don't flinch because I'm too focused on what comes out of his mouth instead.

"You're one of the strongest people I know." His touch is soft. Appreciative. Exploratory in a way that makes my stomach burst with butterflies.

The last time I counted, I had over fifty scars, so that makes me the complete opposite of strong, but with the way Rafael looks at me, I choose to believe him.

His lips brush over one of the older ones. "All I see is someone who chose to live."

My bottom lip wobbles.

"Someone who chose to keep fighting, even when they had reasons to give up." He brushes the tip of his finger over one of my tattoos, and my vision blurs at the edges as tears form near my lash line. "Someone who turned their scars into shooting stars." He leans forward on his knees and kisses my newest scar that always fills me with shame.

A single tear slips out, and I brush it away because I don't want to ruin the moment.

He doesn't seem to care, though, as he repeats the gesture, this time kissing the scar beside the last.

"You're a warrior, Elle." His lips brush over a particularly ugly one. "You put up a great fight, but you don't have to battle those demons alone anymore."

One tear turns into two, and next thing I know, my cheeks are soaked.

Rafael replaces my past memories with a completely new one as he takes his time kissing every single scar.

By the time he is done, my grief has morphed into a yearning so strong, I'm afraid I may combust. My lower half is pulsing, and I desperately want to press my thighs together, but his body keeps them open as he brings out another wave of yearning.

He drops a kiss right over my pussy, and I suck in a breath.

"You like that?" His lips hover over me, peppering me with soft kisses as he makes his way closer to my underwear.

"I know it's been a long, *long* time for you, but I'm sure you can solve that mystery on your own."

His right hand traces a path toward my underwear while his other hand reaches to cup my ass. "Oh, Elle. The things I want to do to that mouth."

Rafael brushes his knuckle up and down my center, sending zings of pleasure down my spine. He presses the pad of his thumb against my clit, and I jolt forward with a gasp. He pushes my underwear to the side, smirking at the wet spot soaking through the cotton.

If I wasn't lying down, I would fall over as he brushes the tip of his tongue over my center.

"You're soaked for me."

"Are you going to continue stating the obvious, or can you actually do something about it?" I wiggle my hips.

A devious smirk crosses his lips. "Keep talking like that and I'll make *you* work for it."

"How?"

He locks his hand around my wrist and drags it toward my center. "Isn't it *obvious*?"

Using my index finger, he traces over my slit, back and forth slowly until I'm quivering.

"Hm. You seem to like that, so I'll have to think of a new punishment instead."

I shudder as he slips the tips of our fingers inside. "Maybe this."

My head drops back, a groan slipping past my lips as he pumps both our fingers in unison. I tremble with every thrust, and a deep pressure builds in my lower half.

He makes a noise of discontent. "Nope. That's not going to work either. You're enjoying that too much."

"Keep trying new things. I'm sure you'll figure it out eventually." My body shakes as he drags both our hands toward my clit. It aches as he pinches it, and my hips buck from the sharp pulsing sensation deep in my belly.

"Good idea." His deep chuckle makes my insides throb. He yanks on my underwear and throws it to the ground on top of my shorts. My lips part, but my protest dies as Rafael swings my right leg over his shoulder before doing the same with my left.

He grips my ass and pulls me closer to his face. His hold is possessive. Demanding. So damn hot, my skin feels like it might catch fire. Perhaps it already is, because I am sweating and he hasn't even tasted me yet.

My thighs press against the sides of his head as he drags his nose across my center and takes a deep breath.

My cheeks flame at the sound of his sharp inhale, but my embarrassment quickly morphs into arousal as his tongue flicks out.

"Rafael." His name is nothing but a moan as I grip his hair.

He groans against me, sending a pleasant vibration straight

to my clit. I sneak a glance at him, only to freeze when I find his eyes glued to mine. Our gazes remain locked as he leans forward and flicks his tongue along my center, collecting my arousal with a satisfied hum.

My brain has officially short-circuited, and I'm too lost in a haze of lust to care.

Rafael seems to feel the same, with his eyes shutting as he stakes his claim on me. His strokes are lazy at first, driving me to madness as he takes his sweet time learning what I like. Every quiver, gasp, and buck of my hips seems to encourage him, and he becomes a master of my body in no time, drawing out my pleasure to the point of tears, only to deny me my release.

Anytime I get close, he pulls back, making me progressively more frustrated with every delayed orgasm.

"I think I found my new punishment."

"Fuck off."

"Why would I do that when I'd much rather fuck you instead?" His tongue plunges inside me again as he resumes his torture.

Minutes pass, and he shows no sign of stopping.

"Rafael," I beg with tears in my eyes as he sinks a single finger inside me.

"Again." He flicks his tongue against my clit before sucking, and my pelvis presses harder against his face.

"Rafael. Please."

"Mi estrella."

Mi estrella: My star.

My heart bursts at the term of endearment.

His pace switches from explorative to punishing as he adds a second finger and pumps. His tongue quickly joins, sliding over my clit before he sucks hard enough to make me jolt.

Stars blaze to life behind my eyelids, temporarily blinding me as I come with a cry.

Rafael doesn't stop stroking, licking, and sucking until I'm limp and panting beneath him. Carefully, he places my legs back on the bed before crawling behind me and pulling me into his chest. His cock presses against my ass, but when I suggest doing something about it, he tells me he just wants to enjoy the moment.

He gives me *cosquillas*, and I nod off for ten minutes before we head back to the house, just in case Nico wakes up.

Rafael drags me into his room, claiming he wants to cuddle, and I don't bother denying him.

Tomorrow, I will need to begin the process of moving out, but tonight…

Tonight, I pretend that tomorrow won't ever come.

CHAPTER FIFTY

Rafael

Morning comes all too soon, although I stayed up for as long as I could before I took Ellie back to her room and tucked her into bed.

I linger nearby, watching over her and sulking about how, come later today, she will be officially moving out. Last night, I tried to shut her idea down, but once she explained her reasoning, I reluctantly agreed.

She wants to take things slow and give us space to figure this out without getting Nico's hopes up, and deep down, I know she is right.

Over the next two weeks, Ellie will still come over to help Nico so he can slowly adjust to life without her, but she will no longer be spending her nights here. She claims it would be too tempting to stay here forever, and I've yet to see the issue with that.

While I don't want her to move back into her parents' house, I understand that to move forward, we can't keep clinging to the way things used to be.

For Ellie's sake, I hope Nico takes the news about her job well, but I genuinely have no idea how he will react. Last night, Ellie and I agreed that she would lead the conversation about her new job, so even if I want to interfere, I told her I wouldn't.

When the temptation to wake Ellie up becomes too great to ignore, I exit her room and head toward the kitchen to make breakfast for the three of us.

An hour later, Nico enters with a yawn. Ellie follows behind him, dressed in another pair of shorts that throws me back to last night, when her legs were—

"*Buenos dias, Papi.*" Nico comes over to give me a hug.

"I made breakfast." I motion to the round table underneath a window that faces the backyard deck and the small pond in the distance.

My son sits at the nook and grins like the pancakes with a smile made of fruit. Ellie and I take seats beside each other, and the three of us enjoy each other's company.

We swap stories and laughs throughout the meal, and it is somehow ten times better than Hawaii, slightly due to being in the comfort of my own home but mostly because of everything that happened with Ellie last night.

She was…*everything*.

A pressure in my chest builds at the idea of no longer

Buenos dias, Papi: Good morning, Dad.

waking up to this, but I promise myself that it won't be for long.

I won't *allow* it to be.

Once we all clear our plates, Ellie looks over at me and nods. I reach for her hand underneath the table and interlace our fingers without Nico noticing.

As much as I want to hold her hand out in the open, I'm not ready for that step with Nico, and neither is she.

Let's take it all one day at a time, she said last night while I held her in my arms.

How am I supposed to take you on dates if you're spending five weeks in Europe? I asked.

We'll just have to get creative. She grinned up at me, and that was that.

Ellie takes a shallow breath. "Nico, I wanted to talk to you about something."

Nico puts his glass of orange juice down. "What?"

"Remember how I was writing a song for Cole Griffin?"

"Yeah?" His furrowed brow reminds me so much of my own.

"Well, he loved it."

Nico holds his hand up for Ellie to smack. "Duh! You're awesome."

Her cheeks flush as she high-fives him. "Thank you."

"So is he going to keep it?"

"Yeah."

"And what about the song I helped you with?"

Ellie smiles. "I'm glad you asked because it turns out Cole wants me to help him with a bunch of songs."

Nico's eyes go big. "Really?"

"Yup. And he told me you could be listed on the credits."

"No way!"

"Congratulations. You may be the youngest songwriter in history."

Nico grins. "If you need more help, I'll only charge you a gazillion dollars."

Ellie and I both laugh at that.

"Well, I don't know if I could afford you, but if you want to help me, you can."

"Wow."

"Pretty awesome, right?"

"Obviously! Congrats!" He holds out his fist this time, and Ellie bumps hers against it.

"Thanks." She glances over at me, and I nod.

Might as well get it over with.

"So, if I want to work with Cole, I have to go with him to Europe."

My son smiles. "That's so cool! You've gotta go."

How can Ellie look so happy yet so sad at the same time? I wish I could erase the expression on her face, but there is nothing either of us can do.

Her hand tightens around mine. "If I work for Cole, I can't be your nanny anymore."

"But can't you come back when you're done?"

"I don't think so..." She bites down on her lip until it turns red.

"How long will you be gone?" Nico asks.

"Five weeks."

"That's not too long. Right, *Papi*? Ellie can come back here after!" His smile dies when he looks over at me.

"*No, mijo*. She can't work for me anymore."

"But why?" His voice cracks.

"Ellie should keep writing music for other people because she's really good at it."

"But—" Nico's shoulders slump with defeat.

Ellie drops my hand so she can kneel beside his chair. "I'm not leaving you, though."

"Yes, you are." A few tears fall onto his lap.

"No. I will *always* be a part of your life."

"But you're leaving." Before I have a chance to reassure him, Nico leaves the kitchen in a rush.

Ellie turns to me with tears in her eyes. "I don't know if I can do this."

"You can."

A sob in the distance, followed by a door slamming, shatters whatever control Ellie had over her tears, and one slips down her face.

My own heart feels split in two as Nico and Ellie pull it in opposite directions. While I wish she could stay with us forever—both because Nico loves her and I...need her—she deserves to choose herself and her future. We will always be here, but an opportunity like Cole's won't last forever, and that is what I tell myself as I rise to my feet and hold my hand out for Ellie to grab.

"He will understand."

She shakes her head. "No, he won't."

"He will once he figures out that I won't make the same

mistake as last time when I fired you." I played a part in Nico's mistrust when I fired Ellie after his accident, and it is up to me to rectify it.

Tears spill down Ellie's cheeks as we follow the sound of Nico's cries toward the source.

I knock against the guest bathroom door located near the elevators. "Nicolas?"

His cries pause as he blows his nose. "What?"

"Can we talk to you? Please?"

"I don't want to."

Ellie bristles beside me.

"I know you're upset right now, but Ellie isn't leaving—"

"Yes, she is!"

"Nico." Ellie tests the doorknob and opens the door a crack. "Can I please come in?"

"Why? You're just going to lie like Mommy!"

While his words feel like a shotgun shell to the chest, I can't imagine how Ellie must feel hearing Nico compare her to Hillary.

She gives my hand a squeeze, and I return the gesture with one of my own, as if to say we can handle this. *Together.*

"I've never lied to you, and I never will." Ellie steels her spine and opens the door.

My son sits on the tiled floor with his legs tucked against his chest and his forehead pressed into his knees.

Ellie kneels beside him while I stand in the doorway, frozen in place, while she circles her arms around Nico and crushes him against her chest. "I'm sorry your mom has made promises she couldn't keep"—*an issue I plan on correcting as soon as possible*—"but I'm not her. I've never broken one since I started working for your dad, even when it meant losing my job because of the secret I kept, and I don't plan on breaking any to come because your trust is important to me."

His forehead brushes against his knees when he shakes his head. "I don't want you to leave me."

"I'm not. I may be going to work for someone else, but I will always be a part of your life, whether I'm your nanny or not."

Nico looks up with red, tear-stained cheeks and bloodshot eyes. "You will?"

"Yes. You're stuck with me forever."

His bottom lip wobbles as his gaze swings from me to Ellie. "You promise?"

"On my life. Nothing could keep me away from you."

"I don't want you to go." Nico hides his face behind his hands and sobs.

Ellie looks over at me in a panic, so I kneel beside her.

"Hey."

Nico's shoulders shake from his ragged breathing.

I lift his chin. "It's okay to be sad."

"It *hurts*." He taps at the spot over his heart.

Ellie dabs at the corners of her eyes.

Something cracks inside me. "I know you're scared Ellie won't come back, but she will."

"But she won't have a reason to anymore."

"I'll make sure she always has a reason to come back," I say with an even voice.

"I'm looking at my biggest reasons right now." She gives

both our hands a squeeze, and it eases some of the heavy weight pressing against my temples, shoulders, and chest.

I wrap my arms around the two of them and drag us into a group hug. "This isn't us saying goodbye."

She nods against one of my shoulders with a sniffle. "It's not."

Nico hides his face against the other. "I'm happy for you, Ellie, but I'm also sad for me."

"Me too," I say earnestly.

Ellie pokes her head out of the crook of my neck. "Me three."

Nico wraps his arms around our necks. "I don't want another nanny."

"Then we won't get one." My original reason for having one doesn't matter anymore because Ellie is plenty for Nico, whether she is in his life as a friend or more.

"Can Ellie visit every day? When she's not in Europe?" he asks between sniffles.

She laughs. "You're going to get sick of me."

"Impossible." I offer her a smile.

"Yeah. What he said." Nico nods.

"You can visit as often as you want. Multiple times a day if you'd like." I wink.

"I mean, it would be a good idea for me to check on the animals. They're practically my children."

"Absolutely. Plus, I'm getting some new additions next week that need names."

"God forbid you name them pigs one, two, and three."

"What about chickens?" Nico asks with an excited smile.

I shoot him a look. "Not yet."

"Aw, man."

Ellie fixes his glasses on his nose. "Chickens do sound fun."

I scratch my chin. "On second thought…"

Nico and Ellie laugh, thinking I'm joking.

While I can easily tell Nico no, Ellie is a different case altogether, and it's only a matter of time before she realizes it.

Julian pulls me into a bone-crushing hug. "I've missed you, man."

My chest tightens as I return his embrace before letting him into the house. "Same."

"Where's Ellie?" He looks around.

"She went back to her mom's house."

"To visit? It's not even Saturday."

I shake my head. "She moved out earlier today."

Nico followed her around all morning while she fed the animals, mucked out their stalls, caught up on all our laundry, and made lunch for the three of us. It was a bittersweet meal, but Ellie already promised to be back tomorrow, so Nico seems in *slightly* better spirits about her leaving.

Despite my plans to take Ellie out later for our first date, I already miss her too. I'm not sure how I'll survive five weeks of her being gone, but I will make the most of the next two weeks before she leaves.

He stops dead in his tracks. "Did you fire her?"

"Technically, yes."

"You're an idiot."

I shoot daggers at him. "She was going to quit anyway, so I figured I'd get her severance pay."

He blinks twice. "That's…"

"Nice?"

"*Interesting*." His gaze lingers on me for a moment before Nico comes running down the hall.

"*¡Tío!*" He jumps into Julian's waiting arms.

"Did you grow a whole foot while you were gone?"

Nico laughs. "No!"

My cousin stands. "Hm. You look taller."

"Really?" Nico puffs his chest out.

I laugh.

By now, Nico is used to the sound, but Julian's head swivels in my direction.

"What?" I say.

"It's really great to hear your laugh."

"You're going to make me blush."

His smile grows wider. "You're joking too? Damn. What was in those Hawaiian Suns?"

"High-fructose corn syrup."

Julian pulls me into a side hug and rubs the top of my head like he used to when we were younger. "Happiness looks good on you."

I shove him off. "Falling in love with Dahlia really has changed you."

"Just wait until it happens to you."

I have a feeling it may happen sooner than I thought.

CHAPTER FIFTY-ONE

Ellie

I've been on plenty of dates before, but I don't remember ever being this nervous, standing in my parents' living room while my mom fusses over me and Burt stands in a corner with a smile on his face.

"You wore the dress I bought you!"

"Is it too much?" I tug at the hem, but it doesn't stretch past my midthigh.

"Of course not! You look *gorgeous*," Mom says.

She was beyond excited to go shopping with me today in search of a new outfit for my date. With the way she cried when I stepped out of the fitting room in this short dress, someone could think I was trying on wedding gowns.

"Should I get my ax and give him a speech on the porch?" Burt asks.

I shake my head. "I must insist you don't."

"It could be fun."

"It could also get you arrested, so there's that."

My stepdad laughs as he pulls me in for a hug. "He's lucky you gave him a second chance."

My lips curl at the corners. "I'm happy I did."

The wrinkles beside his eyes soften. "You like him a lot, don't you?"

"Just a teensy bit."

Mom squeals like she is in grade school again. "Are you joking? You're *glowing*."

"Okay, fine. I like him a lot." As if I conjured him up by just talking about him, Rafael rings the doorbell.

My mom grabs Burt and drags him out of the room, but he still shouts, "Treat her well or else I'll introduce you to my ax," when I open the door.

Rafael holds out a baby pink hibiscus that looks like he plucked it straight from one of the bushes we saw in Hawaii.

I stare at it. "Where did you find that?"

"I have my sources."

My cheeks flush as he curls my hair behind my ear before adding the flower. "A pretty flower for a stunning woman."

I can hear Mom and Burt whispering about it, so I grab my purse and shut the front door behind me.

Rafael dressed up tonight in a button-down linen shirt with the sleeves rolled up to his elbows and a pair of dark shorts. While I was a secret fan of his more rugged outfits and appearance, I won't deny he looks just as handsome right now. "You clean up nice, Prom King."

His narrowed eyes travel over my face. "Never call me that again."

I grin. "Afraid you may like it?"

"I can absolutely guarantee I won't."

I stick my tongue out at him, and he kisses my cheek with an airy laugh before leading me to his pickup truck. He opens the door for me before sliding into the driver's seat and turning the key.

"So, what are we doing?" I ask.

"It's a surprise." He pulls out of my parents' driveway before taking the road out of Lake Wisteria.

"We're leaving town?"

He pushes against the accelerator. "Yup."

"Do you not want to be seen in public with me?" I tease.

His eyes narrow in my direction. "I can turn back around and parade you down Main Street if that makes you happy. I'll even find you a crown and declare you my prom queen."

I glare. "Hilarious."

"Would a sash entice you more?"

"Tempting, but I'll politely pass on that for now." I'd rather keep Rafael to myself for a few more weeks before everyone in town finds out about our relationship. The news would come with hundreds of questions I don't feel like answering, so I'd rather delay that for as long as possible.

He chuckles. "That's what I thought."

"Aren't you not allowed within a hundred feet of Main Street after the fire hydrant incident?" Supposedly, Rafael can't get near any after opening one during Julian and Dahlia's epic high school prank war.

"They lifted the ban last year." His head tilts. "Wait. How do you know about that?"

"Um." My cheeks burn as I fail to come up with an answer fast enough.

Something flashes in his eyes before he squints. "You graduated three years after me, right?"

"Yes?"

"The fire hydrant incident happened when I was a sophomore."

"Huh. I didn't realize. You know how fast word travels around here." I keep a neutral expression despite my entire face giving my feelings away like a mood ring.

"*And* you knew I was the prom king."

I cross my arms. "So did most of the student body."

"But you *also* remembered what my superlative was."

"I was part of the yearbook club."

"And who handled the superlative section?"

"Some junior you weren't friends with." The answer slips out before I really think about Rafael's question.

Shit.

His eyes sparkle with mischief. "Interesting how you would remember not only my superlative over a decade later but also whether or not I was friends with the person who put the page together."

"I've got a great memory."

"You write down notes on your phone about the most menial things so you don't forget about them." His dry tone matches the look on his face.

"Is it too late to plead the Fifth?"

"You're not on trial here."

"Sure feels like I am."

His smile could put the devil's to shame. "Having a crush on me wasn't a crime, but if it were, we both know you'd be guilty as charged."

I lift my chin and accept my fate. "So what if I did?"

"I'd say it makes this all much more interesting."

"Really? *That* makes it more interesting?"

"Of course."

"Please elaborate."

"Because I seem to remember you mentioning that I wasn't your type."

My lips thin.

"So tell me. How deep did this crush go?" He brings my hand to his mouth and kisses the back of it, as if he can distract me into spilling the truth.

Nice try. "*If* I had a crush—"

"Which we both know you did."

Ignoring him is easy. "I would *never* talk to you about it."

"Even if I torture you for information?"

My cheeks burn as his kind of torture comes to mind. "Not even then."

"Hm." He stares at me for a few passing seconds, most likely determining how serious I am. The answer is *deadly so*, because Rafael finding out how much I crushed on him is not an option, especially since I wrote a terrible song about him that will never see the light of day.

He smiles to himself. "I'll find out what I want to know with or without your help."

I scoff. "Good luck."

"If my meddling aunt taught me anything, it's that parents can't help spilling secrets about their kids when asked the right questions."

Shit.

Rafael drives through a town I haven't seen before. Unlike Lake Wisteria and its Victorian coastal aesthetic, this one is inspired by a Bavarian village with its exposed dark-wood framing, colorful exteriors, and cobblestone streets.

I'm surprised when he pulls into a parking spot on what appears to be the main road into town and turns the engine off.

I don't recognize our surroundings, so I ask, "Where are we?"

"Lebkuchen."

"And *what* are we doing here exactly?"

"You'll see in a minute."

He tells me to wait while he walks around the truck, opens my door, and holds his hand out for me to grab. I latch on to it and hop out of the truck. With my hand in his, we walk down the quaint, paved road that seems to feature a lot of the town's biggest stores.

After a five-minute walk, Rafael stops in front of a record shop with a sign on the front door that says *Closed*.

"Cute idea, but looks like they're closed."

He ignores me. "You were looking for a Frankie Estelle record, right?"

I might have mentioned that one in passing to Nico, so how does he—

"The search history." My eyes widen.

His eyes glimmer. "Edibles. Collectible records. What's next?"

I could have *sworn* I cleared the history that night after I searched for—

A vibrator. "Oh shit."

He wraps an arm around me and pulls me in. "So you remember."

A flush spreads from my head to my toes. "Let's agree to never speak of that night again."

"Oh, Elle. It's a little too late for that." His grin holds a devious promise.

I could drop dead.

In fact, I hope I do.

He drops a quick kiss on my lips before swiping at my bottom lip with his thumb. "I've been dying to know something."

"What?"

"Did you ever buy it?"

"I—"

He stops me. "It was a yes–no question."

I'm tempted to wrap my hands around his throat, but I hold back because those things may be frowned upon during a first date, but then again, so is bringing up a *vibrator*.

I glare at him, and he smiles back.

"Shouldn't you be against that kind of thing?" I ask with an arched brow.

"Why would I be?"

"Because if I'm using a vibrator, we clearly have a problem."

His laughter is quickly becoming my favorite sound. "I'm all about teamwork in the bedroom."

My cheeks flush. "What's that supposed to mean?"

"You won't have to wait long to find out." He winks.

CHAPTER FIFTY-TWO

Rafael

When I was thinking about where I wanted to take Ellie for a first date, the house was tempting, but she and I have spent enough time there. Plus, I didn't want her to feel pressured into taking things further than we already have, so I spent my afternoon mapping out record stores within driving distance of Lake Wisteria.

I called them ahead of time and offered to pay whatever amount to keep them empty and open after their usual operating hours, and they agreed excitedly, although Ellie doesn't know that.

She gawks at me when I open the door despite the signage on the front. "It says they're closed!"

"Must have been a mistake." I flip the sign and usher her inside. "See?" The employee waves at us before telling us to look around for as long as we'd like.

I press my lips against her ear with the flower tucked behind it. "Happy hunting."

She lets out an excited noise before grabbing my hand. "You *have* to help me."

"Of course. Whatever you want."

She grins.

"What are you looking for?" I ask.

"I mean Frankie Estelle is great, but I also love Cornelia Jones, Winnifred Carmine, and Astrid and the Treble Makers." She claps her hands together and does a little happy dance, and I immediately know I made the right choice.

I could have scoured the internet for every record she wanted to collect and bought them, but I knew she would be happiest physically visiting record shops and sifting through endless boxes of dusty vinyls together.

I had questioned my idea because when I told Julian and Dahlia about it, they seemed slightly confused, but I should have known that no one knows my girl like I do.

Ellie spends the next hour flipping through vinyls, answering my questions, and sharing her favorite songs and records with me. I always appreciated music, but hearing her talk about it brings the subject to life for me, and I swear I could spend forever listening to her speak about it.

She doesn't find any of the records she was originally searching for, but she has me carry a stack of *possibilities* around the store that grows with every box she checks.

When she eventually asks me to set it down on the checkout counter so she can decide which one she wants to take home, I pretend I didn't hear her as I head to the front door.

"Wait!"

I glance over my shoulder. "Let's go. We've got two more stores left to hit before our dinner reservation."

"We have to pay!"

I laugh to myself and ignore her.

"Rafa!"

I absolutely love it when she says my name like that. For that, I pluck a record from a box that she had been eyeing but never added to the pile and set it on top of the rest.

"Where are you going?"

The bell above the door jingles when I push it open with my foot, and she chases after me.

Ellie runs in front of me and stops. "Wait. Did you pay the store to stay open?"

"Surprised you didn't figure it out sooner."

Her eyes narrow. "Okay. Listen. I know you're rich—"

I fake my surprise. "Who told you?"

She lightly swats my shoulder with a laugh. "Come on. Be serious."

"I am."

"But—"

"You didn't have a problem with my money *before*."

"Things were different."

"How?"

"I was your *employee*."

"And now you're my..."

She raises her brows in silent question.

My mouth suddenly feels dry. I'm not ready to put a label on this—this *thing*—but I know it is serious. These feelings aren't casual, although I'm not ready to categorize them just yet. Doing so wouldn't be fair to Ellie, but I know I want her.

Only a couple of weeks ago, I was determined to spend the next however many years alone, so I need time to process what life with a partner would look like. Can I learn to let go of my past and trust Ellie wholeheartedly? Will I be able to get married again and expand my family?

If I don't stop now, my spiral will never end.

I clear my throat. "Well, you're *important*. And people who are important to me accept being spoiled from time to time."

If I wasn't so attuned to her expressions, I probably wouldn't have noticed her smile faltering or the way her eyes slightly dim, but I observe everything when it comes to her, which is a blessing and a curse based on the way my stomach clenches at her disappointment.

She recovers quicker than me. "You're important to me too." She stands on the tips of her toes and kisses my cheek. "Thank you."

"Ready?"

She nods, and we change the subject while walking back toward the truck, although I can't shake the feeling that I disappointed her somehow.

I need to be better for her, or else I'm going to lose her before I ever truly had her.

Ellie and I spend the rest of our date night hopping around record stores before she asks me to stop at a drive-in chain that brings the food out to your vehicle. I haven't been to the fifties-inspired place since I was a kid, and apparently neither has Ellie.

Turns out she is extremely nostalgic, which was something I hadn't known about her.

Songs. Childhood shows. Her love of family traditions and a blanket she can't fall asleep without despite being twenty-nine years old.

I can't relate to that kind of personality trait, but the way she lights up whenever she talks about the things she enjoys piques my interest and makes me want to appease her love for the past. So I canceled our reservation at a fancy steakhouse as I pulled into one of the empty spots outside of the restaurant.

I don't even let Nico eat snacks in my truck, but all it takes is Ellie batting her lashes and saying *please* in that strained voice of hers for me to cave.

If Julian knew, he would give me shit for a week.

A woman in roller skates and a costume inspired by the fifties comes out to my truck, and we order burgers, fries, and a single strawberry milkshake. I know why Ellie insists on splitting our fries and sharing a milkshake instead of ordering two, and it makes me appreciate her even more than I already do.

Ellie takes over my speaker system and plays Astrid and the Treble Makers, which apparently were big back in the days of jukeboxes and poodle skirts, while we talk and eat our food. I don't have to worry about keeping up false pretenses or overthinking my next sentence, and any lull in conversation is comforting rather than uncomfortable.

She wraps her lips around the straw and sucks, completely unaware of how uncomfortably tight my pants have become in the process of her drinking the milkshake.

"Are you sure you don't want some?" She offers me the plastic cup.

"Nope." I'd much rather watch her, thank you very much.

She laughs to herself. "I thought you did?"

"Changed my mind." My gaze drops to her mouth.

Her face lights up as it clicks for her, and she makes a show of taking another sip.

I narrow my eyes.

She rolls hers with a smile. "Don't tell me you're worried about your caloric intake or something."

"Nope." I readjust my position in my seat.

"You could always work out tomorrow if you're feeling guilty." She waves the milkshake in front of my eyes. "It'll be worth it."

Guilt is the last thing I'm feeling, and based on her teasing smile, she knows that too.

Her voice drops as she says, "I'll even join you."

I blink. "I thought you hated working out."

"I never said I would be participating." She winks. "Turns out I'm allergic to cardio."

"Explains why you failed PE." She had mentioned it once during one of our hikes in Hawaii, and I've never let it go since.

Her nose scrunches with distaste. "The coach was such a dick."

"I know. I couldn't stand him."

"Didn't he coach the soccer team?"

"Yup."

"Why did you put up with him, then?"

"Because my uncle loved me being part of the team."

"Did *you* love it?" Ellie is getting better at asking me pointed questions like this one, and while I appreciate her paying attention, it makes evading the truth harder.

I pause for a second before answering. "No."

Her mouth falls open. "Weren't you the captain, though?"

"Yeah."

"But why would you play a sport you didn't love?"

I stare out the truck's window. "I think you know why."

"I want you to tell me anyway."

"Why?"

"Because you've been holding this all in for years, and I think it would be good for you to open up about it." She touches my face affectionately, and I turn to face her again.

Fine. I can do that. *For her.*

"My uncle always talked about how he loved being on his old team and how he wished Julian would do the same."

"So you stepped up."

I nod. "Julian was too focused on school and his other clubs, so I took advantage of the opportunity to be a favorite for once." My gaze drops, and shame pours out of me in waves. "My uncle was so happy. He went to almost all the games once I joined the team."

"You played a sport with a coach you didn't like because it made someone else happy?"

"I know it seems stupid—"

"It's not stupid, Rafael. It's so damn sad that no one ever took notice."

"To be fair, I was *really* good at hiding it, and it's not like I hated sports."

"Did *anyone* have an idea about how you really felt?"

"Julian had his suspicions, but he never called me out on it."

"Have you considered talking to him about it?"

"Well, no." *Should I have?* The thought of opening up to him like that terrifies me, especially when he has a right to judge me for acting this way for two decades.

I love my cousin, and I don't want him to think I've been deceiving him or acting devious.

I'm just…a little broken.

Ellie seems to sit on that for a moment before saying, "I want you to promise me something."

"Hm?"

"Will you always be honest with me? Even if you think I won't like what you have to say or the way you react to something, I would rather you tell me the truth than ever feel the need to hide behind a lie because you're afraid it might push me away."

"I can do that." I clear my throat. "I *will* do that."

The more time I spend with her, the more I come to realize that she is right.

I've given her countless opportunities to give up and go, yet she sticks around, proving time and time again that I can trust her. That I can *love* her too.

So long as I'm willing to take the risk.

I'm reluctant to drop Ellie off right away, so I take the long way back to her house and extend our date by another twenty minutes, solely because I don't want to let her go. If she were still living with me, I'd take her home and show her just how much tonight meant to me.

How much *she* means to me.

My heart hammers in my chest as I open the passenger side door and help her hop out of the truck, my palm sweating as I press it against the small of her back and lead her to the front porch.

Despite having kissed Ellie plenty of times, I'm nervous about doing the same tonight. Perhaps it has something to do with me finally accepting that we are moving toward something serious, or maybe it has everything to do with the way she looks up at me with a smile that robs me of my next breath and all coherent thoughts.

I can hardly hear her thanking me for tonight's date over the blood pounding in my ears, but I nod anyway.

We stop in front of her door, and she rises on her tiptoes and brushes her lips across mine. "Tonight was amazing. Thanks again."

Instinct kicks in, and I trap her against my chest by curling my arm around her waist. I press my mouth over hers and kiss her hard. She melts into me, and I deepen the kiss until she drops the bag of vinyls by our feet and wraps her arms around the back of my neck.

Heat travels down my spine and spreads to my groin as she returns my assault with her own, tearing through my self-control with the press of her lips and the brush of her tongue over the seam of my mouth.

Before I have a chance to do the same, the front door swings open, and her parents invite me in for a drink.

Ellie is beyond embarrassed at being caught kissing, so I consider declining the invitation to help her save face, but then her stepdad wraps his arm around my shoulder and pulls me inside, declaring he makes the best mixed drinks in town.

Bold claim but who am I to turn down a free drink and an opportunity to spend more time with Ellie?

Her parents are kind, which makes sense given how sweet Ellie is. I've met Burt, but I've never really spoken to him outside of calling his store to book Nico's music lessons.

"Please excuse my husband. He's harmless." Ellie's mom shoos Burt away and offers me her hand. "I'm Mrs. Sinclair." I've seen her around town, but we have never had a conversation before.

"Nice to meet you." I shake her hand. "You have a beautiful home."

"You think so?"

I take in the warm tones and tasteful decor and furnishings. "Yes. Reminds me of my aunt's."

Her smile is bright. "Thanks! I designed it all myself."

"Beatrice! I need your help carrying the drinks!" Burt calls from the kitchen.

"One second." Mrs. Sinclair rushes out of the room.

Ellie's ears tint pink, matching the flower she still has in her hair. "You really don't need to stay for a drink."

"Trying to get rid of me already?" I smirk.

"I'm trying to *save* you."

"More like you're trying to save yourself." I tuck my index

finger under her chin and lift it. "Did you really think I was going to pass on the opportunity to see your baby photos?"

Her mom pops her head out of the kitchen. "Did someone say *baby photos*?"

"I'd love to see some if you have them lying around." I grin while Ellie groans.

"Of course! Let me get you that drink first."

I wink at Ellie. "I'd love that."

Joining the Sinclairs for drinks put a few things into perspective, and I spend my quiet drive back to the farmhouse thinking about tonight.

One, Burt and Beatrice are madly in love with one another despite being married for fifteen years—a fact that Ellie pointed out on two separate occasions when they were caught whispering to each other and giggling to themselves.

Two, Ellie pretends to be annoyed by her parents' antics, but there was a special glimmer in her eyes whenever she looked at them, only for it to fade a bit when she glanced over at me.

I didn't need to read her mind to know what she was thinking. The answer was written all over her face, and it absolutely cut me up inside.

She mentioned wanting to get married, and after hanging out with her parents, I understand why. They really are a storybook example of what it means to find the right person when you least expect it. Of what it is like to choose a partner who can love someone else's child, like Burt does Ellie.

Knowing Ellie's mom, who went through hell during her first marriage, learned to love again hits too close to home for me. The similarities between our lives and past relationships make me reconsider the future I thought I wanted.

I swore off marriage a long time ago, but then again, I said the same thing about falling in love, yet here I am, slowly doing exactly that with Ellie.

Maybe I am more open to the idea than I originally thought, and it is all because of the woman who is putting my heart back together, piece by fragmented piece, like notes in one of her songs, transforming my never-ending sad one into a hopeful symphony.

CHAPTER FIFTY-THREE

Rafael

When are you bringing Ellie to Sunday lunch?" Julian grips his shovel before tossing a pile of dirt behind him.

"I'm waiting." I stick to my task of digging a hole big enough for the plants I bought.

"For?"

"The right moment."

"You can't hide her forever. Ma is going to corner her whether you want it to happen or not." Julian wipes the sweat from his brow.

"I'm not hiding her." I'm *savoring* her without my nosy family meddling in our business.

"Do you have an idea of when you're telling Nico?"

I grind my teeth together. "Okay. What's this inquisition really about?"

Julian motions to the potted hibiscus plants around us. "If

you haven't noticed, you asked me to come over and help you with a shit-ton of plants without any explanation. Forgive me for being curious."

"I knew I should have hired help." When I went to a plant nursery a few towns over, I was only planning on buying one, but then I thought it would be better to have a selection to choose from for Ellie's hair. Next thing I knew, I had purchased the whole store's stock.

He barks out a laugh. "We both know how you feel about having people on your property."

I glare. "Yes, you're reminding me why I don't have visitors."

He flips me off with a gloved hand, and I return the gesture with one of my own. We continue digging a hole along the exterior side wall of the house until Julian breaks the blissful silence with another question.

"Since when do you care about gardening?"

"It's a newer hobby of mine." I smile to myself. Ellie did say I needed to figure out what I like to do without anyone's influence, and the idea of tending to a garden that reminds me of her does sound like a good use of my free time.

Julian groans. "I've lost you again."

"What?"

"You're thinking about *her*."

"You asked me a question."

"And now I have my answer." He stabs into the dirt with the sharp tip of the shovel. "But I've got to hand it to you. This is pretty damn romantic."

My reply is nothing but a grunt.

"To think we will be doing this again next year once these die."

I stare at him. "What?"

"These guys are going to be dead at the first sign of winter."

Shit. I was so hung up on getting the flowers that I completely forgot the obvious issue with my plan. So while I can't save these plants, I can protect any future ones from Lake Wisteria's harsh winter conditions.

"I'm going to need you to build a greenhouse for me."

He points toward the barn. "We haven't even started the expansion."

"I know, but this is important."

"Important enough to put the barn's plans on hold?"

"Yeah."

"Are you telling me we dug all these holes for nothing?"

I laugh. "We'll replant them once the weather starts changing."

"*We?*"

"Did I mention you're the best cousin ever?"

"I'm your only cousin, *pendejo.*" He stares at me for a moment before shaking his head. "I'll get my guys started on the project next week."

"I knew I could count on you."

We spend the next few hours digging. Dirt piles behind us, and my hands ache with every stab into the dirt, but I feel at peace.

My head is *quiet.*

Yeah, I could get used to gardening. Ripping out weeds and digging holes is surprisingly cathartic for me, especially after spending so much time working in front of a computer screen.

By the time we finish the holes lining the perimeter of my house, Julian and I are soaked in sweat. I grab us some beers from inside, and we knock the bottles together and each take a long pull on the back porch.

"Not gonna lie, when you said you wanted to move out here, I didn't get it."

I chuckle to myself. "It's peaceful."

"It's also a major pain in the ass to get to, but yeah, you can say it's peaceful too."

I shrug. "Ellie and Nico like it."

"Do *you*?" He asks me the question in the same way Ellie does, and it makes the hairs rise on the back of my neck. I've always had my suspicions about Julian catching on to my *camouflaging*, as Ellie would say, but I pushed them aside and convinced myself he hadn't.

Perhaps that was a mistake. Julian has always been too smart for his own good, and I clearly underestimated him.

I nod. "Yeah. I like it. A lot." I originally picked this property because I was tired of being too close to the town, but then I realized I loved the land.

He nods. "Good."

"Why are you asking?" The question slips out, and he turns to face me.

"I know how you are."

I fake a scoff. "What's that supposed to mean?"

He looks me up and down, noting the way I grip my beer in a chokehold. "If you want to stop talking about it, that's fine."

I suck in a big lungful of air. "I just…"

He shakes his head. "Listen. I'm not judging you or trying to give you a hard time. I just want you to know I'm glad that you're finally making decisions that make *you* happy because you've spent far too much of your life prioritizing everyone else's happiness over your own."

He taps the neck of his bottle against mine in a toast, and to that, we drink.

After a few sips of courage, I speak up, knowing that if I don't start opening up to Julian now, I never will.

If I want to be a good example for my son, I need to stop viewing the idea of expressing myself as a weakness and start seeing it for what it really is.

Strength.

I swallow back my nerves and speak. "I thought I was doing the right thing for a long time. Best intentions and all that."

"That's how it usually goes."

I stare at the pond in the distance. "Seeking everyone else's approval was addictive."

"Why did you do it?" he asks without a hint of judgment.

I stare straight ahead while tapping my fingers against my kneecap. "Honestly?" I exhale loudly. "After I moved here, I was struggling."

His gaze softens. "I remember."

"Your parents… They were trying so damn hard to help me adjust, but it wasn't working."

"Healing takes time."

"I know that now, but back then, I was scared they would get sick of me and all my bullshit."

"Trauma isn't bullshit, Rafa."

"Says the golden child."

He scoffs. "One of the main reasons I acted like that was because I didn't want to take away attention from *you*."

I blink a couple of times. "What?"

He releases a shaky breath. "You had already gone through so much that it felt selfish to fight for their attention, so I became more independent."

I'm stunned by Julian's confession. All this time, I thought he was perfect because he wanted to compete against Dahlia, but clearly there is more to his story than I originally thought.

Perhaps if we had had this heart-to-heart years ago, I would have understood him better, but Julian is just like me—closed-off and way too prideful to admit any weakness.

"I'm sorry," I confess.

He rears back. "What the hell are you apologizing for?"

"Turning your life upside down."

"Is that what you think?" His soft chuckle makes me frown.

"Did I miss my own punch line?"

"The *joke* is you believing that you need to apologize for being one of the best things that happened to our family."

My eyes roll. "You're just saying that."

He jabs a finger at me. "I never say things I don't mean. Period."

I sit with his statement for a few seconds. "How could you say that when I was faking it the whole time?"

"Because we knew what you were doing and let you get away with it."

My heart stutters. "What?"

Julian's head tilts. "You think my mom wasn't aware?"

"What do you mean?"

He shrugs. "You'll have to ask her."

"You think she knew?"

"You're her son in every sense of the word, Rafa. What do you think?"

Nothing good. I need to speak with my aunt and figure out just how much she knows and, most importantly, why she let me continue the farce for years without ever saying a single thing.

LORENZO

> We'll be in touch about your endorsement.

Oh shit.

I click on the article attached to the message.

News broke this morning that Darius Larkin, owner of MIA Records, has officially sold the company to a rival record label owner, Jack Davenport of Cadenza Records. The sale was made after multiple witnesses came forward to share their personal experiences of what it was like working with Mr. Larkin, which included but were not limited to allegations of blackmail, predatory legal contracts, sexual harassment, and sexual assault.

I continue reading. Some witnesses chose to remain anonymous, while a few spoke out. Their stories are different from Ellie's, but no less disgusting. Some were singers who never got their big break like Darius had guaranteed, while others were promised better opportunities so long as they agreed to an intimate relationship.

Fuck. Is that what Ava did too?

My stomach is in knots as I call Julian. My cousin skips past pleasantries and says, "I just received an email thanking me for being a guest speaker at Lorenzo's political dinner next month."

I choke. "A guest speaker?"

"Yes. And do you know what I hate more than Lorenzo?"

"Losing?"

"*Speeches*, Rafa," he snaps. "This is a damn nightmare. I knew I shouldn't have agreed to the endorsement."

I wince. "I'm sorry."

He takes a few deep breaths before asking, "Did you get what you needed at least?"

"Yeah. He delivered."

"The devil always does."

I sigh. "He's not *that* bad."

"Perhaps I should steal that quote for my speech. What do you think?"

"To be honest, I'm surprised he is asking you to speak. I thought he would ask you to put up a few lawn signs and publicly acknowledge him at Last Call or something at most."

"He wants me to *speak*. In *public*." I can picture Julian sneering while saying that.

"Is there any way I can repay you?"

"Fake an assassination attempt before I ever make it to the podium?"

I chuckle, and Julian reluctantly does as well.

"I'm only doing this because I care about you."

"I appreciate it."

"You owe me," he grumbles before hanging up.

Someone banging on the front door has me tossing my phone on my desk and heading to open it.

"Did you have something to do with this?" Ellie shoves her phone in my face. The article is different from the one I read but the title is similar.

I glance at her face and take in her puffy, red eyes. "Um…"

Before I have a chance to panic about her crying, she throws her arms around me. "Thank you."

"You're not…upset?" I never expected another record label to swoop in and buy Darius's company, so I hope it doesn't mess up her legal case against Ava.

She pulls away. "Upset? No!"

I release a pent-up breath. "Good. I don't want to mess up the case for your lawyer."

"Are you kidding? Even if it does, this is so worth it. He *loved* that company."

The tightness in my chest loosens a bit. "I'm glad he won't be able to take advantage of anyone else."

"All thanks to you." She stands on my toes to kiss me. "You really are a superhero."

"I didn't pull this off by myself."

She smiles. "Julian helped?"

I shake my head. "No."

"Then who?"

"*Lorenzo.*"

After my conversation with Julian the other day, I spent some time stewing in my thoughts and obsessing over the fact that my aunt knew about me keeping up appearances for *years*.

I considered ignoring the subject, but when I show up at her house a few days later for another haircut, it feels like the best time to talk.

Even though the idea terrifies me.

Tía helps Nico get settled in her guest room before she leads me to the kitchen. She offers me a few snacks and a glass of *agua fresca* while I take a seat on a stool. My heart beats rapidly while she gets her supplies ready, and I'm hardly paying attention to the questions she asks about work.

She stops spraying my hair. "Rafa?"

"*¿Sí?*"

"Same cut as last time?"

I swallow the lump in my throat as I shake my head.

"Longer?"

"*Shorter.*"

Her eyes widen. "*¿Qué?*"

"Well, as short as you can go while still leaving it long enough to run my fingers through. And no clippers."

"You want it like before?" She doesn't specify further, but I don't need her to.

"Yeah. Like before."

She smiles throughout my entire haircut. I flinch a few times as locks of hair fall around my feet, but my aunt reassures me that the final product will look amazing.

For a brief time, I thought she was lying, only to be proven wrong when she steers me toward the guest bathroom. I'm overwhelmed with emotion as I check out my new haircut. Like promised, I can still give my hair a good shake with the tips of my fingers, but the length only highlights my features rather than hiding them.

My aunt gives my arm a squeeze. "You look...great."

Our gazes connect in the mirror. Her unshed tears make me feel equal parts happy and guilty, knowing I'm the reason behind them.

"*Por favor. No llores.*"

Her brows pinch together. "I promise they're happy tears."

"I don't want *any* tears. Happy or not."

She looks away with a sniff. "I can't help it. You just look so..."

"Handsome?" I tease.

"*Feliz.*"

I tug her into a tight hug. "*Perdón, Tía. Por todo.*"

"What are you apologizing for?"

"For everything." My voice cracks. "I didn't realize I was hurting you—"

She cups my cheek. "I might have hurt *for* you, but you never hurt me, *mijo. Nunca en tu vida.*"

My own eyes water, but I blink away the tears, not because I'm uncomfortable, but to save my aunt from breaking out into sobs of her own. *Tía* has called me her son countless times, but

---

Por favor. No llores: Please. Don't cry.

Perdón, Tía. Por todo: I'm sorry, Aunt. For everything.

Feliz: Happy

Nunca en tu vida: Never in your life.

today, I allow myself to believe it. To accept that I have a place in this family as my true self.

No more hiding. No more lies. No more pretending that I'm someone else, solely because I thought it would make people like me more.

"¿*Tía?*"

"¿*Si?*"

"I have a few things to tell you."

"Is it about you secretly dating Ellie?"

I can't help laughing. "No, but more on that later."

"Hm. *Que triste*." She wipes underneath her eyes.

My eyes roll. "It's about me."

She pops her head out of the bathroom and calls to check in on Nico before shutting the door behind her. "What?"

"I want to talk to you about *before*."

Her head shakes hard enough to send a few strands of hair flying. "You don't have to talk to me about it."

"I know that but I want to anyway."

My aunt and I spend the next hour sitting on the floor of her guest bathroom, swapping tissues and stories while I pour my heart out to her. Opening up to Ellie, Nico, and Julian was cathartic, but talking to my aunt about my difficulties…

It was everything I needed and more.

At one point during our conversation, she hugged me and hasn't let go since. It's been so long since she held me like this, and it's all my fault. I thought keeping her at a distance would protect

---

Que triste: How sad.

her from getting hurt, but it only caused her more pain, knowing I was suffering and there wasn't anything she could do about it.

She brushes her fingers through my newly cut hair. "You have always been one of the greatest gifts life gave me."

For the first time, I choose to believe her instead of finding a hundred different reasons to deny it.

"For years, I used to feel selfish for being happy to have you in my life," she confesses in a broken whisper.

My chest clenches. "That doesn't make you selfish."

"It does, but I've made peace with it. I just wish I could have saved you from all the pain—both before your parents passed and after."

"I didn't feel—" I stop myself from lying. "You couldn't have done anything to help me through that."

"I could have done *something*. It's not like I wasn't aware of what you were doing."

My chest pinches. "I thought I did a better job at hiding it."

She pats my cheek. "Only because your uncle and I let you believe it."

"You never said anything."

"I wish I had." Her head hangs low. "Maybe if I had stuck to my original plan to get you a therap—"

"I wasn't ready for that."

"Still, it was my job as your mother—"

"Stop."

"What?"

"Feeling guilty over a past neither of us can change."

Her eyes turn glossy again as tears cling near her lash line. "It's hard."

My eyes screw tight. "I know. Fuck. I really do."

She pulls me into another embrace. "Okay. I promise to stop, so long as you do too."

"Deal." I return her hug with one of my own. "I just want to let go of it all and focus on my future."

"Then that's what we will do."

CHAPTER FIFTY-FOUR

Rafael

I knew my happiness couldn't last forever. Ellie and I have spent the last week since coming back to Lake Wisteria in a haze, and it was only a matter of time before reality caught up to me.

I just wish my son wasn't collateral damage as well.

"Nico," I call after him.

He slams his bedroom door and flips the lock. "I don't want to go!"

I test the doorknob anyway. "But you've worked so hard for this."

He and Ellie have been practicing his Strawberry Festival song for two months straight, so to hear that he no longer wants to perform because of her...

It makes me want to rage.

I knew Hillary could flake, but I didn't want to tell Nico

that just in case she kept her promise. He seemed so hopeful about it, so taking that away from him felt unfair.

And look where that got you.

I lean my forehead against the door. "Everyone who loves you will be there."

"I don't care! I quit!"

"Quit what?"

"Music! What's the point anyway?" Nico's sobs can be heard through the door. My chest aches at the sound, and I wish I could take away his pain. Wish I could do anything but stand around, unable to protect him from the one person who always manages to hurt him.

I don't know what the fuck to do. I hate her too, but she is his mother. She has a legal right to talk to and see her son, even if it is sporadic, and there is nothing I can do about it.

I pull out my phone and shoot Ellie an SOS text before testing Nico's doorknob again. "Will you let me come inside? Please?"

He ignores me and tries to muffle his cries with what I assume is a pillow.

"I'm here for you." I slide down to the floor and lean my back against the door.

The helplessness I feel toward my son reminds me too much of my childhood, and it triggers a darkness within me that I can't seem to eradicate.

I'm not sure how long I sit there, checking in on Nico periodically, but I lose all concept of time until a door across the house shuts. The sound of Ellie's footsteps echoes off the high ceiling before she turns the corner and appears like an angel dressed in black.

"Hey." She slides down to the floor and pulls me into a hug.

"He doesn't want to open the door. Says he is quitting music for good."

"Do you want me to try something?"

"I mean, you *can*, but I don't know if he will be willing. He's absolutely gutted."

Fuck my ex-wife. First thing Monday, I'm reaching out to my lawyer and figuring out a better solution to our problem. If she doesn't want to be in Nico's life, fine, but I refuse to let her string him along like she did me.

I don't care how much it will cost me in the long run or if she will feel like she finally won. The cost of my pride is nothing compared to the price of Nico's broken heart.

Ellie's fist knocks against the door. "Nico."

Silence follows.

"Will you let me come inside?" she asks.

The quiet is stifling.

"If you don't want to go today, that's okay. I won't be upset with you."

His sniffle can be heard through the door. "You won't?"

"Of course not. I've heard you play that song a thousand times. In fact, maybe I'll go up there myself and play it better."

"You wish," he grumbles.

Ellie sighs. "Hm. Wanna bet?"

He groans. "I know what you're doing."

"Is it working?"

"No." Although he doesn't sound too sure.

"Will you please open the door? Your dad and I are worried about you."

Soft shuffling, followed by the metallic click of a lock sliding, fills the quiet before the door opens.

I fall back but catch my balance before I hit the floor. Ellie swoops in and pulls Nico into her arms.

"I'm sorry your mom won't be there today."

He snuggles into her and cries. "I really wanted her to see me."

She rubs his back soothingly. "I know."

"I thought maybe if I made her happy, she would want to come more."

Ellie and I share a look. Her glassy eyes add pressure to the one already building in my chest.

Nico's statement reminds me so much of something I would have said as a kid, and it wrecks me to know that will never be the case. He can't make a miserable person happy. They're the only ones who can do that, and his mom is hell-bent on making everyone else feel equally unhappy.

I'll make this right somehow, even if it means flying out to Oregon and having a word with Nico's mother myself. I'm done with her mind games because the stakes have changed. I have *two* people to look out for now, and neither of them deserves her bullshit.

I'm the one who got us into this mess to begin with, which means I'm the only person who can get us out.

"Can I tell you a story?" Ellie asks, cooling some of my angry thoughts.

Nico nods, and she carries him to the bed. He takes a seat on her lap, and I sit beside them both.

Ellie brushes Nico's hair back. "I used to be like you."

His eyes widen. "You did?"

She nods. "My dad never went to my shows or seasonal concerts or listened to me practice. He said music made me soft and kept my head in the clouds."

I wish I could wrap my arm around her and tuck her into my side forever, but I clench my fists and refrain from giving in to the urge.

My son gasps. "No."

Ellie frowns. "Yeah. I almost quit altogether because it made me so sad."

"But you're amazing."

She smiles. "Thank you."

He sucks in a breath. "Wait! If you quit, then you wouldn't have been my tutor!"

"Exactly."

"Or my nanny?"

"Nope."

His mouth falls open. "And then you wouldn't have met Cole Griffin."

"No, I probably wouldn't have."

"Whoa."

Ellie chuckles. "Life is like a row of dominoes. One choice sends the next one falling and so on."

Different emotions flash across Nico's face as his understanding of the world deepens.

"What I'm trying to say is that if I had quit music because my dad didn't like it, then I wouldn't have ended up here with you."

He wraps his arms around her neck. "Thank you for not quitting."

We sit in silence, with Ellie soothing Nico while I rub small circles in the center of her back.

It was always just Nico and me, even when Hillary was here, but now I realize I don't have to share the joys and setbacks of parenting alone. I can count on Ellie too because she loves my son without any conditions, paychecks, or child support payments keeping her here.

It is clear she could love anyone's child, but I'm lucky she chose *mine*.

And for the first time since she mentioned the idea of kids, I wonder what it would be like to raise one as a team.

Together.

Lake Wisteria's Strawberry Festival is the biggest event of the year—even more so than the others that take place in fall, winter, and spring. My aunt, as the town's event planner, puts months into finalizing every single detail, and this year truly is one of the best.

Rows of tents line the festival fairgrounds, featuring everything strawberry related. Food, drinks, clothes. You name it, there is a damn strawberry somewhere on it.

Nico has loved this weekend since he was a toddler, and I'm glad he decided to come regardless of his mother's decision.

Ellie and I arrive at the Strawberry Festival with Nico dressed in his favorite suit and his fanciest pair of glasses that he saves for special occasions like today.

The stage is already set up with a piano that Ellie's stepdad loaned to the event planning team, and a sea of townspeople fills the seats. Together, Ellie and I take him backstage, where he peeks at the crowd from behind the stage left curtain.

"How are you feeling?" Ellie kneels and readjusts his bow tie.

"Good."

"Hm. We need better than good." She reaches to tickle him, and he squirms with a laugh.

"Fine! Great!"

She winks. "Much better."

I lean over and kiss the top of his head. "I'm proud of you for coming, *mijo*."

He grabs his lapels and sticks his chest out. "If I want to become a rock star one day, I can't quit."

Ellie pulls him into a hug before I do the same.

"Everyone, please welcome Nicolas Lopez!"

"That's me!" He rushes out, completely forgetting about us. My son is a damn performer, bowing for the crowd before dramatically brushing his hands across the keys.

The number of people watching has doubled in the short time it took him to check in and get backstage, and it makes my chest swell with pride knowing my son's talent is appreciated by so many people.

With a sigh, I wrap my arms around Ellie and prop my chin on her shoulder.

She steps out of my embrace and turns to face me. "Someone could see us."

"Would you rather they didn't?"

She bites down on her bottom lip. "Yes, but not for the reason you probably think."

"Right." I exhale loudly, earning a small frown from her.

She pulls me away from the stage and deeper into the shadows. "I'm not ashamed of us. It's just…" The words struggle to make it past her lips, and she gets distracted by the first few notes of Nico's song.

I cradle her chin and will her to look back at me. "What?"

Her hand brushes down the center of my chest. "I just want to keep you all to myself for a little while longer. Once everyone finds out, they'll never leave us alone."

"Now that you mention it… maybe we should keep it a secret forever. That way we can avoid my family trying to steal you away from me."

She laughs while giving my shoulder a shove. "I meant a few weeks at most."

"Fine. I can manage that." I pull her deeper into the shadows before circling my arms around her waist again.

She sinks into me as Nico plays the song they practiced a countless number of times. Goose bumps spread over my arms at the melody floating through the air, and my eyes turn misty at watching him.

My son was born to shine, and I'm so proud to be his dad.

"He truly is amazing," Ellie whispers.

"I know."

"No, seriously. He is going to be famous one day. Mark my words and today's date."

"Thankfully, he will have you to help guide him through that process *after* he graduates from high school."

She tilts her head and kisses my jawline. "You're thinking that far ahead?"

"Yeah, I am."

The smile on Ellie's face isn't one I plan on forgetting in this lifetime.

CHAPTER FIFTY-FIVE

Ellie

Rafael presses his mouth against my ear and whispers, "Keeping my hands to myself is driving me crazy."

A shiver skates down my spine, earning a little smirk from Dahlia, who sits across the cocktail table with Julian's arm wrapped around her.

I had a feeling that heading to Last Call after the festival was a bad idea, mainly because everyone we know would be here, but the Muñoz sisters insisted on us going out while Josefina and Rosa took care of Nico. Most of the younger townspeople migrated to the bar once the festival shut down for the night, turning it into a high school reunion.

Lily, who was the main instigator of tonight's plans, disappeared the moment we got here, leaving Dahlia, Julian, Rafael, and me on an impromptu double date at one of the high-top tables near the bartenders working tirelessly to keep up with the demanding patrons.

Rafael and I have done a good job so far of maintaining our distance, but the task is proving more difficult with every stolen glance and sneaky touch when no one is looking. I thought I would be happy keeping our relationship a secret, but with every passing minute, I feel more tortured than relieved.

This was your idea, I tell myself when Rafael reaches under the table and holds my hand while Dahlia tells a story about her earlier run-in with a fan of her interior design show. Julian is too focused on his girlfriend to pay us any attention, although Dahlia shoots me a knowing smile when she catches me giving Rafael's bicep a warning squeeze.

Throughout the story, Rafael's fingers brush across my thighs. Every soft stroke of his calloused hand sends waves of heat rolling through my stomach, and I've drained my vodka seltzer by the time Dahlia finishes recounting her story.

"Thirsty?" Rafael's obnoxious smirk draws a glare from me.

Dahlia chokes on a laugh while Julian finally snaps out of his Dahlia-induced daze.

"I could use another round." He looks down at Dahlia with a soft smile that he reserves solely for her.

"Same," she answers with a grin.

Rafael's thumb brushes across my spine before he rests his hand around the back of my chair. "And you?"

My reply gets trapped in my throat, so I only nod. Rafael's lips curl at the edges as he gives my nape one more fleeting touch before pulling away.

"We'll be back." Julian drops a kiss on the top of Dahlia's head.

Rafael's squinted eyes swing between them and me, and something in my chest twists at the look on his face.

You're the one who wanted to keep your relationship—no, more like situationship—a secret.

The more time passes, the less I like it. When I first suggested it, I thought it would give us time to navigate this new chapter without hundreds of people weighing in and gossiping about us, but after today, I'm not too sure.

Hiding our connection feels *wrong.*

Dahlia leans forward on her elbows and whispers, "So you and Rafael, huh?"

"What about us?"

She grins. "Still keeping everything a secret?"

My face flushes. "I don't know what you're talking about."

"Don't worry. I've been there too."

"Uh…"

Her smile expands. "If you ever plan on winning family poker night, we need to work on your game face."

"I—" Words evade me.

She reaches out and gives my hand a little squeeze. "I'm just teasing you. It's nice to finally see Rafael look happy, so thank you. For everything."

I'm hit with itchy eyes. "You're thanking me? Why?"

"For bringing him back to us."

My throat swells from pent-up emotions. "I didn't do anything."

"And you're humble too. No wonder he is obsessed with you."

Obsessed? With me?

A tingle spreads through my chest before worming a hole into my heart.

"He is, by the way. During Sunday lunch—which we keep begging him to bring you to—he brought your name up three separate times." Dahlia's eyes brighten before they narrow at something behind me.

"What?" I turn and look in the general direction of her stare. It doesn't take me long to find the cause of what disrupted our conversation.

Julian is busy speaking to the bartender while Rafael leans against the countertop, scowling at a brunette woman I recognize from his graduating class. She has her hand wrapped around his bicep, staking a claim that isn't hers to make.

A spike of hot jealousy shoots through the center of my chest when she throws her head back and laughs. My hands clench beneath the table, and my shallow breathing can most likely be heard by Dahlia.

I know Rafael isn't interested in this woman. That much is obvious based on the curl of his upper lip and the tightness in his shoulders, but I can't control the jealousy raging inside, and it scares me.

I've never felt this way in my past relationships. I didn't have a real reason to because I never cared for someone like I do for Rafael.

I want to be his just as much as I want him to be mine, and I want everyone, including the beautiful bombshell with perfectly painted red lips and a veneered smile, to know it.

"Ellie?" Dahlia asks as I rise to my feet.

"Be back in a second."

"He doesn't want her," she says with a hint of panic.

"I know."

She scrambles to her feet. "I could go over there and—"

I toss her a reassuring smile over my shoulder. "No need. I've got this."

I may not know the woman well, but she is about to figure out exactly who I am.

Rafael's eyes find me as soon as I start pushing through the crowd, and my cheeks heat as I follow that tugging sensation in my chest directly to the man holding the other end of my heartstring.

His eyes sparkle with poorly hidden amusement as he turns to face me. "Hi."

"Hi," I repeat back.

The woman glances over at me. "Can I help you?"

"Nope, but I have a feeling I can help you."

Rafael's small smirk turns into a full-blown smile.

Bastard.

A crease appears down the center of her forehead. "Meaning?"

"He's taken."

"You are?" Her hand falls away.

Rafael glances down at me, giving me the power to determine how much I want people to know about our *relationship.*

I nod. "Yeah, he is."

The woman's wide-eyed gaze swings between the two of us. "Oh."

I lift my hand and wiggle my fingers with a smile. "Now,

if you don't mind…" I keep my tone light, not wanting to cause unnecessary drama with someone who lives in town.

After a quick apology, the woman turns in a rush and abandons the bar altogether.

Rafael grabs on to my hand and drops a kiss across my knuckles. "Jealousy looks good on you, Elle."

I brush my palm down his arm, erasing the invisible stain left behind by the other woman. "You're not…upset?"

He chokes on a laugh. "What? Fuck no."

I exhale. "I didn't like her touching you. It made me…"

He curls an arm around my waist and pulls me against him. "Possessive?"

"*Murderous.*"

His lips twitch. "I'd apologize, but seeing you stake your claim was hot."

"I was…" Totally staking a claim.

Shit.

He tucks his hand beneath my chin and raises it. "Now it's my turn."

His eyes drop to my lips, and I sway on my feet. "People are looking."

"Good." A small smile breaks out across his face before he crushes his lips against mine. I can hardly hear the people around us hooting and hollering over the sound of my heart pounding in my ears, but I don't care.

This man is all mine, and come tomorrow, everyone in town will know it.

With time quickly running out before my trip to Europe, I want to take advantage of every moment with Nico, so I decide to spend Sunday morning with him and Rafael despite usually having it off. After breakfast and a morning ATV ride around the farm's property, I head to Main Street and meet up with Willow at the Early Bird Diner. With most of the town still recovering from yesterday's Strawberry Festival, the diner is relatively quiet and empty for a weekend.

Willow props a menu up to cover our faces and beckons me forward.

"Are we hiding from someone?" I look around the restaurant.

"Jessica is good at reading lips." She tilts her head in the direction of the older woman seated at the countertop. "And Cami is an eavesdropper." She tips her chin in the direction of Alana Castillo, Callahan Kane, and their daughter, Cami, eating brunch a few tables away from us.

My gaze swings back to hers. "What's going on?"

She glances around one more time before whispering, "Remember Operation Fake Fiancée?"

"Hard to forget given the growing stack of possible candidates on your coffee table."

She makes a face. "Well, good thing I won't have to interview anyone else."

"You found someone?"

She nods.

"Who?"

Her nose scrunches in distaste. "You're not going to like it."

"Why?"

"Because I'm going to have to ask you to keep the whole thing a secret from Rafael."

"It's always been a secret—" I pause and stare at her for a few beats. "No." There is only one reason Willow would want me to keep Operation Fake Fiancée from Rafael in the first place, and it can only be because...

I pinch the bridge of my nose. "Please tell me you're not thinking of *her*."

Her lips purse. "She wasn't my first choice."

"That's a perfect reason to pick someone else."

"I did."

"But?" I ask.

"Lorenzo refused everyone else."

"Of course he did. Rafael is the least of your worries because once Julian finds out..."

"Lily knows that."

"But she applied anyway?"

"Not exactly."

"Willow." I say her name with a groan.

"I know this isn't ideal."

"Ideal? I like her way too much to subject her to that kind of torture."

"Lorenzo isn't the worst guy out there."

"Does he use that slogan on his dating profile?"

My best friend glares. "With the election fast approaching, we're out of options."

I drop my head into my hands and groan. "I can't keep this from Rafael."

She takes a brief pause before speaking again. "Can you trust him with a secret like this?"

"I hope so because omitting the truth isn't happening." There is no way in hell I could pretend to be unaware of Lily and Lorenzo's fake relationship, especially if it means Lorenzo spending time around the Muñoz and Lopez families.

Her head falls back against the vinyl booth. "If he tells Julian…"

"I know."

"Lily doesn't want her family to know the truth."

Why would she choose to do this in the first place? It's not like Lily needs the cash, seeing as Dahlia, Julian, or Rafael could bail her out in a heartbeat, so I'm not sure what her reasoning is for fake-dating Lorenzo.

"What is she getting out of this?" I ask the question aloud.

Willow drops the menu. "Honestly? I have no idea."

"Does Lorenzo know why she wants to do this?"

"Nope, but he told me that he is determined to find out."

The next day, while Nico is at summer camp, Rafael asks if I want to take Penelope out for a lap around the property together during his lunch hour, and I agree. Rafael has been taking longer breaks from work, both because of Nico's summer vacation from school and because he wants to take advantage of the little time we have left before I head to London. I appreciate his sacrifice, especially when he has to stay awake later to make up for the time spent away from his computer.

Thankfully, Rafael didn't let Lily and Dahlia get rid of his cowboy boots and favorite set of flannel shirts when they were helping him with his closet. His pair of scuffed boots combined with a black T-shirt, faded blue jeans, and a backward ball cap is really doing something for me, especially when he bends over to grab a sugar cube I accidentally dropped while hopping on to Penelope's saddle.

I'm caught in the act of checking him out, and he climbs onto the saddle behind me with a deep chuckle. My heart squeezes in my chest as his arms circle me and his body presses against my back before he grabs Penelope's reins.

I lean back against him with a sigh. "Have you thought about adopting another horse?"

"Why would I do that?"

"Because then we can ride together."

"Do you even know how?"

"No, but you could teach me."

His thighs press against mine. "And miss out on you sharing a horse with me? Hell no."

I laugh. "Fair point."

"Plus, I like to do this." He kisses the sensitive spot on the curve of my neck. "And this." He brushes a hand up the inside of my thigh, making my lower half heat up.

"Focus on the trail."

He chuckles in my ear before making a clicking noise with his tongue. Penelope increases her speed, and my fingers dig into his arms.

"Warn me next time!"

He laughs again as we head off toward the short trail he had made around his property.

"So…" I finally work up the nerve to broach the Lily–Lorenzo subject after mulling it over for five minutes. According to Willow, she plans on announcing their relationship soon, so it's best for me to get ahead of the news.

His arms wrapped around me tighten. "What?"

"I have something to tell you." My hand chokes the saddle's pommel.

"I assumed as much."

I blink twice. "What do you mean?"

"You've hardly said anything since yesterday."

"Oh." Maybe Dahlia was right, and I do need to work on my poker face.

"I thought a quick ride could help clear your mind, but I guess not."

The way he reads me so easily is both unsettling and impressive.

"I—" I pause when he shoots me a look. "I'm nervous."

"Is everything okay?" His grip on the reins tightens.

I stare at his hands. "Kind of."

"Then why are you nervous?"

"Because I want to trust you, but—"

"But?"

"You may want to tell other people."

"So long as Nico isn't affected, you can trust me with anything."

The finality of his words makes me relax against him. "You promise?"

"I promise." He kisses my shoulder. "You can count on me."

My chest constricts painfully. "Okay."

I focus on the trail for a few moments before I work up the nerve to speak. "Lorenzo has been searching for a fake fiancée."

"What for?"

I sink against him again. "The election."

"A small-town mayoral campaign means that much to him?"

I shrug. "I don't know why, but it does."

"All right…"

"Willow's been searching for a while, but they haven't had any success until now."

"What changed?"

"*Lily.*"

Rafael accidentally pulls on the reins. "What?"

"I know. I had a hard time believing it too." I sneak a quick glance over my shoulder to find his face looking paler than usual.

"Is this a joke?"

I flinch. "Afraid not."

"I can't believe she would go through with something like this. Marriage is a huge mistake. Fake or not."

My heart feels like Rafael rammed a thousand needles through the soft tissue.

Thankfully, he can't see my face, but I still take a deep breath and clear my pained expression just in case.

I understand his reservations about marrying someone, but that doesn't make it hurt any less. If anything, it feels worse, because the more time we spend together, the more I consider our future.

I don't want a dead-end relationship. I want a never-ending

highway of possibilities, and I want to go on the journey of a lifetime with *him*.

Give him time to work through his issues.

I understand that dating someone who has countless reasons not to trust someone else isn't supposed to be easy. We're going to go through hurdles, and marriage happens to be one of them.

I clear my throat and the tight ball that formed there. "I'm not sure why Lily agreed to this, but according to Willow, Lorenzo has known her for a while."

He brushes a hand down his face with a curse. "Julian is going to be so pissed when he finds out."

"I thought as much."

"Why would she agree to this?" He sounds so damn confused.

"No one knows."

"Not even Willow?" he asks.

"No."

"And Lorenzo?"

"He doesn't know either."

He grunts something to himself before speaking again. "So Lily just agreed out of the blue to become his fake fiancée?"

"Yes."

He drops back with a sigh. "I don't like this."

I cover his hands holding the reins with mine. "Lorenzo isn't a bad guy." Manipulative and self-serving, yes, but he did help Rafael with Darius and protected plenty of future women from suffering like I did, so I have a soft spot for him.

"Yeah, but that doesn't mean I want him engaged to someone who is like a sister to me."

I sigh. "She won't know that you know."

"I'll make sure she doesn't, but if I sense something is off—"

"Then you and I will kick his ass."

He wraps an arm around my waist and pulls me tighter against him. "I appreciate you trusting me."

"I couldn't *not* tell you."

He shakes his head. "That's not true. You could've stayed quiet, and I wouldn't have known."

"That wasn't an option."

He stiffens behind me. "Why?"

"Because I don't want to keep secrets from you."

He turns my head and kisses any lingering worries away until I'm only thinking about him and how I'm helplessly falling in love with a man who could end up breaking my heart one day. Hopefully, he chooses to protect it instead, but it doesn't matter.

I'd willingly choose to repeat every single moment, so long as it may end with me spending forever in his arms.

CHAPTER FIFTY-SIX

Ellie

Rafael and I go on two more dates within the next seven days—neither of which has ended with us doing anything more than *kiss*. I appreciate him taking things slow, but everyone has a breaking point, and mine officially happened a few hours ago after Rafael had me help him rescue a litter of kittens that were left abandoned on the side of the road.

He *told* me about his days saving Lake Wisteria stray cats, but seeing him in action is truly something else. I can tell he has experience with this kind of thing, because as soon as we found the cardboard box, he knew exactly what to do.

Thanks to Rafael's unlimited resources, we had the cats checked by a vet and cleared for the barn within an hour, which is impressive given the fact that the animal clinic wasn't even open at the time we found them.

"What?" He looks up from the gray kitten he is bottle-feeding. We are both sitting inside the stall, surrounded by blankets and the cutest kittens, but I only see *him*.

I lean back. "You may be the hottest man to ever exist."

His cheeks turn pink. "*May* be?"

"I'm still deciding."

His lips quirk. "Anything I can do to help?"

"Take your shirt off?"

He laughs, and I smile while snapping another photo of my favorite cat daddy. At this rate, I'm going to be able to make a collage of him.

His blush deepens. "Do you want to try?"

I hold up my phone and take what must be my hundredth picture. "Nope."

"Are you sure?"

"Yup. You only have this one left, so I need to take it all in and enjoy it while I still can." My flight to London leaves tomorrow, so I'm collecting memories like the daily flowers Rafael tucks behind my ear.

His lips curl. "*Only?*"

He has spent the last hour taking care of the six little ones, all while I was uselessly drooling, cooing, and filming the kittens.

I fake a sigh. "I'm sad I won't be here tomorrow morning to see you do it again."

"You could always spend the night here."

I choke.

He arches a brow. "Nico is staying with my aunt."

"And you're telling me this *now?*" He made it seem like Nico was visiting, not sleeping over.

"I didn't want to be presumptuous."

"*Presumptuous*? I was starting to get…concerned."

"About?"

"Whether or not you were ever going to fuck me before I left for Europe."

He explodes with a laugh. "I was *trying* to be respectful."

"Feel free to be disrespectful. Multiple times if you're up for it."

His eyes glimmer. "I'll remember that."

I'm easily distracted by a black kitten that cuddles up to my side. I pluck them off the blanket and hold them in my arms.

"I wonder what I'm going to name you." I consider my alcohol options. "We could consider margarita flavors—"

"Absolutely not."

"Hm. Beer brands?"

"No."

"Like I'm going to listen to a man who named his animals goats one, two, and three." I cradle the little black kitten against my chest and sway them back and forth like a baby. "With fur like that, you look like a Guinness to me."

Rafael makes a noise, and I look up to find him staring at me with hooded eyes.

"What?"

"Nothing."

"Obviously something's got you looking like that."

He clears his throat. "You'll make a good mom one day. That's all."

His comment makes me feel unreasonably warm all of a sudden. "You think so?"

"I know it." He glances away.

I can tell his mind is drifting toward unpleasant thoughts, and after the fun night we have had, I can't stand the idea of that happening.

"Well, unfortunately, I have my hands full right now as a cat mom of six."

He groans. "Please don't get attached."

Too late.

"You plan on getting rid of them already? I just started naming them," I whisper, as if the kittens can hear us.

His head drops back against the wood support wall of the stall. "No reasonable person has six cats, Elle."

He stares at me while I grab another kitten. "Look Stella in the eyes and tell her you're putting her up for adoption. I dare you."

His lips twitch. "Based on the blue ribbon around his neck, I'm pretty sure that's a boy."

I glare. "That's what I said."

"*Stella* will find a new home once *he* is big enough."

I point at the gray kitten cradled against his chest. "And Corona?"

"*She* will too."

"Please don't get rid of them." I pop my bottom lip out like Nico does. I'm not expecting it to work, but Rafael struggles to get his next sentence out, so it may do the trick after all.

This time, I hold two gray kittens up for him to see. "Miller and Sam want to stay."

His expressionless face gives nothing away.

I pick up the last kitten. This one is smaller than the others, with light blond fur and a white patch at the top of their head. "I'll let you name this last one."

"No."

"It's important that a father bonds with his babies."

He sighs. "You're worse than Nico when he wants his way."

"I'll take that as a compliment."

He looks at the kitten for the longest ten seconds of my life and sighs. "*Rubia*."

"Love it." I smile and drop a kiss on Rafael's cheek as a reward for his compliance.

"But…"

I turn and hit him with my best puppy-dog eyes.

His narrow. "Don't look at me like that."

"I'll do anything to keep them."

His nostrils flare. "Anything?"

I nod with a grin.

"We'll see about that. Now, get your ass out of here and into my bed before I change my mind."

My core pulses with a need so strong that I teeter as I scramble to my feet. When I reach for the latch on the stall, Rafael calls my name, so I look over my shoulder.

"Yeah?"

"Grab the white box in my closet, but whatever you do, don't open it."

I bat my lashes. "Anything else?"

"Lose the clothes."

CHAPTER FIFTY-SEVEN

Ellie

Taking my clothes off and finding the white box Rafael had mentioned was easy, but following his directions was not. My self-control is put to the test as I battle between following Rafael's command or not.

Part of me wants to disobey, but something tells me to keep my hands to myself and wait, so I spend the next however many minutes tossing and turning in bed.

Rafael takes his sweet time in the barn, which only floods my body with more adrenaline. I've had enough partners to know what I like in the bedroom, but I have a feeling Rafael is going to put those ideas to the test, starting with whatever the hell is in the white box.

It can't be bigger than a shoebox and weighs about the same as a pair of boots. I thought it could be the vibrator from my search history, but I'm starting to have doubts.

Special lube? A set of butt plugs? Maybe some anal beads or nipple clamps?

My mind goes wild, thinking up all the possibilities until a door slams in the distance. The hairs on my arms stand up, and my skin tingles at the sound of footsteps. Goose bumps spread across my arms as I pull at the sheet and readjust my position on the bed.

My heart outpaces Rafael's heavy feet stomping up the stairs, although I can hardly hear him stepping inside the room over the sound of the blood rushing to my ears.

"You didn't take a peek inside?" He pulls his shirt over his head and tosses it to the floor before yanking off his shorts. He stands in front of me in nothing but a pair of briefs that do little to hide his erection.

"Did you look inside?" he enunciates each word.

I shake my head hard.

"Are you sure?" He presses one knee onto the bed, followed by the other. The mattress dips under his weight as he crawls over my body.

"I *wanted* to, but I didn't."

"That's my girl."

I never knew how much I wanted to be *his girl* until he said it. My heart goes into a spiral, the beats climbing so fast that I become concerned about my cardiac health.

He kisses me hard then. No precursor or warning glance. No teasing, biting, or longing stares at my mouth. Just his lips crushing against mine until the whole world goes dark behind my eyelids.

Our mouths fuse together, and my thoughts scatter until

I'm only thinking about him. He breaks away at one point to get rid of the sheet between us, but his mouth is back on mine in seconds like he never left.

The way Rafael kisses me is almost as addictive as the way his fingers roam over my body.

His touch is comforting yet possessive at the same time, and I've never felt more cherished than I do as he crawls backward until he is positioned between my legs.

He brushes his hands over my thighs with such softness, it makes me feel precious. Like he will spend the rest of my life showing me how he finds me a masterpiece.

Not broken, like I had once labeled myself, but *loved*.

He may not have said those three big important words yet, and I don't expect him to anytime soon, but I can tell by looking into his eyes that he is *feeling* it.

And so am I.

My chest warms as he takes his time drawing my pleasure out. Rafael drives me to the brink of madness with his tongue only to yank me back from the edge multiple times before I'm writhing beneath him, begging for him to do something.

"Make. Me. Come," I say between heavy pants, and he grins up at me.

"I am working on it."

"You're a fucking tease."

He chuckles before sucking on my clit hard enough to dull my vision. My cry for him is rewarded, and he plunges his fingers inside me. I push his head down, keeping him right there while his fingers pump into me at a punishing pace.

His head is trapped between my thighs, and they apply

enough pressure to keep him in place until he finally curls his fingers and presses on my clit to make me come.

My pleasure is a wave, rolling through me in a rush of warmth. Rafael doesn't stop touching me until my body finally goes lax underneath him.

I can hardly hear anything over my heavy breathing, but the telltale sign of a condom wrapper ripping piques my interest.

"I thought you got a vasectomy."

"I did." A look passes over his face, and I hate that I'm the reason for it in the first place.

If he wants to be extra cautious about not having any children, that's fine. I don't blame him after his last incident with an accidental pregnancy.

Instead of asking him any more questions, I slide off the bed and grab the condom from his hand. He begins to protest, but the words die on his tongue as I get down on my knees in front of him.

Never in a million years did I imagine I would be kneeling in front of someone I once had a crush on, looking up at him while he stares down at me with hooded eyes and a smirk that could put the devil's to shame.

"*Mi belleza*." He cradles my cheek affectionately, and I melt into his touch before his fingers slide through my hair.

I lean forward and plant a kiss on his thigh. His muscles strain, so I repeat the same thing on his other leg, earning a little sharp inhale this time.

Mi belleza: My beauty.

I drag my finger across his thigh, stopping as I get closer to his straining cock.

After he went down on me in the barn loft, we had a talk about how long it's been for him.

Two years.

"And you call *me* a fucking tease." His gravelly voice makes my body pulse.

With a smile, I wrap my lips around the head and suck. He jerks forward with a curse, and I can't help laughing at him apologizing for accidentally gagging me.

"I'm fine." I brush my hands down his thighs before I part my lips again, flatten my tongue, and slide as much as I possibly can of his cock into my mouth.

His thighs tremble as I slowly pull back, flicking my tongue across his stiff length. His nails scrape at my scalp, but he never forces me to speed up. Never tries to gag me or switch to a new punishing tempo.

If anything, he tugs on my hair in a silent request for me to slow down. At this rate, the poor man may come before he ever has a chance to slip inside me.

"Elle," he rasps when I wrap my fingers around him and pump. His salty essence seeps from his tip and coats my tongue, so I swallow, which earns me a hiss.

He steps away, and I release him with a pop. He yanks me onto my feet and swipes the condom wrapper from my hand before placing me on the edge of the bed.

With a light shove, I fall backward with a laugh while he sheaths his cock.

This is it, I tell myself.

High school me might have *enjoyed* this, but nothing compares to grown-up me who can not only appreciate Rafael *the man* but also Rafael as a *lover*, *protector*, and *friend*.

I'm glad we didn't cross paths until now because I wouldn't have gotten to know the real him, and the thought of that never happening makes my chest hurt. Rafael is everything I could ever want in a partner, and now he is *mine*.

I'll wait however long it takes for him to feel the same because he is worth it.

He pushes my thighs apart, and I wrap my legs around his waist as he presses his body against mine and kisses me. One hand cups my cheek while the other reaches between us for his cock.

There is a slight pressure as he pushes inside me, and his body trembles over mine as he slides deeper. His kiss becomes more desperate, and my lips tingle when he finally sinks all the way.

We both still, and a wave of happiness washes over me. I'm not sure I've ever felt so content—so *complete*.

Rafael trembles as his eyes screw shut and his chest rises with his deep breaths.

"If you come first, I'm going to be *really* mad at you."

"Good girls always come first. I promise." He traces my bottom lip with the pad of his thumb.

He regains control over himself and pulls out slowly. His hands brush down the sides of my thighs and the tattoos of stars as he slides back inside. Once. Twice. Three times, and then I stop counting.

I lose track of time, space, and my very own name, gasping

and moaning as he continues torturing my body with his slow pumps.

"You are the one I never knew I needed." He pauses after saying it, and I do too.

Our eyes meet as a wall around his heart comes crumbling down.

His fingers dig into my hips as he pulls out. "I may not be *the one* you envisioned for yourself, but I won't stop until I feel like I'm worthy of you."

I swore to myself that I wouldn't cry, but fuck, when he talks like *that*, I'm not sure I can control it. Still, I rally, focusing on the sensations in my lower half as much as the ones in my heart.

Rafael doesn't fuck me. No. He takes his time, whispering sweet praises into my ear in between kisses that leave me breathless. Every stroke is a promise, and every touch is an oath.

He will take care of me.

He will love me when I struggle to love myself.

And he is *the one* I was waiting for this whole time.

With a pinch of my clit, my whole world shatters. The pleasure rocks me to my very core, and the world fades around me.

His pumps never stop. Not even after he finally comes with a shout. Watching Rafael come undone must be the sexiest sight I've ever witnessed, and I lock the memory away.

Eventually, despite his best efforts to stay upright, his body gives out, and he lies down on top of me.

I brush my hand through his damp hair and say, "You're the one I was always meant to find."

He wraps his arms around me and squeezes, as if to tell me he feels the same. He may not say it, but I know he does.

And that's good enough for me.

I start to nod off only for my eyes to snap open when I have a thought. "I just realized something."

Rafael grumbles against the top of my head.

"You never showed me what was in the box."

His chest vibrates from quiet laughter.

"What?"

"Nothing important. I was buying myself some time to wrap up with the kittens."

My mouth falls open.

"What did you *think* was in there?" he asks.

I fake a snore, only to have him shake me.

"Tell me."

I sneak a peek at him. "A vibrator?"

His deep, dark laugh tells me it isn't the end of this conversation.

CHAPTER FIFTY-EIGHT

Ellie

I knew this day would come. It was impossible to ignore, especially with how Cole's assistant spent days coordinating the next five weeks of my life, but time flew by way too fast.

"It's only five weeks," Rafael says as we stop outside the glass sliding doors leading into the airport. Earlier, he had insisted on parking his truck and walking me to the entrance, and while I was resistant at first, I'm glad he came to see me off.

I wrap my arms around his waist and hug him so hard, he groans.

"Are you feeling okay about the flight?" he asks.

"Nope."

"Great. What's nine hours of anxiety anyway?"

"Sounds like a typical day for me."

Rafael chuckles. He kisses the top of my head before I let go of him. "Are you sure you'll be okay?"

I put on my best brave face. "I'll do my best."

He stares at me for a few beats. "You'll call me when you land?"

"For the fifth time already, *yes*." Funny how we went from hardly ever speaking to one another to acting like two teenagers who can't go to sleep without talking about anything and everything.

With one last mind-numbing kiss, Rafael heads back to the crosswalk that leads to the parking garage. I'm an emotional being, so I'm already crying before even walking inside the airport.

When he catches me wiping at the corners of my eyes, he laughs, and I flip him off before turning to the sliding doors. I take one step before pausing to glance over my shoulder.

"If you want to make your flight, you should get going," Rafael says.

"I know."

"You've got this."

I throw him a thumbs-up before rolling my shoulders back and heading inside. My anxiety spikes as soon as I enter the busy Detroit airport, but I remind myself that I've been here before and done this once already.

"Here goes nothing," I grumble to myself as I head to the security checkpoint.

I make it through without any hiccups. With time to kill before my flight to London, I check out some stores, although I don't have Nico here to distract me with a hundred different questions.

My chest aches, and I rub at the spot as I think about the

way he looked when we said our goodbyes back at Rafael's house earlier. If it weren't for his father encouraging me to leave, I doubt I would have found the courage to get in the truck and leave Nico behind, especially after I saw the way his bottom lip quivered as he held back his tears.

It's just five weeks, Ellie. They'll be here when you get back.

I head to my gate, only to find out my group was called twenty minutes ago.

"Shit." I hand the employee my phone with the boarding pass before heading down the bridge.

My legs are trembling as I consider my new reality for the next nine hours, but I do my best to focus on the exercises Rafael taught me.

When deep breathing doesn't work, I envision the video he showed me about airplanes and Jell-O, and that seems to temporarily do the trick until I get on the plane and am told by the person in my seat that I got the wrong one.

"No. I'm 17E."

He checks his phone and shows me his boarding pass, confirming that he is in the right seat. With a frown, I tug my phone from the front pocket of my backpack and check my boarding pass again.

6G?

I walk in the direction of the first-class cabin. I'm confused, wondering if Cole upgraded me from business to first-class within the last hour while the polite flight attendant leads me to my seat.

"Thanks." My heart is racing in my chest as I struggle to lift my bulging carry-on in the bin. With one last hard shove, it slides into place, and I shut it before a flight attendant tells me I need to check it instead.

No way am I parting with my prized possessions like that.

I'm jittery by the time I take a seat. The temptation to rush out the door is riding me hard. If I wanted, I could leave and try this all again tomorrow. I doubt Rafael would mind turning around to come pick me up—

"Hey."

My head whips to the side, and my mouth falls open at the sight of my first-class seatmate.

Rafael sits down next to me, and I stare at him for a few seconds before finally recovering.

"What are you doing here?"

"I was in the mood for a trip to London."

"You *what*?"

He shrugs as if he didn't just blow my mind. "I wasn't sure if you needed me to come, so I packed a carry-on just in case and asked my family to watch Nico."

"Oh my God."

"Is it too much?"

It's…

Everything. I reach over the middle compartment dividing our seats and rope my arms around him. "Thank you."

"While I can't follow you around Europe…" He sighs longingly. "I thought I could at least help you through the hardest part."

My eyes mist over. "This may be one of the nicest things someone has done for me."

"We've got to work on setting your bar a little higher."

"Are you kidding? If you keep this up, no one will ever compare."

"Just how I like it."

I laugh, and he kisses the crown of my head.

When he holds out his hand for me, I grab it with a smile. I want to say the three big words that have been floating around in my head all week, and I want to say them now.

"Rafa?"

He looks up from his phone. "Yeah?"

"I love you."

His eyes soften right before his brows scrunch. He opens his mouth, only to shut it again.

"You don't have to say it back. I just wanted you to know."

He brings our interlaced fingers to his lips and kisses the back of my hand. "When I say it back—and I promise, I *will*—it's going to be somewhere without any witnesses."

"I'm holding you to that."

He gives my hand a squeeze. "Deal."

CHAPTER FIFTY-NINE

Rafael

Yesterday, Julian called me crazy when I told him I had decided to fly to London after all, but I corrected him and said, "No. I'm in love."

That seemed to shut him up. While he didn't hesitate to take care of Nico while I'm gone for a couple of days, he did grumble about bottle-feeding six kittens. Dahlia, on the other hand, can't get enough of them, flooding our group chat with photos of Julian frowning at the camera while surrounded by Stella, Miller, Sam, Corona, Rubia, and Guinness.

I probably looked the same while Ellie was convincing me to keep the kittens, although inside, I had already said *yes* as soon as she named the first one and was talking about raising them together.

I had wanted to tell her I loved her there and then, but it didn't feel right, so I waited. Should've known she would beat me to the punch, though. My plan had been to tell her before I took her to bed, but then I got nervous and held off.

It doesn't matter anymore. If anything, her confession gives me more confidence to say it once a cab drops us off at the hotel. Ellie spent the whole ride with her face pressed against the window as she took in the city, all while I watched her.

By the time we enter our hotel room, I'm dying to touch her.

She makes the first move by wrapping her arms around my neck. "I still can't believe you came. Why didn't you mention that you were thinking about it?"

I lock my arms around her waist. "I didn't know if I was or not."

"What pushed you to do it?"

"I wasn't ready to watch you walk away yet."

Her eyes soften. "Because…"

Here goes nothing. I brush my hands down her arms before locking them around her back.

"I know I'm not the person you probably envisioned yourself falling for…"

"I'm curious. Who do you think I envisioned?"

"Someone you could have kids with, for starters."

"You *can*, if you want."

I frown.

She pats the spot over my heart. "Adoption is always an option."

"You say that *now*, but you could change your mind."

"I've thought long and hard about it."

"You have?"

"Yeah, so while I appreciate you being considerate of my needs, it's not necessary. I know what I want."

"And what's that?"

"*You.*" She kisses me softly. "Any way I can have you. Nico with or without siblings. Marriage or no marriage. So long as you're committed to me and only me, then that's all I need."

"You deserve a husband and a nice house on the lake with a white picket fence and a dog or two running around." Although I've considered changing my stance on marriage, I'm still uncertain about the idea, although I wish I weren't.

This is Ellie. Not Hillary.

Ellie steals me away from my torrid thoughts by asking, "Who wants a dog when I could have goats?"

I can't help laughing, and the tight ball in my throat loosens. "Don't forget about pigs."

"And a sheep."

"Did I mention I have a horse too? And six kittens I bottle-feed every day?"

Her eyes shimmer. "All you're missing are some chickens."

"How many do you want?"

"At least a whole coop."

"Consider it done."

She presses her palm against my stubbled cheek. "Can't you see? *You* were who I envisioned for myself, Rafael. It was always *you.*"

I glance away, unable to handle the look of pure adoration on her face.

Ellie brushes her thumb across my skin, silently willing me

to look at her. "You're so concerned about me deserving better that you didn't stop to think about what *you* deserve."

My lungs stutter before stalling completely.

"You deserve to be with *the one* who will take the time to *see* you." She pushes me toward the bed and steps between my spread thighs. "*The one* who will show up time and time again to be there for you, even if you push them away because you're scared, angry, or unhappy." She presses her lips against my forehead. "They don't quit, run, or cheat. They will fight for you, even if it means fighting *against* you, because life is a war zone, but love is the greatest weapon we have." Her mouth brushes over my right cheek and then my left.

"The one *does* exist, but not in the way you thought I meant, like some soulmate or something cosmic. To me, *the one* is someone willing to do everything in their power to be the person you deserve, not because they are fated to love you but because they *choose* to."

She straddles my lap before her mouth claims mine with a passionate kiss that I feel down to my very soul.

Goose bumps spread across my skin. Ellie's fingers dig into my hair, and her hips rotate as she grinds against my cock. My grip on her hips tightens from her maddening movements, and I groan when she rubs against me at just the right angle.

She pulls away, but I seal my mouth over hers again. My grip on the back of her neck is as punishing as the one she has around my heart.

Eventually, my control snaps, and I flip her over on the bed. She lets out a laugh as she slams against the soft mattress, and I make quick work of her clothes, although I struggle for a moment with her sports bra until she helps me remove it.

She matches my rushed movements with her own, and I lose a shirt button from how hard she yanks on the fabric.

Despite the urge to fuck her hard and fast, I slow things down and simply enjoy the sight of Ellie looking up at me without a hint of self-consciousness despite her body being fully on display. Her trusting me like this means the world to me, and I'll do everything in my power to protect it.

"No merezco a alguien tan hermosa como tú."

She doesn't ask me to translate, but based on the way her cheeks heat, she understands enough.

I pepper her skin with light kisses before sealing my mouth over her nipple. She gasps when I suck, and her hands dig into my scalp, tugging at the strands as I flick my tongue over the pebbled peak. Her back arches, and a strained moan escapes her when my teeth scrape against the sensitive bud.

I take my time worshiping one breast and then the other, my movements remaining slow and calculated.

"Rafael," she says with a groan as she yanks on my hair. My head whips up, and our gazes connect.

"Please." She shimmies her hips.

I slide off her with a grin before I wrap my hand around her ankle and yank hard enough to make her gasp. She glides across the comforter before I release her.

No merezco a alguien tan hermosa como tú: I don't deserve someone as beautiful as you.

Her thighs hang over the side of the bed, and I push them apart until she's open for me.

"You're dripping."

"I have a few ideas on how to fix that problem."

"My only problem is that I haven't fucked you yet."

Her eyes go wide as I drop to my knees, widen her legs to give me space, and seal my mouth over her pussy. I stroke, flick, and swivel my tongue until she is writhing and moaning underneath me, bucking her hips while begging for release.

I could spend forever between her thighs, and it still wouldn't be long enough.

Not even close.

Her nails dig into the comforter as she comes, and I find myself smiling as her perfect world shatters around her because of *me*.

Pleasuring her is my newest drug of choice. The high is unlike anything I've ever felt before, and I want to chase it for the rest of my life.

Just like I would chase her to the end of the world and back because I love her.

She goes limp while I sheathe myself with a condom and crawl over her body before our mouths fuse together again. Her kiss is hesitant at first, tainted with the taste of her release, but then her tongue flicks out and traces my bottom lip, making me shudder.

I line myself up and slowly sink inside her. Ellie's legs wrap around my waist, opening herself up even more for me as her heels press into the small of my back. My eyes shut, and my body shakes as I slide inside her inch by inch until I completely bottom out with a sigh.

I want this moment to last for as long as humanly possible. Want to bask in the look of adoration on her face and the pure sense of joy that builds in my chest when I realize I could feel like this for the rest of my life, so long as I don't get in my own way.

She cups my cheek, and my eyes snap open to find her staring up at me. Her hazel eyes look more brown than green in this lighting, the dark of her irises drawing out the deeper tones.

I plant a quick kiss on her forehead before pulling out slowly. My cock glistens in the light, completely soaked with her arousal, and I become distracted by the sight of me sinking into her for a few moments before she drags my attention back to her face.

I cradle her head between my hands, holding her in place as I pump my hips slowly in and out of her. Sex in this position feels intimate. Like I'm being laid bare in front of Ellie with nowhere to hide as the pleasure builds between us.

I rise to my knees and deepen the position. With every snap of my hips, Ellie slides backward, so I wrap my hand around her throat and hold her in place.

Her wild eyes bounce between my face and my cock as my pace quickens, and her heels dig into my back. Pressure builds at the base of my spine as my balls draw up, but I refuse to give in until Ellie does.

My fingers around her neck squeeze harder, and her eyes roll into the back of her head when I shift my angle, hitting the spot that makes her fingers dig into my thigh hard enough to leave marks.

I snap my hips, making her body shake with every thrust, and she replies with a drawn-out moan and a few more scratch marks added to my thighs.

"*Mi estrella*."

She shudders underneath me.

"You like being called *my star*?"

She shakes her head. "I like it when you call me *yours*."

I lean forward until our lips hover a centimeter apart. "If it wasn't obvious, then let me make myself perfectly clear. You're mine, Elle. In every sense of the word, from here on out, because *I love you*."

"Again."

I pull back only to slam into her. "I love you."

A tear slips down the side of her face.

"I love every single thing about you." I grind my hips, making her gasp. "Your mind. Your scars. But most of all, your *heart*."

With a trembling hand, she cups my cheek and looks up at me with glistening eyes full of hope. "I love you too."

With one last shove, she orgasms, squeezing my cock with a cry. I don't stop moving, my pumps only growing more desperate as she rides the wave of pleasure.

Despite the urge to fuck her until the sun rises, I physically can't hold back anymore, and my mind, body, and soul shatter as I come. My balls ache from the need to release, and it seems to last forever.

Eventually, once my cock is no longer jerking, I collapse on top of her with a sigh. Her shaky fingers brush through my hair, sending a zing of pleasure down my spine.

I could get used to this.

To her and the love she is so readily able to give.

And to the love I want to reciprocate because she is the one I can't imagine life without.

CHAPTER SIXTY

Ellie

With Cole arriving tomorrow to play at a local London venue, Rafael and I spend his one and only day here exploring the city. We visit a few famous sites, explore Regent Street and the expensive stores, and hang out at a local pub before heading back to the hotel to get ready for dinner.

When we return to our room, I'm shocked to find three new packages from Liberty London set on a small table beside our bed.

I turn to face Rafael. "Tell me you didn't."

"I'm going to take a quick shower and shave," he says nonchalantly before heading to the bathroom.

Buzzing with anticipation, I unwrap the first box to reveal the exact dress I tried on at the store. I told Rafael it wasn't worth the money, which I still stand by, but clearly, he didn't agree.

The luxurious dress came with a hefty price tag I associate with wedding dresses and ball gowns, and I'm tempted to ask him to return it before I have a chance to stain it, but I reconsider.

Rafael could see my request as a slight against him, and I don't have the heart to ruin his grand gesture with my insecurity.

Even if it means wearing a glamorous dress worth two of my parents' mortgage payments.

The next box has a pair of heels I gawked over—in my exact size too—while the final box has something I never laid eyes on today.

A golden hair pin in the shape of a shooting star that I am going to pretend is encrusted with fake stones rather than the expensive alternative.

Mi estrella, he called me.

I spend the next however many minutes gawking at the sparkling gems that glitter in the light, alternating between tucking the pin into my hair and pulling it out and placing it carefully back in the small box.

"Do you like it?" Rafael asks while catching me in the act of ripping a few hairs out in the process of removing it.

I love it, but I can't say that when I don't intend on keeping it.

"What store is it from?" I stroke the diamond—no, the fake gemstones. For all I know, the array of stones could be lab-created, which, while still expensive, isn't the same as ones mined straight from the earth.

You keep telling yourself that.

"I found it in Lake Aurora, while Julian was ring shopping."

My head snaps in the direction of the door, where Rafael is standing in nothing but a towel.

"What?"

"I'm glad Julian dragged me along, or else I wouldn't have found it." He moves toward me, plucks the pin from my tight fist, carefully grabs some of my hair, and secures it in place beside my ear. "Beautiful." He's staring at me rather than the pin, and a tingling sensation skates down my spine.

"It's expensive."

"What if I told you it wasn't?"

"We promised not to lie."

"Technically, I wouldn't be."

Of course he wouldn't. To a billionaire, I'm sure this barely makes a dent in his bank account, but to me, it means so much more.

I attempt to scowl but fail. "I shouldn't accept it."

"But you will."

"Confident much?"

He leans in and presses his mouth against my ear. "Please, Elle? For me?"

I shudder at his request. "Fine."

His sly grin looks like it wants to be introduced to my fist. "Go get ready before we're late." He turns me in a rush and slaps my ass.

I glare at him from over my shoulder before grabbing the new dress, heels, and my makeup bag.

After thirty minutes of primping in the bathroom and receiving a text of approval from my best friend, I head into the room with my head held high only to teeter on my new heels as Rafael's gaze follows a path from my head to my toes.

"You look…"

My lungs stall.

"*Divina.*" The word rolls off his tongue, along with a wave of heat through my belly.

His tongue darts out to trace the bottom of his lip, and my heart jolts in my chest as he walks over to me and pulls me into a kiss.

"I thought we were going to be late," I say with a rasp.

"It will be worth it." He reaches for my hand, but I slip away from him before he has a chance to ruin my thirty minutes' worth of work.

"No! Stay away." I rush for the door as quickly as my heels will permit.

He chuckles as he follows behind me. "For now."

Another shiver of anticipation spreads over my skin, drawing goose bumps in their wake.

With a wave of newfound confidence, I head toward the elevator bank while swaying my hips, earning another groan from the man who collects pieces of my heart with every passing day.

After dinner and two rounds of incredible sex, Rafael is knocked out while I remain wide-awake thanks to jet lag and some building anxiety about my first day of work tomorrow. I struggle to fall asleep, so I pull out my songwriting notebook and flip through the pages before stopping on one that I haven't touched since we were in Hawaii.

I know some songs are meant to never be finished, but whenever I think of leaving the one I started about Rafael unwritten, I'm hit with a strong sense of loss. So in a rush of inspiration after Rafael told me he loved me, I pick up where I left off on that first day on the boat.

> It was snowing hard on Christmas Eve,
>
> When our paths crossed that first time.
>
> Couldn't believe you hadn't noticed me,
>
> But then again, neither had I.

I stare at the lyrics hard enough to make my eyes cross. The temptation to scribble over them is still there, but it's overshadowed by the urge to continue.

Not for Cole, but for myself.

"Silver Scars" taught me a few hard lessons, including not sharing every song I write with others. So while I can finish the song I started about Rafael and myself, I don't plan on handing it over to Cole for him to use on his next album.

It is *our* love story, not the world's, and I plan on keeping it that way.

My muse remains asleep, completely unaware of me softly strumming the guitar beside him.

Like father, like son. He and Nico could sleep through a heavy metal concert without even stirring.

When I think about Rafael leaving tomorrow, my chest

physically hurts, but then I remind myself that I should be grateful for him being here right now.

We can make it through five weeks because, no matter what, we both *love* each other.

I shake my head and refocus on my song. The process of getting to the final product is different every time, depending on whether I focus on writing the lyrics first or perfecting the melody.

This time, I have a clear picture of the story I want to tell and the melody I want to accompany it. Unlike most of my other songs, which tend to have a similar melancholic vibe to them, this one follows a different beat. One that has sadness, sure, but the underlying sense of wistfulness and longing is present from the very first chord.

"I haven't heard that one before."

I startle at the sound of Rafael's sleepy voice. "Sorry. I didn't mean to wake you."

"Don't apologize—" His reply is cut off by a yawn. "I didn't realize I fell asleep." The comforter I threw over his body falls as he sits up against the headboard and rubs his eyes. "Is that the song you're writing for Cole?"

"No."

He looks confused. "Oh."

"This one is just for me." I discreetly shut my notebook. While I doubt Rafael could put the pieces together since I've only written one verse, it won't take him long to guess who the song is about once I continue writing it.

"Can I hear it?"

"Nope."

"After everything we've done, you're still shy?" His sly smile reminds me of the same one he had earlier while his head was pressed between my thighs.

Color floods my cheeks, making them hot to the touch. "No. It's just not finished yet."

"So you'll let me listen once it is?"

"Sure. Once it's written, I'll let you hear it."

His eyes narrow.

I smile.

"You're scheming," he says with a scowl.

"And you're talking way too much for someone who seemed dead asleep just a few minutes ago."

Without a beard to cover half his face, his rosy skin is fully on display, giving him away.

I sigh. "How long have you been listening?"

"A few minutes. I swear."

My heart rate calms. At most, he heard the whole first verse since I was messing with a few chords while trying to perfect the sound.

"This song sounds different from your others."

My head, along with my world, tilts. "What?"

"It's… I don't know how to describe it. It's just different."

He is right. Unlike my other songs, this one is happy. Hopeful even. Like a never-ending epilogue of our unfinished love story.

A love story that has only just begun, with the best parts still left to be written.

CHAPTER SIXTY-ONE

Rafael

Instead of heading back to Lake Wisteria, I changed my mind at the last minute and switched my flight from Detroit to Portland. My ex-wife hasn't been answering Nico's calls or my texts since she canceled on him for the Strawberry Festival a week ago, and while I don't mind never speaking to her again, my kid deserves better.

I stop the car in front of the gate blocking her driveway, press my finger against the call button on the mechanical box, and wait. Finally, after a couple of minutes, Hillary's voice crackles through the speaker.

"What are you doing here?" she asks in her grating tone.

"We need to talk."

"You flew all the way out here *to talk*?"

"Yes." I grind my teeth together.

The gate opens, and I drive my rental car up the gravel path before parking outside a beautiful house overlooking a lake. I take a moment to appreciate the view, seeing as I paid for it, before taking a deep breath and heading toward the open front door.

Hillary stands with her arms crossed against her chest and a scowl I recognize all too well. Her short, dark hair accentuates her sharp bone structure, and her designer clothes showcase her thin frame and delicate features, the ivory color of her pantsuit making her appear far more angelic than she actually is.

Her red lips pull into a frown. "What the hell are you doing here?"

"Something I should have done long ago," I snap.

She looks around, as if the neighbors a mile away can hear us. "Come inside."

Typical Hillary, always giving a shit about everyone else except those whose opinions actually matter. I used to be the same way, but I've changed.

Ellie opened my eyes to the possibility of accepting who I am without any pretenses, and now that I've gotten a taste, I can't imagine going back to the way things used to be.

I follow Hillary inside, and she shuts the door and turns to face me.

Her nostrils flare. "What are you really doing here?"

"You kept ignoring Nico's and my calls."

"I've been busy."

"Cut the shit." I chose passiveness over passion, but now I'm done. Either Hillary steps up to be a parent or I will fight her for full custody because she doesn't want it anyway.

Her face turns red. "What do you want me to do? Apologize for not being able to make it to the festival?"

"Yes, Hillary, an apology would be nice after you promised to go but canceled only one hour before your son was supposed to perform."

She doesn't look the least bit affronted by my tone, which only fuels my frustration.

"For some goddamn reason, Nico wanted you there because he *always* wants you there, although I can't for the life of me understand why, when all you do is disappoint him."

Her icy facade cracks for a fraction of a second before she schools her features.

Good. It's the least she deserves after making my son cry again.

"I've spent the last two fucking years *covering* for you because, regardless of how I feel toward you, *he* sees the good in you."

She glances away. "I *wanted* to be there."

"But you weren't."

She makes a face. "It's complicated."

"That's always your excuse, and frankly, I'm sick of it. Hell, I was tired long before we ever got divorced."

"Do *not* disrespect me in my own home." She sounds so much like her proper, high-society mother when she uses that shrill tone, and it sends a chill down my spine.

She crosses her arms, and that's when I notice a thin band of pale skin that is different from the rest of her ring finger.

Fuck me.

How long has she been engaged to her boyfriend, and why did it take me this long to figure it out?

My blood pounds in my ears, making my head pulse as I wrap my head around the fact that Hillary has kept her secret for who knows how long, all while I foot the bill.

You're here for Nico. Not yourself.

I take a deep breath and try to dull my rage until it goes from a roaring fire to a burning ember inside my chest. "I get that you can't stand me, but the person you're hurting most in this process is your *son*."

She at least looks slightly unhappy about it. Perhaps there is hope for her after all, although I won't hold my breath.

She takes a deep breath. "I just…"

"*What?*"

Her upper lip curls. "I hate going to that damn town, knowing everyone is aware of my…"

"*Affair.*"

"Yes," she says with a hiss. "Bring it up for the fiftieth time, why don't you? It's been a while since the last time you reminded me of it."

I cross my arms. "We all make choices that have consequences."

"Doesn't mean I want to be reminded of them every time I go there!"

I pause. "So this is all about your reputation? Is that what you're trying to say?"

"You don't understand what it's like to be me."

"No, I don't. I guess I struggle to understand what it's like to be a neglectful parent who cares more about their reputation than their own fucking child."

She flinches. I don't want to feel bad for her, but a small

part of me does because I recognize that she will always be hollow inside, so long as she prioritizes other people's opinions over her own blood.

"We both grew up with two different types of shitty parents, but the main difference between you and me is that you became just like them while I did everything possible not to."

Her face pales. "I…"

I speak when she doesn't. "Nobody can ever fill the void of a mother. You of all people should know that."

She stares at her feet.

I wipe my face. "Make this right and be the mother Nico *needs*."

"Or what? You'll take me to court?"

My lip curls in disgust. "I'm not going to threaten you with money to make you see reason."

I will always pay child support, but her alimony—which makes up eighty percent of what I pay her—will be revoked the moment I call my lawyer and break the news about Hillary's secret engagement.

"How noble of you," she sneers.

I reach for the door but pause and look over my shoulder. "Nico wouldn't want me to, because whether you choose to reciprocate or not, he *loves* you, although if you keep this up, there will come a day when he no longer will. I promise you that much."

"And if he doesn't? Then what?" Desperation bleeds into her every word.

"Pray that never happens, because the moment he wants

you out of his life, I'll make sure you're no longer a part of ours."

"Three bouquets in one week?" Ellie turns the camera so I can get a look at the floral arrangement I had sent to her room before she checked into her hotel in Lisbon. I wanted her to have something of mine there when she arrived in Portugal, just like I'd done in the other countries she visited.

"Do you like them?" I chose a summer arrangement that the local florist recommended, although I was hesitant since Ellie said she wasn't the biggest fan of roses.

"Yes. They're beautiful, just like the others." She spreads out on the bed with a sigh. The sun hasn't even set here yet, and she is already getting ready to fall asleep.

I'm hit with another urge to fly to Europe to see her. It's only been seven days since I left her alone in London, and it feels like an eternity.

Fuck.

I don't know if I've ever missed someone like this before—in fact, I know I haven't. Not even when Hillary left me.

Sure, I missed my ex-wife, but it wasn't like this. I wasn't driven to madness in her absence, nor was I hit with a daily urge to leave my job behind and follow her around.

God, I'm tempted to do just that, but I have Nico and my business to think about.

"I hate that I have to leave them behind, though." She sighs to herself.

Her comment sparks a new idea, and I vow to get started on it as soon as we hang up the phone.

"I miss Ellie." Nico takes a stab at his dinner. I thought he would be hungrier after spending all day at summer camp, but his appetite matches his low mood.

"Me too," I say while pushing a bit of my food around.

"You do?"

I sigh at the pinch in my chest that comes whenever I think of her. "Yeah. A lot."

"How much longer until she comes back?"

"Too long." Ellie's absence is felt from the moment we wake up to a quiet house to the very moment I fall asleep each night.

I miss her more than I could have imagined, and we still have four weeks left until she comes home.

Nico looks at me weird.

"What?" I ask.

"Nothing." His fork scrapes against the plate without picking up any food.

"You sure about that?"

He sighs in that way of his that makes him seem older than his age. "I just…"

"Yes?"

"Remember when I asked you if you *like like* Ellie?"

"Who could forget it?" I tease.

"Do you think she *like likes* you back?"

I laugh, which makes him frown.

"I'm not laughing *at* you," I clarify.

"Oh." He doesn't seem to believe me.

"Your question just caught me off guard."

"Why?"

"Because out of all the things I expected you to ask, that wasn't on the list."

He gnaws on the inside of his cheek. "I was just wondering…"

"What?"

"If she *like likes* you and you *like like* her, would you ever…"

"Date her?"

"What's that?"

"Ask her to be my girlfriend." I know he is aware of that concept, seeing as he had three in the last year.

"Oh yeah. That."

"Would it be okay with you if I did?"

"If you did what? Ask Ellie to be your girlfriend?"

"Yeah."

"Heck yeah! I love her."

I take a deep breath. "I don't want you to get too excited, but…"

Nico's eyes light up as he nods.

Too late. He is practically vibrating with enthusiasm right now.

I pin him in place with my stare. "It may not happen."

"But it could?"

I push the worry away and say, "Yeah. One day."

Nico throws his fist in the air. "Yes!"

Everything between Ellie and me is still rather new, but our connection is serious enough for us to admit we love each other. Hiding those feelings from Nico doesn't sit right with me, which is why I didn't want to ask her to be my girlfriend without my son knowing about us. Ellie had agreed when I mentioned it. She said that he is a big part of our lives, so to keep a secret like that from him feels unfair, especially after our trip to London.

"So, when do I get a brother?"

I proceed to choke.

The photo of Cole and Ellie on my phone screen taunts me, along with the bold headline above boasting about Cole being seen out in Portugal with a beautiful blond.

My beautiful blond.

Ellie may remain anonymous to the general public thanks to her dark sunglasses, but I could point her out in a crowd of hundreds. Cole's hand is pressed against the small of her back while security guards fend off the crowd waiting outside some upscale restaurant. The singer's mouth hovers near her ear, making it seem as though he is passing along some secret the world isn't privy to. Ellie's smile is small but present while her eyes are shielded by opaque lenses.

Based on the photo, I can't get a good read on her, which only worsens the churning acid in my stomach.

Thanks to my masochistic tendencies, I read the article while the knot in my throat tightens with every line.

Cole Griffin was spotted out on the town with his band, although it was the woman on his arm who caught everyone's attention.

On. His. Arm.

Something in my chest shrivels up with the next sentence.

Someone close to the source says Cole and his mystery woman have been seen throughout different stops on the European leg of his tour.

His woman?

Fuck these journalists.

She is *mine*.

Yet looking at the two of them together—looking at how perfectly they seem to fit into each other's lives—makes me wonder if I'm fooling myself into thinking she is.

Wouldn't be the first time a woman cheated on you. The voice I've spent weeks trying to eradicate emerges again, poisoning my thoughts with what-ifs.

What if Ellie and Cole connect on some deeper level and realize they're better suited for one another?

What if Ellie decides she likes bouncing around cities, writing music into the early morning with him by her side?

What if—

Stop it, I tell myself.

Controlling my jealousy proves difficult, especially when I can't get that photo of Ellie and Cole out of my head.

Although I want to believe Ellie wouldn't cheat on me, I struggle to shake off the feeling, which is why I ignore her call that comes in ten minutes later.

I can't talk to her when I feel like *this*.

Jealousy isn't attractive, and neither is feeling insecure about another man, so I'd rather stay quiet than be vulnerable like that, especially when Ellie and I still have four more weeks of her traveling around Europe.

Four more weeks of her possibly falling in love with another man too.

My molars grind together, and I do my best to shove the thought out of my head.

Ellie loves *me*. Not Cole.

Yet no matter how many times I tell myself that, I still worry about the possibility of that happening.

Four weeks is a long time to be apart.

Ellie calls me two more times, but I send both to voicemail. A text follows soon after, and I reluctantly read it.

ELLE

> Hey. I missed talking to you today. Call me when you get a chance? I'll try to stay up.

I wish I were strong enough to call her, but my insecurities dominate my thoughts, turning them toxic with every passing minute.

You're better than this, I remind myself.

Thing is, I thought I was, but it only took one photo to remind me of how fucked up I became because of Hillary's affair.

Pushing Ellie away won't solve your issues.

But I still do it anyway.

CHAPTER SIXTY-TWO

Ellie

My phone buzzing makes my heart stutter. Rafael didn't answer my text earlier asking for him to call me, which only adds to my anxiety about the photo posted by the paparazzi.

I expect to find a new message from him, only to have my anxiety replaced with disgust at Ava's old contact name popping up.

AVA

> I'm suspecting you had something to do with Phoebe and Cole breaking up.

She attached the same photo of Cole and me that has been circulating on the internet and social media apps.

Bile crawls up my throat as I check her next message.

AVA

> Should have known you had a
> thing for taken men. Must be those
> daddy issues acting up again.

I want to reply with something awful, but confronting Ava after a message like that feels like a loss. She will always have this warped perception of me, and nothing I say or do will change that.

Angry tears spring to my eyes, and my body vibrates from a rage so potent, I'm afraid I might pop a blood vessel from the pressure building inside my head. The urge to take the pain away overwhelms me, and my fingers itch for something sharp to grab.

I search my checked bag for the one item I keep hidden deep within an interior pocket. My fingers shake as I grip the sliver of the old mirror and pull it out.

Staring at my reflection feels like taking a punch to the chest, and another strong wave of emotions hits me.

Anger. Sadness. Fear. They all swirl together, creating a tornado of turmoil inside me. My hold on the mirror fragment tightens as I lose grip on reality.

Ava's message replays in my head, along with the sound of Rafael's voicemail, creating a symphony of sadness.

I point the jagged edge of the mirror at my thigh only to stop when the sharp tip hovers beside the quote I had tattooed years ago.

This too shall pass.

I take a deep breath and tell myself that physical pain doesn't take away the emotional kind. That I will only feel worse in the end if I let my demons win.

You don't need the mirror.

I toss the sliver to the floor and fall back on my bed with a sob. I'm not sure how long I cry for, but eventually I begin to practice the strategies my therapist taught me. Deep breaths. Focusing on my five senses. Naming restaurants that start with the letter A all the way to Z.

It takes me longer than usual, but once I calm down, I call Rafael again. When my call goes to voicemail, I'm filled with a fresh wave of disappointment that threatens to consume me, but I focus on counting the stars tattooed on my thighs.

Once I'm no longer hyperventilating, I forward my lawyer the messages from Ava. Ms. Copper replies by telling me that Ava will regret saying that.

I try to call Rafael once more, but it goes directly to voicemail. It hurts like hell to know I'm being punished for something that was out of my control.

It is scary, giving someone that much control over my happiness. I know he is worth the risk, which is why him disappearing when I need him cuts into me like this, but that doesn't stop me from questioning if this kind of behavior will happen every time we face a new challenge.

I pray for both our sakes it doesn't, but after today, I'm not too sure, and that in itself terrifies me.

The next morning, I wake up with a renewed sense of hope. I could have given up and turned my back on the progress I've made, but I fought for myself instead. It wasn't remotely easy, especially when the urge to cut returned, but my future is too bright to get lost in the darkness of my past again.

So instead of packing the mirror back into my luggage like I have done in the past, I toss it in the trash where it belongs, along with any hope of Ava and me making it through this court case civilly.

She might have caught me off guard this time with her hurtful messages, but I won't make the same mistake again.

That much I promise.

I've tried to get in touch with Rafael multiple times since last night, but he hasn't been answering my calls, although he did send me a text late last night apologizing for missing them.

The message was bland, which told me everything I needed to know.

My heart aches throughout the next day and inspires a new song that starts with a sad opening verse that had Cole questioning if I was okay and apologizing for the fifth time about the photo.

"If you say sorry again, I may punch you."

He taps on the bump in his nose. "Anywhere but here, please. My nan already gives me enough grief about not getting it set properly."

I roll my eyes.

He sighs. "I know I can't control the photos, but I still feel guilty."

"Guilty enough to help me finish this song?" I use his same logic against him, earning a glare and a huff from the big man who has slowly become a friend.

We continue working on our song, and I push all thoughts of Rafael and the stupid paparazzi photo aside.

By the time I return to my hotel room at the end of the day, I'm irritable and hell-bent on speaking to Rafael, whether he wants to or not.

Thankfully, he reaches out to me first, saving me from overthinking the idea to death. Relief hits me square in the chest when my phone screen lights up with his name and a photo of us that was taken in Hawaii.

Despite the immature urge to send his call directly to voicemail, I answer right away.

"Hey. Hold on a second." I press the video call button and wait.

With a sigh, he accepts the request, giving me a view of his chiseled face and pouty lips pressed into a thin line.

I don't bother beating around the bush with pleasantries. "I take it you saw the photo."

He doesn't speak.

My frown deepens. "Rafael."

"Yeah, I did." The muscle in his jaw jumps.

"So what? You plan on taking it out on me for the indefinite future?"

"No."

"Well, it feels like it based on the way you pulled away."

I needed you, I want to say. *You were supposed to be someone I could count on*, I mentally add.

I felt so damn lost last night, and you weren't there to help me find my way out of the dark, I'm tempted to confess, even if it starts a confrontation with him.

He brushes a hand down his face and curses to himself in Spanish. "What do you want me to say?"

"Anything, so long as you don't ice me out for something that isn't even true."

"I know it isn't."

"Then why does it feel like you're punishing me anyway?"

His nostrils flare. "I'm pissed."

"Because Cole touched me?" The paparazzi caught a single moment when Cole was trying to help me steady myself after I tripped over a hole in the pavement, and the media turned it into this whirlwind romance meant to sell papers and get clicks on the internet.

He shakes his head. "I know you wouldn't do anything with him."

"Then why are you angry?"

"I'm angry at *myself*. Not at you."

I blink in confusion. "What?"

He looks past the phone's camera and stares into the distance. "I feel..."

"Jealous?" I offer.

His eyes screw shut. "Partially."

"It's normal to feel that way from time to time, especially after what you've been through with your ex. I understand why something like that photo might be...triggering."

He sighs. "I hate being insecure. It makes me feel pretty pathetic."

"It's okay if you feel jealous and unsure, so long as you let me help you *feel secure* about us rather than turning your back on me."

"That's not how a relationship should be."

"Do you mind sharing your relationship rule book so I can get a better understanding of these archaic beliefs?"

"Elle."

I ignore the warmth bursting through my chest. "What?"

"I didn't want you to see me like this. *That's* why I stayed away."

"See you like that?"

"Weak," he says with a sneer.

"The only weakness I see is the fact that you'd rather pull away than lean on me when you need it most." We could have supported each other, but he didn't let me.

His head hangs with a sigh. "You're right."

I consider keeping my feelings about him ghosting me for a day to myself, especially given how torn he looks by his choice, but I decide to voice them anyway.

"Your reaction scared me. I was worried that you might be…done with me."

His eyes snap open. "No. I might have needed a little time to cool off, but it had nothing to do with you."

"Try telling *my* insecurities that."

"Shit."

"*I* could have used you last night," I confess in a whisper. "You disappeared and left me all alone, which only made everything worse."

"What happened?"

"Ava contacted me."

He sneers, although I'm not sure if it is directed at Ava or himself.

"I'm sorry." He curses again. "I should have answered your call, or at the very least, I should have called you back when I calmed down after a bit."

I stare at my hands. "Yeah. You should have."

"Staying away for as long as I did… You have every reason to be upset with me about it."

I release a heavy exhale.

"Do you want to talk about it?" he asks.

I shake my head hard enough to send a few of my hairs flying in front of my eyes.

"Did you…" He lets the sentence hang.

"*No*." I suck in a deep breath. "I thought about it…for a moment…but I calmed down."

He lets out a breath of relief. "I should have been there for you."

"What I do to my body isn't your responsibility."

"No, but you're the woman I love, and knowing you were hurting enough to think about it while I sat around, pissed off and ignoring you, makes me feel like absolute shit."

My chest clenches so hard, my next breath comes out like a wheeze. "You can take time to calm down or work through your thought process, but ignoring me the way you did isn't fair."

"You're right."

I exhale slowly. "I want—no, I *need* to know that you'll be there for me, even when it's hard." If he pulls away every time he gets scared or is triggered by his past, we will never be able to move forward together.

"You can count on me, Elle. I'm sorry I made you doubt that because of my own insecurities, but I won't make that mistake again. I promise."

Over the next few days, Rafael holds true to his promise of sticking by my side, regardless of whatever photos and articles are being published about Cole and me online. He even makes a few jokes about it, including scheduling me a session with my tattoo artist to ink his name on my forehead, which I politely decline.

If I'm going to get a tattoo inspired by him, I would prefer something a bit more discreet, although the gesture is thoughtful.

The next few travel days are long, thanks to our early train rides around Spain. By the time we make it to France three days after my conversation with Rafael, I'm struggling to keep my eyes open throughout the day.

After fighting with inserting my hotel key in the slot at the end of the night, I finally enter my room to find a nondescript box on my bedside table, along with a note attached to the top in a standard typeface.

> Rafael's Relationship Rule Book
>
> Rule Number 1:
> If your girl doesn't want real flowers, make her one instead

With a little squeal, I tug at the pink ribbon and rip open the box. Nestled between layers of protective paper is a 3D-printed hibiscus flower that is painted pink, along with a second note.

> At least you can pack this one in your suitcase.
> —Your Prom King

I fall onto the bed with a huge smile and cradle my new flower to my chest until I accidentally fall asleep without ever texting Rafael thank you.

The next night, I return to my hotel room to find another white box with a note attached to the top. Before I read the message, I send Rafael a text.

ME

You're spoiling me.

RAFAEL

Text me when you open it.

I carefully remove the note from the ribbon and read it.

Rafael's Relationship Rule Book

Rule Number 2:
Never clear your search history...

"Oh my God." With trembling fingers, I pull on the ribbon until the whole bow unravels and I can easily remove the top of the box.

My mouth falls open when I pull out a U-shaped silicone vibrator, along with a second note.

Call me.
—Your Prom King

My heart races in my chest as I pull up Rafael's contact and call him.

"You opened it?"

I check out the device from all angles in search of a button. "This wasn't the one from my search history."

He chuckles. "No. It's better."

"How so?"

"Do you want me to demonstrate?"

My heart lodges itself in my throat. "Sure?" I say with a squeak.

"Put me on speakerphone before taking your clothes off."

I do what he asks and remove my pants.

"All of them," he commands.

Goose bumps spread across my skin. "How do you know?"

"I just do."

I glare at my phone while tossing my shirt, bra, and underwear onto the growing pile in the corner of my room. "Happy?"

"Not yet."

I reach for the vibrator. "How am I supposed to—" A soft buzzing sound stops me midsentence as the vibrator begins to pulse in my hand. "You control it?"

His dark chuckle sends invisible flames licking down my spine. "You didn't expect me to miss out on the fun, did you?"

With how fast my heart is beating in my chest, I could die before I ever have a chance to come.

"Lie down," he says before I hear a door shut on his end and the creak of the leather couch in his office.

I follow his command and settle on top of the mattress.

"Touch yourself first."

The vibrator stops shaking in my hand, and I drop it beside me. With a deep inhale, I trace a path from my nipples down to my wet center before darting away, all while Rafael listens, his breathing getting heavier after he asks me to describe what I'm doing.

A belt jangles, and something drops before he groans.

"Wish you were here touching me instead," I whisper as I drag my index finger through my arousal before brushing my clit.

"I can be there this weekend."

I softly laugh before groaning when he tells me to slide a single finger inside myself. My eyes shut as I imagine Rafael's hands instead of my own, slowly pushing inside before retreating to tease my clit. He is the one who replaces his hand with the vibrator. Just like he's also the one slipping the silicone tip inside before pressing the other end against my clit.

I gasp as soft vibrations pulse through my lower half, sending a surge of pleasure through me that is so strong, my back bows.

"That's it." Rafael's voice deepens.

I beg for more, and I'm rewarded with another pulse of the vibrator, this time different from the last. A moan slips past my lips, and Rafael grumbles something to himself. It doesn't take him long to figure out which vibrations I prefer, and I'm writhing against the mattress within a few minutes, with sweat clinging to my skin and fire spreading through my body.

Rafael pleasuring himself at the same time only ramps up the pressure building in my core. His soft curses and stifled moans amplify my pleasure until I'm pleading for him to let me come.

He switches the vibrations against my clit. The difference between those and the ones occurring inside me and against my G-spot fills my vision with tears, and I come ten seconds later.

My vision goes completely black as I screw my eyes shut and tumble into an orgasmic haze that wipes my brain of any coherent thought. I can hardly make out Rafael grunting before a shout makes my speaker crackle. It sends another wave of pleasure through me that has my toes curling and my muscles spasming, all thanks to the vibrations that haven't stopped despite both of us coming.

We may be an ocean apart, but Rafael won't let me forget about him. Not for a single second of a single day, and it makes me appreciate his love even more.

The next few days go by too quickly, with Cole, his team, and me bouncing between a few cities in France. While the first two weeks were fun and novel, I'm starting to feel incredibly homesick, and not even Rafael's third and fourth gifts of strawberry-lemon fizzy drinks and a pair of fuzzy socks Nico picked out for me can cheer me up.

I confessed as much to Rafael last night. He did his best to make me feel better, but it didn't stop me from looking up flights later that night after we hung up.

When I get to my hotel room after a long day spent at the concert venue, bouncing song ideas off Cole before he went onstage, all I want to do is take a shower, crawl into bed, and call Rafael.

A large white box with the same pink ribbon as my other presents makes me pause. The box is nearly as tall as Nico, although it isn't too heavy. "What in the world could it be?" I grab the note attached to the ribbon.

Rafael's Relationship Rule Book

Rule Number 5:
~~Home is where the heart is~~
Home is wherever YOUR heart is

I reach for the end of the ribbon and yank until it pools on

the hotel room carpet. I'm antsy as I rip at the paper to reveal an unmarked brown box.

I place the box on the edge of my bed and tear into the protective tape with the sharp end of my tweezers, which takes me far too long. By the time I open the box, I'm sweating and winded.

"No way." I pull out a white guitar that is identical to the one Astrid had during her time with the Treble Makers. It looks exactly like the one I commented on, although the black embroidered guitar strap is different from Astrid's and has a unique pattern of hibiscus flowers with stems in the shape of music notes.

It may be the most beautiful gift I've ever received.

I'm so distracted by taking in all the little details that I nearly miss the note Rafael tucked between the strings and the fretboard.

Play for me tonight?
—Your Prom King

The note slips from my fingers and falls to the floor at the sound of heavy knocking on my door.

I don't check the peephole before opening the door.

"Surprise!" Nico runs directly at me and throws his arms around my waist while my mom, Burt, Willow, and Rafael hang out in the hall.

Tears spring to my eyes. "You're really here?" I answer my own question by pulling Mom and Willow into a group hug.

"We heard you were missing us." Burt wraps an arm around Rafael's shoulder, despite hardly reaching it, and pulls him against his side. Rafael's cheeks turn pink, and I'm a goner as I let go of my mom and Willow to wrap my arms around him.

"Thank you."

He kisses the top of my head. "You may not be able to come home yet, but that doesn't mean I can't bring home to you."

One day, I'll marry this man, and no one will stop me.

Not even him.

CHAPTER SIXTY-THREE

Ellie

Cole's grip on the microphone tightens. "I'd like to play a new song for you."

The first row of people standing by the stage go wild, along with my heart. After spending the last month on the road with him, I should be used to watching him enchant a crowd, but here I am, acting starstruck again from my hidden corner backstage.

He continues, "See, I made a new friend this summer."

A few girls shout that they love him, which earns them a deep, raspy chuckle.

"And she and I have been working on an amazing album together."

Traveling around Europe while writing music has been one of the best things that's happened to me. Although I haven't been able to go sightseeing as much as I thought

I would, I've been enjoying myself with Cole and his team. They're professional, creative, and push me to step out of my musical comfort zone and test new kinds of sounds. I've even been learning how to play the banjo and mandolin, much to Nico's excitement and Burt's surprise.

If it weren't for Nico, I'm not sure I would be in this position to begin with. Becoming his nanny and music teacher not only gave me a renewed purpose but also the courage to chase after my dreams once more.

Together, Nico and I fell in love with music again and formed an everlasting bond in the process, and not a day goes by when I don't miss him. He video calls me daily to catch up on what he calls my *European adventure*. I make sure to prioritize at least a few minutes each day for him, whether I'm out and about trying to get inspired or holed up in my hotel room, feeling heartsick over how much I miss him and his dad. Rafael and I talk every day too, which makes me happy and incredibly homesick.

If Rafael hadn't surprised me two weeks ago, I might not have made it through the full five weeks without running home, although he assures me that I would have.

"Is she your girlfriend?" a random person in the second row shouts.

"Oh, no. Definitely not." Cole points at something. "She is happily in a relationship with a decent guy who wouldn't hesitate to kick my ass."

I cover my mouth to stifle my laugh. Rafael has slightly warmed up to Cole, solely because he sees how much this whole tour has meant to me, but that doesn't mean they will ever be friendly.

"I'd love for you to let me know what you think of the song when I'm done. Perhaps we can even convince the songwriter to come out here and introduce herself." He glances over at my concealed spot in the wings, and I take a step back as if the spotlight can find me if he stares long enough.

Yesterday, Cole asked me if he could play one of the new songs we wrote together because he wanted to see how people would react. I was surprised, especially since he hasn't even recorded it in a studio yet, but he told me to trust him.

So here I am, about to listen to a crowd react to my song *live*.

Cole readjusts his fingers on the guitar chords. "This song is called 'Shades of Blue,' written by yours truly and the wonderful Ellie Sinclair."

The volume of the crowd goes up by about twenty decibels.

I suck in a breath. "Oh my God. He said my name. Out loud."

A crew member chuckles behind me before saying, "Better get used to it because, come tomorrow, everyone will know it."

I didn't think it was possible for the crowd to get louder, but somehow it does.

Cole begins playing the first few chords of a song I wrote to a crowd made up of thousands of people. I knew it would make me emotional, but I didn't expect to get teary-eyed within the first ten seconds.

Picturing a future without you

was like looking through a lens tinted blue.

Shades of navy bled to black

until I could no longer remember

what my life was like before you came back and

threw it off-center.

I saw Ava's live concert videos. Listened to her play *my* song after she won the Album of the Year award that I should have also been there to accept. I watched from the sidelines as all my accomplishments were stolen by someone else—as my dreams of ever writing songs again were crushed into a thousand pieces, only to be rebuilt into something far better.

I swipe at my cheeks. Cole's assistant passes me a tissue at one point, which only makes me cry harder.

He gives me a one-armed hug above the waist that makes me wish Rafael were here to share this moment with me. To see me shine from my little backstage corner while the world hears my song.

I push the thought aside and enjoy the moment.

The song goes by too fast, and it makes me wish we'd added another verse solely so I could bask in the glow for a little longer. I'm so caught up in the buzz that I don't notice the silence of the crowd until Cole turns to face the wings of the stage with a smile. "Hey, Ellie. I think they love your song."

My chest clenches as the stadium agrees.

"Do you want to come out here and let them tell you themselves?"

Cole sure has the ability to rile up a crowd. Laughing. Screaming. *Crying.* The man is a true star, and it's obvious why his shows sell out.

The roar of the people attending tonight's show hits me

like a shot of adrenaline, and before the voice in the back of my head speaks out, I step onto the stage and wave.

Cole beckons me forward before holding out the mic for me. "Say hi."

"Hi," I croak.

People break out in laughter in the first row, and my cheeks warm, both from the bright lights and my slight embarrassment.

Cole turns to the crowd. "So what do we all think of Ellie's song?"

It's electric, the way the crowd gets louder as Cole points the mic and spins it in a circle, and I find myself breaking out into a smile as I finally let go of the hurt I held on to for over a year because of Ava and Darius.

What they did doesn't matter anymore because I'm choosing to move forward and pave my own way. Song by song and day by day, I *will* build a name for myself.

And all that starts today.

"I know you were most likely hoping for a better alternative…" My lawyer lets her sentence hang.

With all the packing I need to do before heading back to Lake Wisteria, the last thing I need is to spend time on a video call with my lawyer and Rafael, but Ms. Copper said it was urgent.

According to her team, Ava's legal counsel is looking to settle before the end of the week, so I'm faced with an impossible choice: either accept Ava's settlement money and sign a non-disclosure agreement or have my case heard in court and risk walking away with nothing.

"So no one would know what really happened?"

Ms. Copper shakes her head. "No."

"But Ellie would receive full credit?" Rafael asks.

I look at his spot on the video call while simultaneously wishing he were here, holding my hand while Ms. Copper delivered the news.

Ms. Copper's legal aid reviews something on their tablet. "Ms. Sinclair will be listed in the credits of each song she helped write."

"But Ava will remain in the public's good graces." Rafael frowns.

"There is another alternative." Ms. Copper clears her throat. "We could go to trial and present our case to a judge."

"They may believe her."

"But they could also believe you," Rafael challenges with an arched brow.

I scoff. "Right."

"I don't expect you to make a decision about the settlement today." That's a relief. "Although Ava's lawyers did set a hard deadline for the end of the week."

"Why?" Rafael asks when I remain quiet.

"They most likely want to clear this up before Ava's next album drops."

"God forbid America's sweetheart gets any bad press," I mutter under my breath, earning a deep scowl from Rafael.

Ms. Copper's lips thin. "As it is, her PR team is working overtime after everything that happened with Darius."

Rafael looks rather smug at that bit of news.

"Do you recommend I take the money?" I ask. If I did, I'd be set for life without ever needing to step in front of a judge, and my name would be listed in the song credits, but no one would ever know what really happened between Ava and me. What will stop her from doing this again to someone else one day?

Ms. Copper looks directly into her camera, her piercing stare pinning me in place. "I don't like making recommendations."

"Okay. Fine. But if you were in my position—"

Her lips twitch. "Good try."

I sigh.

"I *can* tell you that I didn't choose this line of work to hide behind settlement paperwork and NDAs."

When I started this legal process, the idea of silently settling with Ava sounded appealing, especially if it avoided any kind of confrontation, but now that I'm presented with the opportunity to do just that, it feels...

Cowardly.

A judge could rule in her favor, and I could never see a dime for my work, but at least I stand a chance of people hearing my side of the story, even if it solidifies my place as the villain in Ava's.

"You can give me an answer by five p.m. this Friday."

I shake my head. "No."

"Are you sure?" Rafael asks with raised brows.

"I don't want to wait until then."

Ms. Copper leans forward on her elbows, making her designer tweed jacket shift with the movement. "Would you like to settle, then?"

"Actually, no. I want to go to court."

All hell breaks loose less than twenty-four hours after my law-yer files my case with the California courts. National news outlets won't stop talking about Ava and me, and while their facts are limited, it doesn't stop people from speculating all about our case. The internet sleuths are actively picking apart my life, and I had to set all my social media accounts to private to stop random people from learning more about me.

If it weren't for Rafael and Willow, I would have given up on the idea of taking Ava to court. My best friend spends hours handling my PR, reaching out to journalists to give them my side of the story, while Rafael does everything in his power to keep me calm, including limiting my internet and phone access.

His attempts at distracting me range from mind-numbing sex to watching him care for all the animals in the barn, including braiding Penelope's hair.

Seeing him not only check on the cats but also all his other animals fills me with so much warmth. Willow accused me of having a caretaker kink, and it's all his fault.

"What are you looking at?" He tugs at the bow he just finished tying around Penelope's hair and restarts.

"You'd be a great girl dad."

He smiles to himself. "You think so?"

"I know so." I check out his handiwork. For someone with hair too short to braid, he sure knows what he is doing. "Where did you learn to braid hair like that?"

"Dahlia and Lily made us play with their dolls growing up."

"They did?"

His cheeks flush. "Yup."

"Well, it worked. You're better than I am at that."

He fidgets with the bow. "I doubt that."

"I'm being serious. Good thing you had a boy, or else you'd be braiding your daughter's hair every single day."

He clears his throat. "Would you want one?"

"What?"

"A daughter."

His question completely catches me off guard. "Um…"

My anxiety grows as I consider telling the truth.

Of course I would want one, but I also understand Rafael may never come around to having kids, so—

"Having a girl may kill me in the process, but I'd want one…in the future."

My heart jolts. "You do?"

"Yup. And I'd be the best girl dad in the world, just so no one else would ever compare."

I laugh before pulling him into a kiss. "Does that mean you're coming around to the idea of adopting?"

"One day, yes. But for now, I just want to keep you all to myself."

Likewise.

CHAPTER SIXTY-FOUR

Rafael

I reach for the doorbell and stop myself. When I agreed to the idea of bringing Ellie to a Sunday lunch at the Muñoz house, it sounded nice in theory. My family wanted to celebrate *my girlfriend* returning to Lake Wisteria, most likely because they no longer have to put up with my grumpy ass now that she is back.

"If they start annoying you with all their questions, let me know," I tell her.

Ellie laughs. "I think I can handle it, but thanks for the offer."

"Lily and Dahlia may team up to get information out of you about us."

"Who says they haven't already tried?"

I stare at her.

She pulls out her phone and shows me a group chat they

share called *The Silver Vixens,* most likely named by none other than Dahlia since it's her favorite show.

I groan. "It's already starting."

"Yup." She laughs. "Don't worry, though. When they asked if we were thinking about a church wedding, I took the bullet for you and said my family isn't religious."

My eyes bulge. "You what?"

"Kidding!"

I exhale. "Thank God. I think my aunt and Rosa would both pass out."

"I mean, I wasn't raised going to Mass like you, but I suppose I'd be willing to make a sacrifice when it's time for us to tie the—"

I struggle to breathe properly.

She swats my shoulder with a chuckle. "Will you relax? No one has asked me about marriage or babies or whatever else makes commitment-phobes like you anxious."

"I am *not* a commitment-phobe."

"No?" Her eyes glimmer.

"No. I'm just not interested in talking about any of that with anyone who isn't *you.*"

She smiles. "So you *are* open to getting married?"

"If you keep trying to send me into cardiac arrest, we'll never make it to our wedding day."

Her smile grows wider. "That's not a no."

"No, it's not." I kiss her softly before ringing the doorbell.

Rosa opens the door to her house with a bright smile that both Muñoz sisters inherited. "Ellie! You're here!" She completely ignores me and pulls Ellie into her arms. "It's so nice to see you again."

Rosa drags my girlfriend inside without sparing me a second glance.

"Nice to see you too," I call out.

"Shut the door before all the AC leaves." She drags Ellie down the main hall toward the kitchen.

"*¡Papi!*" Nico runs down the hall.

"At least someone is excited to see me." I catch him in my arms. "How was your sleepover at Julian's?"

Nico tells me all about his night while I follow him into the house. Everyone is too busy fawning over Ellie to even notice me. I expected as much when I told them she was coming today, but watching it unfold in front of me is a different story.

While I know my family liked Ellie when they got to know her as Nico's nanny, I want them to *love* her as my girlfriend. They are important to me, and so is she, so I hope they mesh well.

After Lorenzo's rough reception as Lily's fiancé two weeks ago, I'm a bit nervous, although it only takes me twenty minutes to realize I was overreacting.

Ellie is fine. Actually, she is more than fine. She happily sticks to my aunt's side while she prepares her beloved *espagueti verde* recipe, and they swap tricks for some of Nico's favorite recipes.

I hang out in the kitchen with them and take diligent notes on Ellie's phone for her. I'd usually be watching a game in the living room, but I'd rather avoid sitting with Julian, Lorenzo, and Lily, who refuses to leave my cousin and her new fiancé alone.

"Your secret ingredient is baby spinach?" Ellie stares at my aunt with wide eyes.

My aunt grins. "How else would I get Nico to eat his veggies?"

"Oh my God." She looks over at me. "Did you know this?"

I zip my lips and toss the invisible key over my shoulder, earning a chuckle from Dahlia and her mother.

"Why didn't you say anything?" Ellie places her hands on her hips and stares at me with the cutest scowl.

I shrug. "It's top secret."

Her eyes sparkle. "Does that mean you'll have to kill me if I tell someone?"

Tía bumps her hip into Ellie's. "He wouldn't, but don't count me out. Julian says he has the perfect place to bury a body should I need it."

"Did you hear that, Lorenzo?" Julian asks from the living room, earning an eye roll from Dahlia and a laugh from Ellie.

Tía sighs. "I told him to behave."

"He's just hangry," Dahlia offers.

Ellie and my aunt wrap up making lunch together while Rosa and Dahlia prepare the table. It's obvious Ellie fits like a missing puzzle piece, perfectly falling into place with our family like she's always been a part of it. In some ways, I guess she has, but I had never paid much attention to the relationships she had with my family outside of Nico.

With every question they ask her, I can tell they gain a bit more respect for her, only for that respect to double when they catch her instinctively passing me her plate with a few forkfuls of green spaghetti. Dahlia's brows rise, my aunt's eyes water, and Lily hides her smile behind a fist. Lorenzo, her *fiancé*, has a look of disgust on his face as his gaze bounces between Lily's smile and my plate.

Take some notes on a real relationship, asshole.

Even Julian, who has a professional poker face, seems taken aback.

Ellie, on the other hand, doesn't even notice as she continues telling Rosa some story about her mom and the music shop.

When they catch me staring, everyone looks away, while Ellie...

She turns to me and *smiles*, and I swear, I fall in love with her all over again.

Later that night, when Nico and I drop Ellie off at her house, her parents invite us inside for homemade brown butter cookies and a drink. Nico was hesitant at first, but after a reassuring squeeze from me and a promise to leave whenever he asks me to, we head inside.

Nico takes some time to warm up to Ellie's family, most likely due to him still struggling with getting close to people he just met. Burt doesn't give up at the first brush-off, though, and it doesn't take long for my son to become interested in hearing about Burt's time as Ellie's music teacher before he started dating her mother.

"So she got free music lessons forever?" Nico asks.

"Yup. She's a moocher." Burt winks.

I smile while Ellie's eyes roll as she says, "I didn't ask you to become my tutor." She mentions needing to use the restroom and disappears down a hallway.

Burt's eyes brighten. "I was trying to impress her mom and spend more time with her." He then tells Nico about Ellie's time on the drumline, and her mom scrambles to find a video of one of the performances.

Nico giggles before looking up at me. "Can Ellie give me lessons forever too?"

Burt grins. "If Ellie says no, I'll convince her for you."

"What am I saying no to?" Ellie reappears in the hallway leading to the bedrooms.

"Burt told me to ask you if I could have music lessons forever and ever."

Ellie pretends to think about it for a few seconds. "Of course. You're my favorite student."

Nico laughs. "I'm your only student!"

Ellie looks over at me with a secretive smile. "Not anymore."

As of last week, Ellie officially became my music tutor too after she caught me messing around with one of Nico's guitars. She claims she is doing my ears a favor by teaching me some basic chords, but I think she wants another excuse to touch me.

Nico gasps. "You have another student? Who? You've got to tell me!"

Ellie shrugs. "Don't worry just yet. They may not last long."

Nico runs over to her and throws his arms around her waist. "Don't leave me for someone better." I snort, earning a dark look from my son. "This isn't funny."

"*I'm* the other student, *mijo.*"

His eyes go wide as they swing between Ellie and me. "You're teaching my dad?"

"He needs all the help he can get."

I scratch my stubbled cheek with my middle finger, which gets a laugh from Burt and Ellie.

"What?" Nico asks.

Ellie's answer is cut off by her mother.

"I found it!" She rushes back into the living room.

Ellie looks horrified while Nico throws his fist in the air. "Yes!"

Burt helps her mother set up the TV. A shaky video of the school band starts to play on the screen, and it is easy to spot Ellie out on the football field with her blond hair and taller frame.

She stares out at the crowd with a look of pure concentration on her face while she plays the drums, and the standard band uniform and hat she's wearing are adorable.

I can't believe I never noticed her back then, but then again, I'm glad I didn't because I wasn't in the place to appreciate someone as special as her.

Life brought us together when we needed each other most, and for that, I'll always be grateful.

"I'm hating every second of this." Ellie's head hangs as she covers her eyes with the palms of her hands.

"Look at your uniform!" Nico giggles.

"Don't be embarrassed, Ellie. You were the best drummer that school has ever seen." Burt points at the TV with pride.

"Yet." Nico puffs his chest out. "When I go to high school, I'm going to be on the drumline too!"

I pull Nico to my side. "I'm sure you will be."

"Ellie loved being part of the band. She even petitioned for them to play during soccer season, but it never panned out." Her mom winks.

Ellie sinks deeper into the couch with a groan.

"Is that right?" I pull her hands away from her reddening face.

"Mom, if you love me at all, you'll stop talking. Now."

"What's wrong? Does Rafael not know about the crush you had on him back in the day?" Burt winks at me.

I knew it.

"I had my suspicions." I shoot Ellie a cutting look. "But Ellie wouldn't confirm them."

"Oh." Her mom covers her mouth.

"I'm assuming you don't know about 'Prom King' either then?" Burt's cheeks stretch with his smile.

Ellie shoots off the couch. "That's it. I'm officially disowning myself and changing my last name."

"Good thing you've been practicing 'Ellie Lopez' since high school then," Burt replies.

All of us break out into laughter except for Ellie, who looks about ready to grab a shovel and start digging her own grave. She mumbles something about needing to use the bathroom before rushing away.

I follow her down the hallway and find her standing at the end of it with her head in her hands.

I drag her against my chest and force her to look up at me. "No need to be embarrassed. I think it's cute that you had a crush on me."

"Let's pretend this conversation never happened, okay?" She doesn't wait for me to agree before saying, "Okay."

I chuckle. "I don't think that's possible."

"Why not?"

"Because you've been fantasizing about me for half your life."

She glares. "That's not true."

"Are you sure about that, Ellie *Lopez*?" I brush my knuckles across her cheek.

Her body shudders as her eyes close. "Never repeat that."

"No promises."

Her eyes snap open. "Why?"

"Because one day, I plan on making your high school fantasy a reality." I brush my mouth over hers and seal my promise with a kiss.

CHAPTER SIXTY-FIVE

Ellie

SIX MONTHS LATER

On the day of my court hearing, I'm a nervous wreck. If it weren't for Rafael sitting in the gallery behind me, close enough to give my shoulder a squeeze every now and then, I might have crumbled under the judge's harsh stare.

Ava looks poised and proper in a designer blazer and pants. She doesn't acknowledge me, let alone look in my direction once. I prefer it that way, although my heart does a betraying squeeze when we accidentally lock eyes while she takes the stand.

I do the same soon after, along with some other eyewitnesses, including Darius. Rafael looks murderous during his testimony, although my boyfriend's temper cools slightly when Darius admits that I played a major role in Ava's songwriting process.

The opposing counsel calls Cole to testify as well, although their plan on catching me in another made-up cheating scandal backfires when Cole explains his breakup with Phoebe.

The final witness—the record label's accountant—seals my future as a millionaire. According to their reports, the profits Ava made from my stolen songs grossed money beyond my wildest dreams, and it turns out her original settlement offer was only a drop in the bucket, especially when music streaming platforms, royalties, and touring revenue are considered.

I'm not surprised when the judge rules in my favor, although I find it hard to believe, even after she slams the gavel and makes her final ruling.

"Congratulations, Ms. Sinclair." My lawyer holds her hand out, and mine trembles as I shake it.

Based on the money I was awarded, Ms. Copper is going to be buying a lot more designer clothes, that's for sure.

"I'm so fucking proud of you." Rafael pulls me into a hug.

I blink a few times. "I didn't do anything."

"You could have taken the settlement money and avoided court altogether."

"I couldn't."

He cups my cheek. "I know."

Willow yanks me away from Rafael, throws her arms around me, and whispers into my ear, "You won!"

My face turns red. "I guess so."

"How does it feel?"

"To be a millionaire?" I ask.

"No! To beat the Wicked Witch of West Hollywood!"

"Is that what they're calling her?"

Willow winks. "Do you like it? I came up with it myself."

My laugh is cut off by a chair scraping against the marble floor as Ava rises onto her stiletto heels. Neither Rafael, Willow, nor I look in her direction, which seems to anger her based on the way she walks over to my side of the courtroom and clears her throat.

"Ava." Cole steps in front of the table, blocking her from view. "I'd say it's nice to see you, but my grandma raised me not to lie."

"Aw. Was your mom too busy screwing her security guard to teach you herself?"

Exactly how small is Hollywood? Because these two seem way too familiar with one another, and I had absolutely no idea.

Cole's laugh is jarring when compared to the ones I've heard before, and it makes the hairs on the back of my neck rise. "Perhaps you should save that sharp tongue for your new songs."

"If I want songwriting advice from someone who hasn't won a single award for theirs, I'll be sure to ask you for help," Ava sneers.

"Speaking of awards, you owe Ellie that Grammy of yours." Willow steps beside Cole, earning a glance from him. His brows furrow for a moment before his sly smile slips back into place.

Ava lets out a long, dramatic sigh. "Ellie?"

I stiffen. After more than a year wishing that Ava had given me a chance to explain my side of the story, I no longer feel the same way.

I'm ready to move on. For good.

Rafael's head snaps in her direction, and his thunderous expression reminds me of dark clouds looming before the sky opens up. "She clearly doesn't want to speak to you, so do us all a favor and go."

Out of the corner of my eye, I catch her squinting at him. "And you are?"

"Your worst nightmare if you don't find the closest exit."

Ava sucks in a breath. "Wait. Aren't you Rafael Lopez?"

He ignores her.

Cole motions toward the exit. "Goodbye, Ava. Tell Darius that I'll see him in hell."

Her heels click against the marble flooring as she walks through the exit.

"What was that all about?" I ask Cole once she leaves.

He shrugs. "I really can't stand her boyfriend."

"You're telling me," Rafael says before he and Cole share a look. Since my trip to Europe, the two of them have become friendlier, especially since Cole visits Lake Wisteria more often now in hopes of us writing another successful album together.

I don't plan on ever asking Cole why he hates Darius, but I have a feeling it is personal, along with whatever anger he holds toward Ava. I'm not sure what happened in the year since I left Los Angeles, but I doubt I'll ever get an answer out of Cole, so there's no point in giving it much thought.

"Anyone up for some drinks?" Cole plasters on his usual smile, although the haunted look in his eyes remains.

"Hell yes." Willow tosses her hair over her shoulder.

Rafael looks down at me, and I nod.

"Just one."

Willow and Cole head back to Lake Wisteria while Rafael and I stay in Los Angeles for the next few days to wrap up the legal process and leave everything with Ava behind. By the time we are ready to meet with Ms. Copper to sign a few documents and receive my first official check, I'm desperate to go back home and never return.

A few paparazzi got wind of our story and the judge's ruling, which means my name is trending on social media. I thought Ava having her America's sweetheart sash revoked would make me happy, but all I feel is apathy toward the situation, which is a clear sign that I'm ready to move on.

"This is it?" My gaze flickers between the check, Rafael sitting beside me, and the lawyer standing on the other side of the conference table.

Ms. Copper tilts her head. "Were you expecting more?"

I stare at the check. "No, but…" I was hoping it would make me *feel* better or, at the very least, make me a little happy to know Ava finally had to pay up for her choices. Instead, all I feel is indifference toward the whole situation.

Hell, a text from my mom confirming Rafael, Nico, and I can come over for dinner this weekend brought more emotion out of me, and we have been doing that every other Sunday for the last six months.

"But what?" Ms. Copper asks.

"I thought it would mean more to me."

Her eyes soften at the edges, which is a rare thing for her. In the few months I've been working with Ms. Copper and her legal team, I've learned she is as ruthless as she is smart.

"I see," she says.

"After waiting this long for closure, I'm just..."

"Disappointed?" she offers.

"Yes."

Rafael grips my hand under the conference room table.

"Cases like these can draw mixed emotions for some people. On the one hand, you get rightful compensation for being wronged, but on the other, you never get the closure you want. At least not unless you pursue it yourself."

"Do I have to accept the money?" The lawyer already took a cut from the settlement agreement, so it isn't like I *need* to do anything else, right?

Her lips purse. "Technically, you have to physically accept the checks, but what you choose to do with them is up to you. Same can be applied to any future royalties earned."

"So, I can never cash it if I don't want to?"

Rafael's lips twitch.

"Not if you don't want to."

Once upon a time, I wanted nothing more than to be compensated for my work, but now that I have the opportunity to be, it makes me physically ill.

While I didn't accept Rafael's severance pay, I'm making plenty of money working with Cole, so I don't need Ava's. In fact, I don't want anything to do with her stolen work or whatever royalties she made from it, especially if accepting it would make me feel worse than before.

I've moved on. I'm making a name for myself that has nothing to do with her, and I want to keep it that way.

After thanking Ms. Copper for everything she has done, I swipe the check off the table and walk out of the conference room with my head held high and my boyfriend by my side.

At my request, Rafael drives me to a local bank to cash my check. I've never seen so much money in my account at one time, but it only remains there for a total of ten minutes while the teller writes me a cashier's check to a nonprofit charity that helps children who are struggling like I was.

I don't need to look up the name because it is the same charity that helped my mom pay for psychological services after my father refused to. Because of donations like the one I'm about to make, my mom was able to find a therapist that helped me, and I hope that my anonymous contribution can do the same for many others.

For the first time today, I have a smile on my face as we exit the bank.

"I'm proud of you." Rafael wraps his arm around my shoulder and kisses the top of my head.

"I didn't do anything but cash a check."

"You could have chosen to keep that money."

I scrunch my nose. "I don't want it." Which is exactly why I plan on donating any residuals I receive from her work.

His eyes sparkle. "I know, but a lot of people would have kept it anyway."

"Yeah, well, a lot of people aren't getting paid to write songs for Cole Griffin, so..." I wink.

He *laughs*, and it may be my favorite sound, only second to his son's.

When our plane lands at the Detroit airport, Rafael asks me how I want to celebrate finally being done with Ava and the legal case, and I tell him to take me home.

Not to my parents' house but to *our* home.

His smile doesn't drop throughout the entire drive back to *our* house on the hill. He has been asking me to move back in for a month, but I kept pushing it off because I wanted us to be certain we were both ready for that next step. To be honest, I'm still surprised he was the one who suggested it first, given his opposition to relationships just over six months ago.

First, he said he was tired of co-parenting our six cats without me and thought it would be best if I moved back. Then, he tried to get Nico to convince me, but I stood strong and said no—much to Rafael's surprise—because I still wasn't sure if it was the best idea.

It wasn't until last week, when he gifted me a set of gold earrings in the shape of hibiscus flowers, that I knew we were both ready.

For the days I'm not able to put flowers in your hair, Rafael said when I opened the box.

I know he hadn't meant to make me cry, but it hit me then how much I *wanted* to wake up every day to him handpicking a flower to put in my hair. The same flowers he spends hours tending to in his new greenhouse, solely because he never wants me to go a single day without one.

I never want to go a single day without *him* because he is the one who inspired the greatest unwritten love song of all.

Ours.

EPILOGUE

Ellie

ONE YEAR LATER

With a smile, I reach for Rafael's latest note that is taped to the top of an envelope. It has been over eighteen months since he started writing notes to me, and I've saved every single one in a medium-sized box safely tucked away in our closet. The small slips of paper never fail to draw a grin from me, regardless of whether there is a gift attached or not.

I unfold the small piece of paper and read the handwritten note.

> Rafael's Rule Book
>
> Rule Number 228:
> When your girl mentions she wants a new tattoo, book her an appointment.

My mouth falls open as I rip at the sealed envelope and pull out an appointment card for the local tattoo studio in town confirming today's date and scheduled timeslot.

I had casually mentioned wanting a new tattoo in passing one night, right before Rafael had fallen asleep, so I thought he forgot.

I should have known better. If Rafael has proven anything over the last eighteen months of us dating, it's that he is always listening and taking notes for his rule book.

With a skip in my step, I rush to his home office and throw open the door.

"You booked me an appointment?" My voice squeaks with excitement.

He holds up a finger, his lips pulling at the corners as he says, "We can meet again in a week to discuss."

My cheeks burn as someone on the other end of the video call says something before ending the meeting.

I wince. "Sorry."

He rolls his chair out from underneath his desk, and I walk over to take a seat on his lap. I drape my arms around his neck and pull him in for a kiss.

He pulls away before I have a chance to deepen it. "I take it you like the surprise?"

I poke at his chest. "Who knew you were such a romantic?"

His nonchalant shrug is endearing. "I have my moments."

"Will you come with me?"

His eyes light up. "Yes."

I drop a quick kiss on his cheek before jumping off his lap. "I need to go figure out what I want."

His brows pinch together. "You don't know?"

"No!" I have a hundred different ideas saved on my phone.

He smacks my butt with a grin. "You only have a few hours, so better get to it."

We drop Nico off at Josefina's house before heading into town. Anika, my tattoo artist, has been seeing me since I received my very first one. It's been some time since I've seen her because life has been hectic.

When I flipped through the concepts I had on my phone, none stood out to me, so I shot her a text and requested a special design.

While Anika preps her station, Rafael paces the small room, grumbling under his breath about me not letting him see the tattoo until she is done. I would hate to ruin the surprise before Anika finished, so despite his protests, I hold strong.

"You can always wait outside."

He casts a stern look in my direction. "No."

"Then quit pacing and come hold my hand." I pat the empty stool beside my chair.

He mutters something under his breath before taking a seat while Anika prepares my right wrist for a new tattoo. She hunches over me, the tip of her needle piercing the blank skin on the inside of my wrist.

By now, I'm used to the temporary pain associated with getting a new tattoo, so I don't flinch while Anika completes the custom-made design. Rafael keeps my mind occupied with a few stories, including one about the six cats who made our barn their home.

I'm so caught up in that one that I lose track of time until Anika announces that she is all done. Like Rafael, I didn't take a peek at the tattoo until now, and I'm glad I waited.

My eyes water as I glance over at the new tattoo. Three hibiscus flowers, one of which is smaller than the other two, share a single stem that forms into a treble clef.

The design is stunning, and Anika's fine-line work is phenomenal, but the meaning behind the tattoo is what matters most to me.

Like the music note tattoo on my other wrist that symbolizes the relationship I have with my mom and Burt, Nico and Rafael will always have a permanent place on my skin to match the one they have in my heart.

A clearing of Rafael's throat steals me away from my moment. "Can I see it now?" The excited twinkle in his eyes reminds me so much of his son.

"Sure." I hold out my wrist for him to see.

Various emotions flicker across his face—excitement, confusion, *surprise.*

I can't handle the silence anymore, so I crack a joke. "Is this getting too serious for you?"

"Not even close." His eyes sparkle, making me feel like I'm missing part of the punch line.

"What does that mean?"

Red splotches appear on his neck. "Nothing."

He quickly shifts the subject and asks Anika about paying,

but I know Rafael well enough to understand he did the one thing he promised to never do to me.

Lie.

"We need to pick Nico up," I remind him as he passes the street that leads to his aunt's lakefront house.

"He's going to stay with my aunt tonight."

"Really? Why?" Josefina never takes care of Nico during the week, mostly because we don't like to mess with his routine.

"She offered to take him to school tomorrow."

"Oh. That's nice."

His fingers drum against the steering wheel, completely out of sync with the music streaming from the speakers. Usually, the silence between us never feels uncomfortable, but tonight, it is filled with tension and some other emotion coming from Rafael that I can't pinpoint.

"Are you good?" I ask once he parks in our driveway.

"Yup."

"You sure?"

"Yes." He cuts me a look before exiting the truck and heading over to open my door.

"Well, you're acting weird," I say before shutting it behind me.

"I'm just…thinking."

Oh God. Maybe the tattoo was a bad idea, despite my mom saying otherwise. Sure, we're in a committed relationship, but maybe getting a tattoo to symbolize it made our situation too real for him?

"Are you sure you didn't get freaked out by tonight?" I try to shield my worries with a light tone.

"No." He uses that no bullshit tone of his.

"Then what's the—"

He doesn't let me finish. "Elle, I promise you that I'm not freaked out or being a commitment-phobe or whatever else you're thinking." He laces our fingers together and leads me in the opposite direction to the house.

"No?"

"No. It's actually the complete opposite."

My heart beats faster in my chest. "Really?"

He leads me to the backyard, where countless stars twinkle above us, and the full moon illuminates the row of hibiscus flowers he planted last week.

"I had this whole plan to take you on another trip to Hawaii next month—"

I interrupt him. "You did?"

"Yes." He sighs with a smile. "But then you got that tattoo tonight, and all I could think about was how much I loved you. Of how one day, I want to add another flower to that tattoo."

My vision turns cloudy. "I knew Nico would wear you down about adopting a sibling eventually."

He cracks a smile as he slides down to one knee. "I want it all with you, Elle. Kids. Marriage. A barn full of animals—"

"Don't forget about the coop," I remind him.

"*And* a coop full of chickens with eggs you send me to collect every morning."

"Don't lie. You like taking care of them."

"I like taking care of *you*, and I hope to spend the rest of my life doing just that, so long as you want me."

"Does forever sound good to you?"

His smile stretches across his face. "Perfect." The flower trembles in his hand as he holds it out for me. "Will you marry me? I don't have a ring yet—"

"Yes. A million times yes," I say right before my lips crush against his, sealing his proposal with a promise to love him as fiercely as he loves me.

For all the days of our lives.

After Rafael's impromptu proposal, he surprised me with a rose gold engagement ring he custom-made for me, a black card with an endless limit, and a request to keep the wedding small and intimate.

Fast-forward ten months, and here we are, about to get married in front of our family and friends in our newly renovated barn. With Lily's vision for floral arrangements, Josefina's party-planning skills, and my mom's eye for details, I couldn't have asked for a better group of women to help me turn my wedding dream board into a reality.

"You're shaking." Willow, my maid of honor, hands me my bouquet while my mom and Josefina fuss over my veil. My dress is fit for a fairy tale and made up of delicate lace and expensive chiffon. It has a sweetheart neckline, intricate detailing along the bodice and skirt, and a train that can be removed after the wedding ceremony.

"I'm just excited." My stomach has been in a constant state of butterflies since I woke up this morning without Rafael sleeping beside me. He and Nico stayed at Julian and Dahlia's place while I remained at the house to get ready for the big day.

Dahlia's hair and makeup crew from her *Dahlia Redesigned* show arrived at the house at 8 a.m., armed with mimosas, an array of hot tools, and enough makeup to stock a Sephora.

Dahlia and Lily arrived soon after. They may not officially be bridesmaids, seeing as Rafael and I wanted to keep it simple with only a maid of honor and a best man, but they are still family.

My family.

Josefina gives my shoulder a squeeze. "Julian told me Rafael has been pacing the house all day."

"Really?"

She laughs to herself. "Yup. He even asked if he could sneak in before you got ready."

"No."

"Yup. Julian had to pry him away from the door."

I choke on a laugh. "It'll be worth the wait."

"Speaking of wait..." Willow checks something on her phone. "The photographer is ready and Rafael is in place."

My heart beats faster. "Oh God. This is it."

With my mom holding my train and Willow tasked with protecting my veil, we slowly walk down the stairs and head to the glass-paned doors that lead outside.

I pause midstride as I check out Rafael's creation that he had prohibited me from seeing until today. He was the one who came up with the idea of keeping the whole thing a secret from me, and I now understand why.

Turns out the zone of the property he had concealed behind a temporary construction fence was hiding an alcove of hibiscus flowers that create the perfect photo backdrop for our First Look. After we share our private vows and take photos, we will have a formal ceremony for our family and friends.

His back is facing me while he fidgets with a cufflink. The click of the cameras around us fills the quiet as a genuine smile tugs at my lips.

"See you soon." My mom blows me a kiss before Willow pulls her away, leaving me alone.

I walk down the pathway that leads to my future husband and stop a few feet away from him. He doesn't turn around right away, so I clear my throat.

"Do you plan on turning around?"

"In a moment…"

"What are you—"

He plucks a flower from the hedge and turns to face me. His eyes go wide, and he blinks a few times.

"You look…" He cuts himself off with a curse in Spanish.

My smile stretches wider, making my cheeks hurt.

"That good, huh?"

"*Mi estrella.*" His eyes darken, and a look of pure desire washes over him as he takes me in.

Goose bumps form, spreading across my skin as I take him in. I've seen Rafael in a suit before, but him in a tux unlocks a whole new fantasy in my head.

"You clean up nice, Prom King."

His dark eyes glitter. "I can't wait to swap that nickname out for a new one."

"Like what?"

"*Husband.*" His blinding smile has my heart stuttering as he walks up to me, tucks a flower into my hair, and pulls me into a kiss that leaves me yearning for more.

ALSO BY LAUREN ASHER...

LAKEFRONT BILLIONAIRES SERIES

A series of interconnected standalones

Love Redesigned

Love Unwritten

DREAMLAND BILLIONAIRES SERIES

A series of interconnected standalones

The Fine Print

Terms and Conditions

Final Offer

DIRTY AIR SERIES

A series of interconnected standalones

Throttled

Collided

Wrecked

Redeemed

Scan the code to read the books

What's next for the Lakefront Billionaires?

You're cordially invited to Lily and Lorenzo's (fake) engagement party that is taking place in 2025.

ACKNOWLEDGMENTS

After nine books, I've come to realize this section only gets longer, which really is a blessing since so many great people have touched my life. That being said, I will try to keep this one short (says the author who went 20,000 plus words over her word-count goal).

First, I'd like to say a big thank you to all my readers. Your continued support with every release means so much to me, and it is because of you that I can continue writing stories that touch not only your heart, but mine as well.

Kimberly Brower—You're such a big part of this author journey, and I don't know where I would be without your guidance, support, and willingness to go above and beyond with everything you do.

And to the rest of the team at Brower Literary, including Aimee and Joy—You are superstars working behind-the-scenes, and I'm so appreciative of your dedication to making *Love Unwritten* the best version of itself!

Christa and the rest of the team at Bloom—I can't imagine working with another publishing team because you all are truly the best. I'm looking forward to seeing what the rest of the Lakefront Billionaires series brings us.

To Ellie and the team at Piatkus—It is hard to believe this is our fifth book together. Thank you for all the work you put into each release, and I'm so grateful to be part of the Hachette family!

Nina, Kim, Ratula, and everyone at Valentine PR—Thank you for keeping me sane.

Erica—I love you more than Reesees' Peecees (Lauren's Version).

Becca—Whether we're talking about Zillow doom scrolling or characters and third-act conflicts, I can always count on you to make me smile and laugh. Thank you for not only being an amazing editor, but also a great friend.

Sarah—I appreciate all the love and effort you put into each book we work on together. I'm so grateful for all you do to help me reach my full potential!

Mary, my ride or die—I always have the time of my life fighting dragons with you. Thank you for embracing your pink era with me, because the cover truly is one of my favorites!

Jos—One of the best parts of writing a new book is getting to create new memories with you. From me excitedly sending you the very first chapter to Kindle versions 1-100, I couldn't imagine sharing this journey (and your tears) with anyone else.

Nura—Sharing chapters with you has become one of my favorite parts of the writing process! Your excitement and our shared taste in fictional boyfriends make each book together that much better.

To my beta readers—It really is an honor to have such dedicated readers like you who want to help push me in the best possible ways. I never imagined being able to have a team as incredible as this one, and I'm truly grateful for the time you take to help me make Love Unwritten so special.

Leticia—Thank you for beta reading and proofreading this one! Your eye for catching little details I may(might SOS I need google) have missed truly is astonishing, and I look forward on working together again!

To my golden retriever—I love you like no otter.

ABOUT THE AUTHOR

Plagued with an overactive imagination, Lauren spends her free time reading and writing. Her dream is to travel to all the places she writes about. She enjoys writing about flawed yet relatable characters you can't help loving. She likes sharing fast-paced stories with angst, steam, and the emotional spectrum.

Her extra-curricular activities include watching YouTube, binging old episodes of Parks and Rec, and searching Yelp for new restaurants before choosing her trusted favorite. She works best after her morning coffee and will never deny a nap.